THE INSTITUTE FOR CREATIVE DYING

For Shirley Dawn Steeneveldt,
who taught me humour's value.

THE INSTITUTE FOR CREATIVE DYING

A Novel

JARRED THOMPSON

Published by Afritondo Media and Publishing 2023
www.afritondo.com

ISBN 978-1-8380279-4-0

Editing by Alison Lowry
Proofreading by Jane Bowman
Cover by Afritondo
Author photograph by Thango Ntwasa

First published in Great Britain in 2023 by Afritondo Media and
Publishing Preston, United Kingdom.

It is a leap of faith to seek the end of a world on behalf of a fantasy.
– Lauren Berlant, *A Properly Political Concept of Love:*
Three Approaches in Ten Pages

If I can stop dying, I can see
the water and the light make peace
here where I do not belong
But remember.
– Gabeba Baderoon, *The History of Intimacy*

So, the very project of survival requires that we take something other into our bodies. Survival [...] requires we let what is 'not us' in.
– Sara Ahmed, *The Cultural Politics of Emotion*

However expressive, symbols can never be the things they stand for.
– Aldous Huxley, *The Doors of Perception*

ON THE SLOPES of Northcliff, between eight and ten Lancaster Drive, there is an unnumbered house. Joggers, dog walkers, commuters don't notice the discrepancy because the house can't be seen from the road and the walls facing the street have been built in seamless face-brick fashion from one numbered house to the next.

To get to the unnumbered house, you must walk up an alleyway that runs between numbers eight and ten. Walking all the way up to the end, on your left there will be a black-lattice gate; you'll recognise it by the vinca vines that wind up, intertwining with the metal and covering its hinges. Above the gate there are two lanterns – both empty – with layers of wax congealed on their bottoms. If you've received an invitation, you will be welcomed by a man with a confident gait. Follow him. He will lead you up a white-and-black-pebbled driveway that curves, at a gradual incline to the left, through verdant, untrammelled gardens.

If you do engage the man, don't expect much of a response. He enjoys long silences. Rather enjoy the willows and their sleepy, perennially sweeping limbs that line the driveway all the way up to the main house. If you have arrived during summer, brace yourself for the gnats that lilt in wispy communities around the willows. You'll have to swat your way through the thick of them.

Very soon, a triple-storey roundhouse will come into view, made of arjun, laurel and sheesham wood and topped with a flat-stoned roof, hollowed out in sections for reinforced glass. There are several entrances and exits to the main house. You could enter via the third floor by taking one of the four outdoor staircases that service each storey. It is the kind of roundhouse where a gust of wind might enter through a window on the first floor and exit out the dining room on the third. Speaking of design, the rocks found here on the ridge have been built around, or incorporated into, the structure of the house, so don't be surprised if a door seems out of place or a window feels skew. The landscape was as much the architect as the owners.

From where you stand now, facing the main house from a worm's eye view, you won't see the outside deck of the second and third storey or the aerial walkways that extend into the trees from the third floor. There will be time to explore all of this during your stay. Those who take up an invitation to live here are obliged to take part in the daily maintenance of the property. This, it is felt, is a fair exchange for the free living on offer.

Do not worry. No resident is given more than they can handle on any given day.

I know, it feels like you have walked into the tropics: every curious footstep or misplaced hand revealing insects toiling in precarious worlds all their own. If you'd like, you're free to wander off the pathway into the curling, webbed gardens, but you do so at your own risk. No, there's nothing out there that *wants* to hurt you. Equally, don't be frightened by the rambunctious dog circling your feet, dashing off through the shrubbery and appearing further up the path on a lichen-covered rock. Abbas shows off for strangers.

Another thing. The ridge is particularly prone to lightning strikes, so when those Joburg thunderstorms come rolling over it's best to stay indoors. The cooling rains do lessen the humidity, somewhat. Because the ridge is such a hotspot for lightning, you will find the property glazed in fulgurite: vesicular masses of glassy, vitrified soil. Like the ones you see on your right. It is astounding, don't you think, that such monstrous force can be fossilised (and look gorgeously alien, too).

Keep up now. Don't let the shimmering sediment distract.

Follow the man. You will be asked to wait outside as he prepares your reception. Yes, the path is uneven and not very forgiving on roller bags. Pick up your belongings with core engaged, pelvis tucked, back straight, knees slightly bent. That way you'll be using your whole self, not just your arms.

DIANNE

The man in purple yoga pants has a bony face but kind eyes; I have to walk twice as fast to keep up with his long strides.

'Willows attract all kinds of creepy-crawlers, as you can imagine. And these ones are quite old.' He reaches out an arm to brush up against the branches we pass, speaking in a deliberate way, as if he's double-checking the weight of each word. We reach a part of the driveway where it splits in two, one path leading to the front and another snaking around to the side of the property.

'This way,' he gestures.

'This place is –'

'– designed with as little human imposition on the landscape as possible, yes.'

I'm a bit ruffled by the abrasiveness, but I try to not let it get to me. I'm tired, and my shawl and legwarmers aren't keeping the chill out as much as I'd like. Up ahead, two tree trunks made into stools flank either side of one of the entrances. He asks me to take a seat and wait. The Northcliff water tower stands above us on the very top of the ridge, its tawniness stark against the blue sky.

There's still time to turn back: Karabo's voice, gentle but firm. I think of us, hiking through Nkandla forest: me panting more than usual, a headache breaking through my forehead. I tell her we've got to keep going, that nothing hard was ever gotten easily. *Wena, you're stubborn for pain, ne?* A click of her tongue and Karabo's gone. If she was here, I know she'd make fun of all these layers I have on. *Kabs, when you're my age the sun doesn't warm you like it's supposed to.*

It's not long before yoga-pants man comes outside and shows me into a sitting room furnished with a small fireplace; each of the ornately upholstered chairs in the room face it. On the right-hand side of each chair is a coffee table with a blank sheet of paper on it.

'Pick a grain,' he says, alerting me to the types of wood the tables are made from.

'Oh, okay then.' I stand over by a greyish one.

'Ashwood. Interesting. We'll begin shortly.'

'Sorry, what's your —' Before I get the words out he's left through a connecting door. There's a pungent smell of burned sage in the air and I open a nearby window to let some out. On the mantelpiece above the fireplace a dark blue statue of Shiva stares me down. The god's long pink tongue, many arms, necklace of heads and waist decorated with blood-stained limbs unnerve me. I rest my eyes on a blue-eyed portrait of Jesus on another wall instead. Below Jesus, on a coffee table, are copies of the Torah, Bible and Qur'an pressed together between two marble bookends shaped like the front and back of an elephant.

The man returns with a glass of water and a set of sharp HB pencils on a silver tray. He points to the page on the ashwood table. 'This will decide whether you're offered a place here, or not,' he says.

'But, the woman I met ...'

'The Mortician.'

'Yes. She told me it was guaranteed.'

He taps the blank page with the pencil. 'This first.'

'Am I supposed to answer something?' I resist the shakiness in my voice, straightening myself in the chair, but it's no use. My desperation shows. If I don't get in, I'll have to go back and explain to Karabo, Tshidi and Lavinia why I left with only a letter stuck to the fridge as my explanation.

'There *are* questions you're supposed to answer. But I don't have them.' He places the water down and leaves.

What do they want? I position the table between my knees. My medical history, maybe? I glance around again. There are no clues. A strange pattern is carved in the wood of the door the man used to exit. It's a series of connecting lines that form little diamond shapes inside it. I pick a starting point and follow the pattern, ending up back where I started.

Focus, Dianne. Give them something.

The last thing I wrote was the letter to my sisters. *You will be mad, but please understand I need to do this for myself. I need to prepare. I'll send money back to cover my part of the bills* … I wrote, not explaining that the money would be coming from this place, which was paying me for my 'exploration', as the Mortician put it.

The page glares at me. I start to write an admission of why I'm here, in big block letters. *I AM D* … but before I can finish the man comes back, picks up my page and folds it several times. Then leaves.

This is too suspect. I have half a mind to let Tshidi know where I am. As I scroll for her number on my phone the man walks back in.

'Your room is ready.'

'Wait, so what, this was all some test?'

'No, not at all, this is important. It's our baseline.'

'Baseline? Of what?'

'Of you. I'm Mustafa.' He looks directly at me for the first time, smiling. 'Now don't forget your luggage,' he says.

We walk towards the door with the carved pattern. 'What is that?'

Mustafa looks from the pattern to me, comparing us. 'It's an endless knot. Come, your roommate is keen to meet you.'

From the sitting room we walk down a wide, curved corridor

with screed flooring. Two sets of pencilled drawings hang on either wall. The drawings change from one frame to the next as we walk, like animation stills. The one on the right is of a skeleton kneeling over a corpse. As we stroll down the corridor, the skeleton goes about picking the corpse up and carrying it on its back. In the final frame, it looks off into white space, the body on its back bearing down upon its bones.

And, on the left, a woman draped from head to toe in velvety cloth kneels over a corpse, as she goes about unwrapping herself and clothing the corpse. In the final frame at the end of the corridor, she lies down with it.

'I'd like to speak to the Mortician,' I say.

Mustafa hasn't spoken since we left the sitting room. 'Yes, of course. In good time. We want you to settle in first.'

'I'd rather it happen sooner rather than later. Please.'

'Comfort is one of our top priorities. The best decisions are made from a position of comfort.'

I slow down a little, looking back the way I came.

'Fear is normal,' says Mustafa, noticing my slackened pace. 'If you'd like to turn back now, you're most welcome to. This isn't Sodom and Gomorrah.'

His body faces forward but his face is turned back to me.

'I don't want to be afraid.'

Mustafa comes up to me and takes my luggage. 'Let me help you.' His demeanour changes; he looks at me as if he knows me. 'The Mortician did not lie when she said we can help. I promise.' He touches my arm lightly, then walks on.

When we reach the end of the corridor there're two doors on our right and left. Mustafa knocks on the right one, leaning in to listen.

'Give me a sec,' calls a woman. After a few minutes the door opens. 'I was just stepping out the shower, sorry.'

Her hair and bosom are wrapped in beige towels.

'Angelique, meet Dianne.' Mustafa steps aside to let me in.

The bedroom is spacious, with a high ceiling and laminated flooring. Angelique's hands are wet when she shakes my hand and follows us inside, dripping water behind her. I resist the urge to tell her to mop up the puddles she's making.

'Nice to meet you,' I say, wiping my hand dry as she walks to what I assume is her bed.

'So, Dianne, what do you think?' asks Mustafa. He shows me to my bed, pointing out my cupboard and drawers.

'It's good for me,' I say.

Our beds are on either side of the room with a large empty space between, filled with only a furry black carpet. The room gets good light at this time of day from a sliding door that opens onto a small, raised patio.

'Are you religious?' asks Mustafa, picking up a rosary that must have slipped out of my pocket.

'Didn't the Mortician tell you about me?'

'She might have mentioned something.'

'I tried to join a convent once. It never stuck.'

'You'll be interested to know we've got a room made entirely of stained glass here. It's wonderful ...' Mustafa stops, his eyes drifting up. '... sublime. It's just through that other door in the corridor. You can't miss it.' He presses the rosary into my palm and walks over to Angelique. 'The Mortician wants to see you,' I overhear him say.

'Now?' Angelique drops the towel tucked under her arms as she lays out different coloured underwear. I'm stunned by her nudity. Mustafa doesn't seem bothered.

'Once you're clothed,' he says, neutrally.

Mustafa leaves us alone. Why would someone like *her* be in a place like *this*?

'You don't mind me getting dressed in front of you, do you?' she asks, slipping a black thong up her thighs.

'No, it's fine.'

'In my line of work I have to be comfortable showing skin. I forget other people aren't like that.'

'What do you do then?'

'I model. Been out of the game, but I'm making a comeback. Don't I look familiar?' She turns her face at an angle to the light, pursing her lips.

'Can't say you do, sorry.'

'Living under a rock,' she breathes out.

Subtlety is clearly not her strength, but I've been around long enough to let people think whatever they want of me. Angelique hops onto the bed and hides her face behind her phone.

Good, distract yourself.

'And you? What do you do?' she presses on, feigning interest.

I go about unpacking, slipping a pack of cigarettes and matches into my pocket, letting her sit like that. Unanswered.

'Hey, you heard me?'

'I heard you.'

'So?' She sits up, prises her face from her phone.

There's a pleasure in keeping her waiting. 'I was the principal of a Catholic school. But I left that a while ago.'

'I went to a Catholic school once. It was ayt. Didn't care for the Masses all the goddamn time. I had this one music teacher though, she gave me vocal coaching after school. Lit times.'

I go out onto the raised patio, desperate for an exit. In the garden below, three guinea fowl idly peck at the ground, before disappearing behind aloe shrubs.

'You're from Joburg, originally, I mean?' Angelique shouts at me from inside.

She can't read social cues. 'Didn't I hear that the Mortician wanted to see you?'

'Oh, fuck me on a biscuit!'

I hear her scuttling out the room as I unlatch the patio gate and step down onto the lawn. All around, the property bristles with trees, flowerbeds, ferns, succulents and tall wild grasses of every colour. There doesn't seem to be any order to the planting. The guinea fowl come back from behind the shrubs and begin to circle me. I must seem like some strange animal to them. Or maybe a statue. When I break their circle, strolling back to the bedroom, the birds flutter a little before resuming their pecking. This is their home. I'm passing through.

FLYING ABOVE THE unnumbered house, a male hadeda swooped in a low glide above the manicured hedge at the back of the property, before perching on a mustard-coloured rock. The rock, outside the property's boundaries but high enough on the ridge to look over it, jutted out – a decrepit face amongst a maroon and hickory landscape. The terrain was inhabited by lizards who warmed their bellies on stones that grew hot as the day waned; while blackjacks, with brazen nettles, waited for rodents to wander close enough for their seedlings to hitch a ride and colonise, elsewhere.

On the rock the hadeda fluttered, letting out a long, sonorous call – the sound of a whining baby extended to distortion. The call was heard in the hedges, where the Mortician walked, tracing her steps through the puzzle she had grown up around her. Because the property was built on a slope, the hedge grew taller and thicker the closer one got to the fly-brick wall at the back of the property. The Mortician heard a hadeda call and searched the sky for its origin. Up above, whorls of cloud were smeared into faint jets by the wind, but no bird. She carried on, rehearsing the false starts, promising leads and dead ends that she had planted; the longer she walked, the prouder she was of the accomplishment.

Another call. Still, no bird. Was it calling for a mate? She was not sure.

The hadeda had been flying all morning and this spot on the rock was his usual stop before a lengthy, circular route back to the roost. His call reached further here than if he was down below, fighting to carve out aural space in the atmosphere of the city. His squawking alerted the lizards nearby; they darted away, squeezing through hairline cracks in the crag.

In the hedges, the Mortician arrived at the centre, surrounded by the mouths of five equally promising corridors. This was something special, she thought, so special she had forgotten the way out. Another call rang overhead: no bird. Sitting on the grass, she closed her eyes. Listened – faint rustling, engine-humming (trucks, cars, lawnmowers), the voice of a man faintly saying her name. She called for Mustafa a few times, loud enough for her voice to penetrate. *He will find me. I must be patient.*

On the mustard rock above the property, the male hadeda spotted a female circling some distance away. He called, furiously flapping so the sunlight illuminated his purple plumage. The female seemed to have heard: a dot in the sky changed course and drew nearer, nearer – now above him, now flapping its wings against the eye of the sun. The female settled on nearby soil. The earth was too hot here. She poked and prodded at her feet, bringing up cooler sediment, and an unsuspecting earthworm.

The male hopped over to where she stood and dipped his head low, revealing a red culmen. She inspected him tacitly, feet restless. The male, intent on attention, jabbed his beak into the ground and pinched the earthworm that she had cleaved. The female leapt to a rock above him and the male followed, carrying the squirming earthworm as his offering. She took the worm from his mouth and ripped it in two. She was hungrier than he'd expected: after swallowing her half she came for his. He let her have it.

In the heart of the hedge, Mustafa appeared at the mouth of a corridor. The Mortician lay star-like, eyes shut; the sunlight pressing against her eyelids created a blurred brightness on their underside. She could not fully look into it, though she enjoyed the pixelated sensation of trying to. The protein fibres in the jelly of her eyes clumped together from all that light.

The grass of the maze was so plush that it removed all sounds of someone approaching. The Mortician only knew she had been found when Mustafa's head blocked out the light above her, turning the reddish-yellow screens of her inner eyelids black. 'That didn't take long,' she said, lifting herself onto her haunches. With eyes open, small retina floaters bordered by rainbows shot across her vision: asteroids disintegrating upon entry into a world.

'It was a matter of time,' said Mustafa.

The pair entered the mouth of a different corridor. With their joint memory, making it out should be easy, she thought.

Mustafa asked if she had heard the hadeda and the Mortician affirmed, admitting that she was not able to see it. They walked on – taking two left turns and one right – before finding an exit. Another call stretched through the air; this time they spotted the hadeda, sailing low above the property, followed moments later by another not too far off from the first.

'Signs of a good harvest,' said the Mortician.

Mustafa agreed. 'Shall we practise? The second cohort start arriving tomorrow.'

'Yes. It'll be good to check in with our sense of separation.' She rested her head on his shoulder.

With a worm in her belly, the female hadeda released a steady, hot stream of shit. It splattered off the edge of the rock, some of it landing on the male's feet. Then she took flight in one synchronous flourish of feathers. The male, unsure if he should follow, watched her lift away. Waited. The female called back once, twice, three times in quick succession, flying above the property. Her call reverberated in the gardens, landed on balconies, rolled in through open windows, splayed on carpets. The male had only the insistent urge to follow. He took flight, leaving claw marks where he once stood.

Quiet. The city's rumble climbed the ridge, dissipating. Lizards emerged from their cracks to resume one last hour of blood-warming. Most had lost their tails as a result of manic sprints through impossible fissures. Tails collected like strings of meat in the gaps while cells in lizard bodies were, already, wriggling to divide.

THERE WAS A room on the second floor that faced west; they had only ventured there once before, with the first cohort. Standing outside a walnut-coloured door carved to appear like threads of rope woven together, the Mortician and Mustafa steadied themselves, deepening their breathing: tensing and relaxing their diaphragms. The Mortician opened the door onto a room that had two barrel-shaped containers, each laid on its side and raised off the ground. Above, a series of translucent pipes snaked out of the ceiling and hovered over them.

They got undressed at opposite ends of the room, meeting in the middle to help seal each other's ears with plugs, double-checking that their underwear was tight enough. Their eyes and mouths went unprotected. 'This never gets old,' said Mustafa.

She led him to a barrel and helped him inside, fixing his hands and feet in straps that came through the bottom of the barrel. Walking over to the control panel in the corner of the room, she toggled a series of buttons which activated the piping overhead. The pipe in question was packed with thousands of micro-bristles, soaked in mild disinfectant. The process took some time to get started but, after a minute or so, a million tiny tip-tapping sounds emanated overhead.

She looked on as cockroaches pushed their way through the bristle-filled pipe, disinfecting themselves and dropping – one by ten by fifty – into the barrel. The fall didn't hurt them; most landed on their backs and tipped themselves over onto jointed legs, flourishing their prickly-haired bodies.

Mustafa closed his eyes, making his body limp. He knew it was useless to struggle. It only agitated them. He tracked the sensations running up and down his skin, imagining the horde as nothing but miniature masseurs, stimulating his follicles. The stiller he was, the more likely their movements would find an equilibrium; with less and less space for them to move around, they would become slight, negligible irritations. The trick was to find a balance on the borders – eyelids, lips, nostrils, anus – each had to be patrolled with a level of tension that did not stiffen the rest of the body. Mustafa imagined his boundaries lined with strings, like those found inside a grand piano. The tapping of the cockroaches, along with the reciprocal *no* they received from his orifices, were his very own felt-covered hammers, playing Rimsky-Korsakov's *Flight of the Bumblebee.*

The Mortician instinctively recoiled. She remembered when they had started out with just five cockroaches. How quickly those five multiplied. How expeditiously the males secreted sugar-rich fluids on their backs for the females to eat, all so that they could trap them in a mating position. At this stage, the females would struggle for a few moments before settling into the predicament of being dragged around by their abdomens for hours. Most of the offspring made it to adulthood; others became food for the brood and, after six months, the tank had close to five hundred. With sets of wrap-around eyes attached to twitching feelers, primed to detect the most subtle undulations in their environment, there was nothing the earth was more efficient at making than these frantic recyclers, she thought. On one end, the recycle, on the other end, the cycle and, somewhere in the middle: them.

A timer went off. The Mortician pulled two levers. The first opened the bottom of the barrel, letting a large portion out into a copper tray. The second released litres of water from another pipe, washing the remaining cockroaches off. Once clean, the Mortician released Mustafa from the straps and helped him out. 'How was it?'

'I kept thinking about my skeleton. How they'd never be able to reach it. At least not yet.'

'And the fear?' The Mortician put her goggles on and stood by the other barrel.

'Slight. Not as much as when we first tried this.'

'Yes, much like weeds, isn't it? The fear, I mean. You can't do anything about it because, somehow, it always gets in. But then you begin to see –'

'– some weeds have a usefulness. Breaking up the mind's hardpans.'

'Hm. Experience, pulling at what grows, planting and praying.'

'I know it in here,' Mustafa said, tapping his temple, removing his goggles, 'but not fully in here.' He slapped his chest.

'This is why we practise. We're never masters, of anything. And why would we want to be?'

Mustafa walked over to where she stood and hugged her. 'Are you ready?'

'No. But strap me in anyway.'

ANGELIQUE

Showers are my fav, but they gotta be hot. The kind of hot that makes you wanna baptise yourself in soap. That's the kind I'm talking about. The hot water never runs out here. There's nothing that grates my tits more than expecting a hot shower and then getting one that just can't rise to the occasion. Like most men.

It's one of the things I couldn't stomach about rehab. You'd have to be first at the showers in the morning if you wanted any hot water. Now, I've never been a morning person so you can imagine what that was like. So of course I complained and of course management assured me a second, larger geyser had been ordered and was on the way. It was supposed to be connected to my room *only*. But did it ever arrive? I don't know. I left before that. But if I ever go back and find that they have the same problem, well, I'll just very nicely blast them on my socials. Then they'll see shit.

The perks of having a blue-tick to your name in these streets.

The best thing about rehab? It bumped up my following. I wasn't even posting on schedule according to my analytics. Even the random DMs, which have always been a thing, were less sexual and actually more encouraging. I had teens telling me how much they 'looked up' to me having 'watched my career'. They made it seem like I was *so* much older than them, like those burned-out presenters on KTV. I didn't appreciate that much.

No, don't worry about the sexual stuff in the DMs: any woman about her business knows how to handle a random dick or two in her inbox. Block. Report. Block. Report. Though without a dedicated socials manager it does get tiring. I just repeat my daily mantra: *Socials are King. Be the Queen.* It works.

Listen, when I saw my room I kinda gagged over the suite the Mortician gave me. It's on the ground floor and opens onto a cute side garden. I'm not really a nature-go-walking person, but it's nice to look through the windows and see green, at a distance. The bathroom is pretty by retreat centre standards: all black granite and round frosted mirrors on every wall. The basin's my favourite, though; it's large enough to hold my creams, ointments, masks, cleansers, exfoliators and moisturisers, as well as the herbal powders that the Mortician said would work wonders for my complexion and hair. It even has a special docking port for my phone so I can play what I want on Spotify while I shower.

My phone is flashing. God, I hope it's a designer wanting me back in the game or an agency checking when I'll be ready to work again. I don't check my phone just yet because I don't feel centred enough to be disappointed, again. If I don't check it, the possibilities are endless: it could be *the* notification that revives my career.

I brush my teeth instead, making sure to brush in clockwise and anticlockwise direction just like my dental specialist advised. The anticipation gets too much and finally I give in. I pick up my phone to see it's just a reminder that I set for my Insta Live today. And just like that: from one hundred possibilities to zero.

There's no hurt in hope so I delete the negative thoughts from my mind; I know I'm not exactly 'most-wanted' right now, but I could make a major comeback. I could.

There's a bright future waiting for each of us. You have to choose it. Something rehab taught me. Positive affirmation – manifesting and attracting everything you want from the universe. They teach you to do three positive affirmations at the beginning of each day in rehab. When I first got there I could only manage one, but now I can do about five, without thinking.

My make-up *has* to be on point for today's Live. It's my only chance to do it before my roommate arrives. Very few people know I've left rehab except some of the staff at the clinic. I made everyone sign NDAs because, wow, the press are vultures. This place, where I am right now, it's not what people expect from me, which is why I chose to come here. Sure, it's a little rough around the edges, and I do wish we didn't have to 'help' with the upkeep of the place, but I guess that's part of the gimmick. 'Getting *involved* in your healing. No longer sitting on the side-lines of your life.' Blah de Blah.

I'm not allowed to say where I am exactly – it's one of the rules – but that doesn't mean I can't titillate the fans. Come to think of it, if I want to make a comeback, I should start thinking about a collective noun to call my followers. Every person who matters has some sort of nickname for their fans. But all the cool collective nouns are taken. It has to be something mysterious and alluring. Like, maybe *my vixens*, or *my fallen angels*. I don't know, I'll need to think about it.

Mystery sells as much as pornography. Todd Nubile told me that on the shoot of my first L'Oréal campaign. He said it with half his face behind the camera and that iconic glass eye of his fixed on me. Todd's glass eye used to freak me out even before I got the chance to work with him, but after L'Oréal it was kind of comforting to know there was zero judgement going on in that eye.

Setting up the tripod for the Live is the easy part. I make sure the audience gets a little view of the outside garden but can't see the single beds on either side of the room (that's ghetto). Only thirty minutes till my first Live in months and I'm so overwhelmed. With my phone set up I go back to the bathroom to apply foundation, nude lipstick, blush and eyeliner. A classic 'I-woke-up-like-this' look. Natural enough, not too showy because, like, I'm doing serious inner healing. I decide to have my white bathrobe on with a little cleavage showing because it'll give an intimate feel.

Fifteen minutes to the Live. The nerves are setting in. Should

I wear something else? I want to give off sex appeal, but the fans know I'm sexy already, right? If they had any doubts about that I'd refer them to my Victoria's Secret catalogue.

Five minutes. I take one last look at myself in the mirror. Damnit. Not enough foundation. I rush back to reapply, giving my face another run-over to cover the discoloration and fill out my cheekbones a little more. No one can see any sign, no one can know. I *will* be the poster child of rehab rejuvenation.

Okay, maybe not so bold. I should go for sincere and thoughtful. Like I've been through a lot and I am learning to be a better person. Yes, that'll work, that'll work because it's true. But I don't want it to get too truthful. Just polite, but authentic. Real, and touching, but not soppy. Nobody likes soppy. It's been done.

Back in the bedroom I reposition the tripod so that the top of my cleavage is visible above the parting of my robe. All ready.

At the start of the Live things are quiet, but it doesn't take long for that zero at the top of the screen to turn to ten, then thirty-five, sixty-three. Sure, not as much as I was hoping for but a start.

The comments start flowing in:

Where have you been?

We're praying for your recovery.

We miss you and love you Angel.

Rehab or not you still look on fleek gurl.

For the first ten minutes all I do is read one after the other, each one reminding me I'm still loved out there, in many lives smaller than mine. I kind of just want to sit here and read comments, but then a couple of followers start asking why I'm being quiet. Argh, interactions. I wish people could just get what they need by looking at me.

'Hey beautiful people! Sorry for my silence. I'm just taking in the love you all are giving me. Wow. I can't tell you what a hard road it's been, like, you really get to face your demons in rehab guys. And maybe what happened to me was God's way of putting me on the right path.' The screen lights up with different coloured hearts; I shift in my seat and part my robe a little more. The number at the top of the screen jumps to eighty-seven.

'I know some of you are wondering what happened between me and Xolisi, and I know, like, there's been a lot of things said in the media and stuff, but let me just put things straight for you, okay?'

Tell us what really happened.

Akiri you were abusing each other?

Are you ever going to model again?

You should run for Miss SA, you're so inspirational – the comments start firing off faster now, too fast for me to read them all, so I keep my eye on the stream of hearts.

'I can't say much because, you know, "ongoing investigation" and all that. But let me say this. I was Xolisi's muse for the longest. We were day one, ride and die shit, and you guys have seen, I was there front and centre when his collections *eventually* got some attention, right? So there you go, what else does that tell you? We inspired one another and, yes, we were the real deal, but I have never ever, swear-to-God, hit that man. I kept it "here". Just modelling. I ain't got time to be beating up my man. I always cater to my king. Anyway, I don't need to explain myself. You all saw those pics of me. Red-eye and all ...' I was now at one-hundred-and-five viewers. Nowhere near my best.

We believe you Angelique.

We stan a queen who speaks truth to the patriarchy!

Tell us more about rehab, how much longer do you have?

Please do more Lives like this, you give me LIFFE – the more comments I get the better I feel about my decision to clear the air with my followers. They clearly wanted – needed – to hear my side of the story. I should continue this, make it like a weekly check-in.

Angelique's Road to Recovery: who knows, I could get a TV show out of it.

'So check here, ne. About rehab ... I'm not there anymore. But don't worry I'm still in SA, just working on myself, like *really* working, like, trying to rise above and become a better person. Maya Angelou guys, still-I-rise kind of vibe. You get me? And rehab, it's just not *the thing* for me. *That thing*: the feeling like you on the right track. And I'm not sure where the right track is for me honestly, but I'm trying something new. It's a top-notch, super-exclusive retreat and I don't know if it's going to work for me, but I had a déjà vu moment this morning when I started this Live with all you beautiful people. And if you know anything about déjà vu, then I don't need to say more.'

All this talking about 'right place right time' is making me emotional; I can feel my throat closing up. The viewer number climbs above one-fifty and it makes me even more emotional – people are listening, they still want to hear what I have to say. With the help of my fallen angels, sending positive energy my way, I can make a comeback. Or at least do one last Fashion Week.

Unamanga!

Once an addict, always an addict.

I believe Xolisi. Men are victims too!

You people seriously believe this crap? Haai voetsek!

The trolls. Fucken weeds, all of them. Eggplant emojis followed by water droplets dominate the comments. All of it is coming from five different profiles with names ending in a random mix of numbers. Bots, or Xolisi stans. I wouldn't put it past him to try smear me. My vixens do their best to defend me; some threaten to report the trolls. Me? I'm chill. I pull my robe up and thank everyone for taking the time to pull through.

Don't leave so soon.

We reported those assholes.

Don't worry Angel. Please do another Live soon – are some of the last comments I read before ending the broadcast and turning my phone off.

I have a feeling the lawyers are going to be upset when they find out; they 'explicitly' told me not to engage in any media till the court appearance. But, like, how else am I going to get my story out?

I slide the tripod under the bed and make space in the bathroom for my new roommate. Mustafa hasn't told me much; in fact, all I know is it's another woman. Thank Jehovah, at least it isn't one of the gays. I'm not homophobic or anything, I just prefer sharing space with women.

I won't lie, the trolls have really shaken me. I can't even do my affirmations for the day. I play Shekinah on loudspeaker and take my make-up off with this wonderful remover made from bee wax (all natural because I'm trying to go full vegan). With a wet sponge, I wipe from forehead to chin; by the time I'm done the basin water is murky brown. The skin around my eyes has an offish hue and my face is all blotchy, with puffiness around my lips and scaly skin along my jaw. I stretch my eye bags with my pinkies, the discoloration goes away when the skin is pulled tight. Why can't it be that easy with the rest of me?

'What are you writing?' asked Mustafa. They had retired to the bedroom, which was suspended between two gingko trees inside a glass atrium: the property's epicentre.

'A letter of condolence. To the Prinsloos.' The Mortician spoke from her desk, her head craned to one side as if a strong wind was blowing through it.

Mustafa considered her, rubbing lotion down his arms. His eyes fell on the mounds of bone poking up from her neck. What did her skeleton look like, he wondered, sitting that way, flesh woven through joints, sockets, discs.

'Are you sure they'll read it? They didn't even want us at the funeral.' Mustafa got into bed. He recalled the stocky men in black suits who escorted them out of the cathedral on the day of Jan Prinsloo's burial, the altercation the Mortician had had with Vicky, Jan's daughter, and how Vicky had promised that they'd get their 'comeuppance' for what they did to her father. Grief was a strange vocabulary, he thought. He had never heard someone use 'comeuppance' at a funeral.

'Vicky doesn't understand. I regret calling her a shallow bitch.'

'Yes,' laughed Mustafa, 'I don't think that helped. Do you think she meant what she said. Our "comeuppance"?'

'People like Vicky have their entire lives handed to them on a platter. And when they think something has been taken from them, in the same way her family took and took, without asking, then people like her want to scream "bloody murder" in the streets. When the streets were always already lined with murder. I think we should be careful.' Her neck straightened as she swivelled around in the chair, dizzying herself somewhat, and releasing the memory of the day that Jan and Bonginkosi had showed them number eight Lancaster, with its enormous back yard, on which stood the ruin of a roundhouse, shot through with green and yellow creepers.

My wife wanted to get rid of the ruin, Jan explained, *but, I don't know, there was a tragic beauty to it. We did try, to no avail, to find out who might have built it, but the previous owners didn't know either. So we left it at that.* Jan went on to explain that the property was so grotesquely spacious that it could, essentially, be split in two.

That was when he placed the keys in her hand.

Bonginkosi, Jan's butler, had taken so many videos of them hugging, teary-eyed, exchanging *thank you*'s and *my pleasure*'s as they toured the ruin, that someone watching the scene might have sworn they'd won the lottery. In each barely recognisable room, they imagined the work to be done, egged on by Jan, who was wheelchaired around by Bonginkosi.

The Mortician observed Mustafa in bed, meticulous as ever with his evening lotion ritual, and wondered if she should tell him about her surveillance. Would he be disgusted? No. Mustafa was part of her story, but not the whole of it, she reasoned. She swivelled back around to face the desk and complete the letter, but her mind trailed off again.

She thought about their time at Bridge Builders Hospice: how people passed through those bedrooms like ghosts on wrecked rowboats, incapable of redirecting course from the approaching cliff. She had witnessed it many times: the moment dying became a letting, and the currents plunged their patients, headfirst, into waterfalls so misty it was like sailing through cloud. Resist or not, it made no difference. She knew that, yet the process of journeying with strangers to their last breath was where she liked to be. It provided glimpses into what could only be felt – the pivot between the flame and its fuel.

Everyone at Bridge Builders was missing something, even the caregivers. A lover. A family member. A best friend. A foot. A respectable CD4 count. A good amount of fat. Enough money to make that one last trip to Cape Agulhas to see if they could spot the difference between the Indian and Atlantic oceans. Longing resonated, impregnating the silent halls, taking on phantasmagorical shapes for the adult-sized foetuses, tucked in their beds. Bundles with two holes for eyes, unable to hold conversation with any of their visitors, yet, when they were alone, rattling off entire conversations to people only they could see. Others were more lucid and could engage their caretakers, but, despite those differences, everyone at the hospice had the world of time to track the sun as it reached through the windows towards their atrophying legs. By evening, the light always withdrew itself into long, vacant nights.

The caregivers worked the silences as best as they could, accentuating them with casual conversation, moulding them with pleasant *good morning's* and *sleep tight's*, sometimes shattering them completely with bouts of comic banter. The Mortician had gone to work there because she believed it had the right amount of existential angst that made her feel part of something monumental. She'd expressed this to Mustafa when they became one another's confidants.

He had warned her about fetishising the work in that way; even existential work was not free from ego, he said. It was these brief, throw-away comments that impressed her. Perhaps this was the segue into their work together?

'Beginnings are important,' began the Mortician, 'but just the right ending can be the cork in the bottle, letting enough air in.' She took to the page, writing what she'd just said in the closing of the letter.

'Reminds me of the new couple we admitted.' Mustafa's reading glasses were on, but he had not picked up the book on the nightstand. She was in one of her moods, he could tell, something akin to the consistency of waterlogged grass.

'I've always had a sense for people, especially couples, you know that. And those two.' She smacked her tongue against the roof of her mouth. 'I don't know, they seem to genuinely care for one another.'

The word 'recovery' cohered in his head. He turned it over, prodding. Did it mean going back to an original state, the way things were before experience bent one out of shape? Or was it more like upholstery, covering the worn furniture with the fabric you had on hand, using whatever technique to bring back a sense of continuity, even if it wasn't the original fabric that had caught your eye when you first bought it? Either way, relationships were lessons in failure.

Out of his nightstand drawer he took a phial with a dropper inside and squeezed a tincture of marjoram oil onto their pillows. Then he took a second phial, filled with a murky dark brown liquid, and squeezed some under his tongue. The bitter ethanol taste announced itself, the nutrients of his sleep concoction dissolving through the membranes of his mouth, into his bloodstream. 'Are you done yet?' he said, lying back.

'Almost.' The Mortician reread the letter back to herself, hoping her words might dissuade Vicky from the threats she'd made at the funeral. She had tried to explain, as best she could, the state of mind that Jan had reached by the end of his life.

Mustafa was dozing off in bed, his nose twitching ever so slightly. Was he aware of this quirk? She yearned for the ease with which he could fall asleep. 'Speaking of endings. Have you given any thought to yours?' she asked, putting the pen down and walking into the bathroom to brush her teeth, assuming he had already fallen asleep.

On the lip of a dream, Mustafa heard the question. 'I have,' he grunted, turning to face the slant of the bathroom light. 'It is early morning. The ocean is calm like an endless smooth mirror. The lone engine of a plane flying over the surface is all you can hear. I'm in the plane, still conscious, barely. And there are a handful of people whom I love. They open the back of the plane together and help me exit. If I can stand up at that time, then I would prefer to stand. If I can't, I'll be on a stretcher.'

'Then what?' The Mortician returned from the bathroom in turquoise pyjamas, her hair tied in a bun.

'If I'm standing, I'll fall backwards, my eyes on those I love. If I'm lying down, they all roll me out the plane – a dot in the sky, plummeting. Hopefully, I'm dead before I hit the water.'

Getting into bed, the Mortician cracked her neck. 'I like that.' She kissed him on the cheek and lay on her back. 'A corpse is for the living.'

'Would you like me to hold you?' asked Mustafa.

'Not tonight. But can I hold you?'

He faced his bedside lamp, curling into the shape of a shrimp, waiting for her familiar octopus arm to round his waist. Sometimes, she held him so tight that, in the morning, he had to peel himself off her. An octopus and shrimp in bed together. The Mortician wrapped her legs and arms around him. During the night, their ribcages intermittently expanded: belly to spine, spine to belly and, as the night deepened into obsidian, they settled into separate solitudes.

LUCAS

At night the world breathes through its mouth. Especially this late, with Daniel next to me. The air is stiff, despite the fan working hard near my side of the bed. I shrug off the blankets and reach for my crutches, needing fresh air. Who knew it took this much co-ordination to get up and toward a window?

Our room is on the second floor. It overlooks the rock pools. Every night since we got here, I've stood by this window, listening to the frogs croaking by the water. That, along with the muffled sounds of cars speeding down the highway, makes me feel like I'm by the seaside, if I close my eyes.

I'm getting good with these crutches. Nikita would be happy. After my surgeries, the physio visited me every day for three months, bending my knees up to my chest, rotating my hips in their sockets, manipulating ankles and toes. She was dedicated, exercising my limbs even when I couldn't stand it. My left leg was damaged more than the right; there were times it felt like Nikita was going to fracture them all over again. That was all in my head, though; she never pushed me beyond what I could handle.

Soft tissue heals through movement. She said that more times than I can count, promising the pain would be worth it. We were seeing good results in those weeks. I was practising how to stand and balance all over again, like an adult baby. After my sessions, the nurses gave me pain meds. That was my favourite part. With benzos you're basically living in a lava lamp: everything comes at you slow and gentle. But, once they wore off, the throbbing from the bolts in my legs always won in the end. It was a game only healing could win. There were nights I'd turn on my left side and wake with a shrill shooting up my spine. I'd never been one to sleep on my back like that and I had to learn how.

Daniel was there when I stood up for the first time. Seeing me struggling to do the simplest of things was hard for him, I know. Before my accident, he had always spoke about how he wished he had a body like mine. Seeing me struggle, he wasn't wishing for that anymore. On the day I stood on my own two legs he made a conscious effort not to let anything slip by that wasn't stamped with encouragement. I could see it in his face and maybe he could see it in mine. I was afraid he'd leave me. He was afraid I'd always be this way. I wanted him to see I was trying to get back to my old self. *Legs shoulder-width apart, chest lifted, hips tilted up* – Nikita drilled all of that into me so often that it became my mantra for standing.

The rock pools are lit with green light tonight. Even by the window, the room is stifling. I opt for the balcony. How the hell does Daniel do it with a pillow between his legs and blankets pulled up over his head? From the balcony I watch fish rise and fall in the rock pools. Must be nice to be surrounded by all that water, moving through it as it moves through you. No matter what you do or where you go, when you're a fish water will always be there, holding you, even as you sleep.

Land is different: you're always working against gravity. When I was able to stand on my own, Nikita moved me to the parallel bars and had me swing my legs back and forth, mimicking some kind of strolling motion. She said this would remind my muscles of how they used to work. She called it muscle memory. I was familiar with the term, having heard about it countless times from my track coach, but these exercises felt different. I wasn't just asking my muscles to remember; I was asking them to forget the accident. It was a crazy thing to experience – the amnesia of my limbs, their slow recall of a previous life.

I look back into the bedroom; Daniel is a heap of snoring blankets. When he first told me about his depression, he said it felt like heavy metals were living inside his head. I had tried to picture it – specks of mercury trapping him. Depression made it hard for him to feel for things he typically enjoyed. That was when he stopped coming to my physio sessions, saying he had mountains of reading to get through for his dissertation on Schopenhauer. No amount of texting or cute emoticon-ing eased the feeling that we were drifting. I was too hell-bent on pushing past my injuries to notice something was wrong. Soft tissue heals through movement, but we were not moving. We were being held in place, by different weights.

The night sky has cleared. Someone is awake on the first floor, smells like bacon with garlic and onions. I back up to a picnic chair and lower myself onto it. Fuck, I could do with a snack, but I'm lazy to go all that way.

'You all right?' Daniel stands by the sliding door, half asleep.

'Can't sleep. Too hot.'

'Take a cold shower.'

'Yeah, maybe.'

'Are you sure it's just that?'

He wants to get closer. I can almost hear him wishing for me to say *I'm fine* so he can go back to bed. 'It's just that,' I say.

'It's good we've come here. Sarah had only good things to say about this place. And we need something different.'

I nod. 'A cold shower is a good idea.'

'Do it,' says Daniel, getting back into bed.

I sit awhile, letting thoughts push and stretch against the quiet, clenching and relaxing my toes the way Nikita recommended. She'd be proud of how well I'm doing. It didn't take long for me to get it right: *weight on hands, crutches first, injured leg second, step through*. Just another way to train the body. If anything, being an athlete prepared me for this. Well, former athlete. Daniel admired my athletic achievements. He used to joke and say that if we ever fused into one person, we'd make the perfect gay man – me with the body, him with the brains. Those were the days we could say silly shit like that. If I had just been there for him during his descent – if he'd been there during my ascent – maybe we'd be more willing to … I don't know.

Okay, get up now. You need some sleep.

I make my way to the bathroom and splash my face with water, drink a glass of it too. When I crutched myself out of the hospital, Daniel wasn't there. The next day I had Ma drive me to his apartment and that's when I found him in bed, pizza boxes and wine bottles on the floor, *Will and Grace* reruns on the TV, the sounds of studio-audience laughter filling up the silence. He needed help. I made him get it. That's where he met Sarah.

I'm cooler, getting into the bed again. We sleep in different layers – me on the top sheet, him buried under three blankets. When we started dating, our sleepovers were my favourite times of the week. We'd cuddle all night, shuffling around, trying to fit together; it didn't matter if our necks or shoulders ached in the morning. Now, we know it's better to claim your part of the bed and stay there for the night.

'Did the shower help?' Daniel asks, eyes closed.

I wait to answer, testing if he is really awake or if this is just reflex. He doesn't ask again. Or maybe he's pretending, aware I'm not answering. I did the same thing to him sometimes: sleeping to avoid speaking. The last time I did it was around the time Sarah disappeared.

We met Sarah when Daniel went into Silver View for his twenty-one-day observation. He talked about her a lot, called her *chatty*, once one got past her scathing wit. Sarah had worked in the police force and apparently this was what had led to her break-down, landing her in Silver View. They got out a week apart from each other. Then Sarah disappeared for three months and no one knew where she was; her family even filed a missing person's report.

The longer Sarah stayed missing, the more likely the possibility that she'd ended things. At least that's what I thought. Then all of a sudden she turned up at Daniel's apartment – hair longer, skin tanned. He was so glad to see her he forgot the stress she'd put us through. He forgave her disappearance so easily too. That made me uncomfortable.

That evening, she told us about a special retreat that had changed her life. She said she had a better picture of how things might work out, that if this was her chance to stand in the clearing then, by God, she was going to *bear witness*.

Daniel commented on how much better she seemed. I wondered what he meant. Did 'better' mean feeling less or more? Did it mean replacing one picture of the world with another? After that she called an Uber and left.

Later, when Daniel came in from saying goodbye, he confessed to knowing where she'd been all that time. She'd made him promise not to tell anyone, not even her family, not even me. *I'm telling you babe, she's different. There's none of that 'wishing' in her eyes*.

I was too disappointed in him to reply.

That night I fell asleep before him, but not before he rambled on about how we should try the retreat Sarah had gone to. I could have said no then. I could have sat up and asked him never to keep something like that from me again. It was easier to pretend to be sleeping, until sleep eventually came.

Thinking about it now, there is no definitive moment when I chose to come to this place. He said it would be good for us and a part of me wanted that to be true. I think it's easier to make choices that don't *feel* like you when all bearings are lost. Because, in those moments, nothing, really, feels like you. Sarah had asked Mustafa if they'd make a special concession for couples. Two birds with one stone. Or two stones with no bird? I should be sleeping, I know. I wish.

'Did the shower help?' Daniel asks again, groggy.

I hum, letting him decide what that means.

JAMS AND MAPLE syrups are spread out on the table. The Mortician has made flapjacks; she and I are watching Daniel and Mustafa do morning yoga on the back lawn. Angelique isn't up this early; her first meal of the day is usually a late lunch.

'Mustafa can pretzel himself into all kinds of positions,' says the Mortician.

We watch Mustafa direct Daniel into downward dog. Daniel's limbs are shaky and he falls several times. When they transition into warrior two we hear Daniel's hip joints snap into place. A few poses later and they're on their backs, in a pose Mustafa calls happy baby. They both have their legs wide open, feet in the air, like women giving birth. After that, they crawl back up to stand at the top of their mats.

'It's taken Mustafa a long time to be able to move that effortlessly,' says the Mortician.

She's right. Mustafa easily brings his head to his shins in a forward fold while Daniel stands stoic, breathing heavily. When Mustafa comes up again his body sways, reminding me of a compass adjusting to true north. I actually never thought Daniel would be into yoga: all that talk of *prana* this and *chakra* that. I know if I asked about it, he'd probably shrug me off. *The body's just a machine to be oiled, babe.*

'You didn't sleep well?' asks the Mortician, drizzling syrup on her flapjacks.

'Is it that obvious?'

'Hm. I'm curious. How did you and Daniel meet?'

'At an inter-schools athletics.'

'Oh, nice. Go on,' she says, eagerly.

Fuck, she wants a full-blown story. 'Uhm, so it was my last year running high school track. There was this guy I used to run against. My only competition really. Sibusiso. From Greenside. Our schools had this historic rivalry, and we were the best runners, so it sort of fell on us to prove who had the better track team.'

'An unreasonable expectation.'

'That's high school for you. Anyway, an hour before the two-hundred-metre I started feeling nauseous. I'd had a dodgy boiled egg for breakfast and for most of the morning I was managing to keep it down. But the closer it came to my race, well, the egg and I just didn't agree with each other. I vomited in a dug-out at the back of the stadium, minutes before my race. After throwing up, I noticed a guy smoking nearby.' I sip my coffee, remembering Daniel and how he liked to roll his sleeves up to make his biceps look bigger.

'Daniel was from the other school?'

'He was in mine. I just never took notice of him. I mean, he was part of the smokers and that group kind of kept to themselves. Being a smoker in high school kind of gives you this aura of badass-ness. Daniel wasn't much of a badass when we met though. He actually offered me a cig and said it would help with the nerves.' I look to where he lies on the grass, in child's pose.

'People will surprise you. One of the perks of only ever being inside your own head,' says the Mortician. 'Did you take the cigarette?'

'Yeah. Didn't smoke it until the season was officially over. I don't think he knows that.'

'That you smoked it?'

'That I smoked it thinking of him.'

Mustafa and Daniel walk up to the table, eyeing the flapjacks. They settle down in between the Mortician and I, both glowing with sweat.

'I miss the smell of sweat in the morning,' I say. The table goes quiet.

'Why don't you join me in the sauna later?' says the Mortician, finishing her coffee. 'Mustafa, you'll be all right if I leave you to welcome Dianne, our new resident?'

Mustafa nods, mouth full. Daniel squeezes my thigh. I want to tell him that I smoked the cigarette he gave me when we met.

'Something wrong?' he asks.

I pick some grass out of his hair. 'All good.'

THE MORTICIAN LEADS the way to the sauna on the east side of the property. We remove our robes and hang them outside before stepping in. It's not that hot at first; it takes a few ladles of water to get the stones going. Her eyes linger on my left leg. 'Train tracks.' She points to the scars on my knee. I notice that she has scars too: train tracks that run down the middle of her chest.

Out of a small pouch she removes a glass bottle filled with amber liquid and squeezes a few drops under her tongue before handing it to me. 'Here, it's a detox supplement I like to use when I sauna.'

I put some under my tongue and, when the heat starts to rise off the stones, my skin begins to tingle. I can feel my pores opening.

'I like to sit for thirty minutes a day. Helps clear the cache.' She takes a seat on the opposite side, resting her head on the rungs of the wooden bench.

'I don't like getting overheated. I struggle to sleep if the bedroom is too hot.'

'It's not for everyone.'

I don't know what she means, but I let the comment slide, easing my bum onto the bench. The stones sizzle, the cabin gets hotter while my heart drums on in my ears. When I take deep breaths a quiver rushes up my spine and somersaults at the base of my head. The hot air holds me close.

The Mortician sighs, stretching her arms to either side. I'm stunned at how relaxed she is.

'You never asked if I won the race,' I say, trying to distract myself.

'Did you?'

'Yes, but it's a lot more dramatic than it sounds. For starters, Sibusiso was winning for most of it. He was a strong starter. Then near the end I just ...'

She throws more water on the stones and the heat sprints through me. I'm lightheaded. 'Don't worry. You'll be fine. Promise. Keep talking. It helps.'

I take a moment. 'Okay, so yeah, near the end I emptied the tank around the last twenty-five metres.'

'What did that feel like? To empty the tank.' She's a lot sweatier than me. Her eyes appear half closed from where I'm sitting.

I lift myself up with the crutches and head for the door.

'No. Leave it.'

'But –'

'Your body will adjust. Sit with it awhile. Please.'

Her 'please' throws me. It's oddly desperate. I sit back down, more upright this time, ignoring the parts of me that say I should leave.

'What did it feel like to "empty the tank"?'

I press my tongue to the roof of my mouth for moisture.

Nothing comes. 'It … burned. My muscles, my entire body … all that mattered was reaching the finish line, coming first. The cheering from the stands had faded, and it was my will and my pain. Mixing.'

'It was quiet?'

'Yes. And no. I can't explain it.'

My vision starts to blur. I think about the race and how I'd crossed the finish line, hoping the boy with the rolled-up sleeves had watched me take first place.

'Control your breathing,' she says finally. 'You can last much longer than you think.'

'Isn't this supposed to be relaxing?' I get up, stumble towards the door. Steam escapes when I push it open. I make it to the railing outside. My knees ache.

'When I was a little girl, my uncle made a makeshift sauna in his back yard …'

Her voice comes up close behind me. I want space from her, but I'm too weak to move.

'… and I was fascinated with the contraption. The things we do to feel something, hey? One day, we're having a big family get-together. Kids are in the front garden, watched over by the grannies, and parents are drinking inside. There I am, curious to a fault, a little girl sneaking into my uncle's sauna to see what the big fuss was all about.'

She hands me a towel and a bottle of water from a nearby table.

'I got stuck. In the sauna. For that whole afternoon I screamed and screamed but no one heard. No one noticed. I was missing until it was time to go home. To rub salt in the wound, I was scolded for wanting "adult things".'

I navigate my way down the steps, not in the mood for her anymore.

'I had nightmares for weeks after that. Until I made up my mind that I'd get stuck in my uncle's sauna again. And again. And again. Do you know why?'

I stop halfway down the stairs. 'Why?'

'I wanted to free myself, without supervision. I didn't know it at the time but that's what I wanted. And if I couldn't do it by myself then I'd sit, patient, for freedom to find me.'

'What if it didn't find you? What if no one found you?'

'I'd probably have used my shoe to break the window, once the fear had evaporated into survival.' She dabs her face with a towel. Steam balloons behind her and for a moment it seems as if her body cannot contain the person inside of it. 'Anyway,' she says, breaking eye contact, '... you'll get used to the heat. Give it time. Sometimes the "you" you think it's up to, is not the "you" that will make it through.'

I walk towards the main house. By the time I look back she's gone inside the sauna. When I reach my bedroom, I feel a nap coming on, the kind that'll leave drool on my pillow. Before I slink onto the bed, fragments of that race, of what it took to push my body over the finish line, return.

How much of that victory was mine?

GUINEA FOWL SKULKED about behind angel trumpet shrubs, pecking at seeds that the morning's breeze had scattered across the grounds. Earlier, the wind had climbed up the back of Northcliff and tumbled down its face, carrying hundreds of red scale crawlers with it. The crawlers – offspring of winged red scales succumbing to little deaths – descended upon cycads, rosebushes and citrus trees planted on the many properties built into the ridge. The crawlers sailed on the breeze towards circuits of sweet sap housed inside manicured gardens – finding a stem, or glossy leaf, or nexus where bud turns to flower, then fruits. They hitched their mouths to the amber pipelines that they found, pipelines made from churning sunlight into sugar.

Most didn't survive because ladybugs have learned to read the wind, knowing infestation leads to feasting.

Across from the angel trumpet shrubs, in Dianne's bedroom, Mustafa hammered St Peter onto the wall above her bed, humming as he worked. The tune was a soft, gently rising melody that crested into gurgling at the back of his throat. *You are here, moving in our midst*, he sang. The tune was an earworm that had been stuck in his head ever since the wind-chimes outside his window woke him. It was what Ms Swanepoel, the head administrator, used to sing on Sundays at Isindiso Orphanage for Boys while she tended to steaming pots, sprinkling fennel seeds, cumin and paprika into her lamb curry.

Swanepoel only cooked for the boys on Sundays and, in her kitchen, Mustafa was the dutiful apprentice. She taught him how to cut onions so that he wouldn't cry, how to tell when a chicken roast was cooked all the way through and, most importantly, how to clean as one cooked so that there weren't dishes in the sink, or the juices of diced vegetables sickly sticking to countertops.

He remembered Ms Swanepoel's amorous relationship with Frank Ledwaba, the head of the hospice that had been built across the road from the orphanage. Every Sunday, Swanepoel invited Ledwaba over for lunch. It was her view that the boys under her care would benefit from being in the presence of what she called 'a man of substance'.

Back then, Mustafa only looked forward to Ledwaba's visits because he usually came bearing gifts. Danish pastries. Carrot cake. Two dozen koeksisters paired with pungent Congolese coffee, which he brewed in a Moka pot. After lunch, it was Mustafa's job to supervise the dish washing, and Victor's to prepare for four o'clock tea. Victor was the only boy the same age as Mustafa, sixteen. Swanepoel had made it clear that they were the role models for the younger boys and had the biggest responsibility to display a proper, Protestant work ethic.

Four o'clock cake and tea only happened at the beginning and end of the month, because that was when Swanepoel and Ledwaba had the money to spoil the kids. In month-middle (a phrase Swanepoel made up) Sunday lunch consisted of corned beef from a can, mashed potatoes and string beans. In month-middle, the boys knew never to ask for dessert.

During four o'clock cake and tea, Swanepoel and Ledwaba often sat on the stoep and watched the boys play an afternoon game of soccer or cricket. When they got bored, they'd split the newspaper into its sections, sharing it. Ledwaba preferred the Opinion Columns and Letters to the Editor. Swanepoel enjoyed the Lifestyle. The boys were only allowed to have cake and tea during halftime or when their game was over, never before. Once, during halftime, Mustafa asked Ledwaba why he never brought the people from the hospice out with him for lunch.

'Oh no, they're far too sick for that, my boy,' he'd said, a scowl steadily spreading across his forehead.

'They can't be too sick for fresh air and sunlight,' said Mustafa, stuffing a whole koeksister in his mouth.

'I've read that every human needs at least fifteen minutes of sunlight,' chimed Victor.

Mr Ledwaba was amused by the boys' precociousness, hiding his embarrassment behind a veil of cake. Later, Mustafa recalled how Swanepoel had pulled them aside to tell them that, for questioning a 'man of stature', him and Victor were to work in the hospice's gardens on Saturday mornings, in return for a bowl of chicken soup and some toast. Swanepoel didn't anticipate that, as reward for their toil, Frank Ledwaba would serve them a tot of sherry with their chicken soup and toast. *Something to soothe the nerves*, he'd say, offering up two shot glasses.

Those memories took on a different texture in Mustafa's mind when he tried to piece them together – something grainy that jumped, like old video footage that had survived a fire. Nevertheless, every feast implies a mass murder, or mass gathering, and while Mustafa sifted through the footage of Sunday feasts, ladybugs in Northcliff's gardens gorged themselves on soft, protein-rich, red scale crawlers. Despite their jubilance, there were some places ladybugs would not dare venture.

Behind the walls of the unnumbered house, over the angel trumpet shrubs and through the fountain grass, stood the sauna. Beside the sauna was a young lemon tree on which red scale crawlers got tended to, and moved around by, white-footed ants who had made this tree their second colony. The white-footed ants' first colony started at number ten Lancaster, at the back of a shed where the owners kept their compost bins.

When number ten dispatched exterminators to root out the colony, the winged males and female swarmed to settle elsewhere, while their wingless counterparts budded and carried the colony's larvae to the fortification of the lemon tree. Attuned to the seasonal downpour of red scale crawlers, the white-footed ants got to work organising their new cattle along the lemon tree's tubules – turning the tree into a farm, of sorts – indulging in the sugary poop the red scale crawlers produced from their sap-eating.

Like ladybugs, there were places Mustafa shied away from too. The face of St Peter (now squarely fixed to Dianne's wall) took him back. He had never noticed the look on Peter's face until now, how similar it was to a painting that hung in Swanepoel's office. *Jesus in the Garden of Gethsemane*. Jesus: warm-blooded Kingdom of Heaven. Jesus praying for angel trumpets to bellow over Golgotha and save him from yellow-teethed mobs, eager to split him to the bone.

Mustafa stepped back to the middle of Dianne and Angelique's bedroom. In the anguished look of Peter's face, he realised that, in both paintings, the men appeared in the foreground of a gnarled, blackened landscape; both casting their eyes beyond the bounds of their frames, looking to the top left and right corners.

What would it mean to pray to one's feet? He chuckled.

In the orphanage, the painting of Jesus in the garden unnerved him. Every time he entered Swanepoel's office, he tried not to look at it. It wasn't so much the anguished Jesus that frightened him as much as the landscape that seemed to want to eat the Son of God. It appeared scorched – the kind of place where rain could fall for days and produce nothing. And there was Jesus in the midst of it, bounded by flesh that feared destruction: flesh so accustomed, so in love with its own separate state of affairs.

He associated the painting with a recurring dream he often got as a boy. In it, a tall, amorphous shadow chased him around the orphanage, in between the double-bunk beds, through the kitchen and out into Swanepoel's beloved vegetable patch. The more desperately he tried to get away from it, the slower his legs became. In one of the dream's iterations, he stood on Swanepoel's balcony, an area strictly off-limits, and the amorphous shadow watched him from the threshold of the office. Then, it drew closer, compelling him towards the only viable option. Flight.

It was at this point where Mustafa jumped. He'd never managed to stay in the dream long enough to see if he floated or fell. Most times, the dream toppled him out of bed.

Of all the dreams he has had over the years, the shadow-dream refused to be forgotten. Over time, he figured out a way to bring any 'chasing dream' to an abrupt end. The trick was to let whatever was giving chase catch up with him. And to do that meant recognising that nothing would happen that hadn't happened before. He'd shock himself awake by running towards the fear, never away.

Metres from Mustafa's reverie, in the lemon tree, a ladybug woke to the reality that the treasure trove of red scales it had stumbled upon was home to a colony of white-footed ants. The ladybug – in the middle of decimating a red scale – realised this too late. It wasn't long before she was surrounded by an agitated horde of feelers and pincers. She tried to hunker down under her outer shell for safety, but there was nowhere to hide. Every feast implies a mass murder, and mass gathering.

Seeking flight, the ladybug raised her shell and unsheathed her wings, but this was not the moment to escape. The ants broke in past her outer border and diligently went to work redistributing her tender insides into hoisted chunks of meat.

Like any dream, the smallest parts of what the ladybug had been will wake again as regurgitated nutrients, spewed from the mouths of worker ants over their nests of larvae, coddled in the husk of the lemon tree.

ON A CUSHIONED roller-chair, in front of three monitors, the Mortician clicked through a series of videos. She watched intently, jotting ideas down on the notepad under her left arm. To see everything not as it appears but as it *is*, she thought. Which is why she must be hidden: in ornaments, pot plants, behind the red eyes of electronics.

She exited the treehouse on the north-east side of the property, locking the door. Daniel was up and ready for their hike, she'd seen him. From the aerial walkway she entered the third floor, taking the elevator down to the lobby. Daniel had locked himself in the bathroom opposite the main entrance to the house. She knocked.

'Be right out!'

'I'll be waiting in the car.' She walked into the garage, knowing exactly what Daniel was doing and not entirely sure how to wean him from his morning masturbating proclivities.

Twenty minutes passed before they were on the road, driving to the Cradle of Humankind. The shifting landscape offered a distraction for them both.

'Something about the wild that demands silence,' she said, goading Daniel to speak.

He grunted, turning on his side to doze against the window.

'We'll be there soon.'

'I'm just resting my eyes.'

She drove on, thinking about the caves yet to be discovered in the area, rocks that had been the perfect theatre for early minds, playing with their symbols in front of flame and shadow, using what was around – ochre, berries, clay, charcoal – to smear mythopoetic visions in the earth's gut. Then dying, passing beyond memory into sediment, quiet as a stalactite, until other hominids, drawn in by storms or harsh winters, squeezed through into the same cavernous theatres, finding handprints like theirs, beside outlines of kudu and buffalo.

Those hominids took up the mantle of maker too, redrawing the symbols on the wall, bringing them new, granular life. Adding to them.

'Are we there yet?' asked Daniel.

'Almost.'

'It's impossible to sleep with the AC.'

She ignored him, trying to recapture her train of thought.

'I read somewhere that they've discovered the Garden of Eden, in Botswana. South of the Zambezi,' said Daniel, rubbing sleep out his eyes.

'It makes sense. It gets deep, in the bottom of Africa.'

'You didn't just quote a house song,' Daniel laughs.

'Doesn't make it any less true.'

They arrived at a dirt road, at the end of which was a compound of thatch roofs. 'We're late,' she said, handing Daniel his backpack. They walked up together to a group of strangers sitting in a circle, most of whom averted their eyes from the newcomers. Two men with long, dirty blond hair, walked up to greet them.

'Apologies for being late. We were held up,' said the Mortician, squeezing Daniel's shoulder.

Daniel smiled obsequiously. Both men seemed indifferent to their tardiness and went about withdrawing capsules of green powder from the back seat of their Hilux.

'Okay,' started the man with a backpack of training weights strapped across his torso. 'Four capsules for you. Six for the lady. You haven't eaten for the day, yes?'

'That's right,' said the Mortician, handing Daniel a bottle of water. They drank the capsules together.

'Is it going to be intense?' asked Daniel, swallowing.

'San Pedro is kind medicine. These people will take care of us either way.'

The man with the training weights introduced himself as Cassock; the other called himself Bambino. They gathered the strangers together in a circle, asking each participant to share what they wanted out of the hike. A man in polarised K-Way sunglasses introduced himself as Sipho and explained that he needed to make a big business decision and wanted clarity on it. A woman with piercing blue eyes, and a penchant for twirling her hair, called herself Jenna and said she had just come out of a messy divorce. The Mortician told everyone that she was looking for reassurance, and Daniel, not expecting to share, said he was open to anything, good or bad.

Not too long after, the troupe filled their water bottles and set out on the hike. Bambino and Cassock had brought their bull terriers and ridgeback along and the dogs raced ahead of the humans through the first part of the hike, which was predominantly made up of flat terrain that bore the scars of a recent veld fire.

There was a sense of anticipation in the air as each distinct digestive tract worked to break down what it had been given. The Mortician and Daniel stuck together, scorched earth crumbling under their feet, staining their shoes black.

'I don't feel anything,' said Daniel.

'Give it time.' The Mortician touched his belly.

Soon after, the group tackled a rocky incline, climbing up onto a higher plane where a massive outcrop shielded them from the sun as they walked. Gradually, as the powdered cactus filtered through the groups' small intestines, the mood became subdued. Each hiker experienced the come-on differently. Some, like Daniel and Jenna, contended with a subtle, rising nausea; others, like Sipho and the Mortician, felt a pressure behind their eyes and the urge to clench and unclench their hands in time with their footsteps.

They had been walking for a good two hours when Cassock and Bambino called for a half-hour silence. Everyone was instructed to sit alone, reflect and rest. The Mortician chose to sit on a fallen tree trunk that had tufts of grass growing through it. The rough bark tickled her hands, the breeze lifting fine strands of hair across her forehead. She felt as if she didn't need anything in the world. The cactus had kneaded itself through her, and she was now a fine gossamer, diaphanous. Whatever self-doubt had managed to sneak its way through to her attention with this group of residents seemed to sink into the grooves of her palms as fodder for the truth – she loved life. Not just her life. Life itself.

Daniel chose a spot furthest from the others, on a weather-beaten boulder, smooth to the touch. He surveyed the landscape, noticing the shed skin of a snake caught in a nearby bush. Why was he thinking of his mother? Why was he picturing himself as a boy, playing on the carpet in his bedroom – one hand holding a Sindel figurine and, in the other, The Fantastic Four's The Thing. There was his father, walking into the bedroom to tell him that the doctors had done everything they could. *Ma is gone.*

I don't believe you, he heard himself say.

Daniel turned away from the crusty snakeskin. From his vantage point he followed the road he'd travelled on with the Mortician, all the way back to the city in the distance. Silver View was somewhere in there, gridlocked, admitting those who'd been short-circuited by life, trying to rewire each of them, replace their worn-out sockets, install trip switches in their habits of thinking.

He saw himself waking up to those clinically white walls, hearing commotion in the hallway outside his room. Someone had tried to take their life that morning and, for the first time, the phrase struck him as odd. *Take their life.* As if the point of healthy living was being reconciled to never having a grasp on any of it. As if the ultimate sin was to hold your life in your hands and crush it, relinquishing all quality of tenderness to those who'd come later to find you – blue-bloated.

Daniel shifted on the smooth rock beneath him and focused

on the remnants of a bridge that the group had passed earlier in their trek. Fragments of the bridge stood over what he assumed used to be a river, but was now a scratch of earth, drawn by the fingernail of air-pressure systems. He thought about mudfish and Sarah. How, one afternoon in Silver View, during group art therapy, Sarah had explained how she was teaching herself to be a mudfish. He had no idea what she meant until she explained how mudfish went without water for long periods. All thanks to their shovel-shaped heads that dug into dry riverbeds, wriggling into veins of moisture below the surface to stay put, hibernating until new rains came.

We all need heads that can shovel, move the dirt around, she had said, showing him her collage of mudfish, made from a mishmash of broken glass, terracotta tile and slivers of glossy magazine.

Once the half hour was up, the group assembled, everyone reapplying their sunblock, making their arms and necks shimmer. When Daniel sprayed some on his forearms, he found himself rubbing profusely. His arms felt like muslin. The harder he massaged, the more acutely he could follow the sensations up his arm and into his shoulder. There was knotted muscle there, and in his hips, Achilles and inner groin. He didn't know what it meant so he ignored it, keeping pace with the others.

It was past midday when the group descended into a shady gorge, the result of decades of water flowing through the middle of a towering hillside. At the lowest point in the gorge was a clear stream that collected at one point into a dipping pool. The men in the group, except Daniel and Bambino, took off their shirts and got in. When they did, schools of silver-grey gobies scattered to their hovels.

Daniel surveyed the scene. On one side of the pool, the Mortician chatted to Bambino, who was holding what looked like a long tobacco pipe. Not too far off, Jenna and two other women, whose names he'd forgotten, boiled water for their tea on a portable kerosene stove.

Jenna walked up to him and offered a cup. 'Have you ever heard a singing bowl before?' she asked, sitting beside him, and inviting him to do the same.

'No, is that one?'

Jenna held out a small, metal bowl with a wooden baton in it. 'Here. Sip your tea.' She held the bowl above Daniel's head and instructed him to close his eyes. As the Five Roses tea settled on his tongue, a sharp-pitched ring unfurled above his head, trickling over his limbs. He felt limp. When the sound stopped, he didn't want to open his eyes.

'The electrical wavelengths of your brain sync up with the frequency of the bowl. Think of it as a toilet chain for your brain.'

'I love it. Thank you.' Daniel looked on at the men floating in the dipping pool, casting his eyes over their drooping nipples and flappy under-arms. He imagined the boys they used to be, reminding himself of the first penis he ever saw up close that wasn't his. It happened in the boys' changing rooms at school. Swimming practice. Sixth grade. Someone had started a competition and a good number of the rowdier boys got in on the fun, pulling down their pants, whipping off their towels. Daniel saw himself changing quietly in the corner, diligently slipping on swimming trunks underneath his towel, stealing glances at the boys who ogled and giggled at one another's lengths, girths, shades and curves.

He was fascinated by each and wanted to hold the shafts in his hands – beacons for a desire he didn't know where to place. Ever since the competition got started, he was first boy out of the changing rooms, ready for the pool.

'Daniel, would you like to try?' asked the Mortician. She stood beside Bambino with the long pipe in her hand.

'What is it?'

'Ceremonial cohoba.'

'Are you sure he's ready?' asked Bambino.

The Mortician looked to Daniel, tilting her head into a question. 'Well?'

'Let's try.' Daniel got up.

'No, no, you'll need to be sitting for this,' said Bambino.

He sat down and braced his hands on the earth beneath him. The Mortician positioned the pipe near his left nostril. 'The first time I blow, hold in your mind all the things you want to let go of.'

Daniel nodded, and the Mortician sent a plume of cohoba up his nostril. Instinctually, he sneezed and coughed, desperately trying to catch his breath from the biting sting in his nostril. The Mortician held him to her bosom and patted the back of his head, muttering to herself. Tears ran from his face and mixed with the mucous dripping out his right nostril.

For the first time since his diagnosis, he wanted Lucas to cuddle him, then and there. He wanted Lucas to know that he had always been a boy afraid of what his looking might give away. He found himself yearning for the night, months before Lucas's accident, when they'd gone out in drag together. How they danced in between stares and lip-smacking gossip, how they'd helped each other out of their thongs at the end of the night, declaring the most outlandish declarations of love that neither of them would remember – Daniel against the frame of the toilet door, Lucas on the toilet seat, sipping champagne, farting.

'The second time I blow, hold in your mind the things you want to receive,' said the Mortician, positioning the pipe in his right nostril and blowing.

The second hit felt different. It was as if he'd been blasted into another realm of his psyche, one not populated with any of his usual senses. All he felt was an overwhelming stirring in his chest – his heart was breaking, but not into smaller pieces. It was reorganising itself, as if being instructed by an ancient string of RNA. This reorganisation liquefied him, pouring out his life into the caverns of his mind – down to its deepest hollow, where the swell of him lapped against natural law, punctuated by chance. And love.

When he came to, he found himself in the foetal position, lying amongst the ferns that populated the gorge. The Mortician sat beside him, eating a sandwich. She reached into her backpack and offered him a banana. He ate in silence.

An hour passed, as Bambino took the pipe to all those gathered. Not everyone took up the offer. Those who did had diverse reactions. Some began to throw up in the stream; others, like Jenna, cried till their tear ducts were empty. And then there were those, like K-Way Sipho, who sat in utter silence on the other side of the stream, tossing stones into a purling reflection.

A cute pun got passed around as the group packed up their belongings to head back: *was this a hiking trail or a hiking trial?* Those who'd sniffed cohoba laughed the loudest.

By sunset, the group emerged from the gorge, wading through, up and over vines and thickets till they reached a breezy escarpment where Cassock pointed to the thatched roofs they had first set out from. As the group drew nearer to the compound, they came upon a baboon carcass, inundated with blowflies celebrating the gunk seeping from its orifices.

Upon seeing the carcass, Daniel turned to the Mortician: 'What did you see when Bambino gave you the pipe?'

The Mortician didn't block her nose at the sight of the carcass like the others; instead she spoke in a heady, detached way. 'My microbiome.'

'Huh? You mean –'

'Yes, all the millions of bacteria living on inside me, as *me*. The whole of us, perpetuating the other, beholden to our horizons, dependent on forces much larger, and unpredictable. Dependent on chaos that one can never draw a circle around. We are gods and grains of sand, Daniel.' The Mortician, lethargic and smelling sour, leaned on his subtle frame. 'Would you mind if you take the drive home?' she asked. 'I have an awful headache.'

'Sure, I saw Panado in the cubby.'

'Ah, bless you.' She interlaced her fingers with his.

Daniel didn't resist as much as he thought he might; instead he tried, with all his remaining strength, to remember what the cohoba had given.

It was no use. By the time they were on the road, heading back to the unnumbered house, that old, familiar feeling of being trapped in his own bell-curved narrative was beginning to creep back into his mind to squat, low and heavy, on his hippocampus.

DIANNE

The door to the stained-glass room is heavy, like it's been rein-forced. The room has the air of a small chapel that extends up into an elaborate dome. All along the walls, floor and ceiling, there are fragments of red, green and blue glass, smelted into thick panes.

Between the panes of glass are a number of large, framed prints. One is of a staircase whose bottom half descends into flames with its top half ascending into clouds, lined with gold. The figures standing on the top half are dressed in silver robes. They stand apart, noses turned up to the light, waiting. Those on the bottom are naked, their bodies embracing, gyrating.

I walk around. Another print catches my eye. It's a collage of a woman, against the backdrop of a black-and-white wilderness. Her bottom half is covered in vegetation, her body made from a medley of textures, shapes and broody colours that peel away like layers of an onion. She reaches for the sky, gripping the top of a palm tree. A snake, with a head on either side of its body, pierces her armpit and wraps around her waist. From the looks of it, she is diseased, but her eyes are sure of themselves. They're fixed to the top of the palm tree, watching parrots nest in its branches.

I take a seat; sunlight angles its beams through the room. How peaceful would it be to be suspended like these prints? With nothing to do but hang, an object amongst objects. The rosary in my hands calls me back. Consoles.

'Surreal, isn't it?' says Mustafa, standing in the doorway, his face awash with orange light.

'This must have been expensive to build.'

He's tight-lipped. 'If you like, I can hang one in your room.' He sits down next to me.

'That would be lovely.'

'I never get tired of this room. I always feel part of something bigger here.' Mustafa draws an audible breath. There's something in the air he wants for himself.

I put some distance between us, circling to the last print. *The Tears of Saint Peter*, by El Greco, the label says. I had a copy of this in my office at Bethlehem Primary, but there's no way they could have known that.

In the painting, Peter looks into heaven, hands in prayer. I could never decide whether it was grief or guilt in his eyes. I suppose the two mix well. Water and salt. I remember when one of my former students, Aluwe, prayed with me beneath a print much like this one. I had instructed him to pray to Mary and ask her to stop the blood from running down the walls.

'That is after he denied Jesus three times,' says Mustafa, looking over my shoulder.

'Guilt will do that.'

'Do what?'

'Not answer when it's called.'

'Do you know the trick with painting eyes? It's the empty space in the pupil that you have to shape just right. Leave room for the light to fall. Do that, and any face can have soul.'

'This one. I'd like it for my room.'

Mustafa lifts the print off the wall and carries it out; he's a lot stronger than I thought.

I stretch out on the couch, blowing smoke from a lit cigarette into the dome, thinking of Saint Peter and how he insisted on being crucified upside down, his feet as his crown, earth substituted for sky.

The smoke leaves me in puffs of white, expanding into grey

sheets that collapse on themselves. I like that about smoke. It has no qualms about disappearing.

I FIRST MET the Mortician in the oncologist's waiting room at Nelson Hospital. She was reading an *O Magazine* and obnoxiously chewing gum. At the time, I'd come up from Nkandla to visit family and was doing the rounds: having braais with cousins, brunches with old colleagues from school.

I'd forgotten how noisy Joburg could be. Taxis. Blaring music. Factories. Sirens. It never stopped. Some days when I wasn't in a mood to socialise, I'd drive out to Krugersdorp and find a stretch of veld to park my car beside. It wasn't the safest thing but I did it anyway. I'd roll down my windows, wanting the quiet, and whenever a lone stranger approached, I'd lock my doors and have my foot on the accelerator, ready to drive off. City paranoia runs deep, even when you think you've left it behind.

By the middle of my visit, I had had enough of the sprawl. I missed Karabo, Tshidi and Lavinia, the women I'd made a home with. Together we had managed to set up an NGO, helping child-headed households (and some adult ones too). We helped kids with their homework, taught the eldest about budgeting, and connected the brightest kids to university scholarships when they matriculated. We raised funds for monthly groceries too and, around festive season, asked for Christmas boxes from schools and businesses.

It was gradual and involved work. On the hardest days, when we didn't know where the next paycheck was coming from, our hikes through the Nkandla forest put a pause on our temporary worries. The bond we shared as women turned into a bond I could only call sisterly. It was an intimacy I don't think I could have gotten from a man.

Before I left for Joburg, I'd been having hot, tingling sensations in my feet that used to climb up my back, ending in my cheeks. When I went to see a GP in a nearby town, he'd said it was a vitamin B deficiency. While in Joburg, the sensations turned into mind-splitting headaches that struck me down every afternoon. The headaches got so bad that all I could do was lie with an icepack on my eyes.

Then a GP in Joburg referred me to a neurologist. The neuro sent me for a routine MRI and then called me back for a second, more detailed picture of what was going on. Two MRIs and a spinal tap later and there I was – in an oncology waiting room, dreading what Dr Hassan had to say.

Of all the things I remember about that waiting room, it's the pamphlets that stick out. A pamphlet for every kind of cancer. Pink for Breast. Blue for Testicular. Yellow for Skin. A soft purple for Leukaemia. I appreciated the ones that shied away from having people on the covers, those that used cartoon illustrations or infographics that looked like they'd been designed for pre-schoolers. I couldn't bear the pamphlets with real people on their covers. A pale woman in a bandana broadly smiling as a doctor placed a stethoscope to her chest; a young man looking down at his crotch, scratching his head; an elderly lady holding a dog close to her breast (the dog seeming like the one who was really in pain). It was all so bloody grim. And to make matters worse, the woman with the Oprah magazine kept popping her gum.

When I got called in to Dr Hassan's office, the woman put another wad of gum in her mouth. Glaring, I walked past, making my disdain obvious. On the cover, a string of red, block-lettered words struck me.

I'M ALWAYS AMAZED AT HOW EASY IT IS TO IMPACT ANOTHER LIFE.

No shit, I thought, shutting the door.

I don't remember much of what Dr Hassan said. After *inoperable* and *chemo* were used in the same sentence I sank back and waited for panic to strike. I was unbearably calm. I knew this wasn't right; I should be angry, ready to fight through whatever poison Hassan promised to drip into me. I was meant to believe in Hassan, in the scientific method.

An hour later, I stood in the hospital courtyard, deliberating if I should go back to my hotel or have something to eat. People strolled past with flowers or balloons in their hands, others nursed drawn expressions above Styrofoam cups. I pictured the brain infographic on the wall in Hassan's office: a cross-section, peach-coloured, with a glob of yellow in it that looked like a booger. This was the tumour, my tumour. A crusty ball of snot. My ending.

I don't know how long I stood there but it was long enough to see a gunshot victim rushed through to the ER and a middle-aged woman ash two cigarettes, with an oxygen tank pumping beside her.

Eat, I told myself. So, I walked into the café and ordered a toasted chicken mayo with a cappuccino. The woman from the waiting room sat a few tables away, browsing the newspaper. She nodded at me and I pretended not to see, switching to a seat that faced the courtyard.

When my food arrived, the waiter brought tuna instead of chicken and I got a lot angrier than I'd meant to. The twenty-something Ethiopian-looking man apologised, but I was having none of it. 'Bring what I ordered,' I said, throttling sachets of sweetener over my cappuccino.

It didn't take long for the order to be corrected. When the waiter put the food down, I mumbled *thank you*, peeking under the bread to double-check. I'd always been the type who chastised people that were rude to waiting staff, and there I was doing the same thing. I needed to apologise but, tasting how good the chicken mayo was, decided against it. The waiter would understand if he knew my situation.

I desperately wanted to think about something other than my diagnosis, so I watched the waiter, speculating about his life outside of the café, away from people's orders. It relieved me somewhat to imagine that inside another body the road ahead looked different. I watched the young man as I ate, embarrassed for assuming he was Ethiopian because the more I really looked at him, the more I spotted hints of Italian, Native American, maybe even Nigerian. He could have been from anywhere, really.

Throughout my meal, the waiter swerved between tables, balancing plates on his forearms, scribbling in his notepad, scanning the café for patrons in need. He was so meticulous in how he wiped and ordered the tables after patrons left. When he got close enough to my table, I snuck a look at his fingernails, most of them were unevenly cut. There was always someone else to prepare for, I thought. Someone coming in to fill the empty seat.

I began to wonder if there was anything inside of him, at that very moment, that would threaten his life. A genetic mutation that weakened his heart. A rogue cell recruiting others to go awry. A predisposition to addiction. From where I sat, he was the captain of his ship, as much as he could be in a job that paid minimum wage plus tips. It struck me how much had to be in place, how much had to go right, for any captain, of any ship, to have both hands on the wheel. Too much credit went to captains anyway. After all, all a captain does is shout orders into a microphone, hoping that whoever is below deck obeys.

I paid for the food, giving a more-than-generous tip, and when the waiter came to collect I searched for a nametag. There was none.

WHEN I GOT to my car, I realised I'd left the headlights on. Starting the engine, the car refused my advances.

A knock at my window. 'Hi, sorry to bother ... do you need a jump?'

The woman from the café: she was standing by my car. No one else had noticed my distress but her.

'Oh yes, thank you.' I got out to retrieve the jumper cables from my boot. Moments later, my battery was jacked up to hers and she revved her engine while I turned my ignition. The car gave a few false starts before the dashboard lit up. 'I really appreciate your help. I was on the verge of a meltdown,' I laughed, half-heartedly.

The woman didn't react. Instead, she asked in the gentlest of tones if I was *okay*.

'I'm fine now, yes.' I untethered the cables. 'Do you work here?'

'Here? No, but I appreciate the atmosphere.'

'What's so great about the atmosphere?'

'Very much like airports. Mellow, with the anticipation of coming and going.' She leaned on the bonnet of her car, considering the hospital like it was the Taj Mahal.

'Okay, well, I have to go. Thank you again.'

'Don't let me keep you.'

She waited for me, waving as I drove off. I didn't know what to make of it, but I was grateful she was nosy enough to help.

I kept the tests, MRI scans, reports from the oncologist and pamphlets for the dying in a plastic sleeve at the bottom of my suitcase. I called home to Tshidi, Karabo and Lavinia every day, each time practising my voice beforehand so no hint of bad news leaked through. For the rest of my visit, that sleeve didn't leave my suitcase.

Near the end of my stay, I went back to see Dr Hassan, mainly because her secretary kept pestering me. I told the doctor I'd made the decision not to do the chemo or any other treatment. It was an unnecessary discomfort, I'd explained, seeing that the tumour was advanced and all I was doing was buying time (by poisoning myself).

'Unnecessary? This will prolong your life, Dianne. It will be uncomfortable, sure, but at least you'll be alive. Don't you want that?'

'No one ever asks us if we *want* to be alive, doc. It just happens. Why wouldn't it be the same with death? We're always getting things we don't ask for.'

'Are you absolutely certain?' Hassan asked in earnest.

'Is there medication for the headaches? And the nausea?'

'I can prescribe some, yes.'

'That's all I need.'

Dr Hassan wrote out a prescription and I left.

Walking out the hospital that day felt different; I'd taken control. That was when I spotted the woman who had helped me with my car. I don't know why I said hello. Maybe it was the way she'd asked if I was 'okay' the first time we met.

She invited me to sit down for coffee and some ganache cake. I had nowhere else to be, so I obliged. I asked her name and she slipped me a business card with her initials printed on it. In brackets beneath it read: *Specialist in Alternative Palliative Care.*

I asked what was so 'alternative' about it.

'Do you have any idea about how you might like to die one day?' she asked.

'Excuse me?'

'Most people usually say they want to go quietly in their sleep, preferably at home, surrounded by people who love them. Which is all good and dandy. I've found, though, that some want to experiment a little near the end. To leave the world with a bang, instead of a whimper.'

'I haven't given it much thought.' I was reluctant to tell her my prognosis.

'The alternative I offer is the bang. Not the whimper. All kinds of bangs. Because, let's face it, death's a scary business.'

'You've been around a lot of people. At their end?'

'My fair share,' she said, calling for the bill.

'What's it like?'

The waiter brought the bill and my question lingered between us as she swiped for the cake and coffee. When the waiter left, she answered. 'There's a moment, near the very end, where the body slackens, as if responding to the tiniest of punctures, made right here: at the top of the skull. And all that pent-up pressure, those years spent making calendars out of days … escapes. It's quite something.'

I turned the card over as she gathered her things to leave. I thought about how I'd break the news to my sisters, about how, when things got unmanageable, they'd likely band together to care for me. My end was so clear. The clarity frightened me. I wasn't ready to step into that ending, though I was certain it was the ending I wanted – surrounded by the women who had taught me genuine friendship.

When the Mortician said goodbye, wishing me a safe trip back, I watched her stroll across the courtyard towards her car.

What could it hurt, I thought, to try something out of my ordinary, just for a while? I wanted more bangs and less whimpers, so I got up and followed.

WHEN I STEP out the stained-glass room, there are four missed calls from Tshidi. I call back, turning the video on. Tshidi answers.

She's sitting in the kitchen, the note I left in her hands, Karabo and Lavinia in the background on either side. 'What's this? You up and leave after telling us you have brain cancer?' Tshidi is crying.

'You don't understand –'

'Make us understand,' Karabo's voice crackles through the phone. 'We have had your back so many times before. We can have your back with this, if you just let us.' She snaps the letter out of Tshidi's hand.

'It's not about that. I need to figure out what this means without worrying about how it's going to affect you all. I know on the outside it seems selfish, but it isn't. Really it isn't,' I say, walking fast to my bedroom for privacy. Angelique isn't back yet (thank God). I sit on the bed, unable to focus on their faces.

'Are you okay at least? Being taken care of?' Lavinia, the youngest, asks.

'Yes. And I *will* come back. Promise. There're just things I need to deal with alone.'

They look to each other, figuring out what they could say to make me come back. I don't have the heart to tell them that there isn't anything to say.

'Funani's aunt came around the other day. She's not looking good,' says Tshidi.

Karabo chimes in: 'She was looking for you. Wanted to know if you'd go with to his grave.'

'Tell her I'll be back soon. I need to go. We'll chat later, okay?' I put the phone down. Saint Peter hangs above my bed and even though his eyes are on heaven, I know he's looking right through me.

MUSTAFA ASCENDED A spiral staircase, built around the body of a varnished kokerboom, to the second floor. The pantry looked a little shallow this morning, he thought. A store run was in order. He made his way past the meditation room and listened in on the Mortician gently prompting Lucas through a meditation.

Lucas, all lean muscle from clavicle to calf; a guy Mustafa would have given a lot of time to in his early twenties. What had changed? In his thirties, he needed more than a firm stomach and single-digit body-fat. If this were his twenties, he would have offered himself up as a vessel for the seeds of men who inhabited bodies like Lucas's. Those days of self-abandon had given him a bliss vaguely tinged with regret. Thinking about that time in his life felt like visiting a different person. Indeed, he had always been drawn to the thought of handing himself over, a kind of sacrifice, to montages of sculpted pecs, veiny arms, taut legs – witnessing men flail and lose their well-composed faces while, in the same breath, grasping with both hands for their pleasure.

At the black-lattice gate, Mustafa double-checked he had his cell phone, bank card and headphones. He didn't like taking the car to the mall, preferring a light jog because that way he was able to take more in. Coming out the driveway, he took a right and jogged to the corner, where there was a metal pole with a security camera fixed to it. These had been popping up all over Joburg and he wondered who was perpetually watching through that opaque, grey dome.

He put on his headphones (Bjork's *Atom Dance* streamed into his ears), and took a left down Frederick Drive. The road's heat cupped his chin as he passed construction workers mixing cement for the foundation of a new home. He nodded in their direction. They didn't notice.

A few streets later, he passed a security guard post situated opposite an island of white rosebushes and turned right down a steep decline that ran into the main road. At the intersection, he caught his breath outside a mechanic's shop, watching as half-greased men leaned their torsos into engines. Turning left, he jogged past three grocery store employees, each with hair netted down, sitting on a concrete bench, sharing a two-litre Coke and a box of masala fries.

At the corner, he stopped outside the International Bed Store wedged between two adult stores. It had been some time since he'd visited; he wondered if it was worth reminiscing. Taking a stroll past a white Hyundai parked outside, he snuck a peak at the driver, who was around fifty, lanky, with greying temples and indented cheeks. The driver scrolled through his phone, gulping down a bottle of water till the plastic caved in. That used to be me, thought Mustafa. Except he would be the one sitting in a dark corner right now, at the back of Adult World, the light of his cell phone as the only sign to furtive faces that he was there.

Mustafa headed across the road into the mall. Here every colour, scent and texture felt designed to funnel people into aisles, fitting rooms and eating booths, subliminally chanting: *there's no reason to be anywhere else.* Malls were, nevertheless, unavoidable. He knew that.

In the aisles of Pick n Pay, packs of pitted olives, frozen peas, bottles of wine, a frozen seafood mix and some prime rib-eye steaks drenched in marinade got tossed into a trolley. The signs above the refrigerated foods read: *Fresh, Making Life Easier For You.* He looked around and noticed other neon signs posted above customers' heads – *See You Soon* – and near the exit: *Before You Go.* There was a mischievous delight in rewriting the meaning behind each.

As a casual exercise, he often speculated about the lives the food in his trolley had lived before being sealed and packaged. Where did the pitted olives once hang? Out of what soil were the peas grown, and by what hand were they frozen? How many nets were cast to fill this seafood mix? Who chose the marinade his steaks would swim in? Thinking about it, he reminded himself that he was just another nodal point, another hand, passing off the plastic-wrapped produce to somewhere else. This always brought Mustafa to the same conclusion. He, too, used to package himself up for others, his worth determined by the hands that handled him, sometimes too roughly, before passing him over.

At the cashiers, in the queue in front of him, a burly Afrikaner fingered his wallet for bank notes. In the till next to theirs, a young girl had had her eyes on a Bar One ever since her mother first pulled up to the till with her two trolleys (the little girl barely able to push one). He watched as the little girl spied the chocolate, asked her mother for it (who said *no*), and then proceeded to slip the chocolate into her jean pocket. It was only when the chocolate was hidden that the girl noticed Mustafa had been watching.

He didn't say anything or gesture a rebuke. The girl was embarrassed, he could tell. She had shown her duplicity, a side he knew everyone had – an impulse woven in each of us to test the sanctity of rules. The girl held his gaze for as long as she could before acting like Mustafa did not exist. Then she helped her mother unpack the second trolley.

Mustafa was placid throughout.

It was only when mother and child were halfway out the store that the girl turned back to steal a glance at him. Still, no smile, no shake of the head or purse of the lips from Mustafa; no indication that he had seen. Before they left, the girl took the chocolate out of her pocket and tossed it into an empty shopping basket near the entrance.

All it takes, thought Mustafa, unpacking his groceries from the trolley.

THE MALL FILLED up as the day wore on. More crying babies and teenagers rationing their attention spans between cell phones and window displays. More desperate salespeople in the middle of the walkways, awkwardly trying to greet you. Fewer old men with crusty feet in flip-flops and aunties idly watching people go by as they attempted to catch their breath on benches, waiting for someone to take them home.

He made his way to the pharmacy opposite the hardware store. The woman at the prescription counter was a peacock-looking lady with round, steely eyes. He hadn't seen her at the counter before. 'Hi, I'm here for a refill,' he said, his bright voice at odds with the woman's methodical and focused typing. The woman asked the usual questions – name, address – and proceeded to read the screen in front of her, pressing ENTER a disconcerting number of times.

'Sorry, sir, it says your refills are up.'

'What?'

'Finished.'

'Yes, I heard you, but …'

'Yes, it says last month was your *absolute* last.'

He must have miscounted. How could that be? He was sure he had at least one refill left. He tried to reason with the lady: 'There must have been a mix-up. Dr Dlamini sent the prescription through.'

The pharmacist was not convinced. She had it on record that this wasn't the first time the pharmacy had given him a bit of 'slack' (she actually used the word 'slack'). She said that, really, he should monitor his refills better and did he want to join their messaging service for chronic patients?

Fresh perspiration shunted down the dried sweat-lines of his body. 'What do you expect to happen now? Must I just go without my meds?' His raised voice made people nearby turn to look at him: vigilant meerkats in the wilderness of flavoured water and cough syrup.

'Please, sir, calm down. You can use our phone to call your doctor. He can email –'

'This is absolute nonsense! What kind of pharmacy refuses chronic medication?'

'Sir, please, it's just our policy.'

It was unlike him to lose himself. He had for so long granted spaciousness to whatever emotion uncoiled itself inside of him. But some emotions are too big, some roll up to you and uncoil themselves on your chest, a family of pangolins.

Moments later, he was escorted out by security. The head pharmacist, a pockmarked man with a bit of a beer belly, said that as soon as he got his prescription he could come back. Mustafa was embarrassed but grateful that his temper didn't lead to tears streaming down his face (a commonplace occurrence when he failed to make room for the pangolins).

He headed for the food court, thinking that a meal might lift his mood, his right thumb dancing a furious foxtrot on his phone screen.

Why haven't you sent through my prescription yet?

He pressed SEND and sat down at an aluminium table in the food court, waiting for Dr Dlamini's response while deciding what to eat.

Victor Dlamini and Mustafa had known one another since the orphanage. Mustafa had been brought there as a baby – a 'dustbin baby', as he learned later, though he didn't like the term. He had just turned twelve when Victor came to stay at Isindiso Orphanage. Victor was the only surviving family member of a horrific taxi accident that had taken place during the long weekend Easter rush out of Joburg to the surrounding provinces. Victor had never talked about his extended family, explaining to Mustafa that his other uncles and aunts were too poor to knowingly let another mouth into their homes. Mustafa had always believed there to be more to that explanation, but never pressed Victor on it.

The other boys at Isindiso saw them as an odd pairing, Mustafa being the more theatrical of the two and Victor being the reserved, bookish type. Victor kept spy novels stuffed inside an old plaid blazer, which he always wore on weekends, retreating into worlds of espionage whenever he had a moment to spare. Mustafa was more social, often convincing the other boys in the dorm to play Crazy Eights or blind man's bluff together, way past their bedtimes.

From early on, Mustafa admired Victor's ability to disappear between the spaces of words on a page and, though he didn't vocalise it, Victor was envious of Mustafa's social mutability. The two boys latched onto one another because they were the same age and, by luck, happened to share a birthday. This fact had a hint of serendipity that even orphaned boys couldn't deny. As they grew into being the oldest in the orphanage, watching others leave to find their way in the world, it became apparent that they, too, would have to enter a world that had so nonchalantly denied them. Realising this, the two vowed to always be one another's family when they became young men.

No moment had confirmed this in recent memory as much when Mustafa landed up on Victor's doorstep, blood test results in hand, needing a doctor's counsel and a friend's embrace.

Hey, man. Shit, I meant to do it, I've just been all over the place. You know, divorce and all … I will do it soon soon. Victor ended the text with a smiley face squeezed between two thumb's ups. Something *was* up, thought Mustafa. Ever since Victor's marriage fell apart, he had been off, not texting as regularly as he used to.

I have enough meds for three days. Please send ASAP. A little curt, but sufficient, he thought. No mutual smiley faces to placate the doctor. This was the problem when one put one's health in the hands of friends: things tended towards the personal. Maybe it was better to remain another medical aid number on a doctor's records than for doctor and patient to have shared late-night polony and cheese sandwiches. Numbers have a brute consistency to them, the kind needed to manage a chronic condition.

A steak and kidney pie would do the trick, he thought, noticing a woman sitting in front of the large fish tank (dubbed 'Aquarium') who was thoroughly enjoying her pie. Seated above plastic shopping bags that made it seem as if she had no feet, the woman withdrew her pie from the grey packet and crumpled it into her mouth. She didn't care about the scraps that gathered at the corners of her mouth or the flakes that stuck to her peach blouse. As more of the packet crinkled in her fists, more of the pie disappeared behind her lips – all the while teenagers, couples, whole families of four passed by, gawking at the tiger-orange and charcoal-coloured fish swimming in circles behind her.

Heaven, thought Mustafa.

He continued watching till the only sign the woman had ever been in possession of a pie were the brown flakes strewn across her pudgy stomach. She rested her hands on her belly and closed her eyes. He imagined the inside of her body lighting up like a Christmas tree, cells in her stomach pounding their chests, singing their national anthem. The only anthem they understood.

Food! Glorious food!

Bite it off. Break it down. Burn baby burn!

He chuckled. A steak and kidney pie would go down well.

AN HOUR LATER, Mustafa was anchored to the curb by his groceries, standing outside the mall, a human buoy in a sea of plastic. The wind had picked up and was rippling across a large puddle of prismatic engine oil in an empty parking spot. Next to where he stood, two men dressed in black shared a pair of headphones. Whatever they were listening to compelled them to bob in unison, like oil pumps going to ground. Not too long after, his Uber arrived.

The Uber made its way through exhaust fumes and whiffs of fried chicken coming from the nearby KFC. It passed the vetkoek and mince vendor on the corner (who had unknowingly crushed a fly into a large pot of mincemeat during the lunchtime rush, serving bits of it to the customers). It then made its way past the BMW dealership that had just sold its newest model to a middle-aged, balding man who gripped the dealer's pen like his own penis, aiming it straight and true on the dotted line. Then the Uber drove by the International Bed Store with its variety of foams and springs (some curving to one's spine, others resisting the shape of one's body, for support). Past the Adult World where men emptied their testes to moaning beams shot at their retinas from TV screens that lit up gloryholes. Past the Eye Doctor where a woman had the strength of her spectacles readjusted (*Can you see the letter now? How about now?*).

At a traffic light, the car came to a stop. Mustafa rolled down his window and handed a young mother and her toddler a packet. The mother curtsied like she was being knighted by the Queen of England while the child threw out the groceries on the street corner, playing cops and robbers with Cup-a-Soup packets and cans of pilchards.

How to keep your heart open in hell, he wondered.

Soon after, the Uber disappeared beneath a canopy of trees, taking shelter in Northcliff's foliage, a louse in a bed of hair, climbing away from the clamorous traffic inching around the mall.

A troupe of walls and intercoms took centre stage in the windows. Walls for every homeowner, reinforced with electrified fences too high for anyone to know there were people living there. Others preferred to offer up slatted views of their gardens through palisade fencing and wrought-iron shaped into floral patterns. When the car pulled up to the alleyway between number eight and ten Lancaster, Mustafa was ready to kick off his shoes and soak his feet in Epsom salt water. The Mortician stood outside to meet him, ready to help carry all that he had foraged.

They walked together through the black-lattice gate, towards the main house. At the top of the driveway, the Mortician turned.

'What is it?' asked Mustafa, the taut plastic eating into his palms.

'That feeling again, like someone's watching,' she said, anxiously.

He dropped the groceries and came up to hold her. 'It's just me. We're okay.'

The pair walked on, disappearing beyond the willow trees. Out in the road, in a van marked Omega Plumbing, someone had been watching, for days.

ANGELIQUE

People are surprised when they find out I'm not squeamish. I've never backed away from needles or picking scabs open, even as a nunus. Not even when Gogo died, and I wanted to see what she looked like, lying in that pretty white coffin with the silver handles, all cushioned and bronzed from the make-up they'd put on her. I knew then that at my funeral I wanted my coffin closed.

I've gotten used to watching the blood curl out of me, returning clean. Mustafa sets up the machine in one of the lounges. It does its job quietly, the way help should. If it was louder, I'd have a hard time doing this, twice a day for two hours. Mustafa knows to put it out of view and to cover the tubes going into my arm. He does it with a light blanket.

Two hours a day equal three episodes of *Are You The One?* It's a juicy enough show where beautiful singles figure out who their 'one' is. The contestants' soulmates are determined by scientifically proven questionnaires, interviews with exes, and compatibility testing. I don't watch it for all that shit. See, what I do is look for the couples who know they're not a match for the show's algorithm but go for each other anyway. Those are the OGs that prove the 'one' is never just one person. The ones are those people you wished you'd met, those you hope you can forget and those who … give you that craving. There's nothing like live heartbreak on television, especially when it's sexy singles breaking hearts for a cash prize.

On days when TV doesn't do it and my phone is too quiet I sit watching the machine. I follow my blood up the arterial line and into the dialyser (funny how a disease teaches you things). The dialyser turns light red after a few minutes as the blood filters through. I don't know whether to refer to it as *my* blood or *the* blood. Both sound right. The machine pumps turn like little wheels; if I watch for too long, I'll get dizzy. When I feel it coming I turn on the TV or scroll for trending topics on Twitter to take my mind off it. My body has gotta be here. My mind don't.

In *Are You The One?* there's something called 'The Boom Boom Room'. The name says it all. My other favourite scenario is when contestants go in and get it on with each other. What usually happens the next morning is that those who weren't let in on the fun feel salty about it. Now, I've dealt with jealousy in my life; whether it was the big-booty girls at the public swimming pool (who said I had no meat on my bones) or the models who said my smile was 'choppy' (I still don't know what the fuck that means). Jealousy, that energy puts up a fight against what it doesn't have. It wants to be in the Boom Boom Room all the goddamn time: making things happen, having things happen to it.

Did you see? There's this video on Twitter of a man and woman doing the dirty in a Sandton high-rise. Someone happened to be looking up and caught them in their own Boom Boom Room. You can't see much, just bodies thrusting. Another video went viral just last month of a prison warden and a convict getting it on. Shem, it's a sweet one by sex scandal standards. If they didn't have their uniforms on, I wouldn't have given it a second look; I mean, neither of them were exactly easy on the eyes. There is this part though, near the end of the video, where the convict unrolls toilet paper (looks like one-ply) and wipes in between the warden's legs, kissing her on her stretch-marked thighs. I rewound and watched that more than I should have.

The machine beeps. Mustafa comes in from the next room. He checks my blood pressure. 'A little low.'

'I've always been lower than normal,' I say.

He double-checks the saline solution and the dialysate. One hour in, and there's tightness in the legs already.

'Can you get some electrolytes for me?'

'Cramps?'

I nod, clenching my toes. He leaves, and I think about how much it'll cost to replace my kidneys. The Mortician said that if I get through their programme, they'd think about sponsoring some of it. That, with a few big modelling gigs and maybe just one nyana endorsement deal, and I'll be on a gurney to the operating room. Nkosi yam, the hustle. Stay strong, buy time, let this machine clean the blood. If there's anything I've learned from being wired up it's that living ain't free. Not by a long shot. Even if you have millions. In my book, to be free is when you need nothing, no one. The definition that gets thrown around is a lie.

I need to secure the bag, like I did with that voting ad I got featured in before things turned to shit. That gig covered my expenses for a year. The man who got me sorted was a politician and let me tell you, baby, he wanted me. Badly. I was familiar by then with how powerful men like Thembikile got beautiful woman like me on their arms. Despite what you may have heard from tabloids, I was loyal to Xolisi throughout that stint; even when Thembikile told me what I'd be earning. Xolisi had been my day one; he knew me before the glitz and glam, when I was just an up-and-comer from the south with a raspy voice in a jazz club.

Fucken cliché, but we move.

What had happened was, Thembikile sent for me days before the shoot. He was staying the week at a penthouse in Sandton, said he had had a couple of other girls who wanted the gig as badly as I did and was wondering whether I was the 'right pick'.

Sitting on his bed, I saw those Range Rover wheels turning in his head: *innocent girl, needs me to show her the ways of the world.* Child, I was no chop. He wanted my cakes, wanted to turn the clock back and make him feel like a twenty-five-year-old again. It wasn't my first soirée, honey.

As intimidating and demanding as Todd could be, he did teach me about power. The type I had. The type I could have. The type to watch out for. So I pulled up the contract on my phone, showed Thembikile, and explained to him that if I was removed without a valid reason I'd go straight to Debora Patta, or whoever the hell was at the forefront of depressing investigative journalism at the time. He grinned, downed his champagne, burped, and offered me the rest of the Moët, for my trouble. Ever since, Thembikile treated me differently, even defended me when the campaign got flak for being, what were the words people used? Oh yes, *shallow, trite, insulting.* All the clever blacks on Twitter came for me. I didn't care. I was making bank.

MUSTAFA COMES BACK with electrolytes. I drink up and the dizziness fades. My legs are cramping less.

'The Mortician would like to see you afterwards,' he says.

'That time again, huh?'

'Like clockwork.'

He leaves me alone with the machine. You can't find the video campaign online anymore. Trust me, I checked. Public outcry works, most times. I don't know why people had such a problem; I hit all the right points – electricity in rural areas, government grants, the importance of getting youth employed. I even threw out phrases like *consolidating policy* (advice from my publicist). Then I added a personal touch by sharing where I was from and how, now, there aren't any water shortages in the area and the garbage is picked up every Thursday. Like, that's progress. Even people on set liked what I was dishing out. But no, people on the socials just *had* to drag me for turning politics into an 'Avon ad', apparently. See what I mean? *Jealousy.*

When the two hours are up the machine beeps three times and I can finally be disconnected. Mustafa rolls it into the corner and turns off the TV. He hands over my waste in a bag. This part is truly kak. I'm not squeamish so I don't let Mustafa see it bother me. The toilet down the corridor gets all of it; I've been told I can't throw this stuff down a sink because it'll damage the pipes. With a cup of bleach, I pour my stuff into the toilet, wait a few minutes before flushing. This is around the time I miss those hardworking little sacs of mine. Kidneys. Those fuckers did me dirty. If they were exes, they'd be the kind to turn the kinky sex videos we made together into revenge porn – like that other politician's dick-in-mouth debacle. They'd be the kind to turn something as effortless as going to pee into an episode of Dr. Phil.

It's what I deserve, I guess, for making Boom Boom Rooms out of them both.

I MEET MUSTAFA and the Mortician in the meditation room. It's on the second floor, and from here you look out over the greenhouses at the back, all the way to the hedges. I haven't been that side, to the hedges, I mean. The Mortician said I wasn't ready. It's a creaky old room, looks like the oldest in the house. The walls are padded and shaped like a studio. Even if you whisper, someone on the other side of the room can hear you like you're standing right next to them. It's freakishly extra, like everything here. If you keep real quiet, the ringing in your ears gets so hectic. Yazi, when they call me in I keep talking just to save myself from it.

Mustafa takes my phone and leaves it outside in a glass jewellery box beside our shoes.

'How are you feeling today?' asks the Mortician.

'A bit tired. I'm used to that by now.'

'Have you had something to eat yet?' asks Mustafa.

I shake my head.

'Good, take a seat.'

They're both on mats and there's a pillow and blanket laid out. I join them on the floor.

'We're going to try something different. A little experiment. I think you'll appreciate it,' says the Mortician.

Mustafa gets close and lays me down. Out of the little bag tied around his waist, where he keeps all his muti, he takes out a bottle and dabs some of its oil on his hands, then rubs me from my chin down to my shoulders. It has a strong rosemary smell. He reaches under my shirt and presses hard on my traps; he does this a few times before grabbing my neck from behind and cracking it. Left. Right.

'The body,' says the Mortician, '… is a repository of niggles, things that have conditioned us from the outside. It's a sponge, soaking up everything, holding onto the trauma in its tissues. It's the ultimate translator, enfolding the paths we've travelled to get here and the flows of time. Human time. Earth time. Microbial time. You name it, it's here.'

I don't know what this bitch is on about, but if I don't listen, girl, I won't get that money.

'Close your eyes. Listen,' says Mustafa. He slides two pillows underneath my knees and throws a blanket over me.

'First. You must breathe, Angelique.'

'Uhh, okay, I'm doing that.'

'… breathe deep, fill your belly to bursting,' says the Mortician.

'Then breathe more and fill your chest,' says Mustafa.

'Then breathe more and fill your head. Breathe so much that you feel the pressure from your belly button to your crown.'

I do as I'm told. It's hard at first. I don't like my belly expanding this way, like someone dogged me raw, and here I'm sitting with the repercussions. It's unnerving, but I do it anyway because, well, I'm here and I might as well buy into whatever they're selling.

'Good,' says Mustafa. 'Do that over and over, getting quicker each time.'

The longer I do it, the easier it becomes. Air flows in through my nose and out the same way. The rush tickles a little on the top of my head. All of a sudden, the Mortician's flute starts up and a lazy drumbeat joins her. My huffing and puffing mixes with the flute and drum.

… *Da daa dum,* **hmmph,** *da daa dum,* **hmmph,** *da daa dum,* **hmmph** …

'Release!' shouts the Mortician.

When I let go of my breath there's a pinging all over me: like phone notifications going off, streaming from my fingertips, into my elbows, down my eyebrows into my cheeks. I feel … filled. There's slight shaking behind my breasts; my heart is a deep-house track with a never-ending intro. Moments pass, and I realise I haven't taken a breath. The urge isn't there.

'Now take another breath. And hold it,' says Mustafa.

'Then let it all go,' says the Mortician.

They're still at it with the flute-and-drum and when I breathe out fully, an uncontrollable laugh pins me to the floor.

'What. The. Hell,' I say, between giggles. There are tiny fingers tapping all over my body.

'Don't fight it. Let whatever it is rise to the surface,' says Mustafa.

When the laugh ends, things get super quiet. Even the flute-and-drum softens. I feel like I've been dangled out a window.

'Good. Do it all again,' says the Mortician.

I go through the entire thing four more times. With each round my need to breathe goes away for longer, my body tense as a snail in its shell. Spaces inside me open and I see myself with Gogo again, picking snails out her garden. We're putting them on bricks and sprinkling them with salt. Gogo shows me how their bodies froth. I get so excited I take the salt-shaker from her and want to try it for myself. I turn a snail over to get as much salt in its shell. *Look! This one bubbles.* I'm excited to watch them die.

The Mortician and Mustafa's music passes through me, each note of the flute, echo of the drum, tickles my eyelids. All this breathing has fucked up my pupils; in the darkness of my closed eyes there are stick birds, made out of pixels, flapping, like the kind a four-year-old might draw. My face starts to feel like a velvet curtain. Heavy. And I remember singing *Haunt Me* by Sade, on a stage in Maboneng. Xolisi looking my way.

Haunt me, in my dreams, if you please … It takes a moment to connect the sound with my voice. When last did I sing? The notes leave me, as clear as when I first sang on that stage. Please, don't end. Not now.

'Angelique.' The Mortician's voice cues the music to stop. She helps me up, touching me on my shins and stomach. When I'm upright, I cover my face. Tears fall through my fingers. I don't feel sad. Or happy. The reasons I could give for them have left a long time ago. I'm all shell.

I lean into the Mortician. 'It's okay,' she whispers.

'Have some milk,' says Mustafa, bringing a warm mug to my lips. I sip. And that's when the diagrams on the walls come into view. Prints of animals – bats, cats, oysters, starfish, frogs – all cut open. The ones that give me the chills are the humans, butt naked, every layer dissected, shaded in different colours.

How had I not noticed them when I walked in? I hide my face in the Mortician's collar, sobbing. She strokes and sniffs my hair.

WE'RE WASHING UP after dinner when the Mortician asks me about my experience earlier and why I chose to sing when I did. I tell her about the velvet curtains.

'… it was when I first moved to Maboneng. A new cocktail lounge had opened that played live music. I wanted to be on their line-up so I asked the manager if I could audition some time. It was a real hole-in-the-wall. I was desperate.'

The steam from the basin makes the Mortician's hair frizzy. It's the first time I've seen it untied, falling over her shoulders this way. She hands me the plates, pots and cutlery. 'Go on.'

'So, picture this, right. I'm on a small-ass stage and each table in the audience is lit with candles. Loadshedding vibes but romantic. At least they invested in a generator. So, I'm pretty nervous but I tell myself, girl, here, here you must fetch your motherfucking life.'

'What song was it?' asks the Mortician, letting water out the basin.

'*Haunt Me*. Sade. A sexy number. When the intro comes in – sax, guitar and piano – it's all live instrumental.' As I get into the story my phone vibrates on the counter.

'Leave it.' The Mortician dries her hands and turns my phone over. She sits next to it and I know she won't let me check until I finish my story.

'Okay, where was I, so I'm swaying to the guitar, piano and sax. Manje, all eyes are on me so when I sing those first lines, joh, that song becomes a juicy peach in my mouth. And fuck, do I bite.'

She smiles in a way that makes me feel uncomfortable. I ignore it.

'*Your breath is with me now and always … it's like a breezze,*' I sing. 'I still got it, baby!'

'I can see why you chose Sade. Your voice has a velour texture to it.'

'Oh. Thanks. So low-key, the longer I'm singing, the deeper I'm swimming in the song. Hell, on that stage I even touched myself a little, just to give that *vvvrr pha*. Check here, the acoustics are vibing and I'm vibing and the audience is vibing, and I *knew* there was no chance that Angelique Mlungisi is not earning a spot on the line-up. And that night, ha, I got a lot of things, let me tell you.'

'What do you mean?'

I hang up the drying cloth and sit opposite her. She turns my phone over, showing me that I've got three missed calls from an unknown number.

'Everything all right?' asks the Mortician.

'Whoever's trying to call can wait. As I was saying, I met Xolisi that night. He was a barman working there in his last year of fashion school. Jeez, I can see him now – slanted eyes, broad back, bit of a 'fro. After my performance, I bumped a skyf off him and that's when we got to talking about my singing and he was all, like, I could be a model, he can link me up with people. But I never took him seriously. Just thought he was trying to score my koeka.'

'Did he turn out to be serious?'

'Completely. Things sorta started with us from then on. I got the gig, performing on Fridays. And after I did my set he'd usually buy me a few rounds. It was two months in when I decided, hell with it, I wanna ride this nigga.'

'And how was it?'

I don't expect the question. Till now, she's been very boujee with me. I half don't want to answer but then I remember how she held me, bawling my eyes out on her neck. It felt good. I won't lie.

'It took us a minute to get over the nerves. He came too quick. And the time after that I was all in my head and couldn't get wet for him,' I say, testing how she reacts. She doesn't flinch. 'Then there was the time I rode him so good I almost broke his dick and the guy goes and loses the fucken condom inside me. Can you believe that shit? A whole musty condom stuck in my koochi for half a day? I had to get a girlfriend to fish it out. Had to even deal with a UTI the following day. It was the audacity of it all for me. Men.'

The Mortician laughs, laying her head on the counter. A reaction, finally. Under all that serenity, she likes getting the tea. I'll admit, she's growing on me. The way she takes up space, unapologetically. Like me.

'I haven't told many people this, but back when I was studying at UJ, I had some encounters with the feminine mystique.'

'And you're telling me this … why?' The Mortician withdraws, sitting back.

'We're clearly not gonna get *any* from the men here, right?' I brush off the awkwardness, afraid she isn't picking up what I'm putting down. I reach for my phone and open my Insta feed to lubricate the situation.

She blocks the screen with a long silky sleeve from her gown. 'Maybe –'

From over her shoulder, I spot Daniel walking down the corridor. 'Maybe you should go check on Dianne. I know you asked me to look out for her, but that owl is way too basic. She probably sent girls like me to detention twice a week in her day.'

'Shame,' says the Mortician, lifting her sleeve from the phone, noticing Daniel, 'try and be kind. She's the weakest of us.' She leaves, walking past Daniel. 'Come see me tomorrow, after dinner. I'll have a special room prepared for you,' she shouts back into the kitchen the way a club owner might order their staff around.

'Did I interrupt something?' asks Daniel, opening a bottle of chardonnay from the fridge.

'I've gotta make a call.' I head out back into the garden, wondering what just went down in the kitchen.

Daniel was masturbating when the Mortician knocked on the bathroom door. They had agreed to be up early for the hike in the Magaliesberg. They were already late.

'Be right out,' said Daniel, lowering the volume on his phone, even though he was sure that it was low enough for the Mortician not to hear. The light from the screen between his thighs made him aware of his stomach fat. He really needed to get back in shape, he thought. Through the open window above the toilet which opened out into the gardens, he heard birds pelt the sky with exultant warbles. On the screen between his legs, two men shoved one another back and forth on a bed; one of them, whose face was masked, pressed the other down into a foam mattress, as if wanting him to merge with it. The second man didn't wear a mask, his mouth shifting into what could be read as pain or pleasure. Even if Daniel turned the volume up, he knew the sounds emanating from the unmasked man would remain ambiguous.

It had been years since he chose this bookmark in his phone's browser. He had half-thought that the video might no longer live in the initial domain he had found it in when he was twelve years old. Yet, there it was, as if somewhere in the vast array of servers that made up the internet this scene would always be playing somewhere, shining between countless thighs. He liked the video because of how vocal the men were; through all their manic thrusting they managed to keep up a lively banter – each half-gasped phrase more salacious than the one before, upping the ante, and doubling the risk, of seeming foolish or, God forbid, banal.

'You'll find me in the car.' The Mortician's voice pushed in from underneath the door.

Did she know what he was doing? No, there was no way she could. He acknowledged her bluntly, hoping she would get the hint, determined as ever to get his quickie in. When the masked man put his face in between the other's butt cheeks, Daniel's pupils dilated. Lucas never liked doing that, he'd said the extra bit of skin that grew to the left of his anus made him too self-conscious. He never believed that excuse because Lucas had been gifted since puberty with a finely sculpted body. And even if Lucas had had insecurities, all that rigorous track training surely pummelled it out of him.

The thought of Lucas feeling insecure was as ridiculous to him as Brad Pitt having insecurities about his jawline. It didn't make sense because everywhere Lucas went, eyes tracked him, a gazelle gliding across a savannah. Plus, how many times had he lain on Lucas's back, reassuring him – *babe, I don't care what it looks like, it's unique and beautiful to me.* Lucas remained obstinate and Daniel began to speculate that, maybe, there was something else going on. That perhaps Lucas had made up his mind to reserve his anus for two purposes. In and out – things went in and things came out, but nothing, and no one, was allowed to lick along the creases that his athleticism could not smooth over.

By now, a translucent drop had appeared on the tip of Daniel's penis. The veins in his pelvis expanded; blood from his quickening heart got sucked into his shaft, the unfolding scene on the screen becoming a gaping mouth of pixels. His attention bottlenecked, so much so that he didn't feel the numbness of his thighs on the toilet seat or the cool air from the window above. Gooseflesh spread.

If there was any satisfaction in being alive it was *this*, he thought. The moments where life dissolved and reorganised into a snow globe. In episodes like these, all his fantasies swirled together at a compounding speed: the harder he massaged his penis the more he became the man in the mask, then the man without the mask, and back again. He couldn't resist not turning the volume up, just a little; he needed to hear the men rummage through their vocabularies, trying to pin down, in bleats and blurbs, what it felt like.

Phrases bulged, begged, caesuras split open into tyrannical demands to be delivered out of their minds. The staccato of their gasps ferried both men into a nether realm where communication consisted, exclusively, of expletives. *Shit. Fuck. Fuck. Shit.* They chanted.

Strained, their baritones shook Daniel, each expletive adding to the blizzard that was now raging. Their incantations summoned the whites of his eyes to overcome their blue pupils, mirroring the white that now spewed and settled, squiggles of curdled milk, in the toilet bowl under him.

Halfway between giddy and languid, he wiped himself clean. He extracted his attention from the scene, that moments before he couldn't imagine leaving. Steadily, the rake and clamour of his penis drew back into the cave of his pelvis. He considered his dick, how soft and elastic it had suddenly turned: a malleable prop, something on which a staged production of a murder mystery might centre. *Colonel Daniel in the bathroom with the elastic dildo.* He laughed. Maybe in this production, the elastic dildo wasn't the murder weapon at all. Maybe it was the seemingly insignificant clue that pointed to who the true killer was.

He washed his hands, leaving useless speculations to float with his white squiggles in the toilet bowl. He felt ready for that hike, prepared for the sun to beat down on him, for that familiar mixture of sweat and sunscreen to leave a grainy film on his face.

OUTSIDE THE BATHROOM window, down the ivy-covered wall, across the dewy lawn, through the thorn trees (with roots so gnarly one had to climb over them) and beside the lemon tree, Lucas disrobed, hanging his gown outside the sauna. He had woken Daniel up for his hike with the Mortician before his alarm went off. Though Daniel often set an alarm, he was a relentless snoozer, often waking Lucas in the process. It was a quirk Lucas still found irritating. So much so that he made a point of being up before Daniel's alarms, making sure he knew the time it had been set to.

Entering the sauna, Lucas took a phial of amber liquid from his gown and squeezed a few drops under his tongue. It tasted like sweetgrass, giving way to a bitter, resinous aftertaste that he washed down with water. He reached for the sauna's ladle and poured water on the hot stones. The water fizzled into steam, his pores responding to the rising heat, blood diverting from the inner caverns of his torso to the upper echelons of his epidermis.

Ah, yes, he sighed, sitting nearer to the stones than last time.

After a few minutes, his skin became damp, his shoulder girdle more pliable. He cracked his knuckles and neck – each crack suspending bubbles of oxygen and carbon in the synovial fluids of his joints. The popping eased him. He had always cracked his knuckles and neck before a big race; it was a silly superstition, but it made him feel lighter. Now that there were no more races to run, idle cracking would have to fit into some other superstition.

He leaned back on the wooden bench, keeping his braced leg extended and his right leg bent, eternally grateful that his right had survived the accident where his left hadn't. The man he'd been before the accident – with a body built for explosive speeds – would never have been able to fathom the way he was living now. He thought of what the Mortician had said at dinner a few nights ago.

The person you think you are, Lucas. That man must die. Though you may resist it, that man is already dead. And you have to use every resource you can to become something new. There is no other way.

He was beginning to appreciate Daniel's insistence on coming here. Though initially he'd seen it as couples therapy, it was nothing like it. It felt more like a place for experiment, where he was being allowed to shatter old habits and shock his system, discovering new ways to hold the world in his mind. He had never been the patient type, though. Every sort of improvement he had ever made on himself had definite steps that could be plotted out clearly. Abandoning control, the way the Mortician was asking him to do, was not a clear path.

Even walking is a kind of falling, the Mortician had said on their third session in the sauna. The phrase stuck with him and, the more he thought about it, the more he came to realise that he was becoming dependent on her infinite resolve.

He stretched his right leg out along the bench, the effects of the tincture taking hold. All the flaps of his mind were opening, the way a plane adjusts its wings at full speed before take-off. *Rebuild your strength in your right and recover some stability in the left,* he repeated, paraphrasing what Nikita advised. He wasn't asking for much, all he wanted was to walk without an aid. He hated the wobbling and cautious favouring he had to do; hated it so much that he avoided walking past mirrors or being inadvertently caught on camera while in motion.

When the mirrors in the lobby of the house first caught him in their frames, all he could see was his past – body in full Herculean torque, coming fast upon a finish line. Was some remnant of that strength still in him somewhere? His muscular frame still held to that illusion, but he sensed that the memory, the know-how, of all his training – hours of squats, sprints, planks, bench presses – was nothing but toxic waste in the landfill of his past.

If memories could be recycled and, like stem cells, directed towards different purposes, different lives, then Lucas had no idea how to go about doing it.

His left leg had gotten the rawest deal, and though he diligently performed every exercise Nikita had recommended, he suspected the leg had popped so far out of joint with its past that not even diligent ritual could reabsorb it into its original agreement of tendon, cartilage and ligament. What would he have done if *both* legs had been forever cut off from their former selves? The possibility unnerved him.

The sauna reached ninety degrees. His heart migrated to his throat and nestled below his Adam's apple. Sweat criss-crossed his chest, creeping over his brow and hanging on the cliff of his chin. He closed his eyes, followed a stream of it from the top of his bald head down past his temple. He stopped the stream with his finger, just before it circled into the curve of his left eye-socket.

When people asked why he stayed bald all these years, he usually said something silly, like it being 'aerodynamic' to keep his hair super short. In truth, as a boy, Lucas had always hated cutting his hair. It all had to do with the immense discomfort stoked in him by the way his mother's electric blades buzzed against his hairline. Whenever Veronica sat him down, flashing that old red sheet that was to go around his neck, she assumed the fastidiousness of a matador. His restlessness stood no chance for as early as he could remember, the sound of blades coming so close to his ears was unbearable. He flinched incessantly during her haircuts, hunching his shoulders, imagining the top arcs of either ear gobbled up in freak accidents – hair bloodily spliced with ear helixes in his own homemade horror movie.

As the mist of memory leaked through his pores, Lucas watched Veronica shave his five-year-old head, angling herself at him with her failing eyesight. Sitting underneath the blades for long periods of time fuelled a creepy-crawly feeling in his groin – it was like needing to pee and scratch an itch simultaneously. Over time, his body was achingly adjusted to the tiny blades grinding his curly hair down into a shimmering scalp, in the same way that

Veronica became adept at moving the blades along the indentations of his skull, mapping his head like any responsible mother would do.

It was becoming hard to breathe in the sauna. Lucas tried to focus, but the mist of memory was too lucid. The outline of Solomon condensed in the mist before him and he began to listen, just as he had done many times before, to one of his father's impromptu lectures.

Mfana wam, I was just like you. Youngest of five boys, it was hard, man. It makes you, what's the word. Antsy. Being the butt of every joke, called a mommy's boy altyd. You must be grateful you're an only child. A brother's cruelty is hard to swallow. It's a sign of love too, remember that. How a man has got to be. You'll learn, boy.

Solomon had said this on the day of his first barber haircut, a month after his parents had separated. He was eight. They were parked outside Fresh Fades and Solomon was showing him all the different haircuts he could choose from. *The barber cuts all styles. Fades, box-cuts, even vinyls. But you can only get that in the holidays. Your ma will kill me if you got it now.*

Lucas was drawn to the handsome men popping up on his father's phone, keen to find out if cutting his hair would chisel his face to look like them.

Fresh Fades was packed that Saturday. He sat down with his father on a ragged red couch, next to boys who spoke a slang he didn't understand. There were four barbers at work, with most of the black clientele waiting in line to sit in the one black barber's chair. *Our people cut our hair*, Solomon had insisted. So they waited, and waited, for an opening, until another man named Patrick called Lucas up to his chair.

'No no, my boy is waiting for bra Zakes.'

'Don't worry, uncle, I can cut your laaitie's hair.'

Looking to bra Zakes for confirmation, Solomon was assuaged. It wasn't long before Patrick was tying a sheet around his son's neck.

Sweat. Sizzle. Hiss. Lucas lifted himself off the wooden bench and shifted his weight to his right leg before pouring another ladle of water on the stones. He tried picturing the photographs on the walls of the barber shop. Ferraris, Mercedes-Benzes, BMWs and Lamborghinis, straddled by bikini-clad women and, below the barbers' work stations, poster-sized naked women in jungles, on beaches, in an airplane, working power tools at a construction site. He knew, even as a boy, that those images were meant to entice. He was not enticed. In each photograph there was an indecipherable code that did not unlock whatever they were supposed to unlock. Yes, the women were beautiful, sculpted from alabaster, no doubt. But they remained just that.

Steam from the stones reddened his face. He felt diaphanous. Rubbing his hands along his wet body, he pictured Patrick: full pinkish lips, gold tooth where his one incisor should have been. Face narrowing at the chin and forehead, diamond-like. That Saturday, the young barber had been working nonstop since the morning. His body was damp; tiny droplets of sweat trickled down his neck and disappeared behind his shirt. When Patrick positioned Lucas's head to face the floor, so he could get a better look at the back hairline, Lucas closed his eyes and imagined himself as one of those droplets, picking up pace as gravity exerted its influence – mixing with all sorts of bodily secretions.

He had been halfway through the haircut when Patrick leaned against him, sighing; the smell of cigarettes and coffee went up his nose. Patrick's leaning alerted Lucas to the bulge in the barber's track pants. Something meaty had saddled up against young Lucas's hipbone. The barber moved around, straightening hairlines in the mirror, unaware of the world he was unravelling for the boy in his chair.

Lucas sat down on the sauna's bench and took off his robe, spreading his legs. He gently flicked his penis, animating nerve tissue in his groin, secreting nitric oxide, as oxytocin flowed into his spinal cord, setting it alight. Of course, he was unaware that this was taking place; in his head he was in Patrick's chair, subtly shifting to anticipate where exactly the barber might brush against him next. And there it was, the bulge: its distinct parts made opaque by track pants. The force of its presence induced an excitement that any boy wouldn't know how to handle.

Patrick thought nothing of his fidgeting. His job was to cut sharp symmetrical lines into heads. Yet, young Lucas walked out that shop feeling amorphous, blurry. From that first cut, he asked Solomon to set up regular appointments every second Saturday so that Patrick could trim his hair and fade his sides and back. A couple of months passed, and it seemed that Lucas had found a loophole in his conflict with razor blades.

His naivety, however, brought all fantasies to a standstill. It was Christmas time, and he had gone to Patrick for a special haircut, one where the barber would cut the outline of the playboy bunny into the back of his head. During the haircut, Patrick asked if he had a 'cherrie by da school', and that was when Lucas understood that he and the bulge in Patrick's pants shared a secret all their own. Patrick was just a barber doing his job.

THIRTY MINUTES PASSED. Lucas wasn't sure how he was going to get out of the sauna. He reached for his crutches and pulled himself upright. Then, feeling his knees quiver, he sat back down, left leg pounding, body feeling like battered chunks of T-bone steak. The humidity crowded his thoughts; all he wanted was fresh air. He leaned over, pressing the emergency button. Mustafa's voice came through on the intercom.

'Everything all right?'

'I can't get out. I've stayed too long.'

'Hang on. I'll be there now now.'

'Hurry.'

Lucas fell beyond the grips of consciousness, splaying on the bench. His abrupt fall sideways wrung synovial fluid into his surrounding joints, forcing the fluid to respond to the weight of the impact and turn itself viscous, supportive.

A long time ago, this egg-white fluid had made a pact with the rest of the human body to be the buffer for bones against the prospect of falling too hard, for too long. Like most pacts made over millennia, there are absolute thresholds.

ABOVE THE UNNUMBERED house, stratocumulus clouds washed across the sky, sluicing all the way south of the city. They folded, ballooned and twisted: galloping chariots in one instance, twirling Sufi dervishes the next, finally collapsing into the faint outline of an old man smoking a pipe, out of which the ghosts of corkscrews drifted.

On the ground, Mustafa drew his arm back through the driver's window into the air-conditioned car. He was parked at a Shell, across the road from the entrance to Sun City Prison. It was almost noon; the man he was waiting for should've been walking out by now. Abbas chewed on a rubber toy shaped like a chicken wing on the back seat, drool drying on the hot leather. Just after one, a man of around fifty, with downward-slanted eyes and patchy salt-and-pepper hair, walked through the archway and dropped his backpack at his feet. The entrance had signs on either side: an ABSA logo on the left and the South African coat of arms on the right. The man shielded his eyes from the midday sun, considering the sky.

Looking on from a distance, Mustafa wondered if the sky looked different on this side of the prison wall. He got out the car and walked around to the passenger side, opening it while waving. The man, recognising Mustafa, threw his backpack on and walked over.

'You got a dog?'

'Abbas. He likes to drive with me.'

The man chucked his backpack through the back window. Abbas, surprised, sniffed it curiously.

'Where's this place you're taking me?'

'North of here. Way north.' The scent of cheap soap and unwashed clothes was unyielding, but Mustafa didn't give his aversion away. 'There's a buy and braai just up the road. Hungry?'

'Fuck ja. All I've had is cabbage and skinless chicken. I lus for some spicy boerewors and chakalaka.' The man didn't need an invitation to get into the passenger's side.

On the asphalt behind him Mustafa spotted a small green book. 'Don't forget this.' He picked the book up. Below the ID number was a worn image of a teenager with high cheekbones and a bottom lip that looked like it had been in enough fights to last a lifetime. *Tobias Meyer*, the book read.

Tobias snatched it away. 'Ey, bra, I'm hungry. Let's waai.'

AT THE SHISA Nyama Tobias loaded the iron drum with charcoal and firelighters. Pork rashers swam in marinade beside him, a glossy brown. The buy and braai was empty so Mustafa let Abbas out to stretch his legs in the parking lot.

'Someone's gonna bust that pup's skull with their bumper,' said Tobias, testing the flames.

'That won't happen. Abbas is a clever dog.'

'Clever or not. A bumper don't care. It bumps, nje.' He clicked his tongue and headed inside for more beers.

Mustafa wasn't drinking, but he'd assumed Tobias would. Old habits and all that. The fire was in full blaze and Mustafa wondered how close he could get before his body signalled danger. He brought his hand within an inch of the flames before pulling back, the instinctual recoil evidence that he still had skin in the game. Or was the pain of crossing over the real obstacle to transformation, he wondered.

'Here, have one,' said Tobias, offering a beer.

Mustafa was surprised. In the HIV workshops he ran at Sun City, Tobias was the inmate who would look to get his hands on most, if not all, of the condoms Mustafa handed out. He later came to understand that there was some form of currency to them. In prison, anything scarce could be currency: cigarettes, toilet paper, cell phones, take-out, sex, murder, deodorant. In the workshops, he observed that Tobias was the kind of man who wanted things, it didn't matter what. He wanted more than the next person. A simple goal.

'You aren't worried what that might do?' said Mustafa, referring to the beer.

Tobias shook his head and slapped the pork rashers on the grill, along with the boerewors. He broke off a piece of raw boerewors and gave it to Abbas. 'Awe, hond,' he said, laughing.

Mustafa sipped his beer, leaving the rest on the table. By the time Tobias had finished his first beer he was already looking to get a second and third. Mustafa had often heard the other inmates talking about Tobias's successful papsak enterprise in Sun City. In fact, when a leaked video went viral, showing inmates drinking wine from mugs and playing music via a Bluetooth speaker in a storage cupboard, most of the inmates knew that it was Tobias who had probably supplied the papsak. No one snitched, least of all Mustafa, who didn't want anything affecting Tobias's release date.

'See, Musty, I don't like my meat tough and dry. You must still taste the vark,' said Tobias, licking the marinade off his fingers.

Mustafa noticed his dark nails, flat and wide like dustpans. On the grill, globules of fat bubbled and popped on the surface of the rashers, while juice from the boerewors dripped through onto the coal, fanning the flames that crusted salt, pepper, chilli and garlic flakes onto the meat. When the meat was cooked, they ate it with buttered Portuguese rolls and chakalaka. Every once in a while, one of them would hand Abbas a piece. As the afternoon wore on, more beer bottles stood empty on the table; it was four o'clock when Mustafa realised the parking lot had filled up considerably. Music played from out the back of Citi Golfs with tinted windows.

'You want me to drop you off in Eldos before we head through?'

'Nah, nothing for me there. Charmaine's house is sold. I had to sell it to pay my fines.' Tobias bit into his roll, crumbs fell over his meat.

There would be nothing for him there, thought Mustafa. He remembered the story. Pastor ran a church from out his garage. Pastor had a real gift of the gab too, so much so that his church community grew exponentially. The pastor was so talented that people didn't mind parting with what little money they had. Word spread, and the garage became too small to house the faithful, so a plan was hatched to buy and renovate a run-down building in the area. The pastor, a less-wrinkled Tobias, convinced the community to seek out more of the faithful to invest in the sacred venture. The more congregants people recruited, the closer to the altar they would sit when The Fountain of the Active Grace of God opened. At least, that was what Tobias promised. The faithful believed because their pastor was a passionate believer: he spoke with them and not at them. He was an amalgamation of TD Jakes and Ray

McCauley; he had watched all their sermons online. He had taken notes.

'You never told me –' began Mustafa.

'What?'

'What'd you do with the money?'

Tobias stopped, scanned the table. 'I partied. More beer?'

'None for me.' Mustafa did not believe it. Was it possible to blow through eighty thousand in three months? According to the newspapers, that was how long it took for the police to find Tobias, cooped up in a guesthouse in Clarens of all places. If there was money stashed away, Tobias would not have agreed to join them in Northcliff, would he?

What was this bra's endgame, thought Tobias. He went inside to order more beer. His gut told him that Mustafa was a scammer; no one got invited to the suburbs to 'experiment with oneself', just like that, without having to pay something. Was this some cult or freaky kak where rich laanies paid to watch poor people fuck, or shit? He'd decided to go along for the ride for as long as it took to find out what the scam was and, who knows, maybe learn some tricks from Mustafa's operation. He had nowhere else to go and nothing else to look forward to so there was no reason not to give the rich people what they wanted. Three meals a day and a roof to sleep under, all for a scam? Not a bad deal.

When he returned, Mustafa had put Abbas back in the car. The parking lot had become a lot rowdier: blaring speakers rattled all the windows in the vicinity. A group of high school girls walked past and men from a band of Citi Golfs leaned back on their bonnets, making comments as they drank. *Ey, those white socks look too clean. Come let me dirty them some.*

Mustafa checked his phone. It was time. 'I have to pick something up from a doctor friend of mine. Then we can go through to the house.'

The food wasn't finished, thought Tobias. This coconut's got geld.

'Take the food with, and the drinks,' said Mustafa. He got in the car to text Victor. He had been without meds for a week, longer than any time before. He wasn't particularly worried. The virus offered a slow death, the ARVs acting as a reminder of what he needed to keep at bay, of his dependency on the ingenuity of others.

By five, Mustafa, Tobias and Abbas were on the road again, heading north, with Tobias sleeping in the passenger seat. Mustafa was wrapped in thoughts of the creature living inside him: the one that hid itself in his fat, intestines and lymph nodes; the one who snuck through in fluids, who swam with his boyhood in a basket down a red river, finding its bedrooms on the banks of lipid membranes. The creature had undressed itself in Mustafa's body almost a decade ago, reading its commandments out loud for its congregants, his CD4 cells, to hear and recite. It was such a persuasive sermon that every CD4 cell the virus came into contact with began to assume that these commandments were preordained, a new law instituted in Mustafa's body, handed down from the mount of RNA. The new gospel spread itself through every cell, ordering them to prepare for the end of days. Mustafa's CD4 cells obliged, believing in their new prophet.

At a red traffic light, Tobias turned towards the window, breath fogging up the glass. It suddenly struck Mustafa that that was what it must have been like for Tobias's ministry. Cutting up the Bible, reorganising it from the inside, fusing so fully to become not just one of the congregants but *the one*.

Mustafa wondered what had become of the people who gave all they had to Tobias's scheme? He imagined them as the kinds of people who yearned to be pierced by any sort of divine message, no matter its shape or vessel. Prophets were shapeshifters, after all, adapted to suffocate the parts of human nature that were hopelessly exposed to revelation, and damnation.

This is what he believed the creature living in the sentences of his DNA had given him too. Revelation, coiled inside the nucleus of damnation.

DIANNE

Walking the first floor, I notice the house is built around a central atrium made of glass. Inside, two gingko trees stand in a miniature meadow, next to a stream pouring over a watermill. It's quite ingenious, the stream seems to run from the atrium out into several corridors; one can only see it in the corridors with glass floors. In between the trees is a treehouse, built in the shape of an eye with windows all around. Lucas told me that's where the Mortician and Mustafa sleep. I think they're a couple.

I pass along the glass pane of the atrium and come upon a reading room that opens out onto the front lawn. It is anything but flat – mounds of green roll down towards burgundy bushes. On the lawn, the deck of the second floor extends overhead and it's only when I'm out from under it that I hear Mustafa from above.

'Looks like folds in a –?'

'What did you say?' I call back.

'The lawn. Looks like folds in a brain.'

There's a Jack Russell in his arms and he's smoking ... a joint? He balances his sunglasses on his forehead while the dog gets fidgety.

'Do you have any pets?' he asks.

Can't he just put the poor thing down? 'No. No pets.'

'You can play with Abbas if you want.' The dog's ears perk up at the sound of his name.

'I'm good, thanks.'

'Playing is good for dogs, and humans.' Abbas is agitated; he clearly doesn't want to be held.

'Don't you think you should put him down?'

'Yes, yes, you're right. Will you catch him?'

'What? No! I meant *next to you*.' I scramble forward, positioning myself under the railing.

'There you are,' says Mustafa, satisfied. 'Don't worry, I'd never hurt Abbas.' He snuggles the dog's snout, letting it lick his face.

'That wasn't funny.'

I walk away before he can reply. The further I get from the house, the more alone I feel. The people here make me miss not having to explain myself, the feeling of home. People here seem so wrapped in their own mystery.

My headache starts up again. I set off on a pathway through the bushes, walking into the unruly gardens, having to manoeuvre under low-hanging vines. The headache slows me down, but I keep on. The path ends without warning, and my foot slips in mud. It's only when I'm balanced again that I make out the Mortician up ahead.

It's a lot muddier where she is standing, but that doesn't seem to be an issue for her. I get the feeling I'm eavesdropping. Is she praying? Maybe I should head back the way I came.

'Are you going to join me or just stare?' she shouts.

'Sorry, I didn't mean to. I mean, I wasn't –'

'Yes, you did. You're on time in fact.'

'On time?'

'Join me?'

'In the mud?'

'How else? There is drier land up ahead. We can climb there together,' she says, pointing.

I don't know if I can get to her. The ground is a lot darker where she is – who knows how deep it gets. I can't even see her feet.

'You'll have better luck with your shoes off,' she says, half turned to me.

I suck it up, take my shoes off and make my way. The mud gets thicker with each step; in some places it reaches up to my shins. My feet make moist, plopping sounds and I can feel the mud getting in under my toenails. I approach with caution, try to step around brown puddles where I see them, gauging which parts are drier, harder, flatter. Some patches hold me; others take my feet down the second I place my weight on them. I cover my nose against the putrid stench of rotting vegetables. The closer I get to her, the more fetid it becomes.

I think of Funani – his bright, fat cheeks, the gap in his teeth that he was so proud of, the way he kicked his feet when he sat on chairs too high for him. *Not right now.* Toes clench: the sour headiness of mud worsens the headache, dozens of electric toothbrushes brush against the inside of my skull. 'That smell …' I say, lurching forward to stand beside the Mortician, keeping my head eye-level, refusing to look down.

'Manure. Mustafa works it in regularly. With the help of Angelique. How else are we to keep these gardens lush and overgrown without the help of our residents?'

I breathe through my mouth, not wanting to smell. Bits of banana peels, lettuce, cobs of corn, onion slivers and eggshells poke up, half rotten. I can't wade through all this.

'We're almost there.' The Mortician takes my hand and gestures to a raised clearing up ahead. Her hands are clean, I think. I feel a gagging reflex coming on and I pinch my nose to stall it. We take a few steps, the Mortician massages a wad of mud through her fingers like a stress ball. I ignore her as best I can.

Finally, we step up, through an embankment. A few metres away stand two big rocks that face one another. She lets go of me and climbs onto one before crossing her legs and goading me with her muddy hand to get on the other rock. 'Here, won't you light these? It'll help with the smell.' She hands me a lighter and a pack of incense sticks.

The sunset casts long shadows across the clearing as I light the incense. 'Smells sweet,' I say, climbing onto the rock.

'Ambergris. A rare scent if you can get your hands on it. Notes of musk and ocean spray. And to think it comes from whale shit.'

'What?'

'Oh, yes. Bile mixed with squid beak. An inglorious symphony, shat into the ocean. Takes months, sometimes years, to decay into what you're smelling now.'

'Did we really have to go through the mud like that?'

'No. Do you remember what I said when I invited you here?'

I think back, trying to ignore the headache, but the ambergris isn't helping. After agreeing to be a resident, the Mortician took me to the eco-park at the top of Northcliff ridge. There, we found a spot under a thorn tree. Being so high up, faced with a panoramic view of Joburg from the CBD to the Magaliesberg, the afternoon sun glinting on everything it touched, I thought of the Bible verse where Lucifer takes Jesus up on a mountain and offers him the world, on condition that he prostrate before him.

'I shared with you how scared I was. How I wasn't ready for life to end,' I say, finally.

'And I told you that all you had to do was trust my methods and leave your expectations behind.'

'Doesn't it ever bother you? Working this much with the dying?'

She scans her body as if looking for an injury. 'It comes and goes. I have doubts like any other person. Then I remember the road it took to get here, the sense of purpose I feel when I've made crossing over that much lighter, exuberant. My work is a kind of midwifery. I can give you techniques and be there to hold your hand but, in the end, you have to climb back up that birth canal. Leave your names behind.'

'And when you're in doubt, what do you do with that?' Her eyes soften. Is she about to cry?

'*I* don't *do* anything. The rock gets pushed up the hill, whether I do the pushing or not. Whether it's something else pushing me, or not. All I can be is what I am in the moment. Whether that's doubt, courage or serenity. I have to practise unconditional compassion, for myself. And it's not easy, not by a long shot. Not when you feel that you should be doing more.'

'So you're the female Sisyphus.'

'Ha! Good one,' she giggles, almost losing her balance. 'No, I'm what's between the woman and her rock. Camus said that the misery and greatness of this world offer no truths, only objects to love. Dianne, when you're reconciled to the reality that you *have been* dying, that death is the condition of your survival, your growth, the very earth you walk on … you feel a shift, an appreciation. Like slipping into a hot spring, way up in the Andes, the world is all around you, frozen in time, and there's your pinpoint self, sweating in the crack. When you live in the world as its absolute equal, how can death not be made *for* us? We, who are so connected to this planet that its very violent processes gave rise to our consciousness and our ability to alter the world to our liking, manipulate its forces.' She presses a finger to her eye, rubbing it. 'In any event, the body's a narcissist. Don't you think? Food and water and self-actualisation, a whole fucken Maslow pyramid. And, and, and, want, need, want, need. It's exhausting.'

I've never thought of things this way; I want to sit and pick her brain some more. Is this why I'm here? To be guided up a mountain and then what?

'Are you happy?' she asks, the question coming at me out of nowhere.

'If Sisyphus can imagine it,' I snort.

'At least he had help, didn't he? The confirmation of a god, the certainty of his curse, the knowledge of what his life would involve till the end of his days. Would you prefer it that way? To know your lot *exactly*. To know why you have been given this brand of suffering?'

The incense forms curlicues on the air; I think of whale shit, mixing in intestines much larger than me, ambergris not fully formed yet, there as possibility.

'If we knew as much to predict our lives down to the exact second, we could probably manufacture great pleasures, and we'd probably dish out a good deal of pain from the buffet too, just for taste. But, I think what we couldn't have are the feelings that rock our roots. Joy. Suffering. Disappointment. Surprise. Grief. Those are harder to come by. And aren't they the kinds that strip us to the truth that, at any moment, our world could be destroyed, remade, saved?'

My legs pull stiff, and I hobble off the rock to stretch them. I want my shoes back. 'Are we going to go back the same way?'

'We'll get your shoes, don't worry. You haven't answered me.' She uncrosses her legs.

'I suppose if I knew the *why* then, yes, the *hows* and *whens* and *wheres* would be a little easier, I think. But maybe you're right. If I knew that much, I'd be less bewildered. Less winded. Or maybe, maybe I'd be at peace.'

'Peaceful as this rock I'm sitting on.'

'No. No, I don't think so. My life's more than some boulder. There are people I love in it. Choices too. However limited. I've always believed every person gets to make two or three big choices in their lifetime. My first was leaving Bethlehem Primary and joining a convent. The second was leaving the convent. And the third ...'

'Coming here?' She saddles off the rock, puts her hand on my shoulder.

'I was going to say joining Hopeful Horizon.'

'Ah yes. I've been meaning to ask you –'

'Why I left the school?'

Her hand travels down my arm, finding my fingers. 'Yes, why did you?'

I pull away and lean against the rock. There's barely the suggestion of sunlight in the clearing now. 'There was a boy. Aluwe. He was in Grade seven when he … started seeing things – visions of blood running down the walls of his classroom. Said the ancestors were calling.'

'Calling him for?'

'To be a sangoma. It wasn't the first time we had dealt with callings as a school. Many times we told parents to deal with these things outside of school time. Most of the parents didn't want their children to have anything to do with ancestors and callings and such.'

'So, what happened with Aluwe?'

'He was a different case because his seeing started affecting other kids. Until it wasn't just him seeing blood running down the walls but five kids in a single week. It was getting out of hand. Aluwe's parents were Catholic, so I didn't see anything wrong with taking him into my office and having daily prayer sessions – him and I, reciting decades of the rosary. It helped. His visions stopped for some time.'

'Until?'

'There were more. A lot more callings. Kids from every grade, boys and girls, the hysteria spread so much that we made it to the news. We had to call counsellors, priests and traditional healers. Can you imagine? Counsellors in one classroom, priests throwing holy water in the corners of another, and traditional healers walking through the hallways burning imphepho. The news ate it up.'

'Did it work?'

'It did. Somehow that combo salved whatever was haunting

the school. I don't know how. When it died down, I felt that I needed to leave. The school board blamed me for the bad press and started looking for any small slip-up as a reason to remove me. I didn't want to give them the satisfaction of retrenching me, so I beat them to the punch. I heard later that the callings were starting up again. At least I'd left by then.'

'That's where the convent came in?'

'Yes. I needed to ground my faith. Witnessing that mix of healers, counsellors and priests all working in tandem made me want to get back in touch with what I truly believed.' I bend over to pull a tuft of grass out of the ground. It resists. 'Anyway, I had very few attachments to Joburg. I was an only child. My parents had died when I turned thirty-five. And when I left for the convent, I wasn't entirely sure it would work: the nuns I was going to were known for their sparse, rigid lifestyle, but I wanted to test it out. To see if I could find the extraordinary in the ordinary, I suppose.'

'It's funny. You think coming here was wildly out of character for you, but you've always been an experimenter.'

The Mortician kisses me on the cheek like I'm her long-lost aunty. Her breath smells of watermelon, her lips are supple. I don't shy away.

'I'm famished. Let's have some dinner, yes?'

MUSTAFA IS WAITING with my shoes tucked under his arms. 'I'll join you all a little later,' says the Mortician, walking off towards the back of the property.

Mustafa leads me on inside, taking a staircase up to the third floor. This floor is furnished with sliding doors made from semi-translucent paper that's fixed into wooden frames.

'They're called shoji screens, known for promoting natural

light and quiet movement,' says Mustafa. He slides one open, revealing a rectangular room with low black tables and round turquoise pillows on the floor, for seats. Angelique gets up to offer me a drink in a small white cup.

'What's this?' I ask.

'An aperitif.'

The liquid has a golden tinge to it. Tastes fruity. Lucas is seated at a table that's higher than the rest; I assume that's more comfortable for him. Mustafa shows me to my cushion and draws the blinds back onto a wide view of lower Northcliff, an urban forest pocketed with houses. To the far left, I make out a section of the highway, recognisable by its tail of orange streetlights. The room is so subdued that the sprinklers out front sound as if they're in here with us. A calm washes over me: what was in that drink? Even the headache has eased off.

Daniel walks in, pushing a cart of plates covered by steel cloches. 'And here, fellow chronics and terminals, is *my* favourite dish. Paella!'

Mustafa helps him lay the plates out in front of us. When they lift the cloches, aromas of spicy saffron fish and garlic mussels greet us. I'm hungry. 'What was in that drink?' I say, turning to Angelique beside me.

'A strong brew of sceletium –' She starts eating before we've had a chance to say grace.

'– to calm the nerves and open the heart,' Mustafa reassures me.

Daniel and Lucas are about to start eating too.

'Aren't any of you going to say grace?'

They look at me, surprised. Mustafa smiles. 'Dianne, will you pray for us?'

Angelique rolls her eyes, making a clang with her cutlery; Mustafa bows his head and the rest follow suit. I say grace. Soon as

I'm done the room roars back to cutting and chewing.

'Hmm, the flavour is quite striking, Daniel. Love the saffron,' says Mustafa. 'Now, since some of us have been here longer than others, it seems opportune to put the horse in front of the cart and for each of us to state clearly why we've come.' He opens a bottle of Boplaas port and fills a stemless wine glass. 'I'll go first. I have HIV, as most of you know already. Living with it has been … odd, but over time it's gotten easier. Almost normal. I say that because I barely feel the medication's side-effects these days. Which I'm grateful for. Medical progress and all of that. The only side-effects I feel now are in the faces of those I share this with. Truth is, the virus and I have signed a treaty, so to speak. It'll live in my body, dormant, and I'll keep its urges at bay; until one day, hopefully, we can be severed from each other. Or at the very least, locked away in separate cells.' He stops, finishes his drink and pours another, handing the glass to Daniel.

'I don't really wanna get into it. But, uh, I've had chronic depression for a while. And, yeah, I've had a friend come here. She said this place gave her a new outlook on life.' Daniel stops, looks to Lucas. 'I need that. Yup, that's me.' Daniel pours another glass and hands it to Lucas.

Lucas drinks before he speaks. 'The doctors say my right leg is set to make a ninety per cent recovery. And the left one, not as lucky.' Lucas hits his legs with his crutches like they're made of cardboard, then hands the glass to Angelique.

'I'd like to go on record saying this isn't proper dinner convo. Anyway, it's my kidneys. They're fucked. And my heart, it's got issues. Nothing as serious as these other psychos.' Angelique drinks the port like a shot of tequila, wincing. Daniel laughs but Lucas doesn't react.

Should she be drinking? Before I can ask, the cup is in my face, refilled. The dark purple liquid sits under my chin; I can see a little bit of me in it. 'I have a tumour. Brain. Inoperable.' The port is pungent when it hits my tongue. The others look on, wanting more. '… I decided I didn't want chemo. Rather be able to taste this paella and enjoy it than worry about whether I'll vomit it into a toilet later.'

They all stare like I'm a second Mandela freshly sprung from prison.

'A terminal is always welcome,' says Daniel.

Angelique leans over: 'Some of us are terminals, others chronics. It's a dumb lingo, just go with it.'

'We're all here for the same thing,' Mustafa pipes up.

'To die before your death. Or at least to try.' The Mortician's voice enters the room before she does. The shoji slides open and she glides in, wearing a kaftan, her hair parted into ponytails.

We all follow her around the room as she speaks.

'There is a prayer by Ananda Coomaraswamy – *I pray that death will not come and find me, still unannihilated.* Think on this.'

Mustafa sets the food down on the table for her.

'So, we're all expected to accept things as they are and not try and be better? Healthier? Safer?' asks Daniel.

From what I can tell, Daniel is the kind of guy who puts pressure on people who think they've found the 'truth'. He reminds me of the kids in Nkandla, those who'll question any adult into oblivion.

'Oh, no, not at all,' says the Mortician. 'It's worthwhile to build, create, fight, rebel, play and work towards our better natures. As long as we have our eyes on eternity.' The Mortician sits and starts eating.

All of a sudden, Angelique speaks. 'We've all had to say why we're here. It's only fair we hear your story. Come on – spill.'

The question doesn't disturb the Mortician. She replies at her own pace, first scooping a baby squid into her mouth. 'My story,' she starts. We all listen as she stops to swallow. 'My parents owned a funeral parlour, back in the 90s. We had a sizeable mortuary and we stayed in a comfortable cottage, just the three of us. Business boomed in the 90s. And my mother ... my mother helped my dad with the work. She was in the parlour mostly, but when bodies piled up, she'd have no choice but to help down below. I was never allowed there as a young girl. That didn't mean I couldn't sense the bodies nearby, on quiet nights, when the fridges of the mortuary whirred in the dark. Initially, it scared me. Then I became fascinated. Obsessed, perhaps. It wasn't long before I got it into my head that the whole business was rather beautiful. We, evolved from chimps, were so conscious, so endowed with the ability to love, that we cared for our dead. For bodies that no longer gave us anything.'

The Mortician spoke as if we were huddled around a campfire. I imagined a flashlight under her chin, giving her the features of a gargoyle.

'A part of the beauty came from the coffins. From your chipboards to your redwoods, your walnuts with gold trimmings to your rose cherries with their distinct sauvignon colours. It's quite consoling to have decided on the kind of wood you'd like to be buried in. I hope you all remember the grains you picked when you arrived.'

So that's what that was about. I glance over at Lucas, eating his paella quietly with a spoon. What grain did he pick?

'Anyway,' the Mortician continues, 'when I turned sixteen, I worked in the parlour on Saturdays for pocket money. I loved it, most of all for what I could learn about a family by the coffin they believed their deceased would like. If I hadn't worked there, I might have never gotten the chance to get into a coffin and close it on myself. I did that once with the Hastings – a white oak that had this exquisite pink finish, trimmed in stainless silver. A little kitsch by my tastes today but, back then, just after closing time, I lay down in that Hastings, its cosiness like a plate of cookies. Wasn't that where we first bumped into each other, Mustafa?'

We all turn – Mustafa nods, clearing his throat, the sprinklers from the garden going on in the background. 'That's right. Although we only made the connection much later,' he says, looking around. 'I had started job shadowing a man who owned a hospice across the street from the orphanage where I grew up. That day, we got to the parlour five minutes after closing.'

'What were you guys there for again?' asks the Mortician.

'We wanted a simple pine box with rope for one of our residents who didn't have any next of kin. Frank and I peeked through the blinds at this teenage girl getting into a fancy coffin and shutting herself in.' Mustafa side-eyes the Mortician with an embarrassed smile.

There's a love there, no doubt. Maybe they *are* together.

'Anyone want coffee? Espresso? Caffè latte? Hot cocoa, maybe?' he asks.

The Mortician raises her fork. 'I'd love an espresso.'

Mustafa leaves the room in a hurry with the rest of our orders as she continues.

'Who's to say what's a normal childhood?' She looks off into the distance, holding something back. 'Any physics enthusiasts in the room? No? Anyone ever heard of the wave-particle duality?' she asks, finishing what's left on her plate.

Angelique offers more tea. I let her pour some for me.

'It is this fascinating phenomenon where an electron has both a particle- and wave-like nature, depending on how physicists measure it. I bring it up because I've always thought that normality is a bit like that. Dependent on what you measure it by, or how you ask the question, or how you observe phenomena and interpret the results: it could be one thing or another, both or neither. An electron acting as particle and wave, and yet, sneakily, neither. Sure, they are workable theories to think why this is so, but when you get right down to it, isn't it all spectra? Slow down and look long enough; you'll see none of us live in strict dualities. Alive? Dead? Come on, it's all jigging and jiving.'

The Mortician grins like she's figured out how to balance an equation. I've never seen someone so satisfied listening to their own voice. Daniel is more concerned with biting his nails and Angelique is picking fluff off her dress; it's only Lucas and I who seem to hang on every word.

'Today, there are physicists who advocate for what they call wave function realism. The fact that two electrons, separated by vast distances, can still affect one another instantaneously seems, for some, to point to the manifestation of higher, wave-like dimensions of reality. If we believe this metaphor gleaned from their experiments, then what we are, sitting here together, could be crests, rising from the ocean – saying *this* is who I am or this is *not* who I am. Either way, we're waving from trough to crest, and back again. Of course, like any wave we need time and space to build up and crash. To froth upon the shore, tickling the toes of children. Anyway, enough philosophising for one night, hey? Let's do some housekeeping. In a day or two, we'll be receiving a new resident. Tobias. He'll be staying in his own room. Other than that, please check the schedule on the fridge for the weekly chores. Tending to the space around us is just as vital as –'

All this talking is making me woozy. Mustafa returns, rolling a tray of steaming drinks. I reach for my hot chocolate, my hand not feeling like my own. Everything I touch (serviettes, cutlery, plates) adjusts against me. I'm losing control. The Mortician is speaking, but I can't make out what she's saying. I want to signal that I'm not okay, but there's a pane of glass between my brain and mouth.

The Mortician stops. *Dianne, are you all right?* Her voice

comes at me as if through water.

'Lie ... down. I ... need –'

Angelique helps me to my feet and out the room. I know what this is, but I cannot tell them what to do or how to help. I have to trust ... strangers.

Once out of the room, my tongue grips onto some words: 'I need to lie down. I can't feel my feet.' Angelique is right beside me, holding my arm. There's a pitter-patter on the roof.

'Oh, it's drizzling,' says Angelique.

I don't reply. The pitter-patter is loud; it's crashing inside my skull. I hit the floor, convulsing, muscles locking me inside the rhythm of a fish out of water. Angelique yells for Mustafa. My head bobs in her hands.

'How is she?' asked the Mortician.

Mustafa shut the bedroom door. 'All right, considering. I sedated her. She's gaining some of her strength back.' He zipped up his small satchel. 'The last seizure was brutal. It will get worse. We may not have enough time.'

'We'll be there for her as much as we can. Where are the others?'

'Cleansing. I'm heading over there now.'

'Very good.'

Mustafa nodded, walking off.

He was unsettled by Dianne's prognosis; the Mortician could tell. She walked up to the third floor, thinking back to the time Mustafa interviewed her for one of the caretaker positions at the hospice he used to manage. She recalled their intense eye contact, kept throughout, and the incense burning in the corner of Mustafa's office – a mixture of cinnamon and myrrh.

Mustafa had asked if the incense was too much (in his experience, people found his tastes overbearing). She had smiled, said it was soothing.

On the third floor, the Mortician strolled onto the wooden deck. *Why do you want to work here?* a younger Mustafa had asked.

I feel as if I've come full circle. This is where I could help. She hadn't prepared for the interview, believing the best conversations were the ones where people felt around inside themselves for the words that could crack open just right – glow sticks. She'd always believed language had light in it, perceptible only by the objects it came in contact with. Without something to touch, something to obstruct their speed, words whizzed through space. Inert.

Tell me more about this full circle. Mustafa's enquiry, light through slatted blinds. The Mortician unlatched part of the deck's railing, stepping onto the aerial walkway. She tried to recollect how she had answered. The walkway was a series of interconnecting bridges sprawled amongst the trees, each ending in spherical treehouses hidden from view. They had made sure to reinforce the walkway, double-bolting every section to the nearest tree.

High above the ground, she wandered through moonlight that filtered through the canopy in blotches of luminous pearl. Shadow and light remapped her body. Yes, she thought, she had told Mustafa about her family's parlour, and her father's dream to revolutionise how people were buried. About her father's fall into disrepute, how he was ridiculed by his peers, forced to remain 'sane' and, in the process, became disengaged from his fatherly responsibilities; about how her mother had stepped in to carry their family as he slipped into purposelessness.

I came to understand that a person could really just give up. After she said this, Mustafa broke eye contact, looking at her CV on the desk, putting it to the side. She thought the interview had been ruined, that she had overshared and revealed a part of her very few people, if any, got to see. That was not the case. Mustafa asked if she wanted a tour of the hospice and when was she prepared to start.

They would discover much later that they had met before as teens: Mustafa looking in through the blinds of her father's funeral parlour at the girl disappearing into a Hastings.

THE WALKWAY DIPPED slightly with her weight on it. From where she stood, she could make out each treehouse: large eggs in their nests. This late, this dark, most things were emptied of detail; she moved through the trees' brushstrokes of black like an action painter trying, and not trying, to let the paint speak.

She couldn't help but read into things. It was her nature.

Holding her palm out to the bark, she thought: *Tributaries. Roots. Bronchial tubes. Capillaries – a path's destiny is to divide, completely.* Why were some shapes more conducive to breathing or transporting blood than others? A single path can't reach everything, she reasoned.

Onto another section of the walkway, she ascended to the topmost part of a palm tree. From here the hedges in the back yard and the dominating cliff face above Northcliff came into view. There was the neighbour's cat too, on the wall between the properties, grooming itself. The cat was as surreptitious as she was, but then, without forewarning, it darted into the grass below. She considered the roof of the main house all the way to the rows of pine trees swaying delicately in a blanket of branches she couldn't see through. A body of sorts stirred there, she thought, its limbs vaster than the horizon. She felt an old, familiar ache: the sense of being inconsequential. Years ago, this frightened her. Tonight, it was a thought that drained the murkiness from her mind.

She made her way down from the palm tree and circled back to the house. Abbas was howling, provoking other dogs in the neighbourhood to join him. From house to house the howling spread, gathering – every canine looked up to its slice of sky and added to the chorus. High-pitched barks rattled alongside deep, wide growls, every size and shape of dog offering its evolutionary echo, the air above Northcliff quivering with canine instinct. No matter how long and loud the howling got, the air would settle.

SHE HEADED TO the treehouse on the upper north-east of the property. This was a room of her own. She had explained this to Mustafa when they first moved in. Mustafa, familiar with the phrase, didn't question her motives; in some ways, the greenhouses were his sanctuary. He never asked her what was inside.

She unlocked the treehouse and sat down in front of the monitors. She scrolled over to watch the cleansing, turning the audio up.

Mustafa, Daniel, Lucas and Angelique stood in front of two doors. 'Right,' began Mustafa, 'I've drawn Lucas. Daniel and Angelique, you have each other. Each of you, pick a totem. One that calls to you.'

Spread out on a table were stamps. Some shaped like animals; others were symbols that stood in for elements, and still more that looked like plants and geometric shapes. Angelique picked a cloud. Lucas chose a circle. Daniel picked a stamp with four triangles all turned inward, pointing to its centre. Mustafa picked the symbol of an eel.

'This is a ceremony of care. A practice of devotion for someone you barely know. If at any point you don't feel comfortable, you are welcome to leave. A word of encouragement, though: stay with the discomfort. Make that inner voice imperceptible, microscopic. Let it no longer inhibit you.'

The group split into pairs and walked into their separate rooms. The Mortician split her screen so she could look into both simultaneously. In each, there were two pods filled with water and, beside them, a table with essential oils and tubs of body paint. She watched them undress to their underwear. Mustafa took Lucas's circle stamp, dipped it into the body paint and began stamping circles all over Lucas's body. Daniel did the same for Angelique. The pairs then switched. Once the painting was complete, one half of the pairing sat down beside their pod and let the other lather them in essential oils. Over a loudspeaker, Mustafa instructed that one person from each pairing fully undress and get into the water.

From her vantage point, the Mortician noticed Angelique's hesitation. She zoomed in on their room to listen.

Angelique was about to unclip her bra when she stopped. 'I

think I'm gonna call time of death on this.' She reached for her clothing.

'Don't let me do this alone. If we're going to be doing weird shit, I'd rather be doing it with someone as confident as you. Plus, you know your bits don't interest me.' Daniel held out his hand. Angelique took it.

The two were developing a bond worth watching, thought the Mortician.

In the other room, Lucas had stripped and gotten into his pod. The longer he stayed in the water the more the circles on his body started to fade.

It seemed as if Lucas was about to question the validity of this ritual when Mustafa instructed those outside the pods to wash those inside. 'If you cannot find a sense of devotion, of service, to your fellow human being, then we really are lost as a species.' His voice echoed in both rooms, coming through to Daniel and Angelique over a speaker. He spoke in a hushed tone. Not accusatory, but plain, as if forecasting weather.

Mustafa and Daniel lathered soap onto loofahs and washed their counterparts. The Mortician watched with interest. For both of them, the only way to relieve themselves of uneasiness was to pretend that the body they were washing was their own. Even though they hadn't seen it before, it was, nevertheless, a form to which they were tethered.

When the washing was complete, Mustafa spoke. 'At the bottom of the pod, there is a see-through suction hose. The person who is outside the pod must take it and give it to the person inside. Press the intercom button to confirm when this has been done.'

A few minutes passed before Daniel's voice came through and confirmed that the instruction had been completed.

'Good. The people in the pod, Lucas and Angelique, insert the hose into your rectum.'

Suddenly, the intercom switched on again. It was Daniel. 'You can't be serious! What kind of fucked-up ceremony is this?'

'The ceremony of care is one that asks us to look beyond our programming of disgust. To witness the workings of another's bowels is the height of intimacy. If you cannot do it, it is fine. But what's so terrible? The waste you'll vacuum out of your partner will go on to become manure that will sustain the life of these gardens. It is your way of giving back to us. In any case, it'll eventually leave you in a few hours. Again, you're welcome to decline.'

The Mortician listened, admiring how genial and persuasive Mustafa could be. This ceremony was his idea. She did not have the patience for it. Either way, it was an erudite technique – one that brought you face to face with the body's own transformative capabilities. She wondered whether the residents would see it that way. For them, it was disgusting from every angle, and perhaps it was asking for too much, too soon.

The Mortician watched Angelique slide the tip of the hose into her rectum, signalling for Daniel to turn the suction on. Angelique giggled at first as sprites of water shot up into her. Then, as the suction became more intense, she grimaced, biting her bottom lip. The process, once one got over themself, was quite pleasurable, thought the Mortician. One felt twice as light after the ordeal.

Mustafa and Daniel watched Lucas and Angelique's brown matter snake away out of the room. It was surreal for Daniel to see the fragments of Angelique's day pass overhead. Pieces of yellows, greens and reds, not even distinguishable as forms of breakfast, lunch and dinner, suggested, at least for Mustafa, that fragments always met up with a whole somewhere down the line. It took some intuition to see that. And a whole lot of stomach.

The Mortician had seen enough. The pairs would swap places and the entire ceremony would be done within the hour. She made a mental note to check the treatment tanks in the composting greenhouse the next day. Her shoulder girdle had started to ache, as it usually did this time of night.

SHE LOCKED THE treehouse and walked back down the aerial walkway to the deck of the third floor.

Imagine all of it is you. This was what Mustafa had advised on her first day at Bridge Builders Hospice. This was soon after she'd cleaned up the mess Frank Ledwaba had made in his bed. She didn't know it then, but Mustafa's equanimity at the soiled sheets was a sign that they both shared similar experiences of being squeezed and spread, like paint from a tube, by a cosmic child who spoke no language, who was all play. It was also an indubitable sign of Mustafa's love for Frank, the man who'd offered Mustafa his first job as a caretaker at the hospice and who, growing fond of the young Mustafa, roped him in to take over its running.

Back on the third-floor deck, the Mortician entered a carpeted corridor. African masks were hung all the way down the passage walls. Some ochre-coloured and oblong, with pointy chins and diamond-shaped eyes, and others fashioned with horns that curved like praying hands or delicate arcs of water. She noted the contours of each: the places where what was carved out had allowed something more-than-human to surface.

The masks drew a memory from her. She had invited Mustafa to watch a rare Liberian Dan Ge performer. They stood together in an open field late one afternoon, a sizeable crowd having gathered in a circle, awaiting the performer's arrival. Anticipation grew. The world outside the gathering took on a bronze hue, thanks to the sun setting in the distance. There was, for the Mortician, the distinct feeling of being extracted from a sepia photograph and inserted among a band of technicoloured enthusiasts.

When the Dan Ge performer entered, everyone went quiet.

The performer – dressed in red, black, orange and white raffia feathers, ankled in bells of different shapes and sizes, and wearing a ridged black mask – swayed to drums and stringed instruments, played by musicians who stood to one side. At first, she was aware that a person was beneath the lustrous black mask and its foreboding presence. As the performance deepened and the crowd clapped and whistled, the performer's legs moved at an incendiary pace: feet kicked up dust, arms thrashed fine earth into transient whorls. Her mind slipped, and she forgot the person beneath the bells and feathers.

Here was a different intelligence. An intelligence that did not speak, formulate or define. It listened, touched, opened up unreservedly to the Malleable, the Mutable, the Manifest.

At the end of the corridor was a spacious bathroom filled with candlelight. In its centre was a large bath of an unusual depth; it was so deep one had to step up to the rim and then descend, step by careful step.

The bath had been drawn. Mustafa must have made it for her before the ceremony. The Mortician slipped off her clothes, the fabric sticky from the day's heat, and got in. Castles of crinkling bubbles surrounded her.

A surgical scar ran down the centre of her chest; she didn't take note of it anymore. It used to bother her, stirring up a dry, bitter taste at the back of her throat. It was now a signature of the doctors and nurses who had kept her in one piece.

One piece. One peace. She ebbed water over the scar.

Sometimes, the memory of what had happened rustled in the underbrush of her body (flocks of sparrows taking off in unison, knowing in an instant which way to turn). The trip away to the Magaliesberg with her parents, the solo hike that she took, the fall. The fall so fast she had no time to catch up to her body being bent over trunks, slamming against rock.

Half of what had happened was couched in imagination, the other in gut feeling: the two interpenetrating so that no amount of recall came close to the real thing. The bare facts. It was some time into their friendship before she told Mustafa about the fall. About the vision that she had had and the purpose it gave her.

The water bordered on scorching. With a coarse sponge, she lathered herself, scrubbing along the furrows, folds and steppes of flesh. When the soap washed off, it tingled. She thought about Frank Ledwaba and his loose bowels. The face he wore when she woke him earlier than usual because of the mess he had made. She tried to be as gentle as possible, repeating that it was *okay*, that he had nothing to be ashamed of. But mentioning shame woke Ledwaba up to it. By that time, Frank's body was emaciated, his eyes carrying what little energy was left for shame. Though she smiled her way through the tender process of turning him over and cleaning his backside, she sensed that he wished someone else was doing it. A child? A sibling? A lover? A relative? Mustafa? She wondered what had become of his family, if he had any, and why he had taken such a liking to Mustafa, so much so that he'd trained Mustafa as his successor.

The following day, laughter emanated from Frank's bedroom. Upon closer inspection, she found him chatting to Mustafa, who was serving chicken soup and weak tea for lunch. Standing by the door, she noticed Frank had a diaper on, a diaper Mustafa must have helped him with. Mustafa gestured for her to come inside. *I was just telling Frank how you've come full circle. Nothing fuller than wiping a grown man's bum.* At the time, she couldn't decide if the men were laughing with her or at her. It was the first time she'd encountered Mustafa's brand of humour, his ability to provoke laughter out of the most sensitive situations. Of course, not everyone at the hospice was a fan of it, but there were patients who yearned for it, requesting Mustafa for nothing else but a good laugh.

Some people just get it, Mustafa said later, passing her soapy lunch dishes to rinse and dry. *There's a difference between seriousness and sincerity.*

Though the Mortician had scrubbed every inch of skin, biomes of bacteria remained. The microbiota had learned, over generations, to survive on the scraps human skin provides: sweat, sebum, organic matter clinging to the upper epidermis. The upper layer, the stratum corneum, had dead cells for microbiota to feast on. A layer of death acting as fodder and a protective barrier, preventing water loss, prohibiting too much of the world from getting in.

The Mortician got out of the bath and dried herself in front of a full-length mirror, applying lotion to her skin, combing her hair back. She clothed herself in satin pyjamas from a cupboard next to the mirror and let the water out.

There was no way she could see the squirming bacteria that she was displacing down the warbling drain. She hadn't noticed the pruning of her fingers either, the way cells took on water, swelled and turned flaccid once more. Already, bacterial communities on her skin were back at work, breaking down secretions from her pores, turning oils into acidic coatings for greater adherence. Skin was an unforgiving place: desiccated and nutrient-starved, like the fringes of outer space, or the ocean floor. A war zone. Still, colonies had been finding ways to live in the striations of the Mortician's elbows, the crease of her knees, and the nape of her neck since she was born. The landscape was diverse here – humidity, dryness, oiliness – and the bacteria that were most successful were the ones who knew how best to work together, metabolising sweat into nitrogen, producing enzymes that alchemised decay.

The Mortician entered the glass atrium and climbed to the treehouse. Mustafa was lying on the bed, shirt off, reading.

'Thanks for running the bath; you didn't have to,' she said.

'It's okay. I wanted to.'

He did so much. Did she do enough for him? 'Do you want a massage?' she asked.

Surprised, Mustafa turned onto his back: 'What's the occasion?'

'I was thinking about the time we saw that Dan Ge performer.'

'What about it?'

'It was the first time we got to speaking about things. You know, experiences that *do* something. That show us there's more.'

'Come to think of it,' he said, lifting himself onto his forearms, 'that might have been the beginning of all this.'

'Lie on your stomach,' she said, gently. With massage oils in her hand, she straddled Mustafa from behind, her fingertips applying pressure along his shoulder blades, her hands transferring traces of bacteria to Mustafa's skin. Some bacteria would not be welcomed into the communities already established there, while others might offer synergistic benefits to his biome.

As she rubbed and prodded, dabbed and squeezed, the temperature of his skin rose.

'Remember what the musicians said after the performance?' he asked.

'What?'

'How the music's gotta be *hot*, the perfect pitch and rhythm. It has gotta be so hot that the performer dissolves in the presence of the *genu*. They have to be taken over. And once the spirit's in, that's when the crowd feels it.' His face disappeared between continental pillows.

She massaged until her palms were flushed and his back tender.

DANIEL

Depression is the flaw in love … I stop reading. The clouds above me have moved; the sun burns my neck and I shift over to the other side of the lawn for shade. It's cooler here. I settle to read the line again, *the flaw in love.*

It reminds me of Prof Obenhaus and the day he taught Schopenhauer. Of all the lectures I was late for (and there were a few), I'm glad I was on time for that one. Prof Obenhaus was old school, a lecturer who liked getting his fingers chalky. He always said a real philosopher isn't afraid to get his hands dirty. I was majoring in philosophy, with a minor in film, when we crossed paths. He wanted me to do postgrad, said I showed potential, whatever that means in philosophical terms. But I'd made a pact with Pa; we'd agreed I could get my 'fancy degree' (as Pa put it) if I took over the butchery when he retired. Triomf Meats had been in the family for decades and no amount of German Idealism was going to stop that generational handover.

Out of nowhere, a tennis ball flies over my head, barely missing me. Abbas gallops through the treeline and onto my blanket, paws muddy.

'Hey! Watch where you're throwing that!'

Tobias, the new resident, comes into view. In a word, he is – *irritating.* One of those men who believe their brawn to be an achievement. The day he arrived, Angelique was asked to show him around. Big mistake. According to Angelique, Tobias had ogled her throughout, 'like a piece of pork rib'. I have nothing against straight men, but the catcalling reminds me how much of our reptilian brain survived natural selection.

'The little guy is mos cute, ne, getting all excited. Over a ball nogals.' He takes the ball out of Abbas's drooling mouth, acting like he's never played with a dog before. Or maybe on some level he recognises part of himself in the mutt. 'What's so funny?' He digs something out from between his teeth and flicks it at me. I'm unable to hide my smirk.

'Nothing.' I go back to reading, *to be creatures of love we must be creatures who can despair.* Hmm, isn't it eerie how, once the sluice gates of pleasure open, it all runs back down into the catchment of suffering? At least that's what Uncle Schopie thought.

'You like reading, huh? Me, I've never. It doesn't do anything.'

He's still standing over me, wanting my attention. Isn't Abbas enough? 'You and my pa would get along,' I say, in the most neutral tone I can manufacture.

'Relax, bra, I'm older than you, but not *that* old.' He throws the ball across the lawn. Abbas scampers after it. 'Your kind have a thing for daddies, isn't?' He twiddles his fingers as if sprinkling salt, then walks across the corner of my blanket, streaking mud.

'My kind?'

'Ag, don't be sensitive now. You know … moffies.'

I notice the tattoo on his forearm, letters squiggled in an unreadable font.

'Come here, boy, ja, that's it, bring it here.' He keeps making this disgusting, wet-slapping sound with his lips.

I roll the blanket up and head inside. I'm halfway to the house when the tennis ball flies past my head again. 'What the fuck is your problem?' I yell. His facial expression is like that of a teacher whose student has finally figured out the answer. As I approach, I notice that we are more or less the same height. The yellows of his eyes remind me why he's here with the rest of us.

'Nothing. No problem.'

'I've known people like you my whole life,' I say.

Abbas comes back and I take the ball before Tobias can get to it and throw it into the bushes. The dog rushes after it. I hope the bloody thing disappears and neither of them find it.

'Not bad,' he says. His breath is musty, it's like his insides need airing. 'Clever boy like you, hai, I don't think you've met someone like me before.' He pokes me with his index finger; he hasn't cut his nails in a while.

'Leave me alone!' I shove him, much harder than I mean to.

Tobias topples back onto his bum. Laughing, he wipes grass off his hands. The way he is looking at me makes me want to call for help. But it's too late; before I get the words out, he punches me in the gut.

'Feel that? I can do worse!' he shouts into my ear.

I'm still drawing breath when I turn to see the Mortician twisting his left hand.

'Stop! You gonna break it!' he yells.

She's calm. Her hands manipulate his fingers, all conductor like. Every jerk snaps a new sound out of him.

'What are we going to do with you, Tobias? Daniel, I'm sorry you had to go through that.'

He resists her instruction to apologise, grunting and shrieking; it's only when she yanks his middle finger all the way back that he stops resisting.

'We'll get Mustafa to bandage that up nicely for you, don't worry.' She kisses him on the cheek before he falls to his knees.

I know I shouldn't, but I feel sorry for him. Why would he stay, after going through that?

THE NEXT TIME I see Abbas, his head is on Tobias's lap, who is passed out on a patio recliner downstairs. I'm on the second-floor deck, trying to finish this chapter, but I can't stop replaying what happened earlier.

I'm surprised Tobias didn't pack up and leave. I mean, the Mortician really hurt him. For a man like him to be put to shame, by a woman, no less, must have been difficult. Maybe he has nowhere else to go; maybe the luxury of the institute is the best he'll get. Some men, as brash as they are, get whittled down to size pretty easily in the end. All one has to know is where to pull and they'll sing like canaries (or weep, in this case).

It had happened with Uncle Ronnie. Old in-your-face Uncle Ronnie, who worked with Pa in the butchery; the uncle who shook my hand so hard every time he greeted. Ronnie loved squeezing my fingers together; his face wound up into a grin each time like he was measuring me for something. Or was he training me? Whatever it was, he enjoyed inflicting it. There were times he would sneak up and scare me with a loud shriek, laughing when I jolted. And how could I forget when he 'accidentally' locked me in the freezer for half an hour?

Pa shrugged off my complaints, saying Ronnie was *just like that* and that I should learn to deal with people like him. I was grateful when Pa finally drew the line with the freezer incident. That day, he lambasted Ronnie in front of the other workers for his 'absent-mindedness'. Ronnie was not an absent-minded guy; even as a kid, I knew him to be conniving.

He did calm down after Pa roasted him, but he still shook my hand way too hard whenever we greeted. I tried to squeeze back just as hard, but his fingers were much thicker than mine. He barely felt me.

Abbas's body lies limp on Tobias. Animals fall for anyone. Every now and then a bird in the gutter gets the dog's attention and his ears flap up like a submarine scope. I'll admit, a part of me is jealous of the dog. Animals: the present incarnate for Uncle Schopenhauer. I sometimes wonder if it would be easier not to be so involved in 'the life of the mind', as Prof Obenhaus termed it. Knowledge seems much like the bandsaw that cuts no matter what you put in front of it. Take this place, for instance. I can deconstruct every experience I've had since coming here – from the San Pedro hike to the cleansing ritual – and still I'd be left with questions.

Take last week, for instance, when Mustafa took me to the senseless tank. We had gone up to the aerial walkway; the tank was kept in one of the treehouses. The room was bare, except for geometric prints on the walls. Mustafa called them yantras. He then asked me to stand in front of the one that appealed to me. I played along, choosing a yantra with a geometric red and yellow flower in its centre, an upside-down triangle as its pistil and a background of purple running through each petal. He told me to observe the yantra, to take in as much detail, without blinking.

It wasn't long before my eyes hurt. The yantra did seem to shift slightly, its geometric layers – square, circles, triangles – assuming significance one after the other, creating an illusion of depth. I kept my focus. After some time, the triangle in the middle started to look like a bird's eye view of a pyramid. I put all of it down to cheap magic tricks. Obviously, my brain was trying to figure out what it was looking at, deciding how important the different parts were for the whole. The illusion was nothing but the neuronal circuitry getting tripped up on the interface between it and the outside world.

After that, I got into the tank as Mustafa instructed. The water was lukewarm and held my weight as I lay in it. Once the pod was closed, silence overtook me. Maybe silence is the wrong word; it was more like … absence. I felt uneasy. I thought that this must be what being buried alive was like, except with water. The living dead, and there I was, playing the part. And for what? Shits and giggles?

I really tried putting my scepticism aside and following Mustafa's instructions to *pay attention*. So, I started paying it to my shoulder blades, and the rise and fall of my belly. It was hard to lie there, doing nothing. I felt so ready to get up and do something. At one point, I wanted to pretend that I was drowning, just for the drama. The water was too shallow.

I was completely safe where I was and yet I felt like I had to be somewhere. Anywhere but here. In absolute darkness, I echoed, filling the space with my thoughts. I wondered what it must have sounded like for God's voice to ring out at the beginning of the cosmos. That's if you believe in an all-powerful deity who gets to stalk your dirtiest thoughts and weighs your heart on a scale against a feather. Or am I mixing up mythologies? Anyway, I daydreamed about the Big Bang, and my mind strained to imagine what things might have been like before – all condensed matter.

I wanted so badly to turn down the volume on my thoughts. How did Mustafa and the Mortician do it so easily?

And then, like the effortless changing of gears, there was a sliver-of-a-moment where the edges of my thoughts crumpled and softened, getting too small for me to read. My eyes relaxed, and I lost all sense of direction. The beating of my heart went on without me. The feeling was too brief to matter.

When Mustafa opened the tank, the world rushed back. He asked me how it went, and I told him I wasn't the type for gimmicks. If I wanted to relax, I would take a sleeping pill with a glass of Merlot and conk out for twelve hours. Simple.

He laughed and walked out.

Before I followed him, I went over to read the inscription written beneath the yantra I had chosen. *The ability to alter, for a time*, it read.

Of course the body is going to react to new experiences. That moment in the tank was nothing; it's like the first time you have sex, where everything appears larger than life and then, over time, all that you're left with is skin thrusting into skin. Maybe that is just the way things are, but it doesn't mean I can't try the tank again. For shits and giggles.

'Daniel, I'm ready.' Mustafa's voice perches on my shoulder.

I close the book. 'Oh, already? Okay.' I leave my book on the deck chair and follow him into the house.

'You can hang your clothes on the hooks,' says Mustafa. He leaves the room for me to get undressed and lie on the padded table. The blinds are turned down and several oil lamps are lit. I lie face-down on the table and wait. When he returns, he puts on some music and drips warm oil on my body.

'What instrument is that?' I ask, referring to the soft-hollow percussion coming through the speakers.

'A Hang. Fascinating instrument. Looks kind of like a flying saucer. Come, relax now.' He pats me lightly from my traps to my feet. 'You're not relaxing. *Relax.*'

'I'm relaxed,' I say, annoyed.

He places his thumbs in the middle of my back, the pressure stark on my skin. His thumbs bring Uncle Ronnie back. Uncle Ronnie's thumb, to be exact. And the cooking oil that I'd put on the floor by his cutting station when he wasn't there. Nothing will ever be as vivid as Ronnie losing his balance just as he pushed a large cow tongue through the bandsaw and … *voilà* … severed thumb next to cow tongue. Ronnie screaming. Blood pooling on white tiles.

The bandsaw did not distinguish. How could it? It ran on – like the present. A decisive, irreversible line.

'People assume a massage depends on the one massaging, but it's a joint effort. You have to trust. Allow yourself to be touched and to follow the sensation,' says Mustafa, his voice bordering on a whisper.

He finds the knots in my back quite easily, taking the time to press each one out. I grimace, but the pain is … enjoyable. After a while, he changes technique: using the full width of his hands, he glides up my back.

'First, we press where it hurts, then we move the hurt around.'

Again, Ronnie's severed thumb flashes past. The hurt I inflicted on him was too big. It couldn't be moved: there was the blade, there was the thumb, and there was the blade-and-thumb, one succumbing to the other, despite itself. And there were the workers, rushing to Ronnie's aid, and customers too disgusted to look away.

Mustafa presses firmly on the small of my back, circling round to rub the side of my stomach.

I squirm. 'That tickles.'

'Good sign.' He treads lighter up my side. Lucas surfaces. He is holding me in a crowd on Constitution Hill, with Busisiwa exclaiming (*Her Majesty the Queen is in the booth, come to the dance floor*) on stage. The bass slaps, the crowd a mass of rippling kelp. His beer breath paints my neck; the buttons on my jeans clink against his belt buckle.

'Harder. Press harder,' I say, sighing.

Mustafa goes to town on my legs, spreading them apart. He rubs my thighs as if he's going to eat them, the same way Pa used to marinade legs of lamb. Dutifully spreading sauce in every cranny. Lemon-and-garlic marinade on prime leg; Pa and I with our hands in bowls of meat, rubbing the sauce through.

One evening, after marinating the meat, I closed my bedroom door and danced to Candi Station's *Young Hearts* on my iPod. *It's high time now … my mind must be free to learn all I can about me.* I twirled around and there was Pa, wanting to know how rare I wanted the rack of lamb he was going to put on the braai. His eyes sort of hovered above me, as if he were imagining a taller, stockier son. Someone he hoped I would grow into.

I told him I wanted it medium-rare. He never commented on my dancing.

'Everything okay?' asks Mustafa.

'Everything … is … fine,' I say, between the cracking of my toes.

'You mentioned Sarah at dinner the other night,' he says.

'Uh, yeah, why?'

'No, just curious. Did you know she wanted to live here, with us, permanently? Naturally, we couldn't let that happen.'

'I didn't know that. Last time I saw her, she seemed less afraid, still struggling but … different.'

'Is that what you want? To be less afraid?'

'Sorta. I don't know. I don't usually walk into things with high expectations.'

Mustafa hums, agreeing, and walks to the head of the table. He massages my temples and I think of Sarah at the clinic, alone near the back fence, the one separating it from a veld where, a year before, police found an unidentified, burned body amongst refuse bags.

I spotted Sarah just as I was unloading my bags from the car, getting ready for my twenty-one day stay. She was scrunching magazine articles into aerodynamic balls and launching them over the electric fence. Her randomness intimidated me, which is why I only asked her much later why she'd been doing that.

Her version of an explanation was sarcastically quoting the titles of the articles back to me.

How to Sell Yourself.

Tap into the True You.

Top Ten Ways to Biohack Your Self-Esteem.

The massage is over in an hour. I can barely lift myself up from the table. Mustafa says not to rush. He takes out a small glass jar filled with yellow powder and mixes it into a glass of water. 'It's pine pollen,' he says. 'Very rejuvenating for men's health.'

I watch the mixture from my place on the table. The pollen eddies, turning the water a bright yellow. The urge to move filters slowly into me again; I'd rather stay here even though I know, eventually, I *have* to get up. There is no living without getting up, again and again, ad nauseam.

Maybe depression isn't the flaw in love as much as it is an unbearable stasis. A not wanting to move the pain, or the pleasure, around. When you're in the thick of it, the simple pleasures start to look like the beginning of a long arc of hurt.

Is that what Lucas saw when he found me in bed, having not gone anywhere for two whole weeks, ordering take-out until even the bank called, asking if I had noticed the unusual activity on my account. I'd noticed all right. It didn't stop the delivery men from knocking, or me gladly swiping the day away with burgers, pizzas, booze and, when I was feeling fancy, sushi.

Get up!

That's what Lucas shouted then, and that's what I do, taking my clothes off the hooks.

WHEN I GET back to the room, I find Lucas sitting in a rocker chair, the book I was reading in his hands.

'*The Noonday Demon: An Atlas of Depression*,' he says, lowering it.

'Sarah gave it to me when I got out the clinic.'

'Is it helping?' He pages through it.

'It's relatable. Puts words to feelings.'

'Like therapy?'

I don't answer, knowing that, really, all I want to do is lift him from the chair and kiss him.

'Are you okay?' He reaches for his crutches.

'No, don't get up,' I say, unbuttoning my shirt.

'What are you doing?'

'Just, stay there.' I throw my shirt to the floor, kick myself loose of my trunks and walk over to where he is. I sit, spread-eagled across his lap, tossing the book on the bed.

'This is a development,' he laughs, nervously.

I shut him up with my lips on his, forcing his mouth open with my tongue. 'Give me your tongue,' I say.

He does it reluctantly. I suck on it like an ice lolly.

'Ow, you're hurting me, babe.'

I stand up and start to undress him. 'Don't do anything. I want to please you.'

There's a mixture of terror and excitement on his face. I keep going.

'Careful with the –'

'I know,' I say bluntly, yanking his trousers off.

'Hawu! That's sore!'

'Sorry, I just want you in me so bad.'

When I get back on his lap, he's nervous, just like me. He holds my head and kisses me, his dick semi-hard. I try my best to make it harder, doing the things he used to like: sucking on his earlobe, kissing his neck, flicking my fingers on the tip of his dick. He stays semi-hard. This has to work, or else. It doesn't matter that we haven't fucked since the accident or that I haven't bottomed in months. He is cumming in me – hell or high water.

We try for what feels like ages. Me grinding while he avoids eye contact by sucking on my nipples till they're numb.

'It's too tight, babe,' he says, trying to make light of the situation by chuckling.

'It's fine. You're too soft anyway.' I get off, irritated, and pick up my clothes.

'Ey, you don't have to say it like that. My body is still sorting itself out. The doctor said it would take time before I feel like myself again.'

'Can I fuck you, at least? Did the doctor say that was okay?' I throw my clothes in the washing bin.

He looks as if I've just told him I've murdered his pet. Then, something shifts, and I feel guilty for asking so crudely.

'If you can pass me the crutches, I'll lie, face down on the bed, how you like it.' It sounds as if his voice and his body have decided to part ways.

I pass the crutches, not saying a word. He lies face down, a pillow under his torso, his hips as high as he can raise them.

'Can you use the numbing cream,' he mumbles, through the bedsheets.

'You know how that makes my dick feel.'

'Just get it!'

A crack in his voice. I don't know how to respond so I do as I'm told, lubing him up with the numbing cream. He lies as flat as a board, not moaning or reacting. I'm about five minutes in when I can't stand it; I get off and wipe myself clean in the bathroom.

'Did you cum?' he asks, turning over, staring vacantly at the ceiling.

I lie.

THE SUN CROWNED Northcliff's roofs, dressing walls in butterscotch; on the other side of the cliff, the sunlight turned gauzy – covering the buildings and roads. The first to wake were the flowers. Not too long after, men pushing plastic trolleys with wonky wheels lunged up steep avenues into culs-de-sac, faces socked in balaclavas. It was garbage day. And all kinds of paper and plastic would be siphoned off from the suburbs and townships into large woven bags, hauled through the streets of Joburg, clots extracted by unlikely doctors.

The eyes of houses, raised high above fences, blinked their morning Morse code. Tungsten filaments, resisting morning currents, burned hot white; light poured out of half-opened doors, cutting across kitchen floors. Cornflakes and muesli were tipped out of Tupperware into bowls, while boiling water stripped ground coffee beans of their history.

Identities rose, bubbles jetting to the surface. *Pop* – eye gunk got scrooped out of tear ducts. Fluoride fizzed on teeth: Rorschach inkblots, made from wine and too much tobacco, smiling wide in mirrors. White spots of Lumière were pinkie-dabbed on drab cheeks and baggy eyes. Neckties made tourniquets above men's hearts. Pairs of Achilles tendons, shortened over years, welcomed the height heels offered.

Geysers hurled insults into themselves; washing machines spincycled jeans and shirts into creatures made of buttons, pockets and zips. Cars in driveways coughed up carbon monoxide, while intestines, bundled up in car seats, massaged last night's midnight snack – accordions tuning themselves for a mid-morning toilet run.

All this, and nothing stirred in the unnumbered house till ten.

Nothing, save the red light of the alarm sensor in the kitchen taking blinking contests with the microwave while, in the lounge, a TV decoder whirred guttural, seeking sounds, updating itself. In the basement, a generator hummed the only song it knew. Occasionally, blankets ruffled, shoulders cracked while switching sides on a pillow; door hinges, wall units and stairs gave feeble thuds — expanding. But, overall, nothing.

IT HAD BEEN three days since Dianne felt the sun on her skin. When she woke, she was surprisingly rested. A yearning to be outside drove her feet to the laminated floor. She clenched her toes a few times. The tingling wasn't so bad today. Signs perhaps that her body could manage a walk.

Out on the veranda, weavers darted between branches of a plum tree. Agile and swift, their tiny heads twitched in unpredictable motions. They took turns flying off, returning with limp haulms in their beaks. Nests slowly took shape in the tree, clumps of brown growing larger, like tumours. Below, their previous homes lay discarded. Dianne took the stairs down to the rejected nests, inspected each one and picked them apart. Still warm, each had a balminess to it. Did birds sweat? She imagined families of them huddled together, with hearts the size of mulberries.

She took to peeling them apart to decipher how they'd been made (feathers, grass, leaves, twigs). There was no clear beginning or end — everything dried together into temporary shelter. She came upon a caterpillar in one of the nests, soft and blind, and was unsure if it was dead or alive, or how it had managed to tuck itself so discreetly into the brown mesh. She prodded it with her pinkie; it didn't move.

She continued walking beneath the treehouses on the west side of the property and wondered what each of them contained. More ways of dying, she assumed, or techniques of breaking through the hardened shells of perception, as the Mortician liked to quip. Of all the things she had been put through so far, the metronomes were the most interesting. The session had taken place in one of the treehouses, but she couldn't recall which.

Mustafa had led her into a room filled with them: metronomes all balancing on a plank that was fixed to large rolling pins. He had instructed her to get comfortable in the centre of the room, propping her body up with cushioned bolsters. Then he offered her a phial, filled with a liquid that reminded her of olive oil. She allowed him to put some under her tongue and she held it there, letting it absorb into her mucous glands.

She started to feel at ease: the birdcalls from outside seemed to open themselves up to her. Listening, she distinguished their squeaks from their squawks, the tittering pinches from the throaty clattering. When she closed her eyes, the melodies rippled across her eardrums. She sensed Mustafa moving about the room, the distribution of his weight reaching her via the floorboards.

Mustafa tapped each metronome, building an out-of-sync, tick-tocking rhythm that grew louder with each metronome he recruited.

All she had to do was allow her mind to be absorbed by the sound. As she listened, the out-of-sync metronomes interrupted one another, reminding her of the turning of a rusted screw. As time wore on, the sound found new shapes to inhabit – a screw-driver, stapler, heels clacking down a tiled corridor. One by one, each metronome fell in sync with the other, becoming absorbed in a baseline rhythm that she recognised as the sound a horse makes when galloping. When she opened her eyes, the metronomes had fallen in line, leaning left and right in unison.

She felt the most urgent need to join in and be carried along.

That had to be it, thought Dianne, looking up from a path in the garden at a treehouse suspended above. That one held the metronomes, she was sure. She'd have to ask Mustafa to take her there for another session.

She continued past the angel trumpet shrubs and came upon a secluded alcove with a sculpture of a woman in it. Taking a seat at the foot of the sculpture, Dianne tried to understand why the unison of the metronomes had brought up so much emotion in her. Maybe it was the eeriness of the whole affair: the uncanny ability objects had to influence, reflect and sync up. *Come with us*, the metronomes seemed to ask, *there's no need to be afraid.* Maybe that was what she wanted them to say. She gazed up at the face of the stone sculpture. It was a woman, kneeling and combing her hair (the hair itself made from thick glass, the type used to make the marbles kids played with). The woman barely had a face. The weather had taken its toll.

Dianne had never mentioned it to anyone, but there was a time when statues like this one were her only friends. She had been a shy girl, too quiet for anyone to take seriously. It wasn't that she didn't want to play with other kids; it was that there were always two or three other conversations going on inside her head. These conversations got started by voices that didn't quite feel like hers. She was never able to say for sure where the voices came from. One day they were just *there*: telling jokes and making up games for her to play.

Befriending statues was a way for her to give the voices their appropriate bodies. At primary school, she remembered the statue of Mary, stationed in an alcove not too different from the one she sat in now. During breaktime, she would eat lunch by it, talk and laugh with it, bring it flowers or shiny quartz from the school garden.

Amongst the other children, she was known as *the Mary girl*. Kids teased her, and when some had asked why she never played with anyone else – why she insisted on spending her breaktimes with a statue – she had no answer. It was when a girl named Naledi started spreading rumours about her being a saint that things spiralled out of control.

Dianne touched her hand to the cool stone of the woman's leg and the moss growing up her calves. She didn't know if she had the strength to make it back to the main house. She would have to try. No one had seen her go this way.

ON THE NORTH-WEST side of the property, Mustafa led Lucas into one of three cylindrical greenhouses, each facing the other in a triangle. In the first one, rows of sativa and indica grew from leaking buckets stationed on tables. The tables drained excess water back into a reservoir in the middle of the room. Sunlight slanted through the glass roofing, drawing apricot, mauve and tan hues from the ripening buds.

'The pump in the tank runs water through the drip lines,' said Mustafa.

'And the drip lines run through each bucket?' asked Lucas.

'Exactly.' Lucas was picking up fast, thought Mustafa. He showed Lucas around, explaining maintenance, the ratio of premix solution to water and the optimal moisture for the rockwool and clay pellets in the buckets.

'How long did it take you to figure all this out?'

'Couple of months. It was trial and error mostly, and what I found online.' The room smelled earthly sweet; dripping water, the hiss of the air pumps created an elemental melody. The flowers were almost ready. It would be Lucas's job to see them through to curing and smoking. 'I'll be with you every step of the way, so don't worry about fucking up,' he explained.

It was the first time Lucas had heard Mustafa swear and that seemed to mean something. He leaned in close to one of the plants, his lips inches away from leaves that gleamed with translucent, spindly-wet hairs.

'Those gooey parts are trichomes. We keep the females and males on separate tables. That way they build up desire. It gets the females to produce more oils,' said Mustafa, cradling a leaf in his palm.

It was strange for Lucas to hear someone speak of desire in plants; he had never thought of it that way. For him, there were just cycles of seeding, growing and ripening that, under the right conditions, *happened.* Then again, separated in buckets like this, how did the females know their counterparts were nearby? Did they sense or smell or have some other way to gauge the air? And how different was that to people? The last time Daniel tried to 'pollinate' him the conditions weren't so optimal, and look how that turned out.

'So, you think you can manage?' Mustafa handed him a book filled with notes, sketches and instructions. 'Those of us who imbibe are counting on you.' He spoke in a jokingly serious way.

'If I have any questions, I'll ask.' Lucas took the notebook. Most of the plants seemed close to ready, stalks heavy with promise. The small project at least gave him something to look forward to. A high he'd have a hand in making.

OUT OF THE first greenhouse, across the lawn and up the side patio stairs that led into the kitchen, Angelique made breakfast. She held a generous sprig of coriander on a cutting board and diced it up. For her, the best part of cooking was its sounds: snips, cracks, snaps, like feet tiptoeing over autumn leaves.

She placed two cubes of butter beside one another in the centre of the pan, watching them melt towards each other, before tossing in onions.

'Smells lekker,' said Tobias, hovering over her shoulder. 'Give me some.'

'Make your own.' She brushed him aside, scooping more ingredients in. The aroma lilted, composing into a bassline pitch of onion with riffs of garlic, snare-drummed by ginger and the twinkling keys of chilli.

Ever since arriving, Tobias had scouted opportunities to engage her. It was getting uncomfortable, and she was considering bringing it up with the Mortician. She moved the wooden spoon through the pan after the tomatoes and peppers were thrown in. Saliva pooled beneath her tongue. She was starving.

Tobias leaned against the kitchen island, and even though her back was turned, she felt him watching.

'Jeez, you eat omelettes every day?' said Daniel, who was rummaging in the pantry.

'There's no excuse for not dining like royalty,' said Angelique. She reached for the pot of coffee on the stove and poured a mug for them both. Out of everyone, she got on with Daniel. His saucy remarks reminded her of the models she used to run around with – the ones that gave you dirty looks if you came across as a basic bitch. Luckily for Angelique, by then she was already doing all the things models were supposed to be doing. Stoking envy via her Insta page. Snapping pics with bottles of Moët on ice. Giving followers a live tour of her wardrobe.

Daniel and Angelique had led very different lives up to this point. Neither was entirely sure what was at the centre of their burgeoning friendship. For Angelique, her attraction to him took the shape of a window; for Daniel it was a revolving door, as he struggled to pin her down, once and for all.

Tobias held out a mug for her to fill and she reluctantly obliged. 'So, what are we doing today?' he asked.

'We?' said Angelique, cracking eggs into the pan.

'Ja, *we*. Mustafa and his cherrie are supposed to be gone for the day, so … You know what? We should throw a housa.'

'Should you be partying in your condition?' asked Daniel.

'That's the joy of being terminal, my guy. No reason to care.' Tobias slurped his coffee, throwing the rest in the sink. 'It'll be fun. What do you say, Angie, my skat?'

'It's Angelique, and Daniel and I have plans, so maybe you can find someone else to bother.' She judged the omelette to be the right consistency; when she flipped it over, it fell apart. 'Fuck it! I never get this right. Scrambled eggs it is.'

'You gotta cook till it's hard. Then flip it, babes,' Tobias smirked. He got a Savanna from the fridge, opened it with his teeth and headed for his room. He sauntered past the reading room, with its smell of leather and fingered books, and over the glass floor in the corridor, through which water flowed, channelled from the stream that ran through the central atrium. He wished this bougie place at least offered some form of excitement. A thrill. Where was the arcade room? The foosball table? Strippers? Thank the gods of Zamalek that there was a lounge with a big flat-screen for him to watch his Kaizer Chiefs play.

Through the lounge window – over a bed of lilies, freshly peed on by Abbas – he spotted Dianne, sitting by the rock pools. This was the very sick one, the one they said didn't have much longer. He had not met her yet because she had been cooped up in her room ever since he arrived. She looked fine to him, just a little sad; all she needed was a lekker dop to get her right. Or even better, a dop and a skit.

DIANNE MADE HER way back from the alcove to sit by the rock pools. The sun had sapped what energy she had left. On lichen-covered rocks, she contemplated whether she needed to eat or just sleep the day away. Mosquitoes skipped along the water behind her, tempting fish to snap at them, as she began to measure the number of footsteps it would take to get to the kitchen and back to her bedroom.

'So, you're Dianne,' said Tobias.

She squinted through the sun at the man with the half-drunk Savanna.

He offered her the bottle. 'Tobias,' he said, shaking the drink and making it foam near its neck.

'It's too early for me.'

He sat down next to her and finished the Savanna, burping. 'You look familiar. I know you from somewhere. What's your surname?'

'Hendricks.'

'Hendricks … from Bosmont? You were a big shot principal somewhere, ne?'

'Ja, that was *very* way back. Who are you?'

'Tobias Meyer. I'm sure you've never –'

'Weren't you that pastor that stole money from your church community?'

'My community, listen to you,' he scoffed. 'Nah, I don't have a community. But yes, that's me.'

'Prison has reformed you then.'

'The tronk? Joh, that place makes you worse. Kills whatever spark you got left.' Tobias flipped the bottle upside down, turning it into a baton. On the balcony of the second floor, he spotted Angelique and Daniel having breakfast together. 'You get along with those two?' he asked, pointing with the bottle-turned-baton.

'They're all right.' She dipped her fingers in the water, making the fish scatter.

Her tone was so matter of fact that Tobias had no way of replying. When he had arrived at the unnumbered house, he thought losing all cares and worries equated to parties being thrown every day. Sitting next to Dianne made him feel uneasy. Her frailness reminded him that parties were the least of his needs. Nevertheless, he still cradled the idea of throwing one and getting big-booty strippers and liquor and good music on big speakers. He was not prepared to let an old, sick woman deter him. Even when a familiar, stabbing pain erupted from his side – brought on by the alcohol travelling through scars etched into his liver – Tobias was adamant that only one thing could make being here worth his final days. 'I'm gonna get us more drinks. You want a blanket? You're shivering.'

Dianne could see he wasn't taking no for an answer. He *needed* to lift her spirits, she sensed, as if his happiness depended on her. Or maybe this was one of those times when she slipped too eagerly into believing in the goodness of others. It was more likely that he didn't want to drink alone, and she was the weakest in the pack, the easiest to persuade.

'If I'm going to drink, I'll need food first.'

'I'll make you some eggs.' He walked back towards the house, rubbing his lower back till the pain subsided.

Dianne didn't know why she was indulging him. Was her resolve that weak? Was the tumour soiling her principles? Or was his eagerness to party enviable? All she wanted was to nod off.

Mustafa led Lucas into another greenhouse. This one was all walls and roof, without a floor. It was dark, its small round windows covered with thick curtains. Mottled logs, inserted into the earth, towered over them. They drew deeper into the room, mud belching as they went. Mustafa turned on a dim light: all the logs, licked with flaming fungi, wondered what the two men were doing there.

'And this?' asked Lucas.

'My pride and joy,' said Mustafa, showing him around. He went on to explain the process of log culture making. How one first drills holes into the logs, then fills them with sawdust before inserting spores into the substrate. Out of each log, fluffy-white, burnt-orange and turmeric-brown fruiting mushrooms grew. 'Lion's Mane. Reishi. Chaga,' he pointed.

They were exquisite, thought Lucas, noting how some took the shape of dried-up mopane worms clumped together, and others fruited like fan-shaped palettes, glossed with paint and varnish. Then there were those that had the texture of burned bark. 'What do you do with these?' he asked.

'I harvest and sell some. They're medicinal. Lion's Mane is for the brain and immune system. Reishi is an overall, balancing tonic. And Chaga is a potent antioxidant. It's a booming market.' He took Lucas to the back where, in several trays on a low-lying shelf, another set of mushrooms grew. 'All my mushrooms are special, but these over here ...' In each tray white stalks, topped with bulbous brown tips, stuck out.

Each tray was its own city for Lucas, who crouched to get eye level with the mycelium metropolis sprawling beneath the fruiting bodies.

'Have you ever tried it?' asked Mustafa.

'Never.'

'You're in luck. These babies are just about ready.'

'What's it like?'

Mustafa paused, trying to come up with a satisfactory explanation. 'Have you ever seen the crystallisation of a saturated liquid?'

'Joh, are you really asking me that?'

Mustafa giggled. 'Go look on YouTube, and you'll see. It's like that. Your body is this super-saturated solution, and the mushroom is the seed crystal. Once inside, the mushrooms conjure bridges and staircases throughout your being, interlocking in every direction, shifting under your feet like a game of snakes and ladders. And by the end of it all, you're a crystal, in awe of how everything just fits together.'

Mustafa was rambling. Lucas figured he'd understand once he tried some. Out of the corner of his eye, on another shelf, a large fish tank caught his attention. Instead of fish and water, there was sand, tunnels and, were those ants? 'I've never seen an ant farm in real life before,' he said, walking over.

Mustafa didn't answer, his attention given to spraying the mushrooms with a water solution. 'Was. It *was* an ant farm.'

The tank was eye-level with Lucas. On its surface above the tunnels stood a miniature town, taken straight out of an old Western: saloons, horse-drawn carriages, log cabins and plastic men on horseback. Small cacti and succulents sprouted in several places, much larger than the town itself. The ant tunnels reminded him of the underside of tripe. But the ants – there was something wrong with them.

Mustafa sensed Lucas's interest and walked over to explain. Months before any residents arrived, he had acquired the spores of *Ophiocordyceps unilateralis*. He decided to place some in the tank with the ant colony. Curious as to which species would outmanoeuvre the other, he watched and waited as ants became infected with the spores. In their exoskeletons, the fungus wove round their muscle fibres – thorax, abdomen, legs – creating networks of communication for its reproduction. *Climb. Climb*, the fungus compelled, co-ordinating its mycelium, directing all the infected ants. A puppeteer.

Powerless to resist, ants watched themselves do things they wouldn't normally do, while their insides were dissolved into soup. The ants not infected tried to save the rest by shunting the sick away to a corner, distant from the hive. But *Ophiocordyceps* spreads its climbing message far and wide, preserving the ants' brains for the very last moment – when their mandibles are ordered to grip the underside of a leaf. Purpose served, the infected ant is allowed to rest, its brain having been cultivated into loam, out of which a wiry body fruits to spore again. A magician pulling itself from a hat.

Lucas backed away suddenly. 'What the fuck, that's messed up.'

'What's wrong?'

'Why would you do that?'

'I didn't *do* anything. I put two species together. The rest is up to them.'

'Yeah, but.' Lucas had never felt this strongly about ants. He wasn't the type to care about squashing any crawling thing that inconvenienced him. Why was this bothering him?

'Think of it this way,' began Mustafa. 'The cordyceps moves through the colony, rapacious, insatiable. What foresight can it have? As far as I can tell, it doesn't know it's inside a tank. It doesn't know its food source is limited. It eats anyway. Then spreads until every organ has been turned to mycelium mush. At some point, its own hunger and some sturdy glass limit it. Cordyceps becomes its own enemy. Its own threshold.'

Lucas looked again. Ant carcasses lay decimated all over the town – on top of carriages, outside saloons, on the highest leaves of succulents. Spores were scattered on roofs, toy horses, stuck to cowboys with guns in the air. Everywhere the wiry cordyceps left its mark, its tentacles growing out of heads the way Lucas imagined souls left people's bodies – winding up, out of their skulls, stopping halfway and bursting into … he didn't know what souls burst into.

Once outside, Mustafa offered Lucas some water and went over how he should care for the plants in the first greenhouse. 'It would be ideal if Daniel could help you,' he said.

Lucas knew what they were trying to do, getting Daniel and him to 'bond' over something innocuous. He appreciated the idea but couldn't see Daniel taking care of plants in the meticulous way Mustafa was doing. He found Mustafa's focus admirable and, dare he think it, attractive? There was something unapologetic and dynamic about Mustafa, but not in an overbearing way.

Some distance from the men, near the path that led to the garage, they saw the Mortician pacing frantically on the phone. Whoever she was speaking to was on the receiving end of words that were way past their boiling point. They couldn't help but stare.

'Everything okay with her?' asked Lucas.

'I'm not sure. You go on inside. I'll check.'

'What about that one?' He gestured towards the remaining greenhouse, the largest of the three.

'Don't worry. Just compost in there. I'll tell you all about it later. Maybe you can help with that too, but only if you're up to it.' Mustafa had not taken his eyes off the Mortician's frantic scene. He walked away from Lucas, who went inside a little disappointed but unable to articulate why.

As Mustafa drew closer to the Mortician, nebulous sounds collapsed into syllables, words, phrases.

... title deed ... sound of mind ... court papers ...

The Mortician turned; he caught her panic. 'Yes, we can meet you. At three? Fine. We can't allow this to happen, Shona. You've seen the title deed is all above board. I'll come through with Mustafa. Okay, bye.'

'And that?'

'The Prinsloos. They're disputing.'

'Can they do that?'

'Apparently.'

'But, what's the argument?'

'Unsound mind. Manipulation. Psychoactive hallucinogens.'

'Shit man! They were there every day at the end. They saw how lucid he was.'

'We have to go today, before we go see my parents.' She stopped pacing, shoulders sinking.

He sensed her trepidation at going to see both the lawyer and her parents on the same day. Ishaan and Saisha liked him, at least, probably because they assumed he was dating their daughter, like most people did. He never had the heart to dispel that myth from their grandchildren-expecting eyes. 'We'll go and sort this out. We've got this.'

'Too far. We've come too far to be stopped, Mustafa,' she said.

When she spoke this way, Mustafa picked up on the tension in her throat – the way she swallowed hard, pressing her tongue to the roof of her mouth. Beneath her skin, he pictured her hypo-thalamus, pituitary and adrenal glands co-ordinating her cortisol. He tried to remember cortisol's molecular structure from the short course Frank had him take in palliative care. Plug prongs, that's what it looked like. There were plug prongs cycling all through her now. Prongs occupying her power sockets, pulling levers, marshalling blood to major muscles, sounding the alarm for sugars to rush into the streets and side alleys of her neighbourhood.

Neutral. Live. Ground: they were going to have to rely on each other in the uncertainty of their meeting with Shona Molefe, the lawyer they kept on retainer. Mustafa was grateful they had one another to conduct their frustrations through.

'Let's get ready. Don't forget, we've got a delivery to make as well. We can do that after the lawyer and before your parents,' he said.

'I'll pack the car. Tell the residents we're leaving.' The Mortician took the gravel path to the garage that was nestled in the shadow of the willows.

Mustafa went inside to announce their departure, explaining that he could be reached via phone in the event of an emergency.

TOBIAS

In the tronk the ouens make noise; their echoes are endless. All night and day, cells open and close, the buzz of fluorescents and voices bounce off the walls. You get used to it. The white noise helps you sleep, or you figure how to keep a grain of silence, deep deep in yourself, where no one can get it.

In these laanie hills, it's tjoepstil. There's no toilet flushing, or skelms whispering behind your back. It's not so lekker. The other cons used to call it papa waggies – when you're asleep and you feel a spook sitting on your chest. It first happened to me when I was young, way before prison and even before my ministry. I don't know why it started happening to me, but, ja, I couldn't sleep heavy because of it.

Mustafa calls it 'sleep paralysis'. Said he got it when he was a boy too, and that the Mortician may be able to teach me how to get rid of it. Hey, you'll be surprised by how many cons go through it. When papa waggies sits on your chest it is another kind of initiation. I won't lie, I started saying Our Fathers for the first time in a long while during lights out. Just thinking about papa waggies gave me goosebumps.

The only way to escape papa waggies is to dig a hole deep in yourself so that he can't find you. Like an empty well you can fall down every time you need to sleep. Buttons help with that, those small pills Lunga put me on. Joh, those ones knock me over the head and throw me down the well easy easy; for most of the day I'd be staring up from the bottom, drugged up, nca.

When Lunga couldn't get me buttons, a small part of me

154

stayed awake and papa waggies got hold of me. I used to think that if only I could make that part of me shout and pray and demand deliverance, then the other ouens in the cell would get it in their heads to wake me. But it don't work that way. When that small part of you is crying, snot en trane, running from basement to attic in your kop, trying to find a window to climb out of your head, all it looks like on the outside is an old skelm having a restless night.

Mustafa has put me up in this room, big enough for a whole corridor of skelms. When I can't sleep, I make five-by-five-metre squares on the carpet with my feet and open all the windows to smell the garden. Rather that than the mif memory of unwashed armpits and damp sheets.

Eish, I don't know when I'm gonna be able to sleep proper. If it's not the silence it's papa waggies, who squats on me just as I doze off. I never see him directly; I can just make out the outline of something that looks like a gorilla. Joh, it's kak scary when you can't defend yourself; that's what makes papa waggies a true terrorist, scarier than anyone who's gonna try and steal your skyfs.

I started seeing him again after Daniel and I had words. I still say he *deserved* that punch: making me look all dom, like I couldn't handle myself. Fuck, if I was younger, he'd be face down in a gutter right now, teeth skew. Without a sweat. It's lucky for the moffie that I'm falling apart. See, that night, after the bitch nearly broke my fingers off, papa waggies came and sat on me. The only thing I remember from the dream was my Aunty Charmaine, calling my name.

Tobiass!

She always shouted the 'ass' part louder when I was in trouble. A lot of the time I deserved it because I was beating up on one of the smaller shits in our street, the goody two shoes who thought they were better than me. Aunty Charmaine's calling woke me, but not all the way. And that's when I felt papa waggies, swaar on my heart. I say this to anyone who'll listen: your body doesn't belong to you. If it did, then why does it say *no* when you really need it to say *yes*? It'd be better if we were all kingpins of our bodies, not this fake power we think we have. Me? I'm a voice box, trapped in a throat, and when papa waggies comes all I can do is watch and pray, hoping he doesn't get it all his way.

What made me turn to prayer? Ey, that feeling of someone or something wanting to climb up inside you, it's like the devil is sommer operating at full capacity. And I'm not going to let that happen without a fight. That's what praying is mos: fighting the world with words. Even today, I have my Our Fathers locked and loaded, like aunty taught me. If prayer makes me feel better and papa waggies disappears, then it must be doing something. I blame those evangelical channels aunty kept on all day and muted at night. I wasn't allowed to change the channel for nothing, not even my poppetjies. Not even for *Days of Our Lives*. Lucky for me, watching TD Jakes and Prophet Benny reruns after school helped me make my own prophecies and start my enterprise.

Why is papa waggies scared of prayer? You really wanna know? Fuck, who can answer that. All I know is when I pray, half asleep climbing out of dream-stickiness, those words build a dam between me and anything that wants to hurt me. Brick by brick papa waggies fades away and I'm free. But being a free man doesn't matter much, not when you've stayed locked up for as long as have. There's a good chance prison won't ever leave; if you ever spend time in the tronk you'll get like me, mapping cell blocks on the carpet of a big fancy house in Northcliff, if you're lucky.

Pace – that's what I do at one in the morning, remembering the size of my cell with my feet. That's where Lunga called his cherrie, and there is where Pieter and Adriaan played cards. Here where Keano got shivved. People came and went, and sometime the group of us felt like a family. We were just ouens, trying ou best to stay out the other's way. Those were my survivor days, when all I wanted was to scavenge some comfort in a cell with eight others. Humanity? Say that with too much passion and the young fast ones will think you're a chop. Us swak ones, us old brommers, nah, we won't look at you funny. We just know there's better things to talk about than humanity. Like the best naai of your life.

From the window of my bedroom, I check Mustafa over there, walking across the grass. Why's he up so late? I put on my gown and take the balcony stairs to the ground. It's dark-dark, only a cut of light from one of the greenhouses. Out on the deck, I take the stairs down to the grass. It's papnat from the sprinklers; my slippers are gonna be slopping. I hate that mif smell.

When I get close enough to the greenhouse window, I bend low, bringing my head above the windowsill. There's a compost heap in there, and rows of wire in the shape of cocoons. What is this ou up to? I move to another window; Mustafa packs the compost into bricks and slides them between the wire. There are rows of trees lined up against the back wall. All of them in big pots. I should head back, but before I can, Lucas comes out of another greenhouse and walks in, where Mustafa is working. Hier kom a ding! The night brings out all sorts, ne?

I go round the other side for a view. Lucas packs the compost into a brick, hands it to Mustafa, who secures it in the wire. It goes on for twenty minutes before they take a break. My legs are tired and I'm ready to call it when Lucas puts his head on Mustafa's shoulder. Mustafa rubs the boy's head and that's when I know.

I don't even have to stay and watch them kiss. I just know. Check here, in the tronk life's a poker game. There are men who raise themselves into prison royalty (who don't wanna leave when their time is up). There are those who bluff themselves into respect and protection, making people believe they're much more danger-ous than they really are. Then there are those with balls enough to call one another's bluffs – in showers or storage rooms, or late at night. Prison has enough shadows for almal. Do what needs to be done, wardens and convicts, no one is untouchable forever. Those men who call each another out either get a fist to the face or strangle marks across their neck or overalls pulled down to their ankles. There are a lot of us who want to serve our time quietly, that's true. Those are the ouens you stick with.

Lucas and Mustafa are serving a different time. I leave them to do their business and walk back across the lawn, up the staircase, onto the second-floor deck and back into my room. There's a scratching at my door and when I open it Abbas comes running in, acting like he doesn't need sleep, like me. I pick him up and get into bed, letting him run beneath the covers and lick my toes. He reminds me of Bulldozer and Betty, Stephen and I's pit bulls. We had this game where we would take them onto the veld, tie Bulldozer up by a tree and then one of us would take Betty across to the other side of the veld. Bulldozer would go befok! Pulling, biting, getting himself tangled in the chain, almost choking himself, trying to get free so he could be with Betty.

I don't know why we liked to see the dog get all mal. It was dangerous because Bulldozer would get so befok that he'd turn on us, sometimes. But Bulldozer never bit us too badly. When we let him free that dog diced across the veld like a souped-up V6, revving all cylinders. The dog ran so fast that it couldn't slow itself down; most times he ran right past Betty. I think by the time he reached the other side of the veld, Bulldozer forgot why he was running in the first place. He just wanted to feel like a bullet.

'How's your hand?' asks Mustafa.

I'm still groggy from last night. We're on a walk with Abbas at the top of Northcliff. 'It's seen worse,' I say, holding the leash with my other hand.

'I see it's still swollen. Don't forget to ice it, okay.'

'Ey, man, Musty, this isn't for me, hoor.'

'You want to leave? And go where? You said it yourself, there's nothing out there for you. No one to take care of you. You're in no condition to look after yourself.'

'Fuck, I'll go to the Salvation Army or something, bra. I'm not like the others, not like you. I can take care of myself.'

Mustafa is min. He's been waiting for this.

'Tobias, listen to me. You're very sick. And have no money. No family. This is as good as it's going to get. Out there ... it's designed to break you.'

'Look what your poes of a friend did? Where were *you* when she was hurting me, huh?'

'You've done a lot worse to a lot more.' He taps my swollen hand a few times and I wanna bliksem him right there on the spot.

'We all have our tricks, baba. What I did, was done to *make* it. Check the politicians on the TV, you think they're doing any different? They just do it in a nice suit.' I let go of the leash; Abbas runs off.

We're the only guys up here and I know that if I could throw Mustafa off, I could disappear for good. Then what? How would that help? He's not lying when he says there's no one to take care of me. And things, they're getting worse – fevers, stomach aches, itchy skin. Can I just vrek uit and call it a day already?

I climb onto a rock and lean over the edge. I can see where Northcliff turns into Bryanston, then Rivonia. The world is too big for anyone to handle alone. I want to be done with it. Chew it up and spit it out. The same way it did me. The world's ma's se poes.

'What're you thinking?' Mustafa puts his hand on the rock I'm standing on.

I step to the side and help him up next to me. 'I'm done. I'm tired of having, then not having. Make it soon, Musty, the way you promised. When are we doing *that*?'

'Have one or two more sessions with us first. Let us lay the plank before the leap.'

'Ey, you know I don't like your riddle kak. Give me my session sommer now.'

Mustafa pulls out a bottle with a dark brown liquid in it. 'Drop a little under your tongue.'

The liquid tastes kinda like alcohol, but not really. 'What's this?'

'It's a bronchodilator, mixed in with some cannabinoids.'

'A what now?'

He lifts up his arms, gets on the tips of his toes and starts screaming. It's crazy. He does it for at least ten seconds.

'Hey! You're making noise. People are gonna kick us out.' I try shoving him, but before I do he steps back.

'Since when are you worried about other people?'

This one, he's making me dom. 'I can't scream like you. Just walking up here and my lungs are pumping.'

'That's what the tincture's for. Here, keep it. Use it every morning and night. You'll begin to feel more space in there.' He touches my chest.

'Bra, don't touch me like that.' I hit his hand away and look around for the dog. 'Abbas!' The bloody mutt doesn't come when he's called.

'You know queer men aren't infectious.'

'Ja, I mos know that.'

'It isn't unmanly for men to help one another. To express intimacy. And I'm not talking about the "bro's before ho's" kind of intimacy.'

I spit over the edge of the cliff, watch the spit dry on a rock further down. 'I had a chomie like that. You would have liked him he was touchy like you, but he didn't take it up the bum. Nah, he was an original. They don't make them like Stephen anymore.'

'Scream about it.'

'Say what?'

Mustafa shows me where to stand – right by the edge of the cliff, over all the pragtige huise with their tennis courts and blue pools. 'Ball up your fists, clench the soles of your feet, breathe in deep and shriek it out. Just try it. What have you got to lose?'

I give it a try like he says, taking off my shoes. Then I make fists with my hands and dig my nails into my palms.

'Breathe in deep three times, then do it.' Mustafa stands back. He is a voice on my shoulder.

Whatever he gave me works fast. My ribs expand and my belly fills with air. I scream – full, long, loud. I scream till my throat tightens and my heart punches, wanting to climb out of me. I don't stop till I'm lightheaded.

'Woah, don't do that.' Mustafa catches me before I tip over. 'It's not your time yet.'

'Yussie.'

'The body is a reservoir of charge. It builds and builds, and we repress and repress. Every feeling we have lives, in between bone and muscle, and needs action to unchain it. The voice, it's a powerful resonator. Like a sonar for feelings, and thoughts if you're so inclined.'

I lean over the edge. Jinne, it would have been a vreeslike fall. 'Give me a pull of that Swazi you were rolling earlier.'

'Go find Abbas first.'

I go looking for the dog. A security guard comes up to me and asks what's going on, who was screaming. 'Chill, man, it's no one getting raped or anything, don't worry.'

The security don't believe me. He spots Mustafa and calls him over. They start getting into a back and forth about how dangerous it is to be up there, by the edge; how a few months ago a lady fell over and it took paramedics two days to find her. On Valentine's, nogals. The world is fucked.

I leave Mustafa to deal with security and go find Abbas. That's when I come across a group of boys who're using their school bags as pillows against a tree. They pass hookah between them, laughing. As I walk by, they go quiet, like I'm going to snitch and tell their mothers that they're bunking. Is that what I look like now? A skelm for rules.

Stephen used to say rules were for the people who made them, not for those who followed. Some of us aren't born to benefit from the rules. I miss him. He was the only fucker who got me; the only one whose father was more by the jol than by the house, like mine.

I can still see our daddies lekker hot from the brandy and Coke, skelling ouens who owed them money from last week's dice. You could exchange Stephen's father for mine and we wouldn't tell the difference. Both useless. We were brothers, kinda, joined at the hip by the things our fathers didn't do for us. We even took bets to see whose pa would stay absent from the house the longest. Mine won most times because Stephen's loved drinking on the corner near our high school. So when we came out in the afternoon he'd wave us over (all red-eyed, slurring) and Stephen would make a point to call him by his first name. That stung the old ballie. It didn't bother Stephen because, by then, he had decided that his pa was a dog that couldn't be tamed. A dog that, every now and then, came home for its bones.

You get to an age where blaming the people who brought you into this kak becomes useless. It's like blaming the wind for the direction of a stray bullet. The bullet is going to do what it's going to do. You know, one time, Stephen and I were walking home from school and out of the blue there he was, my father, sleeping on a merry-go-round in the park, across from Anils Pharmacy. Stephen points him out to me like he's a pile of bird shit. I didn't avoid him, nee; that day, we took the path right past the park just so I could make sure the hobo in rags was *my* father. *Knocking on Heaven's Door* was playing nearby from the speakers of some no-nonsense aunty who ran a spaza shop out her garage. We were on our way there to buy fireballs. If my mother was around then, I'd have asked her why in the FW de Klerk did she choose *this* man, out of all the men.

We walked past and my father opened his eyes and almost recognised me, before falling asleep again. I hadn't seen the man in weeks and he looked right past me. It was confirmation that I didn't have a pa to begin with. All I had was Aunty Charmaine.

Abbas's leash has him stuck around a tree. He's not bothered with being stuck; there's something in the grass that he wants.

'What is it, boy?' I get close and see a snake, long as my fore-arm, light brown with black stripes, lying on its side, lifeless. I lift the leash through the crack in the tree's trunk and Abbas creeps around the dead snake, excited. 'Leave it!'

Eventually he runs to me, and we head back, but when I turn to take another look, the snake isn't there anymore. Abbas knows to test many times to see if something is dead.

We share the Swazi on our way back. Mustafa's in his own thoughts so I can finally take in the houses, picking which ones might've been fun to break into and how I'd do it. It's not hard to break into a house, but I wouldn't recommend it for amateurs be-cause it doesn't matter who you are, if you're in someone else's yard when you're not meant to be, you are enemy number one, bra. We all got our special places where we like to pee. Territory.

I only broke into three houses before I decided it wasn't for me. The first one was an old deaf tannie, which meant it wasn't hard to move around and take what we wanted. We didn't get much – an old TV and some gold-plated brooches. Stephen and I didn't feel bad because the tannie's kids visited all the time in Audis and Volvos; also, they were always having big parties by her place whenever she turned a year older (because at her age every birthday needed a celebration).

There wasn't anyone home for our second one. Being in someone's house when they're not there is like stepping into a life that could have been yours, with different underwear and photo albums. Now this particular house, it had all the family's achievements front and centre – graduations, marriages, degrees, trophies. I took a degree for myself, just because. And a trophy of a man's golden torso: *3rd Place, Men's 90KG Weightlifting.*

After the second one, we went out on the jol, and that's where Stephen confessed he only liked robbing when the mense were home. That now made no sense to me, so I pushed him on it. He said when the people are in their homes, all you wanna do is get in and out, but when you're alone, with all their stuff, curiosity makes you open more cupboards than you should. You wanna know what pills they're on, where they keep their water and lights bills, what's in the metal box at the bottom of the bedside drawer and why's it filled with old love letters and unopened presents?

Stephen didn't like being left alone with all that detail. *In and out, Tobes, that's how simple the job has to be.*

A week later, Stephen asked if we could stop with the houses and find another hustle. I was enjoying the challenge and was in no mood to give up. After four weeks of trying to convince him, poverty crept back into his wallet and he was up for another round. He couldn't say no. *Okay, bra, but let the people be home this time, asseblief. In and out.* Stephen, one of a kind.

You mustn't think it was all easy sailing for me, please. I just found a way to separate the homes from the houses. Look here, a house is like an old charity store. Red Cross or Salvation Army. People don't know what they don't need so they keep more than they can ever use. That's where I come in, to help. The trick Stephen never got, and what I should have told the boytjie, is never to look at the pictures in the frames, no matter how happy they seem.

'Mmmm,' says Mustafa, with the last of the joint between his fingers. He's facing me but looking past, back to a car with tinted windows, four doors down.

'What's it?'

'That Nissan has been parked there for weeks now. The other day I could've sworn someone was following me on my run.'

'My broer, you've been spending too much time with me. You're in the burbs, why so para?' I unclip Abbas's leash, he runs up the alley. 'You then told me this place isn't on the GPS, or in the Yellow Pages. Hell, didn't you say the neighbours at number ten have been paid off?'

He waves me off, and I start to think the weed's making him dom. This ou that likes to act all gangster.

'I know the cars gatas use for stake-outs. That's not it.'

'Who says I'm worried about police?' He turns, serious, following Abbas.

The Nissan starts up and drives our way, blaring John Vuli Gate; heavy bass shakes the windows. I can't see whose driving. There's a jol going on and whoever's inside knows exactly what they're doing and who they're going to do it to.

DAMNIT TO HELL, I can't sleep, again. One in the morning in a proper deluxe suite and still this kak. Not like being five to a bunk and being forced to become spectator to snaak things. Ja, it happened. When Lunga was new to the cell and the ouens took all his food for a week. It was only Keano who shared some of his toast and cabbage.

Let me tell you, one night, I see Keano waking Lunga up,

chiming that he owes him food. Lunga doesn't know what's up until Keano says he better find a way to pay him back. I turned around to sleep against the wall before Lunga picked up what Keano was putting down. It's best to be sleeping before that time of the night comes around.

And even if papa waggies is gonna paralyse you, in the tjoekie it's better to let the devil you know have his way. Rather that than squeaky bunks. This other time, there was a lice outbreak in our cell and they had to shave us bald. Ha, Lunga, Pieter, Adrienne and Keano – we all looked like cancer brothers with our pale, bald kops.

I get off the bed and pace the edges of the carpet. It feels lekker; how I imagine ladies feel in salons when they put cotton buds between their toes to keep them apart while the nail polish is drying. With my feet I mark out the places in the carpet where the ouens would've slept. It's the only thing that makes me calm enough to feel tired.

'Tobias?'

Haai, how could the lady of the house know I'm not sleeping?

'I was out walking in the garden and noticed your light on. You mind if we chat for a bit?'

This tief won't quit. She already bruised my hand, now what, she wanna apologise? 'Uhh, ja, I can't sleep.' I open the door. The Mortician's hair is down over her shoulders. Her eyes are puffy. She can't sleep?

'I hope you understand that what happened between us earlier had to happen.' She presses her hands on the door, wanting to open it further.

I block her with my foot. 'Is that right? You are lucky Mustafa convinced me to stay. I could charge you with assault.'

'This is why I'd like to make it up to you.'

'Is it? And how you gonna do that?' Is this cherrie coming

onto me?

'You want to be able to sleep, am I right? I can help you. But, you have to trust me.'

'Lady, I got no reason to trust you.' I'm about to shut the door when she stops me with her foot.

'Aunty Charmaine's house. Mustafa told me that's what you asked for. Shut the door now and that becomes less likely for you.'

'Okay,' I say, opening the door. 'Let's see what you got.'

The Mortician guides me onto the deck from my balcony. We head up onto the walkway, towards a treehouse. The lights are on. Did she plan this? We go in and sit on leather chairs with a small table between us. The room is empty, with weird paintings on the wall. And the wall – it has these wooden spikes.

'Angelique comes in here to sing every day. I've had the room treated acoustically. So she can hear herself. Are you a fan of Dali? Those are his works on the wall.' She shuffles a deck of cards, slapping them together and splitting them apart in a rhythm.

'Dali Mpofu?'

'No, no. You're a lot funnier than I'd thought you'd be.'

'You should do MMA with that grip of yours.' I put my hands on the table; she goes for my wrists, rubbing them like I'm her man.

'You don't mind me touching you?'

'Nah, it's nice.'

When I call it 'nice' she pulls back and carries on shuffling the cards. I keep my eyes on how she works the cards like a dealer at Gold Reef.

'So, what's *that* for? We playing Blackjack?'

'We're going to tell a story, together. A story about you. Using these.' She slaps the cards and spreads them out on the table, face down.

'Jy's a sangoma.'

'Just a fellow traveller.'

'Okay, missus. What's this story we telling?'

'Pick three cards. Let's find out.'

The cards are a slick black. I keep my eyes on her as I pick. Before I turn them over, she stops me.

'Past … Present … Future,' she points. 'Tell me what you see.' She turns the first card over.

'Two people, falling from a tower.'

'A flash of the possible is waiting, only if you learn how to fall.' Her voice is like an earbud going for an itch. I feel swak. A shiver runs down to my bum, but I don't wanna get up. 'Is this –' My voice doesn't sound like mine; it's thick and far away.

She turns the second card over and asks what I see.

'A man. With sticks in the ground behind him. He looks, like a bangbroek. His eyes are too big for his body.'

'Nine of wands says it's time to mend.' She looks at me, expecting an answer.

'Rest?' I ask.

She nods, her face lighting up: 'All the sticks are already in the ground. There's nothing left to do but –'

'Rest,' I repeat. The room gets darker, like her hair.

She rubs my bandaged hand the way a mother would. 'Do you want to see the next card?'

I try to nod, but my body doesn't listen.

'Don't be afraid. You are in control, Tobias. Why wouldn't you be? When you are resting, when the wounds scab, *you* are in control. It's always been that way. Hasn't it?' She turns the last card over. 'How does the story end? Tell me.'

On the last card there's a goblet filled with beer, in a cage. A hand reaches through the bars to pick it up.

'How does the story *end*?' she asks, her voice rising. 'Stories can only ever tell the truth. One way or another. Yes?'

There's a bag of sand in my mouth; I can't speak.

She comes around the table and turns my chair to face the door, kissing me on the cheek, whispering: 'Tobias has fallen out of the tower, but he hasn't hit the ground yet. He impales himself on a row of sticks, sticks that have been worked into soil long before he arrived. Up walks a woman who looks a lot like him, but is different, somehow. The woman reaches into his flesh, through the ribcage, towards a bare heart. She squeezes its haggard chambers. A heart that was meant to give and give and give.' She lifts my chin up towards the top half of the door.

The chair I'm sitting on has gotten ten times bigger, its leather sticks to me. All I can do is follow where she leads – on the back of the door is a carving, links of a chain in a funny shape.

'The knot is endless. Tobias. Take succour.' She kisses me on the top of my head.

Yasis, I feel vrot. The chair chows me. Finish and klaar.

WHEN I WAKE up in my room I'm not sure which day it is, but I know it's morning from how the sun is shining through the windows. I feel strong, rested. Ready for a jol. Mustafa better have remembered the Old Brown sherry I asked for.

SHE HAD CUT her thumb on the lawyer's letter. It was tiny, nothing to worry about. Her index finger kept returning to the raised flap of skin at the corner of her thumbnail. Playing with it, she resisted the urge to peel further along her cuticle. For a moment, she considered the flesh beneath. It was red. All the way down to the bone, there were enough injuries in her past to confirm this much and yet she still felt an incessant curiosity to look again, make sure, poke more.

Mustafa was driving. She enjoyed the canopied trees on either side of the road and how they patterned sunlight through their leaves. *Komorebi*, dance of shadow. As the day waned, she anticipated the segmented sunlight to shift, bend, all but disappear, the shadow dance entering many phases along the walls of people's homes. It had always been this way: things moved at angles to each other: intersections as far as the eye could see. Beneath the tarred road, she imagined the roots of the trees on either side wrap around one another, a meeting of species. *Deep enough and there's union.* There was no way to verify if the image in her mind matched what was really happening under the road, she knew. Such a confirmation would require destroying all that construction. How then would people get to work, feed their families, live?

Mustafa turned left into the main road, passing the comic-bookstore, and switched on the radio. 'I've really been enjoying this character. And then the author goes and kills him off last week Friday,' said the radio host. 'I mean, he killed him off at different times for different people, but for me it happened last Friday. I want to find out whether you, our listeners, have you ever been attached to a character and upset when the author decided to kill them?'

Mustafa thought about the question. *Charlotte's Web* came to mind. He thought of the horror he felt when a kid in a grade above him had ruined the ending; he'd always felt it unfair that that final death of the beloved spider was taken from him.

The kids in higher grades had moved on to reading larger, grander stories, and there he was in Grade four, trying to anticipate the page where the pig-saving spider might die, curious as to what Charlotte's babies might do with her body. Someone in the class suggested to the teacher that the babies ate Charlotte when they hatched. Mrs Arnott said there was no need to discuss that since it wasn't in the story, and, look how happy the pig was with his new spider friends at the end.

Mustafa was undecided. Adults hide things from kids; it was their nature to decide, beforehand, what parts of the world should be revealed to them. But then, who was peeling back the layers for adults when they were the eldest in the room? That had to come from somewhere else, from something greater and unpredictable.

The car turned on the highway, heading south. Both passengers listened to callers on the radio express their sense of loss for beloved characters who'd been living with them for many years. Characters who died multiple times, all over the world, for different people, and who would keep dying far into the future; characters whose lives meshed, unevenly, with the world. And where did such a web end? Whose web was it, anyway? Mustafa looked to the Mortician, curious about her thoughts on the conversation being had on the radio.

The cows on a cattle trailer in a lane beside theirs drew the Mortician's attention. They were stacked back to front and filled the trailer to capacity: one's face next to another's rear. She assumed this was done to give the cows the feeling of being *with* their kind, without letting them get spooked by the fear in one another's eyes.

Fear arising, most probably, from the intermittent rocking of the trailer.

Some of the cows appeared stronger than others, while some had resigned themselves to being jostled into corners, cramped into a half-squat position. The cows' bodies were shaped like the maps of continents. She wouldn't be surprised if once the trailer was unloaded, there'd be hustling and a lot of bruising amongst the herd, trying to get out. Some of the prized meat would be damaged in the process, some would have to be cut away. The ones weak enough to be stifled into corners would get the worst of it.

The car veered off the highway, turning into a street jammed with cars. Linked by metal in their frustration, some drivers tried to break the chain of engines by attempting sly dashes up any of the empty side streets that availed themselves. This behaviour slowed everyone else down. It didn't surprise Mustafa or the Mortician. The traffic lights at this intersection were always out, and even when they were replaced, they never lasted longer than a month. Reasons varied: sometimes it was a drunk driver who skidded onto the island and swiped a robot clean out of the ground (disconnecting the others); other times it was the result of theft. Any metal not bolted into its concrete was up for grabs these days. By whom? No one seemed to know.

At least here the poles of the traffic lights were still standing, thought Mustafa. He knew that in the intersection closer to the lawyer's office there weren't any robots to speak of. Those traffic lights had been replaced far too many times, so much so that someone in a high-rise office somewhere must have decided to give up on the repair effort entirely and let nature take its course. People's ability to take care of themselves – this was essentially what was happening at the intersection they were stuck at now, he thought. Each driver tiptoed over their respective white line, entered the crossroads and announced their presence. Some did it tentatively others were more brash. Yet, despite the methods of approach, everyone had a single-minded purpose – *get across* and *don't collide.*

Four-way stops: the prime example of spontaneous order, multiple minds reading the environment, syncing their bodies, and their cars, in some ethereal realm of anticipation and estimation. So much depended …

'… on trust,' Mustafa blurted, the weight of his thoughts dropping from the highest branches of his brain onto his tongue.

'What'd you say?' The Mortician turned the volume down.

'It all depends on it. Trust. Without it we're in the wild.'

'Hmmm.' The Mortician cranked her head like she was emptying water from her ear. She followed the same routine whenever she faced an idea she hadn't considered before. In her brain, synapses came alive: lighting in a dark sky.

'Yes,' she said. 'It's about how best to cordon off our basest natures. How to channel them to the appropriate place where they're allowed to be let out. The procedure of it all, it's repetitive enough to break anyone's back.'

Mustafa inched forward into the intersection, crossing without a hassle. They often spoke this way, one offering an observation and the other taking it in several directions. There'd be plenty of caesuras in between, a patient listening for what came next. For Mustafa, their conversations were like ornate compositions of music; for the Mortician, his questions set stepping-stones across the inner lake of her mind.

But too many ideas, packed on top of one another, ended up sounding like kitchen cupboards caving in, thought Mustafa.

Indeed, the Mortician felt similar; that sometimes their meandered way of talking left her in the middle of her mind, stranded amongst reflections.

The car stopped at the second intersection, the one bereft of robots. In the rear-view mirror, Mustafa's attention rested on a white Corolla driving up in the left-hand lane beside them. The car wasn't slowing down like it was meant to; in fact it was maintaining speed – right up until it slammed into the bumper of a black Hyundai. Buckled metal and screeching tyres made everyone drive slower; the whole intersection eager for what would happen next. Even the lady on the corner, the one selling samosas and curry balls from a large plastic container, stopped what she was doing.

The woman in the white Corolla calmly got out of her car and apologised to the man bending over his rear bumper. They exchanged details as the stream of traffic slowly curled around the collision, centipedes around a pillar. Mustafa found himself disappointed somewhat, but, then again, what was he expecting? What was everyone else slowing down to see?

'It is amazing when trust comes from recognition,' said the Mortician, breaking into his thoughts.

'That could have been us. If I'd chosen *that* lane instead of this one. If I had felt like switching lanes, for no reason save for fact that I *could*,' said Mustafa.

'See, recognition. It could have been –'

'In a different skin. Recycled fictions.'

'Clichés giving birth to clichés.'

'And the wheels keep turning.'

'Except no one believes that, do they? Not *really*.' The Mortician checked the time on her phone. Her father had already messaged his customary *ETA?* She wouldn't reply, not until she was outside their house. As Mustafa drove up the side street, he realised something vital had passed between them. The Mortician had felt it too. It was the way their conversations took the world apart, and rebuilt it in the air, which made their friendship worthwhile.

In their world, ideas sometimes vibrated, aligning their inner landscapes with flashes of connection that burned, white-hot – straight from the mind's eye into a deep, mutual, understanding of the other. An understanding as steady as the Mortician's hand on Mustafa's, shifting gears.

THE PARKING LOT was full. Law was a thriving business – so much so that the sewage pipes leading from Molefe Attorneys had a steady stream of rank passing through: signs of client satisfaction and the small relief that comes from getting custody in a divorce, winning a lawsuit, or claiming a lump sum from the Road Accident Fund.

Ms Shona Molefe was adamant when she first bought the residential building that the renovations had to turn the place into a respectable, law-practising establishment. Making sure the bathrooms were comfortable and clean was top priority. She knew her clients would face some of the hardest moments of their lives in her cubicles, taking their private moments to prepare a poker face before facing her in the office. Dealing with the estate of deceased loved ones, taking employers to the labour court over wrongful termination, choosing whether to drop assault charges over lack of evidence – Molefe had seen her share of war. Law was war, in her mind, and to win any war required knowing your terrain better than your enemy.

The reception's terrain was sparse. Ferns stood in corners and a large rug with printed seashells stretched across the tiled floor. Two couches rested on either side of the room and the walls were a pristine white, the kind that reminded Mustafa of a doctor's examination room. They were sitting on a couch, eyeing the receptionist speaking at a pace into his headset. A Nigerian from the sounds of it, thought the Mortician, taking interest in the receptionist's moustache. 'Doesn't that make him look a little like Captain Hook?' she whispered.

Mustafa nodded, hiding his amusement. The receptionist's tick-tack typing filled the room. Whatever he was doing looked serious, world-saving serious. The receptionist's fingers co-ordinated with his brain in an impressive display: basketball players in training, running up, one by one, catching the ball and dunking it; each dunk summoning pixels onto the computer monitor, assembling letters into subjects, predicates, clauses, full stops. Mustafa imagined the computer beaming emails all over the city, encoding strongly worded messages of 'disagreement' and 'final clarification' and pumping them out through servers that spanned the globe. The whole world bound together by endless corridors of blue-flickering lights in darkened rooms, kept at a steady twenty degrees Celsius.

He looked to the wi-fi router, on a shelf behind the receptionist, and imagined its signals flooding through brick, bone and perhaps the palisade fence outside. Everything that was not within its spectrum got scaled to insignificance. His attention drifted to the windowsill, where dust motes wandered in and out of the sunlight. They seemed so lifelike: an illusion produced by dilations in airflow. Maybe they were alive, just not in any way he could grasp.

'Ms Molefe is ready to see you,' said the receptionist, snapping bundles of paper together with a stapler and taking a swig of coffee.

He already looked wired, thought the Mortician. Did he really need more?

The receptionist seemed to think so as the caffeine entered his bloodstream, flooding synaptic clefts with dopamine, turning the avenues of his mind into five-lane highways.

Ms MOLEFE WELCOMED the pair into her office with her usual one-armed hug. She showed them to her Chesterfield armchairs that formed part of a lounging nook she'd made for important clients; other, lower-paying clients were shown to the L-shaped, hardwood desk where stiff Rickstackers made them sit upright.

'Can I offer you anything? Cranberry juice? Tea?' said Ms

Molefe, adjusting her shweshwe headwrap.

'No, thanks. Let's get right to it,' said the Mortician. In a cul-de-sac of her mind Ishaan was putting scones in the oven, waiting for a reply to his text.

'Right, yes. Let me get the file.' Ms Molefe ducked down into a drawer – columns of green and red leather-bound books towering behind her – and pulled out a manila folder. 'Here we go. As I said on the phone, Vicky Prinsloo, the executor of Jan's estate, is claiming the signature on the title deed of the Northcliff property was forged. She's also contesting the validity of the lump sum allocated to both of you in the will.'

'So, coercion, is it?' asked the Mortician.

'Correct. To be sure, there's very little Vicky can do against the will's directives, for two reasons. Mere suspicion and speculation won't hold water. The court needs evidence and, from what her legal counsel have shared, there is nothing for her to base her allegations on. Also, a year had passed between the creation of the new will and Jan's death, more than enough time for Jan to alter the will, if he saw fit.'

'Where does that leave us?' The Mortician crossed her legs and sat back, braced.

Ms Molefe sensed her clients' tension. She had really hoped they'd say yes to the tea. 'In my opinion, proving undue influence at this stage is a tall order for any legal counsel. So the funds are safe, and the process of transferring them should be enacted as soon as I get the matter thrown out of court.'

'What about the funds we received while Jan was alive? Are those safe?' Mustafa wrung his hands together, the memory of selling Frank Ledwaba's hospice crawling up from deep within him.

'Those funds are safe, yes. The real issue here is Vicky's grab for the property.' Ms Molefe sat down on the third armchair in the nook. She looked from Mustafa to the Mortician, trying to read for any sign of acknowledgement, guilt perhaps. There was none.

'She cannot do that! We made sure that all of the procedures were followed. Signed and dated,' said Mustafa.

Molefe stopped him, pointing her index finger in the air. 'Yes, that's exactly it. *Procedures*. We're going to need to get hold of the witness.' She held her hand to the blue-beaded choker on her neck, caressing it.

'Bonginkosi,' said Mustafa and the Mortician, seconds after each other.

'His signature is barely legible, but at least it's there,' said Molefe, pulling out a copy of the title deed from her manila folder. 'And, just to confirm, he was there at the time of the signing?'

'Yes, yes, he was there.' The Mortician began pacing the room; she felt better in motion during tense conversation. 'I just have no idea where he could be now. Last time we heard, he'd been fired.' On Ms Molefe's shelf, next to an intimidating tome titled *South African Property Practice and the Law*, stood a framed photograph of the lawyer, speaking into a megaphone to a group of students. A bus was on fire in the background. The Mortician remembered seeing Shona on the news when the FeesMustFall protests took place – it was real gutsy, she thought, for an established lawyer to be so public with her rage.

'If I'm going to save you from the dubitable evidence of forensic handwriting experts, we will need to trace Mr –?' Ms Molefe squinted at the signature on the title deed, then gave up. 'What's the man's surname?'

The Mortician looked to Mustafa. 'Mahlangu,' he replied, scrolling through his cell phone. 'I have his number right here.' He pressed the CALL icon and the cell phone was put on speaker. The room fell silent.

The number you have dialled does not exist. Please check the number and try again.

'We need to find him.' Molefe scribbled something down on her notepad in long, curling letters. Her incised fountain pen briskly roved across the crisp notepad; Mustafa felt a tingle pirouette on the back of his neck in response.

'And what if Vicky has done something to him?'

Both Mustafa and Shona turned to where the Mortician stood. She had ventured over to a pencilled sketch of The Kingdom of Mapungubwe hanging on a wall above a fruit bowl. The sketch was a bird's-eye-view rendition of what the kingdom might have looked like centuries ago: bustling with people trading livestock, fabrics, precious metals, with guards patrolling the outer perimeters. If she squinted just right, the view resembled a human cell: cytoplasm coddling organelles, semi-permeable membranes acting as both buffer and doorway, an inner life maintained through chemical tango.

She smiled. The more she looked for what she felt to be true, the more resonance there was of it, in everything.

'Do you mean –?'

'Yes, Shona.' The Mortician's attention shifted back to the armchairs.

Ms Molefe reached over into the satchel at her feet and pulled out a tube of hand lotion, rubbing it between her fingers.

'If we do find Bonginkosi, if nothing has happened to him –'

'There's no use, Mustafa. Vicky's got to him. I just know it.' The Mortician leaned against the side counter, picking out a naartjie from the fruit bowl.

Mustafa was surprised by the turn in the conversation. Why was she so ready to believe that Vicky would stoop so low? What did she know that he didn't?

'Let's not jump to conclusions without evidence.' Ms Molefe headed over to her desk and made a call. 'Hi, yes. Get hold of NMU Consultancy. Let them know we need their best detectives on the whereabouts of Mr Bonginkosi Mahlangu. Last known address –' she squinted at the scribble below the signature '– twenty-seven Ray Street, Flat three, Sophiatown. Yes, top priority.'

The Mortician broke her naartjie in two and threw the other half across the room to Mustafa. She knew something about Vicky he did not; this much was clear to him. 'If it does end up with forensic experts,' began Mustafa, 'wouldn't we still come out on top? I mean, neither of us forged anything. Does that not count for anything?'

'Your testimony is tinged with bias because you both stood to benefit,' said Ms Molefe. 'And when it comes to forensic document analysis, don't hold your breath either. We'd be putting one expert witness up against another, comparing whose training is more prestigious. I'm afraid that sophistry is not guaranteed to land in our favour. What *is* guaranteed is if we get Bonginkosi in a courtroom to testify.' Ms Molefe felt satisfied: the terrain of the case was becoming clear; silhouettes that first appeared like arthritic hands, idling in the air, revealed themselves to be climbable branches. If law was war, she thought, then the terrain was mapped with judges, precedence, evidentiary burdens and, most vital, witnesses. They interpenetrated – all in an effort to arrive at an asymptote of the truth. She had to remind herself that, no matter how prepared she was, a map was not a territory, and the Mortician may end up being right about Vicky Prinsloo. If it came to that, the battle would have shifted scenery entirely; she would have to adapt to that kind of guerrilla warfare.

'Right,' said the Mortician, 'you'll look into this then?' She stepped away from the fruit bowl and stood close to the door, signalling it was time to leave.

'We'll see what we can do on our side. I remember the one cleaning lady Bonginkosi spoke fondly of. Gladys, I think her name was. Maybe she'll have a lead on him.' Mustafa went over to shake Shona's hand. For a woman as sharp as she was, her hands were soft. He could smell the moringa and aloe on them.

'I'll be in touch,' said Ms Molefe, watching the pair leave. Taking them on as clients was a risk, she knew, but when had that ever stopped her? Law was a practice, and there was no better way to practise one's eloquence in the social contract of a nation than when it came to defending the necessity of alternate ways of dying that, inevitably, scorched the earth as they got going. She believed in their enterprise.

Molefe peeled a banana from the fruit bowl, mulling over the trajectories the case might take. Her gaze rested on the sketch of The Kingdom of Mapungubwe. In the corner of the frame, there was a handwritten note.

Mapungubwe Hill was only accessible by two very steep and narrow paths that twisted their way to the summit, and yet over two thousand tons of soil were transported to the very top by a prehistoric people of unknown identity. A lot of the details surrounding the discoveries at Mapungubwe were suppressed and were only released after 1994.

She'd often reread the note as a reminder of how much was left to be discovered and uncovered; how much had been desperately kept hidden before '94. One thing was certain: the sketch was a reminder that entire civilisations could, and would, turn to ruin if the climate rejected them. No amount of hoarding or hill-climbing or censoring was immune to the mood of soil.

ANGELIQUE

Every photographer knows that the beginning and end of a day is the kind of light you want for selfies.

'You want me to take it for you?' Daniel holds his hand out for my phone.

'Nope, I'm good.' I position the plate and mug at an angle on the coffee table; we're on the second-floor terrace, the view of lower Northcliff's treeline facing us: an audience of green for the comrades. Being this high up suits me. Soothes me. The still-I-rise life ain't so bad after all.

Daniel's on the lounger beside mine, coffee in one hand and a cig in the other. Lucas isn't going to like that: sneaking one in behind his back. Definitely going for bronze in the boyfriend Olympics, this one. I say nothing – glass houses and all. The angle of my pic is just right: high and to the left (my good side). Enough to show the scrambled eggs at my waist, sunlight on my face, palm trees in the background. Must get the palm trees in.

What would Todd say about this composition? *Always leave them begging for more, not gasping for less.* Yes, he'd pull out one of his ready-made phrases, always aimed at other photographers he thought weren't doing anything worthwhile. Fuck, that man could take a photograph! People called him the 'love-maker'. Todd could take any model at any stage of their career and teach them how to give up every last bit of themselves to the camera. Just when you thought you were *giving*, he'd show you how much more you still had left to offer. I'd walk out of his shoots sometimes feeling like he'd extracted precious pieces of cut diamond from me. Ay, that

Canon, those speedlights. With those tools and that one working eye, Todd came looking for *the* Angelique Mlungisi. There was no hiding; over the years he took so many photos of me, in so many poses, that I wonder where he keeps them all, now that I'm no longer an 'it girl'. Probably in some folder inside another folder on his laptop or catalogued in a book that doesn't get opened.

Despite what you may have heard, Todd was the quintessential professional. All he cared for was bringing something *real* out of whoever stood before him. He told me his job was simple; all he had to do was wait for the 'exact moment' in a model's face, the kind that enticed a viewer with a promise. The average Thembi on the street can come as close to perfection as a glossy page and that's what makes them want *it* even more, he said.

When I asked him what the 'it' was, he didn't answer.

Todd was my big break. That first Mercedes campaign where he picked me out of thousands catapulted my face onto billboards and across TV screens. It must be some wild kind of power to turn a person into a persona like that, just with the snap of a camera and some airbrush nyana. It makes sense why Todd was hardly seen with any romantic connection. Who needs romance when you have that power?

On the terrace, I fix my phone to the selfie stick and take a pic for my Insta story, deciding on the right filter. Rio has too many colours going on and isn't natural enough. Tokyo shows up my sunspots. Cairo brings out my warm undertones, and that's a bit better. Lagos might work; it gives off a matte finish. I'm putting together a compilation on InShot – it's gonna be a collage of vids, pics and memes that've made me laugh – and the plan is to post it just as I get out of here. I want it to be a reveal, obvs not as big as Beyoncé's album drop or Kim's breaking the internet. But close enough, for my fallen angels.

'What do you think? Postable?' I hand Daniel the phone.

'Are you sure it's okay to post from here?' Daniel swipes through the filters and settles on Lagos. 'This one.'

'She said it's fine as long as I don't say where we are.'

'You know they can't afford paparazzi skulking about, what with those greenhouses.'

I go back to my eggs and coffee. The secrecy of it all reminds me of a nameless club in Sandton where a concierge takes you down into a lounge lined with crystal decanters, all in the shape of women's bodies. Truth is there's nothing more exclusive than the underground – the places you can get into via invitation only. The kind whispered in your ear at loud parties.

By the rock pools, Tobias is bothering Dianne. Can't that skebenga leave the aunty alone? She's going through enough; now she's gotta deal with his alcoholic ass too?

'You should add a song to your story,' says Daniel, lighting another.

'What song says, "Namaste, but will still cut a bitch"?' I ask, finishing off the last of my eggs. He laughs, but I'm serious; I don't want people out here thinking I've gone full hippie. I type in 're-flective' into the Search tab and Azealia Banks's *Heavy Metal and Reflective* comes up. Something like:

> *I be V.I.P.*
> *You be guest list.*
> *I been knew cheddar*
> *You been that ex bitch.*

Too much electronic bass, not enough rhythm. I scroll to a lo-fi beat that's softer on the ears and attach it. I'm not sold on the angle for this pic, but I'll take a different one for the feed later. Maybe in the garden? Next to some flowers. Yoh, I really miss the days when my publicist did this.

'How many followers do you have?'

Daniel looks at me like I've asked him to get naked. He looks behind him and back at me. 'Do I look like I'm on Insta?'

'I mean, I didn't wanna *assume*.'

'Go ahead, assume.'

Something's bothering him. 'Where's bae?' I ask, keeping an eye on Tobias, who's walking back inside with an empty Savanna. What is that skelm up to? He better not be giving Dianne alcohol; she's in no state for that and I'm in no mood to be looking after her raggedy ass again. Angelique Mlungisi is the permanent exec of lush living. Emptying a stranger's bedpan ain't the look we're going for here. I could barely make it through the occult colonics we gave each other days ago. Like, I know it's supposed to humble us and teach servant-leadership and all that jazz but damn, do I have to go full Mandela to get better?

'With Mustafa,' says Daniel.

'Huh, what?'

'Lucas … he's with Mustafa. Had something to show him apparently.'

'Oh. Right.' I track Tobias till he disappears under the deck. My phone blinks. Reactions! They're flooding in – faces with hearts for eyes, flames popping up in the DM, 100s tallying up, one after the other. I double-tap everyone. A gesture, the Queen giving her dutiful wave. The Queen, blowing on dice and hitting jackpot.

'What's funny?' asks Daniel, putting his empty plate on mine.

'Nothing. Just nice to know there's people out there waiting for me. Let's take one together.' I turn my back to him and balance the phone on its popsocket, trying out the other side of my face.

'Let me take one of you.' He blocks his face with his palm.

'Okay, what's up? You seem, I don't know, frustrated?'

He takes another cig from the box we're sharing. Argh, a DMC is on the way. Let me check the views on my story before he gets into the nitty-gritty. One fifty in the space of fifteen minutes, not my best but something. I scroll up and click on the message requests. All random strangers: most lack originality, but then I come across a guy offering to e-wallet me if I take a pic of my feet soaked in a tub of milk. That's new.

'Since Lucas's accident … we haven't –'

'Fucked,' I say, trying to move the convo along. I open another DM from a sneakers brand based in China that's asking me to wear their latest. Seems like a bot.

'Been intimate. I mean, we tried a round the other day. It wasn't the same. We've lost something.' His voice firms up.

I put my phone away and try to listen.

'We cuddle, and kiss sometimes. It's starting to feel like every time I initiate, things get weird. It's not like he's even doing it consciously, I don't think. The signals, my signals, they're not landing. I just don't know how to break through. Do you think that when two people go through separate traumas so soon after the other, that it can either bond or break them?' He drags the cig till it's half ash and crushes it in the ashtray.

My phone vibrates against my leg. It's fucken hard to ignore. 'Lucas has been through a lot. With the accident and his legs, it's not easy having your life … derailed. I know. *We* know. And you've been getting your mental health right and tight. It's hectic in these streets, but you guys are putting in the work and that's, that's Africanacity.' I pinch his arm, trying to lighten the mood.

'I want things to be like they were.'

'You gotta give it time, babes.' My phone vibrates some more, but I hold off. 'Also, you need to be saying all this to *him*.' The vibrations fire off in quick succession and I need to know what's happening on the other side. Bekind27 is going through my profile, like *really* going through it, liking pics from when I allowed cheap synthetic to touch this scalp. Wow. I was out here, hey.

I forgot about this one: Xolisi and me at The Bungalow. He is in an all-white linen two-piece, green shades on, and I'm in a mint-green halter top and skirt. Platters of prawns, calamari and mussels laid out in front of us with caviar on salted crackers and champers ready to be popped on either side of the table. It takes me back. We were on the come-up then; nothing was off-limits – endorsements were coming through as often as we changed phones. Receipts were things we put our used gum into. We never saw the ugly side of anything. Our windows were too tinted for that.

'Are you listening to me?' Daniel's voice is sharp, direct.

I quickly turn my phone over.

'You know I adore you, Angelique, but sometimes –'

'Look, I don't know what you want me to say? I can only give you the same advice you've heard hundreds of times. "Communicate. Be vulnerable. Open up".'

'I don't want your advice. Damnit, just be here, for fuck's sake!'

Bathong, we're in a situation now – the silence thicker than cheap platforms from Mr Price. I check to see where Dianne and Tobias are; I can't believe the old hag is actually drinking with him. Maybe I do need a drink. My kidneys can take it. 'I'm taking these in,' I say, collecting the plates and mugs.

Daniel doesn't reply.

I get up and take the long way round back to the kitchen, down the ramp that's covered in ivy on the east side. I end up having to pass the gym on the first floor. That's where I bump into Lucas.

'Everything all right?' he asks, sipping his water bottle, all geared up in track pants and a green muscle top.

'Yup.' My eyes wander down to his braced leg. 'Working out?'

'My body is craving a good burn.'

'I bet it is.' I wink, walking away.

People always talk about the high from exercise. I've never understood what the hell they were going on about. Never felt such a thing. Never had a reason for it, with my metabolism. In high school I usually just said it was that time of the month so I could skip PE. The PE teacher and I had a little thing going on; it wasn't serious, just some over-the-school-jersey action.

Should I tell Lucas that Dan's been smoking? No, Ang, just leave things be. Don't be petty.

My phone vibrates, and a part of me doesn't want to roll the dice anymore. I should delete Xolisi's pics – every hand on my shoulder, arm around my waist, silly biting of my earlobe. Certain things are only good for forgetting.

With the breakfast plates in the sink, I sit at the granite counter, knowing I'll need both thumbs for this job. Scrolling to the bottom of my profile, I begin removing all signs of Xolisi and his friends from this page and every other page that has my name on it. It takes a kind of surgical precision. But I have time to spare. If anything, I have that.

IN THE AFTERNOON, the sun finds its way through the palm trees, reaching flowers that remind me of Gogo. I've forgotten their name, but they are perfect for pics. Gogo never had much space for flowers outside her flat; each person in the retirement block only got a rectangle of hollowed-out concrete outside their door where they could plant anything they wanted. Some planted spinach, herbs, cabbage. But not Gogo. All she wanted was to plant this flower. What's it's proper name again?

There's movement above me on the walkway. It's Daniel, but he doesn't notice me. Or maybe he does and pretends not to see. Why are the gays so sensitive? See, these are the kinds of things a person like me isn't allowed to say (let alone think). I'd be trolled on all the socials for 'stereotyping', for 'blah this' and 'blah that'. You can't just say anything anymore, not if you want to keep your name unblemished. One day I hope every marginalised group gets its day to be called out on its bullshit. It is only fair. They'll call it Anti-woke Day, and anyone who's anyone will get to say all the racist, bigoted, homophobic, classist shit they go around thinking, without being cancelled. I guess that's kind of what comedians do anyway? Maybe we should all be comedians then.

Akiri, there's times you can't help but miss an ex. If nothing else, Xolisi didn't mind me sharing my unpopular opinions on people without worrying about the 'problematic assumptions' of what I've said. Everyone's gotta have their issue to stay relevant; that thing they're an ambassador for. Save Palestine. Queer Rights. Legalise Sex Work. Mental Health Awareness. Body Positivity … the list goes on. I mean, I care, sure, but I don't wanna fill my socials with these causes all the time. It's depressing. And sometimes, it's like you're expected to have a degree in race and gender studies and the horrors of colonialism. Either that, or people will figure you out and discover that, really, you're just trying to live with what little life you have, getting as many hearts in your DMs along the way. People always expect you to get behind a cause. Use your platform. Normalise this and that – people love *that* shit. But, like, what if the things I'm expected to know and react to happened decades before I was born? Why should I care? It's not like it will change anything if I retweet a photo of a raised black fist. Right? What did Andy Warhol say about being deeply superficial? Now there's a queer who knew what was what.

Argh, the sun's too bright to get the flowers in the background of my pic. I'll have to wait for it to move over behind those evergreens. Maybe I need a better camera. I mean, I've learned to believe in everything these days. Energy. Wicca. Hinduism. Star signs. Chakras. The Secret. I've gotten to the point where I know, in my heart of hearts, that one day we'll all have cameras inserted into our eyes, and then we'll be able to livestream with a flick of a thought. I saw somewhere that scientists hooked a man up to a computer and he could control his house through his thoughts. Convenient much?

While the sun takes its own time to shift to the left, I'm halfway through removing Xolisi from my page. He's a stubborn little shit. I'll give him that. I'd forgotten how many we took together. Here's us at Fashion Week next to David Tlale in a shimmering all-black ensemble with purple shades. Ah, that show – mocha-coloured models in sheer white-and-black motif fabric, spotlights catching splashes of gold in their collars as they burned up the runway. David was charming, getting us front row seats. He was trying to get me to be his 'centre piece' for the next collection. Front row seats were part of the seduction, but Xolisi was playing unimpressed, even though he knew this was a big opportunity for me. As much as he denied it, he resented David.

Delete. No need for that mess, especially since what happened after, when we got home from the show. That's when I told Xolisi I'd decided to do it, work with David. He didn't like that, said he needed me for *his* collection. It was almost ready for showcasing and my name, in his show, could get the attention he needed. I told him the Patrón at the afterparty had gone to his head because, last time I checked, all he had were torn fabrics pinned to mannequins. He knew his time to make his mark was running out. If you're lucky, like I was, you look back and realise that the younger you rise to recognition the more of a 'sensation' you are. And Xolisi wanted so badly to be like me.

The trees have stepped in to do their job. Finally. The shade is enough to break the sunlight and make it softer. I crouch down to flower level, double-checking my angles, contrast and focus. None of it is really giving me that *showing flames* allure I'm looking for. I twist my neck, lift my face to the right, then the left. Nothing pops. I get down lower and couldn't care less that the grass is wet.

Gogo would've helped me if she were here. Even with her arthritic hands she'd have gotten the job done. When I used to sleep over by her flat, she'd move the furniture to one side of the lounge, which was really her bedroom, and make like I was a su-permodel. Supermodels always seemed taller than life, with jaguar eyes – that's what Gogo called it.

Show me those jaguar eyes, Angie, she'd say, holding two flash-lights, pretending she was the light technician. She'd turn the lights low, use her flashlight fists to make it feel like I was being praised by an audience that was too far away for me to see. Then she'd put me in one of her blouses that reached down to my knees, old leather gloves, and high-heels too big for my feet. She even let me hold an unlit cigarette and pretend to smoke it down the 'runway'. I tried to show Gogo all the jaguar eyes I had in me. The fiercer I was, the happier she became. She always wanted *more*.

She got more all right, especially when she fell into some money. An uncle who had had the hots for her back in the day had passed away, leaving her with a substantial portion of his pension fund. I didn't understand it at the time, but now I realise how much of a bad bitch Gogo was to keep men panting after her well into her sixties.

Anyway, first thing Gogo did was move out of that flat and buy a three-bedroom in Mondeor; then she got a lawyer to make my mother sign over custody. I didn't feel the 'sign-over'; my moth-er lived with a man who never wanted me around, who said I was gonna grow up to be 'bad news' and that I was 'always showing off my legs' around him. What did that mean for a girl who liked playing in the dirt as much as I did? Skirts that went down to my ankles just did not cut it.

It is not ideal. I've had to take my Nikes and socks off and get into the flowerbed. Just one good pic. The Gram needs it. With my face above the flowers, I start snapping – as many as possible –

hoping I'll catch the right one. Like fishing. Above me, Daniel exits one of the treehouses. He passes, shaking his head my way.

Never mind him. I'll get my pic. I continue, using every face I've been trained in (neutral, flirty, thoughtful); every contour needs to come through by force by fire, right down to my breasts – it has all got to *serve*. When I think I've gotten enough material, I get out and wipe my feet on the grass. Strelitzia! That's what they're called. Knowing their name makes them seem different, somehow. I google strelitzia (Google corrects my spelling) and there it is: Bird of Paradise. Yes, that's right. Birds mid-flight with Fanta-orange wings. I can see Gogo above her concrete rectangle with her watering can, soaking them. *Come help water my birds, Angie.* Her voice croaky from the pack of cigs she smoked every day.

Heading back to the house – Nikes in one hand, phone in the other – there's music coming from the front patio. Tobias's voice is louder than the others and I just know he's going to say something crude when I rock up. *Strelitzia* – I repeat the word so I won't forget, thinking about how I tried to make those birds fly in the back yard of Gogo's complex, near the bundles of cut grass I wasn't allowed to roll in. I'd removed the strelitzias from their stalks and was throwing them as high and as far as I could. Mr Douglas, Gogo's neighbour, a real flaky mlungu, yanked me by the arm all the way to her door. She didn't like that at all. Actually, Mr Douglas saw flames; he thought he had me, but Gogo said 'back to sender'.

Don't ever pull my child like that. Have you no sense. I was confused: was I or Mr Douglas in trouble? Mr Douglas just clicked his tongue and mumbled something I didn't catch. When we'd gone inside, I felt so proud of Gogo for sticking up for me. She had had my back, guilty or not. It was only when she brought me in and locked the door that she dished out what she really thought of what I had done. A beating my bum didn't forget.

But if they're from paradise they should fly!

Now. They're. Going. To. Die. Gogo sounded out each word as she hit.

After my post-hiding nap, I found her burying the birds back in the same concrete rectangle, next to headless stalks. Would the stalks make birds again? I didn't know. I told myself if they would, I wasn't gonna force them to fly higher than they were meant to. I was gonna let them live on their stalks. In mid-flight, always.

When I get to the patio, the party is in full swing. Lucas is chatting to Dianne and she's hunched over a mug, a blanket across her lap. 'Join us,' he says, alerting the others. Tobias asks what I want to drink. I ignore him and head over to the cooler-box, pouring myself a vodka and soda water.

'A spirits girl. Nice,' says Tobias, changing the song on the speakers from the phone in his hand.

'Anyone see Daniel?' I ask.

'He said he wanted to check out the floating room?' says Lucas.

Dianne asks before I do – 'What's the floating room?' – since neither of us have tried it yet.

Lucas says it's a tank where you're supposed to float in absolute darkness: 'No light, no sound, just you. And your thoughts.'

'Sounds like too much,' I say, checking Twitter. What the hell … I'm trending. But how? Wait, it's not just me. Xolisi and I are trending. I go into the thread, my thumb scrolling like a hundred-metre sprinter.

'Is everything all right?' asks Dianne.

I don't answer. Instead I leave the patio and head for our room. Once inside, I try and get a grip on what I'm seeing. How could they have given Xolisi bail? He's a flight risk. I bring up Insta to search for Malik. His followers have shot up by 10K, but I haven't got time to congratulate him. He's online.

Malik, my friend, did you see the news?

Hey boo. Long time. What news?

Xolisi. He's out.

What?

I minimise Insta and leap over to Twitter, where I pull up an article and share its link to Malik's Insta inbox. He takes a while to respond so I wait, finishing my drink.

'Angelique? Can you unlock the door, please?'

Fuck, Dianne, not now. I preferred when she was out for the count and bedridden for days. It's a horrible thing to think but at this point I don't care. *Deep breaths.* Remember the Mortician's teachings. *Feel your body. Give whatever you're feeling space. Don't do anything. Just give it space. Change your relationship to what you're feeling.*

I slow down my breath, watch my thoughts like they're not mine. *He's gonna find you. Are you sure he had no clues about where you are?*

As hard as I try, I can't get to that peace that the Mortician led me to – the place where the knots untie, and I slip out from under it all. I need another session with her.

No, I need to be coming up with a plan, calling the police, making sure I am safe. Malik's replied:

We should do a call. Can you talk?

Yeah, is Insta fine?

Sure. Hold on, let me video call.

When the call comes through, I can tell he's not in his usual apartment. I ask if he's moved and he tells me to hold on while he turns his Live on.

'Wait, I don't wanna go Live.'

'I kinda have to, boo. I'm signed to this reality show. It's pretty dope. *RealityX.* You didn't hear about it? They do in-depth raw footage, and they pay.'

I guess I could do a Live. Malik's always been the better trend forecaster than me. Maybe this will help me rebrand? We haven't spoken since rehab, but I think he's been following my name online.

'Okay, wait, let me just set up my ring-light real quick.' He fixes his phone into a tripod. With his face so close to the screen I can tell he's got some work done.

A part of me knows this is great content; if I ever want to have some sort of comeback, this might be the start. The drama, a real-life thriller. Whether it's in Malik's show or someone else's, I'll be getting airplay – in conversations, via curious thumbs googling my name, sharing articles about Xolisi and me and, who knows, maybe even an interview on TV. I could be in mid-flight again. Ascending.

'Askies, friend, now tell me. What's this you sent me about Xolisi getting bail? I mean, with GBV what it is, how can they do this?' he says. We're Live to all his followers, all five hundred and counting. He's a lot better than I am at this. 'Angie, your connection okay?'

He presses me to respond, but I don't know what to say. Then, like a born-free singing the national anthem, something else takes over: a way of speaking I've learned on the road to blue-ticked-dom. 'Yeah, you know, friend, I'm just going to stay strong. I know what's right and wrong and I'm in the right. We all know the wheels of justice turn slowly and, you know, letting the police and courts do their work. It will all come out when we go to court. When the verdict's made I am going to move on with my life. You can't keep a hardworking woman down. Strike a woman strike a rock. Am I right? I'm gonna go back to being a permanent MEC of the lush life department!'

Despite Malik's Botox, his face leaks. It's not in the skin around his mouth, or from his smooth forehead; it's the way his ears drop so slightly, like a dog who's realised their owner has played a trick on them.

Malik, like me, is a pro. 'Angie my friend, we've come a long way together. I'm here for you, no matter what. And what some people on my page don't know is that I was there when you called the cops on that scum. Yes, people, your boy Mal Ding was there at the very beginning.'

Professional or not, he's thrown a curve-ball. The comments come streaming in:

Malik, you're such a loyal friend.

What was it like to call the cops on your fiancé Angie?

You two are Friendship Goals!

It's so inspirational to see such beautiful people show the ugly side of fame and dating.

It's true. The night it all turned to shit Malik was the one to hand me the phone. We were different then: he was a talented, emerging model, too eager to please, in my mind. I thought I could mentor and help him avoid the tricks the industry plays to exploit newbies, like photographers offering 'exposure' and 'free merchandise' instead of money. I was making soup that night, cauliflower and pea, holding the liquidiser with my good arm while Malik steadied the pressure cooker. Xolisi was out doing a fitting for a wedding. The garlic bread was almost ready.

You can't go on like this – Malik had dialled the number on my phone and put it on loudspeaker. I continued liquidising, even when the voice on the other end repeated their greeting for the third time. With his other hand, Malik stopped me, letting the soup in the pressure cooker settle into bits and pieces. He shook the phone in my face above the cooker, the number on the screen fogging up. I wanted him to drop my phone in with the soup. *Yes, hello, my name's Angelique Mlungisi. I need to report an assault. Multiple.*

Malik tries to keep the Live going, interacting with the comments, trying to distract from my on-screen silence. Does he even know that he's crossed a line? We had never set one in the past, but, come on, this isn't a game show. If it was, Malik would be winning, the audience would be on his side, and I would have used up my one and only call-a-friend.

I hold the shutdown button on my phone; the screen goes black before I toss it onto the bed. That night we ate cauliflower and pea soup with the police officers in my apartment, waiting for Xolisi to get home. The first thing he said, walking in: 'Baby, that food smells so good. I got the paprika you asked for.'

I kept spooning soup into my mouth, letting it burn my tongue. Xolisi knelt in front of me, raised my face to his, pleading, the officers' hands on his shoulders. I kept eating as he got escorted from my line of sight. I'd never been so hungry. I finished four bowls of soup that night, with the garlic bread.

The music from the patio is soft, but as I step out of the bedroom and walk down the passage the bass slides up into me. Smooth. Solid. I wanna drink and jive and forget that Xolisi is out, that he will try and find me. A part of me is scared. Another excited. Eyes have finally turned my way. Does it matter what it took to get here when my name and face are flashing across screens again?

BENEATH THE CITY is a conglomerate of rock, shot through with veins of gold that have seen their fair share of invasion. Stories have been told about the quartz with an elysian lustre, and the city that rose up from it. Most malleable and ductile of metals – twisted into wire, stretched into sheets spanning kilometres, smelted into intricate shapes (while resisting rust) – the veins of this city have alloyed with generations, taking on the warmth of earlobes, fingers and promises as their own.

No one knows how the sweat of the sun got here. Some say before there was a word for 'world' there was only force-and-fire – housed inside a cosmic egg as small and as dense as the tip of a fountain pen. There, a tyrannical symmetry reigned supreme, so much so that whenever force-and-fire congealed into form – a spot of ink with which to write – it was pulverised in a zero-sum game of Whac-A-Mole.

In the miasma of the egg, force-and-fire gradually grew to know itself as pure appetite. It willed a fissure, a coup d'état from the tyranny that would later be called 'void'. And when that crack came, when pure appetite felt 'yes, we, too, want to matter', one of the billions of dreams it conceived of was gold. Gold as confetti, scattered upon the marriage of neutron stars. Gold as the eulogy of supernovas. Gold shot through the vacuums of space, plummeting in pregnant meteorites towards an earth that was all molten soup. Volcanic vomit.

Over millennia – as metal collected deep inside earth's fist, and water settled on the surface of its knuckles – microbial mats of cyanobacteria in a large, inland lake, on an African highveld, began metabolising the metals in their water. In so doing, these bacteria concentrated the flows of alluvial gold, inadvertently depositing layers of it in the sediment of the highveld. The lake became known as the Witwatersrand Basin, and its surreptitious veins birthed a gold rush.

Today, there are mine shafts all over, running through the urban underland, marking space for dreams, disease, death. In the south, near New Canada Dam, men with photographs of old shafts (their only maps) go in search of gold dust previously lost to the folds in earth's crust. They hunt for nuggets of the alien snuff, dissolving and purifying what they find with liquid mercury (or cyanide), inhaling the toxic fumes of their trade, fumes that appear – strident exclamation marks – across their lungs.

When you've travelled to the cavernous labyrinth like these men have, death waits for you behind every boulder. This deep, disease is airborne. The Zama-Zamas leave the surface of a citied world and brace themselves against the jagged, narrowing depths, where a different cosmopolitanism lives. Throughout the underland, in cavities the width of thumbs, flatworms, nematodes, rotifers, arthropods, annelids and protozoa commune in metabolic partnership. Thriving this far from the sun is no easy feat; it demands that nutrients are shared in the hope of defeating a common enemy. Lack.

It requires slowing down too, like the nematode does, suspending its life cycle when things get too extreme. For the nematode and others like it, getting close to the razor edge of death is a lifesaving strategy. This deep below the surface, there are aquifers billions of years old, pools that first formed at the beginning of the world. More cells reside in these ancient lakes than in all the world's open oceans. Between fractures and faults, oxygen-deprived water boils, bombarded with gamma rays from untapped uranium. In this immanent hell, life finds its appetite every thousand or so years when a micro-organism re-ignites its engines to divide, and pass its story on, along the gamut of tectonic time.

By the time Zama-Zamas have completed their daily toils around thumb-sized metropoles, the *E.coli* in their guts will have reproduced several times over. When they surface, their pupils contract against the light. Then, they *feel* it – time having passed, without a signal from the sun, without cardinal points. For them, there is only the counting of heartbeats against eardrums and the rumblings of quartzite when one of their pickaxes invades a fault line – widening it.

All it takes is one strike where the reef is weak for the conglomerate of rock to be brought together in an opera of stratified vibration, belting out an aria that rocks the Witwatersrand. That's measured on the Richter scale.

'… *THIS MORNING'S TREMOR was one of the largest recorded in recent times,*' began the newsreader. '*Experts say illegal mining activities in abandoned mines may have some role to play –*'

Mustafa turned down the radio. Neither of them had felt the tremor, although it was reported that areas in the north were affected. The damage was general – some cracked windowpanes and driveways, nothing to write home about.

They were finishing up with the deliveries. Their last stop was Gabriella September. Gabriella was a national sensation on account of her car-spinning talents. The Mortician had first introduced Mustafa to her at the Wheelz and Smoke arena around the time Bridge Builders Hospice lost its manager and owner, Frank Ledwaba.

'Is she home?' asked the Mortician.

Mustafa checked WhatsApp. They were parked outside a townhouse complex, waiting. Gabriella had read the message. 'I think so. Give it a few minutes.'

'What did she order?'

'A few Golden Teachers and some Northern Lights.'

The Mortician got out to stretch. She messaged her father that they would be on the way soon. She thought about her cousin Gabriella and how her fame had reverberated through their extended family. *First woman in a male-dominated sport*, uncles and aunts repeated whenever the family got together for birthdays, Sunday lunches and braais.

It wasn't jealousy, the Mortician reassured herself. How could it be when she had been an integral part of Gabriella's awakening? Did she yearn for some recognition from the family of that fact? Was that the reason she had undertaken her own project at the institute, without Mustafa's knowledge? The greatest innovations in science and art happened on the fringes, as far away from ethical considerations of right or wrong, she reasoned. The history of humankind could be rewritten as a rebellion against what people claimed was normal.

'There she is,' said Mustafa, handing the package through the window. Gabriella walked through the sliding gate of the townhouse complex, past the empty security checkpoint and onto the pavement. She was petite and nimble, her body well suited for quick escapes from cars revolving on their tyres at nine thousand revs a minute.

'Hey, cuz, you good?'

'Hi, Gaby. Yes, I am fine, thank you. Here you go.' She handed the package over, waiting for Gaby to tear it open as she often did.

'You always bring that good good,' said Gabriella, holding the package close.

Gabriella hadn't ordered anything from them in a while, she thought, sensing how long it had been since they last spoke. There was something different to Gaby; she seemed a lot surer of herself.

'When's your next spin?' asked the Mortician. 'It's been a while since we've seen you in action.'

'Joh! It's been long, hey. Last time I was first up at Wheelz and Smoke, right? Now I'm *second to last* on the line-up. I'll be there tonight, if you're free. I might pull out a suicidal swing for ya'll.'

'I can't. Promised I'd spend tonight at home.' The Mortician checked her watch. She needed to get going.

'Oh, okay. Say hi to Uncle Ishaan and Aunty Saisha. You know, cuz, my parents, they still asking me to get "a proper job".'

'You were born to be behind the wheel. Don't let them take that from you,' said the Mortician, in a solemn tone Gaby was not expecting.

'No, of course. It's just things parentals say. Nothing major. Hey, Mustafa! Looking good. All that yoga paying off! I see those bi's and tri's.'

Mustafa waved as the cousins hugged awkwardly and said goodbye. He overheard the Mortician invite Gaby to come check out the 'retreat centre'.

'Is that what we're calling it now?' he asked, as the Mortician got back in the car.

'It should be whatever it needs to be. Retreat centre. Institute. Ashram. Temple. Escape pod. Take your pick.'

The air around the Mortician had turned acerbic. 'Why does Gaby bring this out in you?' he asked.

'What do you mean?'

'It's not the first time you go "off" after seeing her.'

'You don't always need to know everything I'm thinking and feeling. Haven't we shared enough?'

'That wasn't our pact when we started this. Have you forgotten?'

The Mortician kept quiet. All that lay between them for the next half hour were the sounds of the engine shifting in and out of gear and the squeaks of brake pads at every intersection.

As much as she resisted Mustafa's suggestion, the Mortician knew where the ache in her chest came from. As cousins, they had loved the idea of spinning cars. It had started around the time Ishaan lost the funeral parlour and Saisha found work as a seamstress for a boutique in Fordsburg. She always had it in her mind that the funeral parlour would belong to her one day, and that she would carry on the tradition of preparing the dead. She blamed Ishaan for them having to sell the parlour to pay for the civil lawsuit that left them bankrupt. The lawsuit that saw them move into a flat in Fordsburg. She had just turned twenty and was desperately looking for any excuse to be somewhere other than that god-awful flat, stuck between a bunny aerial TV and her father's brooding resentment. That was where Gaby and her new BMW E30 came in.

Gaby had suggested they take the car to the spinning arena and learn some tricks from the seasoned drivers. They sought out all the drags they could (without their parents' permission) and found themselves captivated by the technical skill needed to manipulate a vehicle in such dramatic fashion. Being close to spinning cars, teetering towards danger, invoked an amalgam of terror and exhilaration in the Mortician. Gabriella, on the other hand, was interested in mimicking what she saw of the drivers' hand-eye co-ordination from where she stood amongst the spectators, behind the concrete and metal barricades.

'Do you remember when we went to watch Gaby perform for the first time?' asked the Mortician, breaking the uneasiness in the car. Mustafa was clearly upset from the way he had been speeding up and braking suddenly behind drivers who were driving too slowly. He needed to be quelled.

'I do. Prinsloo had already signed over the Northcliff property and given us all that money.'

'We sold Frank's hospice around that time too, didn't we?'

Mustafa grunted, clearing his throat.

'Yes, I think it was just after that. We'd gone to see Gaby spin and remember there was a *Sunday Times* writer there. That was the night Gaby did her first suicidal swing and the crowd lost their shit. You know *I* gave her that move. Well, the idea. I gave her the idea, back when we used to take the BM out behind Highgate Mall to practise. Gaby always had raw talent and I ... I was her passenger. A second pair of eyes.'

Mustafa thought about his first time at the drags. The gleam of Gaby's dark purple BM, the engine rapidly spluttering like an exuberant sports commentator. Gaby, all confident in the driver's seat, entered the Wheelz and Smoke arena, taking a high-speed left turn that bent the car's velocity, forcing its rear tyres to lose just enough grip on the tar to allow the car to drift along a sweeping, circular trajectory. Just when he thought Gaby no longer had control of what was happening between the tyres and the tar, she swerved the steering-wheel in the opposite direction, reasserting her friction. She did this several times, alternating between right and left turns, before locking the steering-wheel out completely. This 'lock-out' seemed to hypnotise the metal, convincing it to glide along in a doughnut-shaped orbit.

Then, Gaby jumped out of the driver's window, exiting the BM's orbit, and let the car spin on its own. She looked on as part of the crowd: the car in its own trance, driverless. When she raised her hand and shrugged her shoulders, the crowd cheered and whistled. How utterly divine she was then, he thought. Instantiating a pattern that the BM could not escape. Moments later, Gaby climbed back into the vehicle through the driver's window and locked her legs on the inside of the driver's door. Then she leaned back, close to the ground, her hair sweeping the gravel like a human broom.

It reminded Mustafa of the scene from *Titanic*, where Jack held Rose at the tip of the ship. Except, in this version, no one held the damsel; the damsel held herself, upside down, out the window of a whirling BMW – wholly bound to the laws of traction and slippage.

Afterwards, people swarmed Gaby for her autograph. Young girls wanted to run their fingers through her hair. Men offered her drinks.

'She never gave you credit,' replied Mustafa, finally.

The Mortician nodded. 'When I bring it up, she's adamant the suicidal swing was all her idea.'

'Does it matter? You both lead different lives now.'

The car pulled up to Ishaan and Saisha's home. In the dead end, opposite the house, the Mortician caught a glimpse of Ishaan, breaking empty glass bottles in the road. What is that man up to, she thought.

Mustafa didn't pursue his own question, letting it dissipate as he turned the engine off. 'What you said at Molefe's. Why are you so sure about Vicky?'

'I don't want to get into it right now.'

'If you've been keeping something from me, I want to know.'

'Can we do this later? They're waiting.'

Mustafa looked to the house; Saisha was sweeping outside. 'Fine, later. But you will tell me.' He reached around to the back seat and drew the wine they were asked to bring for dinner.

THE YARD WAS littered with soot. It fell from the sky like the singed edges of love letters. Saisha tried sweeping it up. It was useless. 'Jinne, this burning people do! Hello, you, come inside.' She changed her pitch once she saw Mustafa.

'Still talking to yourself, Ma. Good to know some things don't change.' The Mortician hugged her mother: her hair smelled of the red rose incense she liked to burn.

Saisha brushed soot off her daughter's shoulders. 'Every year they start this shit earlier. Autumn's at least a month away.'

'Where do you think it comes from?' Mustafa asked.

'The community group says it's that veld near the N1,' said Ishaan, coming up behind them.

'WhatsApp group? You use that now?' said the Mortician.

'Your father's the admin. Resident Mr Mini-mayor over here,' said Saisha, taking the wine from Mustafa and tucking it in her armpits.

The family followed one another inside, a heavy aroma of tomato and basil alerting Mustafa to his hunger. He took his seat at the dining room table, which was already set, and cast his eyes around the room. Black and white photographs of remote landscapes adorned the walls, along with ruined, face-brick homes in the middle of nowhere, half-broken windmills lazily turning near the edge of a barren cliff, a train track curving off into a mangy bush, a horse sleeping against the back of a cart, a misty shoreline dotted with driftwood. The photographs changed the quality of the light coming through the windows. The space felt contemplative, despite Saisha's spirited toiling in the kitchen and the voice of Luther Vandross swooning on the air.

The Mortician brought the food to the table, filling the centre with a bright rocket salad, tossed with walnuts and pomegranates, dressed in balsamic vinegar, a plate of crispy chicken pieces, a pot of pasta in red sauce and a side of nutmeg-and-cinnamon-spiced pumpkin. 'What's with the broken glass?' she asked as everyone settled.

'Ever since the squatter camp, we've had to augment our surroundings. They love to park at the end of the road and get up to all kinds of mischief,' said Ishaan. 'I mean, the other day, after the soccer match on the veld, there were three cars parked opposite and people were drinking and playing music. And loud, hey. They even pulled out a braai stand. Mind you, this is a residential area, so we had to ask them to move it along.'

'Did they?' asked Mustafa.

'We asked nicely,' said Ishaan, biting down on a leg of chicken. 'The glass is a deterrent. Helps keep it clean over there. Wasn't it last week, Saisha, when a young couple were doing "things" under the tree? You must make your boundaries clear for people. Otherwise they walk all over you.'

'If we don't take pride in our surroundings, who will? The municipality?' Saisha clicked her tongue, reaching for the chenin blanc.

The doorbell rang suddenly and voices of children – all yelling 'Aunty!' one after the other – interrupted the conversation. Saisha got up to open the kitchen door and listened to the kids' request for food. She went over to the breadbin, buttered some slices, and put the bread in a plastic packet before passing it through the gate, with some apples from the fridge. 'Not a day goes by where someone doesn't come asking for food or old clothes,' she said, returning to the table.

'It gets so bad you start wondering where the parents are,' said Ishaan. 'The other day, the caretaker of the primary school up the road caught some boys emptying Duggie's tyres.'

'Luckily I was there, or your father would have bliksemmed them,' said Saisha.

'They need a good hiding. Little shits. Anyway, we took them to the police station, just to make them a little bang, you know –'

'– first we took them to their mother, there in Thornton,' said Saisha.

'Oh, ja. Mustafa, you should have seen how this family lives. A back room, children everywhere, small two-plate stove in the corner. Thin foam mattress against the wall. Everything reeking of mildew.' Ishaan scrunched up his nose and looked to Saisha.

'The mother, spaced out of her mind, busy telling us that *we* must take *her* boys to the police to teach them a lesson,' continued Saisha. 'Can you believe that?'

'Did you go through with it?' asked Mustafa.

'We couldn't just do nothing or those kids would do it again, to someone else. And they were crying snot en trane already, so, yes, we took them to the station, and a constable gave them a lekker scolding. Definitely put the fear in them, shame,' said Saisha. 'Hopefully it was enough.'

Mustafa had always assumed divorce equated to irreconcilable differences, that proximity to an ex-lover meant a sustained form of torture. The Mortician had told him that her parents chose to continue living under the same roof because it made financial sense; they'd always had a knack for looking after each other. His pragmatic side believed that explanation, but what moved between the Mortician's parents felt like more than just the logic of balanced books. He couldn't quite put his finger on it.

As the meal wore on, each dinner plate looked like a ravaged wilderness: chicken flesh forked and separated from the bone, strands of rocket lay spent in puddles of red sauce.

'I saw Gabriella today,' said the Mortician, breaking the consuming silence, interested to see how the news would filter through.

Saisha got up and took her plate to the kitchen. 'Her parents tell us that she still doesn't want to study,' she began. 'She can't do that spinning all her life, God!' She came back with malva pudding and Tin Roof ice-cream and set them down on the table. 'I'm glad *you* stopped with that. It's not safe.'

'I never wanted to do it full-time, Ma. After my fall I had enough thrill to last me a while.'

The room went quiet. Mustafa took the opportunity to dish up some pudding and ice-cream. He sensed a painful memory had been pried open; its stench surrounded them, making the family focus on the syrupy-sweet taste of malva.

Another voice, this one booming, came from outside. 'Uncle! Uncle!'

'It's like a halfway house,' said the Mortician.

Ishaan opened the kitchen door and told the dishevelled man at the gate that he should have come earlier, like he had promised.

Through the curtains, the Mortician watched as the man pressed his hands together, pleading.

'Bring your ID. Ja, I know you're not from here but bring it anyway. They need a form of identification. Remember this is a proper gardening job that I got for you, at a *good* school. Don't fuck this up, okay?' she heard Ishaan say before he closed the kitchen door and returned to the table.

Ishaan's face didn't emote a lot, but when it did it was the quiver of his lips that gave him away. 'Edwin's a good guy, young and willing to do any work he can get. I swear, we have so much untapped talent in this country, desperate for anyone to give them a chance,' he explained, his lips taking on a strained, prune-like shape. 'You try where you can. Change one person's world, that's all.'

Everyone at the table tacitly agreed as they finished dessert. The first bottle of wine was emptied with efficiency and the second was well on its way to the same fate. Saisha made sure everyone's glass stayed above a level that she deemed appropriate for a jovial family dinner. 'And how is your health these days, my girl?' she asked, pushing through the lull.

'It's been all right, Ma. I don't get back pain so much. Sleep comes easier.' The Mortician looked to Mustafa, who was focused on his ice-cream.

'Mustafa, did she ever tell you what happened on that mountain?' asked Ishaan.

Ishaan and Saisha frequently asked him questions about her life in order to gauge how intimate they were. At least that was what he assumed. 'She's told me some things, but I've never heard the story from all sides,' he said, swallowing.

'Do we have to go into it now, Da?'

'If it wasn't for that, do you think you'd be who you are today? Mustafa, did she tell you what she saw, what appeared to her at the bottom of that cliff, while she waited for help to come?' Ishaan leaned back in his chair and peered through the curtains. Dark clouds had gathered above the factories across the veld and cracks of lighting broke through their bellies, illuminating their size. 'When clouds come from the mine dumps there's a proper storm on the way. You two should stay the night. We haven't had company in so long.'

'Uncle! Aunty!' Another voice at the gate.

'Clearly you get enough stories from all these visitors,' said the Mortician.

This time it was Saisha's turn to open the kitchen door. 'No. No. Not today. I gave you yesterday,' she began. 'Oh, you don't remember? Yesterday you said you needed taxi money for a job interview. And? You forgot? Please, ne, don't take us for poese in this house.' She slammed the kitchen door.

'Shuu, Ma, what did that lady do to you?'

'No, your father and I don't mind giving, but when you start lying and thinking you can take us for poppetjies, then that's when I draw the line. People abuse kindness.' Saisha sat back down and reached for Mustafa's hand. 'Please stay the night. The retreat centre will be fine for one night, I'm sure.'

'Actually, I think it would be nice if we did,' replied Mustafa, before the Mortician could get a word in.

He should never have come with, thought the Mortician. There were parts of her that Ishaan and Saisha inadvertently exposed, perspectives on her life they supplied without reservation. Although, what was she so afraid of? Mustafa had never given any inkling that he couldn't be trusted or that he couldn't handle her eccentricities. If anything, she was the one taking advantage by not telling him what he needed to know. Maybe this was his way of intuiting just how vulnerable she was under her parents' roof.

'We planned on watching *The Woman* tonight. It was your favourite,' said Saisha, sensing her daughter's hesitation. 'You and Mustafa can sleep in the same room, if you want?'

'Saisha! They aren't together like that,' said Ishaan, apologetically shaking his head at Mustafa.

'It's all right. People often assume …' said Mustafa, not finishing his sentence before taking his bowl to the kitchen.

'Ag, I'm sorry. I can be a little too forward. Of course, you are "business partners" for your retreat centre,' said Saisha, play-slapping herself on the wrist.

'Ma … the kind of work Mustafa and I do, it's intense spiritual work. We help people come to an awakening of their true selves.' The Mortician stopped. She had never gotten this far in explaining her job to them. Was the wine betraying her?

'Awakening?' said Ishaan, his tone akin to someone who recalled the meaning of an archaic word.

'Yes, Da. We help people have the best death they can imagine for themselves. It is not easy work. It requires dedication from both of us.' As she found the words, a surge of gratitude for Mustafa enveloped her. He was in the kitchen, out of sight, but she knew he had heard. Now her parents finally knew exactly what was on offer at the 'retreat centre'. She hadn't planned on doing this, but maybe it was better that they knew.

Saisha's attention shifted to Ishaan. 'See this,' she said, her voice shaky. 'This is *your* doing.' She began clearing the table, gulping down the last dregs of wine in her glass.

'We're honestly doing amazing work,' Mustafa said reassuringly, trying to ease the tension.

'My boy, are you and my daughter registered with the proper councils? What gives you the right to help these people, who are probably not in the right emotional states to be making such decisions in the first place?' asked Saisha, touching his cheek.

'As much as we've grown accustomed to policing what people get to do with the end of their lives, I think we offer a valuable alternative to bleak hospital rooms and hospices,' he replied.

Saisha scraped the leftovers into the dustbin. 'I had my suspicions, Ishaan, didn't I? Now look,' she shouted, to no reply.

The sound of cutlery against their good china filled Ishaan with dread. 'Mustafa, let's go out for a smoke, boy.'

'I don't smoke tobacco.'

'Ja, I know, but come anyway.' Ishaan led Mustafa out by the shoulder onto the back stoep.

The fumes of fermented yeast spewing from nearby factories stained the air, making it sour. Ishaan was hoping the storm would clear it. He drew his pipe from his pocket and stuffed it with tobacco. 'There might be a power outage tonight.' He pointed to the power lines liberally swaying overhead in the street on account of the wind.

'Why are they so loose in the first place? That's a hazard, surely,' said Mustafa.

Ishaan nodded. He peered through the window into the dining room. Saisha would attempt to talk sense into their daughter, but children, as he had come to understand, were born with their own compasses. Though he would never admit it to Saisha, he was proud that some part of his vocation had rubbed off on their daughter. He wanted to hear all about the retreat centre, about the death work she was undertaking, but first she had to face her mother in the same way he had done all those years ago – when his dream of turning corpses into forests had cost them their livelihood.

'It *is* a hazard,' said Ishaan, taking so long to reply that Mustafa had forgotten his comment. 'It does make for one hell of a show, all those sparks. You know, Mustafa, Saisha and I were rebels in our brave days too. When we turned away from Islam and pursued our life together, our families didn't like it at all. Imagine how much we saved on the wedding.' Ishaan coughed, sending a wad of spit into the garden in front of him. 'But when the parlour became a thriving business, ah, then people didn't care who we prayed to. Family members who hadn't spoken to us from the get-go suddenly knew our names. What I'm trying to say is, every new venture gets some push-back, sometimes from those closest to you. You will see, if you two manage to get this retreat centre off the ground nicely, people's minds will be changed. Even Saisha's, though she has always been more of a hard arse.'

Mustafa stood amidst the smoke gushing from Ishaan's pipe. Behind them, the Mortician and Saisha fenced off with one another – bits of retorts and rebuttals escaped onto the stoep and got swept away by the billowing wind.

'In the end, how much can a father be blamed?' asked Ishaan.

Mustafa wasn't sure whether Ishaan wanted him to answer. The tone of the question seemed directed at no one, but he couldn't be sure. Perhaps Ishaan had tortured himself so much with this question that now its asking was pure habit, a spit bubble Ishaan mindlessly toyed with, between puffs of his pipe.

DIANNE

String lights in mason jars above our heads give the feeling we're not ourselves tonight. Not exactly. Maybe it's the marigold glittering in them, looking like trapped fireflies, or the silhouettes pasted on the glass, mixtures of human and animal – a snake with the body of a man, a springbok with the face of a woman, a child with the limbs of a mare. Some combos are unsettling, some aren't so bad, like the old man with praying mantis hands, silhouetted in purple.

The day's been stifling. We're all sweating. Lucas dances in front of me, shining the brightest. I must say, he's got great skin. Me, I can hardly move; checking on Angelique took more energy than I cared to give.

I drink the rest of the cider that Tobias offered me, something with two kissing strawberries on it. It's so good I find myself reaching for another from the cooler-box. There's a point in any party where *having* fun turns into *becoming* fun. And maybe this is *it*: on my fourth cider, swaying to whatever's playing on the speakers. Last time I felt this boozed up was at my matric dance, praying over a toilet bowl and promising the Almighty never to drink again, if He would only take the retch away. (Never to drink, except communion wine on feast days.)

I see that girl now: finally feeling like she belongs in the class of '65, walking out of the bathroom, stares coming at her from the soccer team sitting at their tables near the back of the community hall, all smug. News of the church girl having her first throw-up travelled fast. I didn't care. I had the best marks CJB had seen in a long while. I was going to be in the *Bosmont Daily* and no matter how versed my peers were in brown liquor, there was no taking that from me. So, I smeared on rose lipstick, popped a peppermint and joined Noah at our table.

'How're you gonna ask me to dance and then stay sitting?' says Lucas, balancing between his crutches. He's tried moving around the house without them all day, without much success. Now it seems he has resigned himself to using them. A cool breeze wafts up from the gardens and the mason jars gently clink together. The silhouettes and trapped fireflies flirt with our limbs – snake-on-ankle, firefly-on-cheek, hoof-on-heart.

'Okay, I'm coming.' I say. 'Let me finish this off.' I down my cider just as Angelique steps into view. She avoids me, walks over to the Bluetooth speaker and scrolls through the phone on top of it. Looking at her, I realise I believe too much in the goodness of people. It's not that I don't like her; it's the fact that she's so consumed with herself. There is tenderness in her, but don't ask me how to get to it.

'Play something we can move to,' Lucas says to Angelique.

I join him under the mason jars. Abbas darts under the patio tables, racing over to Tobias, who scratches him behind the ears. Tobias is lekker hot – a whole afternoon of the devil's juice will do that. Angelique puts Michael Jackson on, that song where he rises out of liquid gold to remind the Egyptian queen of the love they used to have.

'What's this called again?' I ask.

'*Remember the Time*,' says Lucas.

He and I dance, not too vigorously. He can't move too fast, and I can just about stand on the spot and deliver myself over to the music. At least the headaches have subsided; in fact, I'm quite at ease now. I hold Lucas by the wrists as he steadies himself with my waist. I haven't been touched this way since Noah asked if I wanted whiskey from the flask his father gave him for his eighteenth. I let him give it to me – tilt his flask, pour its contents into my mouth. Noah was devout, like me; we ran the church's youth group together. I felt safe with him.

'The first time I saw this music video,' I tell Lucas, 'I was sitting in between the legs of a boy named Noah, looking over at another guy named Cedric make Freda Abrahams giggle.'

Lucas nods his head vaguely. The music is loud and I'm not sure he's heard me. It doesn't matter. Saying it out loud sets the memory off: a marionette puppet show in my head.

'What kind of a name is Freda? Sounds like she was destined for the convent,' says Lucas.

He's not wrong, but Freda never joined a convent. I did. And the boy who outshone all boys, even Noah, was Cedric. Cedric in his buttoned-up black-collared shirt and red tie, tickling Freda's earlobes with his pinkie (the finger that always had a gold ring on it).

After the matric dance at the community hall, a bunch of us went back to Cedric's (his parents were out at their own dance). I went along because of Noah, not wanting to embarrass him in front of the other guys. At least that's the reason he gave for insisting I come – *all the guys are bringing dates, don't make me a moegoe.*

I didn't. I wanted to be curled up in bed with warm milk steaming my chin, but Noah needed me. Well, he needed some part of me. So, there we were, boys with their dates in Cedric's lounge, watching Michael Jackson moonwalk for the first time.

Lucas attempts some dramatic moves, copying what he's seen of Michael. It's cute, but Michael is hard to imitate. I'm grateful that my body works well enough to feel the beat and move to it. These moves, Michael's voice ...

It was warm in between Noah's legs, I'll admit. Cosier than my bed. And listening to Cedric hit his Michael-esque falsetto runs from across the lounge, impressing Freda, was a bonus. I'm not sure why I liked Cedric. That version of me lives somewhere else now, caught in her own chorus.

'Haai, man. Let me show you.' Tobias catches a second wind. We stand to the side and he shows us his version of the moonwalk, finishing off with a local jive I don't know the name of.

'Okay, Mr Vosho, I see you,' says Angelique, joining in to show her own Michael moves: the iconic snap-kick-hip-thrust.

Tobias is happy that she's noticed him. He wipes his face and dances around her. Lucas and I watch, unsure of where this is going, hoping he doesn't do something stupid.

'If we were in Michael's video, Angelique would be the Egyptian queen, throwing men to the lions,' says Lucas.

'Or chopping their heads off. Wait, that means Tobias is … Michael?' We look at the unlikely pair, amused. The song has broken something between them; they may not be from the same worlds, but their bodies move in sync. It's uplifting to watch people give their bodies permission. As if Lucas hears what I'm thinking, he takes a seat and refills his drink. He scoops Abbas up onto his lap (though it's clear the dog would rather be on the floor) and turns away from Tobias and Angelique's knee-bending and tiptoeing.

The mason jars have attracted the mosquitoes from the rock pools. They are going to town on my ankles. I take a seat, scratching their bites.

Don't make me a moegoe – Noah slipped his hand up my skirt. I supposed seeing slender, boy-faced Michael slide all space-like across a stage must have aroused something in Noah. Who can tell? After so long a memory gets over-edited: *clammy hand on thigh*. All I have is the journey his hand took underneath a paisley blanket in Cedric's lounge. It was only when I caught his wrist, forcing him to stop, that I noticed it was happening to the other girls too.

Each of us under blankets, beside a boy who took notes from the King of Pop on what impressed queens. Dance moves summoned by dark arts.

'Shuu, that was now lekker. Another one,' says Tobias, half-limping to his seat. He takes off his shoe, exposing a swollen foot. No one sees except me. Everyone in their own way is trying to wring more fun out of this than it really is.

'Geez, what's up with your foot?' says Daniel, walking out in pjs.

Tobias pulls up his sock before Lucas and Angelique can see. 'Nothing.' He gets back up and joins Angelique by the speaker. 'Another one!' he shouts, louder than necessary.

The rest of us look awkwardly at one another, signs of exhaustion showing.

'Here! Pick one,' says Angelique, pouring some wine and offering it to Daniel. A moment of hesitation passes before he takes it. They stand over to the side, away from the rest of us, speaking in private, side-eying Tobias and his drunkenness.

What little space dancing mended between Angelique and Tobias has been broken. Feeling sorry, I offer myself as substitute. 'Play another Michael.' I hold my hands out for Tobias to lift me up on my feet.

'There we go, Di-Di. For an ou vrou you don't disappoint, hey.'

I squeeze his forearms against my sudden vertigo. My nails dig into his skin. Either he can't feel it, or he's felt it all before and doesn't mind. Once the vertigo subsides, our bodies tick-tock, back and forth, his right hip against my left, our backs to Daniel and Angelique.

'It's close to midnight, something evil's lurking in the dark,' raps Tobias, speaking at the melody instead of singing.

Lucas smacks his crutches on the slatted wooden floor in time to the beat.

'Babe, you'll damage your crutches,' says Daniel, to no reply.

It's just Tobias and me dancing hip to hip, turned to the garden, its own kind of nocturnal animal. One that flexes, rubs its back against the sky at this hour, with a voice halfway between an exhale and a purr. (I've been spending too much time with the Mortician.)

'This ou had vision,' says Tobias. 'No one thought to sing such a song, make such a video even.'

His eyes are shut, and I wonder if he's picturing it – the transformation from man to zombie that Michael takes, the moment where decay becomes its own dance, with an eye dangling out of socket. A gothic disco ball.

'This video was unsettling when I first saw it,' I say.

Tobias grunts, not interested. His swaying gets violent and my legs start to ache.

'They will possess you. Unless you change that number on your dial.' He sing-talks louder with each verse.

Daniel and Angelique tell him to keep it down, but he won't listen. I break free from him and head over to sit by Lucas, who's stopped drumming.

'Let him have his moment,' says Lucas, shifting up to make more room for me.

'Clearly.' I place my head on his shoulder; he plays with my hair, wrapping it round his fingers. With liquor interceding the way it does, we get comfortable. More comfortable than I was in Cedric's lounge when his parents returned from their dance. I remember the click of their front door, how it sent every boy to attention: hands above blankets, bum cheeks pasted firmly to the spot. Even the girls, not wanting to let their compatriots know what had happened, tightened around their chests. Hunched over. I never let Noah travel further than my kneecap.

While on our way home from Cedric's, we stopped under a highway overpass, next to a mulberry tree that was growing through the pavement. His car climbed the sidewalk, nicking its undercarriage. He didn't care, he said, all he wanted was 'time alone' with me.

There was no Michael Jackson, no bad falsetto, no parents to distract when he tugged at me, nervous, and a fiery urge broke across his body – pelvis to pectoral.

Yes. Come. Like that.

I was calm in the tumult: the hull of a ship at night.

While forcing our bodies together over the gearbox, the beads of my rosary pressed into my collarbone. Noah tried to climb across, positioning his body against the stereo and incidentally turning it on. Gospel music played through the speakers. It gave him pause, enough for me to voice an excuse. *It's late. Can we do this another time?* He knew I was just being polite. I'd never let myself be *that* alone with him again.

He got out of the car for some air, lit a cigarette. I got out too, keeping the car between us. On the pavement, there were red and black mulberries smeared and crushed into dry paste. I nipped a couple from a low-lying branch to have when I got home.

Tobias leans on the table with the speaker as the song ends. His heaving grows urgent. 'I'm moeg,' he says. He takes another cider from the cooler-box and walks inside.

Watching him, I can't help but picture a young Michael, hugging his girl at the end of *Thriller*. All human, again, with a sly, snake-like twinkle: the trace of zombie.

'You should try it, Angie. Might be good for you,' Lucas and I overhear Daniel say. We start to clear up the patio, all of us doing the bare minimum. We're tired and have had enough of each other for one day.

'What's this?' I venture, butting in.

'Sounds too claustro for me. I don't enjoy spaces like that,' says Angelique.

She goes inside while the rest of us clean up. I have half a mind to call her back and tell her to help us, but, then again, I'm more at ease when she's not around.

'The sense tank. Maybe you'll like it,' says Daniel, coming over with a plastic packet. I chuck some empties in; their tinkling competes with the crickets.

'If you want, I can set it up for you, Dianne' says Lucas. 'It'll help you sleep. It helps me when I can't.'

The boys are using me as a buffer. Maybe they're afraid of what liquor might bring out behind closed doors. 'I'm tired, boys. Let's do it another time?'

Daniel carries on clearing, unperturbed. 'You two go on. I'll finish here.' He waves us off.

'Be quick, the wind is picking up. Don't want you catching a cold,' says Lucas.

Lucas tries to hide his relief as he helps me down the passageway. I start to feel sorry for these two. Though I'll never admit that I don't whole-heartedly agree with their lifestyle, I can't deny their feelings. I want to tell Lucas to go back and talk to Daniel, but would that be condoning too much? By any measure, they've found something I never quite managed to get hold of. I do hope, for their sakes, they try not to break apart in each other, like shrapnel.

I have my arm around Lucas, his fists on the crutches' handles. Our frailty holds.

Power lines rocked in the rain. Each time they touched, sparks erupted with a snap heard throughout the house. The storm was relentless: the wind kept changing the direction of the rain; it fell in thick currents on the windowpanes, changing course in abrupt spurts, traversing the glass in criss-crossing strokes. Water leaked through the older frames, pooled on the sills and found its way into the skirtings, which were already bulging from the damp brought on by previous storms.

Mustafa stood in front of the guest bedroom mirror. It was dark except for the candle he'd lit by the bedside. He heard the instant *pop* of the electric wires incinerating on contact; each time they did, he suspected more houses had their power knocked out, like theirs was now. A mirror was the best place to practise death meditations. He pictured the skull beneath his flesh, opening and closing his mouth. He observed the mechanics of his jaw, not knowing how, exactly, it all fitted together. He pressed his finger-tips to his face and felt around for the spots where his eye-sockets connected to his cheekbones and his cheekbones to his jawline. Who was he without this to hang on? Even bones, compact and resistant, formed part of a matrix very much alive with time.

He turned from the mirror and lay down on the bed.

Lightning struck nearby, momentarily igniting the room in a flash and causing the windows to vibrate. Collected on the top of a small cabinet in the corner was a trove of empty perfume bottles, each fashioned from different cuts of glass: tall and pointy, round and dainty. Whose was it? Saisha seemed the more pragmatic of the two, he thought, a woman with no qualms about getting rid of sentimental excess. It was reasonable to assume that the collection was Ishaan's. He was the type to admire the varieties of distilled, textured scents that could be housed in glass, and how this housing added to the scent's story.

He had not expected Ishaan to tell him so much on the stoep. He'd been content with standing, speechless, beside the man and his smoking pipe. But the Mortician's revelation had stirred something in her father. *The corpse, who is it for, Mustafa?* Ishaan had asked. The question appeared to have an obvious answer. It was for those left behind. Those looking to hold onto any sign of a life lived. Even a mass of pale, limp tissue, voided of its vitality, would do.

What's more honourable than soil, hey? Did she tell you that that was my big crime? Human composting. Can you believe it? Such an innocuous thing. Ishaan hadn't ever conversed with him so openly. The conversation had started to feel like some kind of call-and-response ceremony.

Mustafa opened the blinds and peered into the storm. A figure, draped in a large raincoat, hurried across the lawn towards a shed, moving with a gait similar to Ishaan's. Mustafa watched the figure carry a large container out of the shed and back into the house. Was the water off as well?

Lightning tendrilled through the sky, illuminating pot plants on the shelf above the bed. Venus flytraps and butterworts, he noted, raising a candle to the leaves. The Venus flytraps' mouths stood open, trigger hairs eagerly spread, patient. Other petioles had their traps closed, having already ensnared a fly or bug drawn by the plant's promise of fruit.

He thought of Ms Swanepoel. It was a tradition for the head of the orphanage to gift a Venus flytrap to the boys on their eighteenth birthday. She did so religiously, often instructing them not to feed the plant dead insects or, God forbid, sticks or stones. That, she'd said, didn't help the plant at all because it could tell what was living and what wasn't. When Mustafa had asked how the plant could tell, Swanepoel, sensing young Mustafa's botanical interests, leaped into a description of the plant's stimuli thresholds, and how its fluctuating calcium channels helped it figure out the size, and nutritional value, of its prey, storing that information away for future generations.

That, along with the plant's ability to detect chitin, insect exoskeleton, stunned young Mustafa. Plants were just as alive as animals, and if they could remember past moments of stimulation then they had their own form of memory, right? When young Mustafa posed this question to Ms Swanepoel in her office, she reached for a book from behind her desk and gifted Mustafa a copy of Morton's *Eating the Sun* – saying that, yes, memory is movement, through an instant, a year, a lifetime.

'How much of it is a trap?' he said out loud, speaking to the butterworts, each of their leaves dotted with gnats held in place by gland-secreted mucous. He placed the tip of his pinkie on a leaf, testing the stickiness, then brought his face close to the plant's surface. There, struggling to get free while being digested, was a mosquito, alive for the time being. Nature always found ways to feed on itself. The trap. And the trapped. A game of Lego brought to life.

It's a black hole. The corpse. Nothing returns, Ishaan had exclaimed, emptying the ash from his pipe into the bushes. *I saw soil where they saw holes, Mustafa. And that's how come I've no licence to practise anymore.*

It was not as clear-cut as that, thought Mustafa. The past never was. Before the '90s, death had played its role in maintaining political dominion. Post '94, circumstances surrounding the disappearance and execution of people who'd been opposed to the regime were recorded at the TRC. The commission was an attempt to map the lifespan and reproduction of a flesh-eating disease in the nation's viscera. An especially virulent disease, one that turned the country into a trypophobic's nightmare. Holes, clusters of them everywhere, never quite healing.

On some level, it made sense to Mustafa that the '90s were not ready for Ishaan's human-composting. Maintaining a corpse for its viewing was a gift of dignity given by the living to the dead. Perhaps the process of embalming was a kind of salve, he thought, rubbed in and around the edges of absence. A way to stave off time for the living to run their grief through the dead, returning not fulfilled, but less piercing.

He wondered what was more surreal than seeing the cushioned face of one's mother or father, expressionless, eyes glued shut, jaw fastened. Being an orphan cauterised one against those lofty expectations of belonging and bereaving.

The Mortician had been the second person, after Victor, who had accepted his eccentricities and unusual ideas. That reminded him: he needed an answer from her. There was no better time than tonight.

Mustafa opened the door and walked down the passage.

HAIL STRUCK THE house: hundreds of racketing fists upon the roof. Saisha stood at the basin, listening to the pipes. Nothing. Water's absence drew eerie moans from the faucet, ending in sad spits.

'Saisha! Water's off. I'm leaving a bucket here by the door!' Ishaan shouted from the corridor.

Saisha listened for Ishaan's footsteps and the swishing of water-in-jugs. 'Thank you,' she called, opening the door. He had already turned the corner.

She brought the bucket in, grateful for Ishaan; to some extent they still looked out for one another, though the terms of engagement were different. Ishaan was the caretaker, the person in charge of screwing bulbs in and out of sockets. Her responsibility was to prepare meals, wipe down surfaces, gather dirt and sweep it out. Together they maintained the textures of their separated lives, under one roof. No one knew her mannerisms better than him (and vice versa), so it made sense to live together, shoring up what resources they'd amassed against the trek towards entropy. If anything, she had always believed that owning a funeral parlour made them stiflingly aware of the passage of time and so splitting up completely, at the end of their marriage, seemed an unnecessary acceleration of decay. It would all come to nought, anyway, she admitted, so why not share the burden under the same roof? After all, even the human body at its very limit was a *thing* – something to be made, maintained, recycled. No?

Saisha brought a palmful of water to her face, cupped tiny puddles in either hand and dabbed her armpits, abdomen, and groin in equal measure with soapy water. In an empty bathtub, crouched over a plastic bucket, she brought the black-silver water to her face, remembering her younger self, bathing a wrinkled woman.

Ma, she whispered. Darkness this deep made her mind run wild. She could almost grab the nape of Ma's neck – that spot overgrown with fuzzy grey. Bathing Ma was something only she experienced fully because, by then, her mother had become a husk, her brain having split into its composite parts. She found some comfort in reciting the basic facts of Ma's life back to her, squeezing the sponge into soapy-luxury below Ma's breasts. It was an incantation spoken, patiently, into Ma's ears.

There were moments, she remembered, when the jigsaw pieces of Ma's brain clicked into place, and she recalled some of the details of her life without any prompting. Those moments were few and far between, the surprise of which was enough to signpost to Saisha that Ma had not completely vanished.

Saisha lifted the bucket over her head and emptied it, directing the streams down her arms, wondering if her daughter would look after her the same way she had looked after Ma. If there was any need for memory, she thought, it was to taste experience a second, and third, time. More than that, and you were languishing in fermentation, risking some form of melancholic intoxication.

Saisha got into bed, turned up the radio loaded with batteries, and listened to Etta James belting out *I'd Rather Go Blind.* The argument at the end of dinner would not let her rest.

Have you learned nothing from your father's and my struggles?

Times are different, Mommy. Mustafa and I are pioneers.

Your father thought that too. Rubbish!

You don't understand. We're trying to help people.

Is that all you're doing, huh? Come, tell the truth.

There is some experimentation that everyone is invited to partake in, within reason.

Reason? Reason isn't much to go on.

Saisha grabbed a pillow and placed it between her legs. The doctor said it would help with the hip pain that woke her during the night. In the ceiling above the bed, a desperate scratching was heard. That bloody mouse, impervious to the poison Ishaan had laid out for it. How had it managed to get into the roof? Why had Ishaan not bought the rat poison that she recommended? She wondered about the path the rodent took to get into the ceiling – scurrying through hollow channels in the walls – and marvelled at its ingenuity to seek higher ground in a storm.

Wasn't that what she was trying to do? Convince Babita to change course for a safer shore, one not plagued with ethical issues. Of course, she understood Babita's views because they were her father's. Become intimate with suffering's edge, transgress the limits of sensibility, keep enough of yourself left for the sobering end of a life. Why wouldn't a child so intimate with death from an early age grow up to be that woman who had sat across from her at dinner. Why was she surprised?

Comfort. Care. Someone to reach for ... Saisha feared that Babita's work would draw her far away from them. She would be left without a daughter's tenderness, guiding her to the bathroom. *Most of all I just don't, I just don't wanna be free, no* – Etta James' belting made the room feel empty. The song stood no chance against the thunder.

Below Saisha's bedroom, Ishaan rummaged in the storeroom for more buckets. Water had become an unreliable resource, just like electricity, and so with every storm that came around Ishaan took it upon himself to gather as much rainwater as he could, primarily for the cisterns. Saisha never missed an opportunity to deride his feeble attempts at recycling water; as wise as she liked to act, she was never one for action. Always criticising, but the first to congratulate when things worked out.

Ishaan carried four empty buckets to the front door, two on each arm. It occurred to him that he could have asked Mustafa for help, but he figured the boy had had enough of an old man's ramblings for the night. He had meant what was said about corpses and soil though (something he would never repeat in Saisha's presence).

When it came to the family history, Ishaan was reconciled to being cast as the irresponsible father; the one blamed for the loss of the business. Truth was, he'd never regretted going against funeral parlour regulations, sourcing John and Jane Does and renaming them *Baobab, Knobthorn, Jackalberry*. Morticians should be more than preservers; they should be repurposers – taking what was left and letting it become more than rubbery tissue stuffed in a coffin.

He left the buckets out in the rain. Water poured from the gutters, gushed through drainpipes, flooded the road at the end of the cul-de-sac. The drainage system was blocked. Despite reports to the municipality to unblock it, the garbage in the storm-water drain had not been dislodged. It had formed an impenetrable plug that grew thicker with each season. The real problem, he concluded, was the narrowness of the system as a whole. It was never meant for this amount of waste, and no number of violent storms, charging from the mine dumps, could release it.

The buckets filled up quickly. Ishaan carried them in two by two, dropping one off at each room, ending with his daughter's. He half-expected Saisha to ridicule him, mutter 'silly man' and close the door. But as he turned the corner towards the guest room, he heard a gentle 'thank you'. The tone of her voice made him want to go back and check in on her. From what he'd heard earlier at dinner, Saisha's remonstration had ended in a dramatic walk-off – one to the kitchen, the other to her bedroom. A door slammed. Pots banged. The outage had brought with it a forced silence in the house that wouldn't have been there if there had been electricity.

'I'm leaving a bucket for the toilet in your room. Water's out.' He knocked once at a door plastered with faded stickers of bubble-gum ice-cream cones and headed for his bedroom. His daughter was not alone; Mustafa could be heard muttering in a frantic tone, almost pleading. Ishaan had believed his daughter when she'd explained that there was nothing between her and Mustafa save for their joint venture. He knew her well enough to know that once an idea enraptured her, it took a lot to distract. Mustafa would have to transform into a cold corpse if he were ever to stand a chance. He laughed, replaying the first time he'd noticed her interest in the work.

She was ten. He was working late on account of the Gauteng bombings. Two on consecutive days, one at Germiston taxi rank, the other at Bree. Thirty-one people killed. One of the craziest two days in '94. The bodies that weren't burned beyond recognition had been sent to their mortuary because he was considered one of the best embalmers in the business.

Saisha had decided to sleep at her mother's. It was a nervous time. People held their loved ones close. Law and order felt its most porous, as if at any moment the entire country could be made, dismantled, and remade.

Ishaan undressed at the foot of his bed, piling the wet clothes in a corner. He imagined what Babita had looked like at the top of the stairs leading down to the mortuary. Hair braided, Mickey Mouse slippers on her feet. She couldn't sleep because a stinkwood branch kept banging up against her window. He saw no option but to invite her down into the sterile, white light. She knew what was down there because Saisha had warned her not to go to the basement when Ma and Da were working on bodies.

Come see. Come, he had said. It took some prompting, but once she was on her way down, nothing could stop her. The dead were calling. Babita never flinched at the sight of them: singed, in metal trays, heads rested on blocks of wood. He used to fear his work would traumatise her but, on that night, she showed curiosity. *How do you make them ready, Daddy?*

Ishaan climbed into bed, skin damp. The storm had faded into a listless drizzle against the window. He listened to the water dripping off the roof, thinking how drenched the garden must be. *First, we wash them. Here, while I do it you can massage the feet. See how stiff they are.* He turned onto his right side, coaxing sleep, breathing deeply to slow his thoughts, the same way he had taught her to do. *Good. Now, with the lady's mouth wired shut, you can shape her mouth into anything you want it to be. Happy, angry or sad? Most people prefer the face blank. Like this, see?*

Ishaan cupped his cheek with the palm of his right hand, smelling the plastic from the buckets. Sleep came, unexpectedly, his mind drifted down towards the mortuary, his daughter, her Mickey Mouse slippers, ducking and diving in between blood that ran from the drainage tubes of corpses, across the white embalming tables, towards the blue, bean-shaped buckets where it pooled, thickly.

ISHAAN'S FOOTSTEPS FADED down the passage. 'Thanks, Da!' said the Mortician, gesturing for Mustafa to lower his voice.

Mustafa's face tightened around the ambivalence taking residence on his tongue. He turned away from the Mortician, who sat crossed-legged on the bed, towards the window. The trees in the yard hung heavy with water; one good shake would free them of their weight. With the storm subsiding, the whining of the factories from across the veld grew more distinct. He held her cell phone in his hands. Pressed PLAY. The video showed Jan Prinsloo and the Mortician, in a lounge at the institute. Jan sat blanketed in a wheelchair and the Mortician was feeding him soup.

Be careful of Vicky, said Jan. *She is exactly the kind of child I wanted to raise. A shark.*

I'm sure she'll understand —

No, you don't understand. See, back in 2012, we were having trouble with a couple of major shareholders who wanted a different accounting firm to perform an in-depth audit into our procurement processes. The whole affair would have embarrassed the family. Vicky did what any loving daughter would do. She protected the family.

Jan coughed several times before the video ended.

'What does this have to do with us?' asked Mustafa.

'I did some digging after that conversation. Around the time Jan refers to, things started happening to board members of PSA Holdings. Food poisonings. Car accidents. Sensitive email leaks. The timelines match up.'

'You're saying Vicky intimidated those people. Or worse?'

'If the shoe fits.'

'This isn't much to go on, though.'

'Mustafa, don't be naive. Do you think people like Vicky leave traces?'

'So she's gotten rid of Bonginkosi. Just like that? Is that what you're saying?'

'I'm saying that I'd put nothing past people who're accustomed to getting everything they want.' The Mortician felt surprisingly triumphant.

'Okay. Say I believe you. It doesn't explain this recording.'

'Say what?'

'You heard me. This isn't a cell phone recording.' Mustafa noticed her body shoulders clench; she tried to hide it by pretending to be stretching her neck. 'It looks like CCTV.'

The Mortician shifted to the edge of the bed. Words she had previously dreaded saying seemed to effortlessly bubble up from inside her. 'So what if it is?' She look straight ahead, towards her dresser, unable to meet his gaze.

'I started the institute with you because I believed in what we were doing. There was a need for it. For us –' he stammered. He thought of Frank Ledwaba (Frankie, as he liked to call him), the man who'd taken him in and made him the gardener of the hospice, who later paid for his certificate in palliative care. Frankie, who became a ballast in a world Mustafa didn't ask to be part of. 'And now you're telling me you've been surveilling the property. The residents. Me. People who've placed their trust in you.'

'Don't be so melodramatic.' The Mortician got up and approached him cautiously. She'd never seen him this upset. 'If I hadn't taken the initiative, we'd never have known what Vicky was capable of. Thanks to me, we know our enemy.'

Mustafa opened the window. A rush of air made the hairs on his forearms stand erect. 'You can't justify recording the residents because of that.' He could tell she was trying to get close enough to touch him, like he was a child that needed shielding from the world. Her world. 'Frankie would be disappointed to see what you've made me an accomplice to. Why are you doing this? For what?'

'For our legacy! How can the institute grow, if we don't record and learn from every little triumph and failure? Don't you get that? Everything must be seen, by us. There must be nowhere for our residents to hide. Observed, without the observer effect. Are those not the optimal conditions for experiment? What we are gathering can be passed down. Outlive us. Don't you want that?'

He walked over and sat on the bed. She closed the window behind him, her line of sight resting on the sodden lawn.

'All I wanted was for us to do our work peacefully. Respectfully. Give what we could to the few who came,' he said.

It became clear to her that Mustafa misunderstood, despite her straining towards clarity. 'I want more, Mustafa. I want real change. Broad-stroking change. It must come fast and hard and true. Rev –' She couldn't bring herself to finish the word.

'But at what cost, Babita?'

'At the cost of going beyond good and evil. At the cost of forgoing permission and privacy so that we're able to witness some sliver of the real, the unencumbered, a life given over to itself. Irrevocably.' She was unable to decide whether she was huffing because of the pace of her speech or the knot in her throat.

Mustafa cracked the joints in his neck. Sighed. She had prepared for this, he thought. He couldn't believe that he hadn't noticed her setting up cameras and microphones all over the institute. With the clear intention of not telling him. Was this what trust led to? Too disappointed to speak, he made for the door.

'Where are you going?' She grabbed for his limp arm.

He shook it violently, as if it was useless to him now, until she let go. 'You know all the right things to say.'

'Mustafa … please.'

'Babita. Let me be.'

The bedroom door dragged across the faded carpet, crackling static behind it; the latch punched into the door's socket, final a a full stop.

What had she done? She should never have confessed. It wa inevitable. The moment she'd shown him the video of Jan, he wa on the way to figuring it out. Now that it was out in the open be tween them, she felt exhausted. Frazzled.

She walked over to an old chest – repurposed for Ishaan' screwdrivers, nails and hammers – and jerked a drawer box out o its slide. Reaching into the cavity it left, her fingers found what sh was looking for: a collection of floppy plates. She spread the X-ray out on the bed and searched for a light strong enough to displa their details. A cell phone's torch would suffice, she thought, mov ing the bright, white light from plate to plate. Fractured ribs Popped shoulder. Pins inserted along the spinal column. Bolts in knee. Metal plates for each shin. Broken apart and fused togethe Was there anyone to blame for all this artificial fusing but her ow weight, steadied on a rock loosely held in place by sediment?

Her tumble off the cliff face was effortless. A sneeze of gravit An evanescent collage of colour as her head tilted back – earth an sky exchanging places in her eyes – so much so that she had to shu them – recoil – and prepare to be pierced, battered, cinched o all sides, through vines and branches wielding her body like spu pizza dough. *Plop*.

At the bottom of the cliff, she had briefly glanced up, wit the eye that was still able to see, at the route of the fall right up t its origin. Dust, leaves, flies and, much later, mist, obscuring an attempts at rescue for hours.

How could it have been? That after falling from such a heigh she was floating above her own strewn body? She had never gon into great detail with Mustafa about what those misty waters of hallucination felt like. How could she explain that the pain, cruel as it was, mushroomed her consciousness into bursts of colour. She was not her body. Not the undergrowth entangling it. But the in-between.

All Mustafa knew was that the experience made her seek out hospice work. If the fall hadn't happened, she would have returned to the family's chalet, a young woman unable to bear her parents' imminent divorce. Unable to watch Ishaan wallow in his mistakes and Saisha march, headstrong and callous, into a future none of them wanted.

The Mortician pondered the opaque spaces between her ribs on the X-ray, thinking about Ishaan, and the listless lump-of-a-man he became when they moved into that one-bedroom flat in Fordsburg. They were in the Magaliesberg that weekend because Saisha had wanted a break from the city, speculating that a remote chalet at the foot of a small mountain might ease Ishaan's depression. At the time, she knew her parents were heading for calamity, that the mistakes her father had made were too severe for Saisha to forgive. They were going to get divorced. The trip to the Magaliesberg was Saisha's attempt at salvaging some semblance of a family.

The Mortician placed the X-rays in an old school bag beside the bed and settled herself in for what remained of the night. It was quiet, except for a cat crying in the neighbour's yard. The crying mingled with her memory of Ishaan lecturing on how *an individual is only as good as the ingenuity they offer humanity*. She had to wonder – how did she survive her father in that Fordsburg flat, while Saisha was barely earning enough from her seamstress job. Her mother, practical as ever, knew there was no time to mourn Ishaan's dreams or the possessions they had to sell to pay the costs of the civil lawsuit. There was no time for recuperation, it was either fines or jail time. It was her father's fault, there was no way around that fact. His fault that they leaked money through every orifice. She wouldn't have called herself a mortician if she had not found a way to embalm Ishaan's rot.

Babita got up, fetched the bucket Ishaan had left by the door and filled the toilet cistern. In the pixelated dark, she pushed, pressed, grimaced until her rectum gave way, filling the toilet bowl with scat.

TOBIAS

It's mos easy to get out of bed when you're this thin. If Aunty Charmaine could see me now, she'd fry up vetkoek and sit me down in front of it to vreet. *Tobias, jy's te maer. People will think you're a hobo.* I can see her now even, standing by the fryer, trying not to get hot oil on her apron.

The bedroom tiles help my feet when they get swollen like a pregnant woman's. Some days, the fevers are so kak that I'd rather lie kaalgat on the floor than be anywhere else in the house. The ouens in the tjoekie had a saying – the longer you're inside, the bigger the baby. You would think they were talking about their women waiting for them on the outside, with laaities growing in their bellies. But me, I know it's about being locked up; how it's like carrying your own self. Check here ne, in the tjoekie your body changes and you get cravings for things that you took for granted. Like getting dikgesuip with the bras on the corner, talking all kinds of nonsense.

The difference is that when you're jail-preggies, there's no one that wants to deliver you. Most guys I know land up right back inside after a few months. Going back is the only thing that makes sense, really. There are those lucky fuckers, like me, who get so sick they got no option but to let you out. They don't care if you got somewhere to go.

It burns when I try to pee. Maybe a hot bath with Epsom salts will heal the barbie? Mustafa's left me some salts on the counter with the herbs he told me to take every day. He said the medicines will detox me and keep me stable till I've decided how I want to go.

I run the bath and pour the salts in the water. My hands are red and puffy: good old skrr-o-sies joining with my barbie to make my day. If Stephen was here, he'd give me a Jack and Coke with lots of ice for the hangover. He was lekker agtermekaar that one, saying the cure for any barbie is to go back in time, and the only way to do that is through a bottle of brown. Any kind did the trick.

The thing about being drunk is that it's not a forever thing. You can't be *that* sauced all the bloody time because the body crashes into shit the next day and the next day and the day after that. The harder the dop, the easier you turn into a marshmallow in the morning. My feet itch when I get in the bathwater; it spreads as I lower myself in. I get the tissue oil and pour it on my arms, chest and legs. That helps. Aunty Charmaine would have used coconut oil; she swore by the stuff, used it for everything from her skin to her teeth. I used to rub coconut oil on her feet when she got home from double shifts at the hotel. The more doubles she worked, the larger the very-close veins in her legs got. Check here, the ones on my thighs are just like hers, but these are not ready to burst. When the prison doctors saw it, they told me the mampoer I was making in the cell was killing me. I said, ja, I know, that's liquor's return policy.

The skrr-o-sies is done with me already so there's no point in stopping; I'm the warden of this body and liquor's my key. It opens the cells, lets the inmates play soccer for a few hours a day. Who are my inmates? You really wanna know? Secrets, bra, all the things that have been done to me, and all the things I've done. Without my dop, my dizzy tyd, fuck, I don't know what my inmates would do to me.

The Mortician's muti helps. That week when she took me into the treehouse and played her freaky card game with me, ever since, I've been having the same dream. I'm standing in an empty train station. No trains are running; the train tracks and power lines have been stolen. Nyope addicts do their things in the ticket booths. There's grass growing through the rubble; when you walk you don't know if you're going to cut yourself on broken glass or meet a family of rats. Alles is vrek and vrot.

On a half-broken bench there's this white lady, prim and proper vrou, dressed to the nines, staring at the arrivals board on the wall across from the platform. There's me, being the gentleman I am, introducing myself. I can already see she's a have and I'm a have-not so the instinct is mos to see what I can get from her. This tief turns to me and says, 'You're not real,' then shifts down the bench so I'm not in her way. I'm now befok, so I stand in her way again and she says, 'Do you work for PG Glass? You're not real,' and shifts to the other side of the bench again.

'Excuse me?' I'm now pissed. 'Lady, do you know what I could do to you? Right here, without breaking a sweat. Jou doos.'

The white lady checks me gone; she lights a gwaai, looks me up and down, and says, 'This is *my* dream, and you're ruining it.' Now she's smoking and talking at the same time, so fast it looks like she's breathing smoke out her nose and mouth.

So now I'm thinking: *Tobias, how are you gonna make this bitch believe you're real? This is* your *dream. She's in* your *dream!* That's when I pick up a brick and moer her over the head with it. Except, when I do, she don't move or scream or nothing. She's tjoepstil. Solid. Then blood starts running from my temples and dripping onto my shirt; that's when I think, *shit it, the white woman is right. I'm in her dream. And if I'm in her dream, what does that make me?*

Jussie! I forced myself awake fast from that one, bra. It didn't matter how drunk I got though (because Musty stocks all the lekker stuff), when I went to sleep I was there with that woman, at that train station, and every time I spoke, she'd say, 'You're not real. You're in *my* dream.' I tried breaking the arrivals board, sneaking up and scaring her, even putting on the old Tobias Meyer charm to see if she'd give me some rounds. A vuilpop that one; I couldn't touch her, hit or distract. She looked focused on getting somewhere, anywhere but where she was. All she kept repeating, making me mal, was, 'You're not real. This is *my* dream, you're in my dream, and you're ruining it.'

The Mortician knew what she did that night in the treehouse. It happened more than once too. There were nights I swore I wouldn't go to the treehouse with her and then, all of a sudden, I'd find myself sitting across from her, telling that same story about the tower, the sticks and the heart that wouldn't stop giving.

That lady got muti, jong; it's her fault I can't escape the white woman at the train station! Ey, I never wanna get on the Mortician's bad side; the bitch'll make you go insane. Her games are strong, I'm starting to remember things I thought I forgot, things I promised to never think about. Aunty Charmaine's secrets.

See here, one night after rubbing my aunty's feet, she decides, just for just, that I'm old enough to know the true story about why Mommie Ellen never wanted me. Just so, no warning. At the time, knowing why Ellen left me didn't matter; she was never around so I made sure she was never on my mind. Fair is fair.

Aunty Charmaine didn't care about fair is fair; she was a skinnerbek, through and through. And, yerre, sy het my stukken geslaan that night – saying Mommie Ellen left because I was too brown to be taken to her new family. Simple as that. Like looking up the definition of 'poverty stricken' and finding dark-skinned children with boeps. I had my daddy's skin so passing me off as the child of a white woman was never gonna happen. But Mommie Ellen was *not* a white woman; she was a fair coloured enjoying Whites Only swimming pools, parks, restaurants, daai dinge. In those places she met the man who would give her the key she needed to the life she wanted. Marriage.

I asked Aunty Charmaine why I was so easy to leave behind.

I don't know why I asked (such a dom question). She never gave a proper answer. As old as I am now, I'm only starting to understand what Mommie Ellen did. If I was her son, it then made sense we were tricksters, always hustling for ways to scam the world into giving us what we weren't meant to have. She left me the same way I left my congregation without a pastor. For once, I got to abandon people who depended on me. And it felt kwaai, I won't lie.

Barbies always mess me up this way. The rum from last night on my breath; the steam from the bath fogs up the mirrors; I'm sweating out the dop along with what water is left in my blood. When I'm feeling this way, my ideas are all over the place. I know I'm not the only one that's been through what I've been through. Somewhere in the world, this poes of a life is being replayed in different skins, some better, most of them worse. One way to survive is to imagine that there are thousands like you, in shittier places, running from people in their dreams that tell them they're not real enough to matter to anyone. For me, a good life is when you convince the world to give you things you don't deserve. I told the ouens I was locked up with that they've gotta work smart, not hard. Like me and my ministry: you've gotta be Bushiri enough to slay people in the spirit (and their wallets).

I let the water out and the bath starts to press into my back slowly. Arme Tobias Meyer, alone at the bottom of a bath, stuck with dirt that won't go down the drain. Boeta, let me tell you, I'm ready to die the way Mustafa promised. Let all my inmates out, onetime. Burn the prison down. Let that white jintoe have her dream all to herself – going nowhere, alone.

I get out the bath and don't look in the mirror. Kaalgat, the skrr-o-sies has given me ou vrou tits. If I was in a better mood, I'd jiggle them. But not now.

'Don't you ever stop?' says Angelique, to me. Lucas stands next to her with Abbas in his arms.

I'm scratching in the fridge for what's left of last night's jol. There's only a bottle of red and white wine. 'It is my human right to suip!' Abbas jumps out of Lucas's arms and runs to me. 'This pup, he's a real one, ride and die, ne, Abbas, me and you.' I bend over and make a fist; the dog puts his paw against it.

Angelique and Lucas walk out before I finish. In my day, if a girl was so jas, I'd press her to show who's boss. Aunty Charmaine would have pinched them both by the ears with her purple nails and sentenced them to a month of scrubbing skid marks out her panties.

I go out with my wine to the hammocks near one of the garages. Abbas follows, biting my ankles in a game he's made for himself. I throw a stick down the path so he can stop bothering; he doesn't know what to do with the stick, so he carries on biting.

The garage hasn't been cleaned since my session with the Mortician. There are burns all across the windows. I pick Abbas up to stop him from going near. When I get to the hammocks and open my wine, I look back at the wreck. What the Mortician let loose.

I'd been helping Mustafa treat manure that he planned on mixing in the garden. He wanted to plant Chinese flame trees near the garage and tie hammocks between them. We were busy mixing the manure with wood chips and dried grass when the Mortician came up, saying it was time for another session. By then, she wasn't aggro over what had happened with Daniel; our late-night sessions was making us real chommies. Her muti was helping me sleep, even if it did replace papa waggies with a white lady. I was at least sleeping. Also, every time we were in session she asked about my hand, a real mommie that one.

I followed her through the willows towards the garage. She pressed a remote, opened the door and we went inside. It was chock-a-block with electronics, jewellery, name-brand clothing and a car that I'd never seen on the property before.

'Where'd you get all this stuff from?'

'We have the means to do whatever it takes. And it can all be yours, if you want.' She reached for a dimmer switch and brightened the room. That's when I saw the money, stacked high on a table.

'Hold on. Make me understand.'

'In our sessions you spoke about your aunt's old house in Eldos. I know losing it to the courts hurt you; that much is certain. I see how much that house means to you and, I've been thinking, maybe you want to end things there. So, you have a choice to make today. Take all of this and leave, use the money to buy back the house, if you want. Or stay a little while longer with us. Stay and see how much more you can discover with our help. Use the tools on that wall over there and liberate yourself from these … things.' She pointed to a wall that had a set of baseball bats, a sledgehammer, knives, hammers, a chainsaw and a flame thrower.

I didn't know where to look or what to do.

'Some bodies are primed for rage. And that's not entirely their fault. From the time we're swimming in the womb, our nervous systems are exposed to so many environments, all converging on that most delicate sphere, the amniotic sac. From the very beginning, the unpredictable outside incites, creates, trains, predisposing foetal dreams to chaos. Take up arms against your conditioning. Decimate what the world has said you'll never be.'

The weapons on the wall stood out to me more than the laptops, TVs, watches, clothes and glassware. The Mortician grabbed my wrists and kissed me on the forehead. Stephen entered me, and I remembered his love for machetes. How he'd called me his 'blood bra' after cutting our palms with his pocketknife and pressing them together.

My eyes focused on the money. That was my guarantee that I could leave, go back and buy Aunty's old house.

The Mortician closed the garage door behind her, leaving me alone. The first thing I did was check if the money was real. From the few watermarks, it seemed so. Even the Honda Jazz had that fresh-car smell in its seats. I turned the engine on and saw a full tank on the dashboard. Looking around, there were gold necklaces, platinum rings, diamond-studded grills, racks of luxury suits, Rolex spelled correctly, Gucci with two 'c's, Samsung, Apple, HP gadgets on the floor near the car's boot. I could sell all this for profit.

Why didn't I? Bra, this was a test. Like, if I gave in to what she expected, then I'd be missing out on what else she had to show me. In our late-night sessions, she promised to make me understand my life, saying I would never have to be scared of papa waggies, not even of the skrr-o-sies fucking me up. She said I'd be able to drink myself to death, with no guilt, if that's what I wanted and *still* land up in a heaven that I chose. I decided, then and there, if this was a test to see if I was worthy of learning her muti, then I'd take only the money and car, and get rid of the other stuff.

So I went to work on the flat-screen TVs, smashing them with the sledgehammer. And, before I knew it, I'd gone to town on the laptops as well – bits of glass, wires, microchips everywhere. I got the biggest hammer and laid into the speakers, one by one. All that breaking was nogals kwaai.

In my head, Stephen called me a *poephol*; he was always better at moving radios and sound systems. He'd have lifted those Apple speakers just for himself. If we had carried on with the break-ins, we would never have been rich because Stephen never wanted to sell the expensive shit. We were too greedy for good times to be rich, I guess. Sneakers, jewellery, cell phones: anything we could pocket, that was the motto. It didn't matter how much we stole, sold, how much we kept for ourselves or gave to our cherries, there was always room for more.

I picked out a baseball bat and started on the Rolexes lined up in rows on a table. Their tiny hands bent under my blows. By the time I shifted to the cabinet of figurines, I knew I was rêrig enjoying this. Elephants, wolves, giraffes, all crystal – my baseball bat murdered each. When I got tired, I threw some against the door.

I thought of that time when we poisoned those two German Shepherds from the house in Parktown with the big pool and lapa. Remember how powerful it felt to step over those dogs knowing *we did that*, Stephen?

When I was done with the figurines, I sat on the car's boot, swak, heart beating in my temples. I hadn't used the flame thrower or chainsaw yet. I was saving them. When I lifted the flame thrower off the wall, it didn't take long for it to chow the clothing. Buttons, zippers, silks, cottons, all melted; women's and men's, all sizes and colours, turned to ash, baba. The fumes got so bad I had to open the garage door for air.

I walked out of my wreck. The Mortician sat nearby, cutting her toenails, not interested in me. I went back in and moved the money onto the grass so the smoke couldn't damage it. Then I reversed the car out.

'You're taking the car then?' she said, still cutting her toenails.

'You gonna stop me?'

'No. Like I said. You have to want to be here.'

What she said made me think about the guys in the tronk: the ones who got out but chose to go back because they knew life was simpler when someone else told you what to eat, when to sleep, how much time in the sun you can get. It's mos maklik to be pressed under the bosses' rules. There was enough money on the grass for me to make up my own rules, for once.

Stephen, my broer, you would have told me to leave, I know.

But I'm an old comrade with very few festives left in me. Even with the car and money, it don't really feel like winning. All of it can be lost in one game of dice.

'How did it feel to do all that?' she had asked.

'Like getting my Sunday-seven-colour meal.'

'Come again?'

'It felt good.' I went for the baseball bat and bliksemmed the car's windscreen. It felt good. Then I pulled out a butterfly knife and dug into the car's leather seats. It felt good. When I picked up the chainsaw, the Mortician came to me and put a mask on my face.

'Protect your eyes,' she said, stepping back.

I chopped up the car's doors, shouting, 'I'm keeping the Mandelas.'

Another half-hour had to pass until I gave up and put the chainsaw down. I knew that if Stephen were there, he wouldn't understand. He would have called me a poes for believing in the Mortician.

'This is a big step,' she said, helping me onto the grass. 'Those things you've disposed of, they're the scabs on your life. And that, that wreckage is the wound.'

The Mortician looked from me to the gemors, comparing us.

'Take this. You'll feel better.' She handed me a dropper with a white liquid in it. I squeezed some below my tongue, letting it sit for a few seconds before swallowing.

She left me on the grass and walked back to the house. From where I sat, I saw Mustafa planting his Chinese trees. I was papnat. The smell of burning gave me a headache.

As soon as the Mortician's medicine set in, the smell had disappeared. All inmates were silent. I felt light.

THE HAMMOCK'S SWINGING wakes me. White wine has spilled on the grass; the other bottle of red is empty on my chest. Groggy. I don't lus to get up. I try and go back to sleep. It's better this way. If I'm awake I'll want more dop.

The Chinese flame trees are growing fast. The one above me has a lot of seeds already. Mustafa said he liked them because they're shaped like lanterns; when the wind blows it sounds like tiny choir shakers. That brother is a little touched in the head, but ek kan nie kla nie. So am I.

'Tobias, wake the hell up!' Dianne yells like a crazy bat, shaking the hammock.

I feel funny. 'What? Why?' My eyes sort out the shapes standing over me. There are six people. I fall off the hammock when I realise what's going on.

'You two! Take him inside.'

Mustafa and Dianne pull me up. Four skelms wave guns in our faces.

HAIL FROM THE storm had cracked several windows in the lounge. Saisha was out in the garden digging holes for sparrows that had, the evening before, been battered to death by abnormally large hailstones.

'Ma, we're getting ready to leave,' said the Mortician, leaning on the gate that separated the garden from the driveway.

'Okay,' said Saisha, her back to the gate. 'Drive safe.' She nudged the birds' limp bodies into holes, covering them.

Her mother would need time, thought the Mortician. She clearly was unable to separate what she was doing from what Ishaan had done. If only Saisha knew how careful they were being; how selective they were. Ishaan, when his composting was in full swing, had become lax about the illegality of his project. The Mortician had always been bewildered by the twists of fate that led to the collapse of the family business.

Ishaan had reached an agreement with a buddy he used to study with, Henry O'Sullivan. After they graduated in mortuary science, Henry went to work at Joburg General and always kept in touch with Ishaan. They were good friends, and what made them so congenial was the fact that they agreed on most things, from politics, to relationships, to which rugby team to support. What they agreed on most of all, and what cemented their friendship, was that both men yearned to be a part of a revolution in the death industry. One that was kinder to the environment, that integrated the natural processes of human decay into the immanent cycles of regeneration with which the planet sustained itself. Whose idea was it? To this day, Ishaan will tell you the idea belonged to them both. The Mortician knew better, however, believing her father t be the most lateral thinker of the two, the kind of man whose ideals were held so passionately that they had an infectious quality to them.

The plan was simple. Henry would keep aside John and Jane Does who hadn't been identified or claimed by family members. He was meant to be highly selective, not taking more than what was needed, making sure those taken were absolute nobodies. What they didn't expect was that even nobodies could stoke public outrage, especially when strewn across the M1 highway on one of the hottest days of the year.

The Mortician recalled the sight of Ishaan, pacing in front of the television on a Saturday morning, yelling to Henry on the phone, who was at Joburg Gen's morgue. It was a pure accident, the convergence of a poorly maintained bakkie and an over-zealous driver. Who could have anticipated the bakkie's tyres bursting on that road, in broad daylight, amidst cars zooming past at high speeds? The driver had lost control, the bakkie had overturned, John and Jane Does went fly-flopping all mannequin-like across the tar.

The media descended like vulture bees, demanding answers from the Department of Health. It made matters worse that none of the corpses were white, but that was just the beginning. Soon, families came forward to identify the bodies: anonymous faces were made famous through national media coverage. When the long-lost families of some of the deceased came forward the Department of Health sat up, wanting it to seem as if they had been acting all along. Investigations into the driver led back to Henry, who in turn gave Ishaan up, without much provocation. When it emerged that the morticians' smuggling of unclaimed human remains was orchestrated in order to develop, and patent, methods for human composting – with the vision of turning cemeteries into forests – Ishaan and Henry were under no illusion that they were as good as dead in their industry.

Henry O'Sullivan, whose life revolved around his job, self-immolated with a can of petrol in his driveway weeks before he was set to appear in the civil case instituted by the families of the deceased. Ishaan couldn't bear to escape the way his good friend had, and he didn't have the stomach to put his family through that kind of hell. So, there he stood: the face of a corpse-smuggling cabal – a face that would later be sold as a plastic Halloween mask for years to come. The media had dubbed him the 'Monstrous Mortician', relishing in the sinewy details that emerged from his testimony. During litigation, the presiding judge ruled against an in-camera hearing, claiming it to be of 'public interest' for the case to be covered in the media.

Every step of their enterprise was excruciatingly exposed on television. Henry would harvest the bodies, picking ones that seemed least likely to be claimed. Homeless. Vagrants. Illegal migrants. He'd pack them in separate black bags, paying a different driver each time to take them to Ishaan's parlour. The drivers were always paid enough not to ask any questions about the cargo. Ishaan, in turn, never asked for more bodies than he could handle. All he needed was a handful, which usually lasted about a year at a time. Ishaan confessed to believing that the long periods between harvests was his foolproof way of not getting caught.

It wasn't easy for the Mortician to see her father appear on television for the better part of two years. That, in addition to being named 'Morticia' – a name that didn't even make sense to her – by former high school classmates, made it extremely hard to socialise, especially since all her former friends had distanced themselves. During those years, she learned that nicknames didn't have to subscribe to any kind of sense; they just had to be memorable. And this one was hard to shake, so much so that she decided to embrace it. Around the same time, she went about removing herself from all protean, social media platforms: Mxit, 2Go and MySpace.

The only person willing to associate with her was Gabriella. She was with her cousin – spinning Gaby's BMW in an abandoned parking lot – when details surrounding Ishaan's methods broke on the news. He'd done it in the new Wendy house that the family recently built in the back yard, a space fitted with high-powered air-conditioning units and freezers, like the ones he used in the mortuary. It had taken Ishaan several attempts to figure out the ratio of ingredients and the correct method of storage, monitoring and mixing that would make the best quality soil. At the start, some of the corpses turned to mush in the barrels. Which was not conducive. Then came the bodies that had been infected with highly resistant pathogens; bodies that, through trial, error and research, Ishaan realised were too toxic for the surrounding organic material. Finally, after burying several failed batches of compost behind the Wendy house (late at night, while wife and daughter slept) he came upon the method that was to be patented.

He had appreciated that, unlike embalming, composting depended on trusting the microbes to do their work. Each human body had its own microbiome and this needed to be stoked to do its work undisturbed. He decided to only bother the bodies every thirty or so days after storage, remixing the straw, alfalfa and wood chips in the containers that housed the corpses. Depending on the progress, he might add more organic material (leaves, dried grasses, fruit peels). After some time, as flesh gave way to bone, he would pick out any dental fillings, prosthetics or implants. Then, for another fifteen or so days, the remains were sealed in rectangular iron vessels which he'd made specially for them. These vessels were kept cool and sterile on the outside, while the shed that they were stored in was regularly cleaned with hospital-grade bleach and disinfectant.

Ishaan testified that Saisha had no knowledge of his activities, a claim contested in litigation. The Mortician never believed this. She remembered seeing Saisha take Ishaan meals in the Wendy house, although she never stayed long. When it came for the Mortician to testify, she didn't divulge this to the judge, convincing herself that Saisha had no idea. At the end of the testimony and evidence, the judge's verdict was unequivocal. Ishaan would have to pay damages to the families of the deceased. The judge also stated that though the individuals had already passed away – and would have been buried in anonymous graves were it not for the scandal – it nevertheless did not excuse the lack of human dignity Ishaan had shown to the deceased.

The Mortician remembered that day, driving home from the civil case, the car so quiet that the noise of the city felt muted against the windscreen, unable to rouse anything but forlorn stares. She sat on the back seat, repeating the amount of money the judge had ordered her father to pay. What were they going to do, she had asked, to which Saisha replied: *change how we live*.

MUSTAFA WAS ALREADY sitting in the car when the Mortician said goodbye to her father. The electricity was still off, and Ishaan was boiling water and milk for his coffee and oats on a portable gas stove.

'I'll invite you around to see what we've been working on,' she said, hugging him.

'I'd love that. I'll see if I can get your mother to come too.'

'She won't. She doesn't understand like we do.'

'She used to. Be careful, okay?'

'We have each other's back, Mustafa and I. When the time comes, people will know what you sacrificed, Da, what we gave up. They'll understand.' She kissed him on his stubbly cheek and got in the car.

Ishaan watched them drive off. Yes, he was proud of her courage to carry on his project in her own way, but there was something tainted about it all. Later, over a cup of coffee, he tried to figure out where the feeling originated.

He had become an awful man after the civil case, the target of consistent scorn and ridicule from industry peers and family members, all the while being forced to sell their assets and pay for the lawsuit. In those dark days, in that one-bedroom flat in Fordsburg, he embodied a self-pitying tyrant – barking orders at Saisha, refusing to get another job, mumbling resentments and admonitions about the lack of vision in the country during the meagre meals they shared.

After several months of treating his family like used furniture, his anger accumulated into a bolus of grief, lodged at the back of his throat. A desolate solitude possessed him; he barely spoke in full sentences anymore. The most he accomplished was getting out of bed and standing in front of the fridge, whose staple contents were small rings of cheap white cheese and liver polony.

He never blamed Saisha for wanting a divorce. A part of him was relieved when she finally came out with it, not because he didn't love her. Because he loathed himself. The divorce was the plank that his self-pity made him walk. What came after would no longer hold him to any of the ideals he once held. He was committed to handing his life over to an ocean of regret, from which only drowning could save. Then came the trip to the Magaliesberg, a trip Saisha had wanted to break the news of the divorce to Babita.

Saisha walked into the lounge and sat across from Ishaan. 'How are you feeling?' she asked.

'I can't help but wish I was different when things went to shit. If I hadn't –'

'There's no point in "what ifs", Ishaan. You were who you were.'

'If I *was* different, maybe she wouldn't be on this vendetta to –'

'She's doing this for herself. Not for you or me.'

'You can't believe that. After all we've been through.'

'Are you proud that she's following you?'

'She is following us. And yes. That doesn't mean I don't think about how it could be different. How she could be different.' Ishaan got up and headed for the kitchen, dumping milk from his bowl in a pot plant.

Saisha got out her yoga mat from the storeroom and laid it out in the lounge. Electrical outages were the best periods to get in some yoga because all the electronic sound of the house disappeared. She entered the child's pose, her hips sluggishly opening with each breath she drew into the deepest parts of her lungs. Though she had intended on an active asana, the child's pose felt too good. She stayed like that for a good fifteen minutes. Her shoulder girdle, rib-cage and tailbone bloomed with blood, pumped into the crannies constricted from a night of restless sleep. She farted – a rumbling, drawn-out, sulphurous emission that relieved her.

Lying there her mind meandered into memories of the Magaliesberg trip. Their plan had been to tell Babita about the divorce and how things were going to change. Ishaan would have to find his own place, and Babita could go visit every weekend. But Babita wasn't ready to give up on her father; she pleaded for Saisha to stay, for Ishaan to get his act together, for all of them. She held steadfast to the idea they could still be a family. It was possible, she had said, they weren't trying hard enough.

That was the problem, thought Saisha. Babita was the type of person who'd cut the corners of a puzzle piece just so it could fit where it didn't belong. She would peel the coloured squares off a Rubik's Cube and re-stick them to prove she was the smarter one. This was not a game. Saisha knew back then that if she did not get out of her marriage, she would go down with Ishaan, wallowing in the past, like him, till the past suffocated her. That was when Babita took off, angrier than she'd ever been, into the late afternoon sun, claiming she needed space. They let her hike the mountain, alone.

When Babita hadn't returned by late evening, they spoke to the owners of the lodge, telling them what had happened. A search party was scrambled with what little staff lived there. The hiking trail was dense and unforgiving; nature clamoured at anyone daring to make a way through, leaving bruises and insect bites on everyone. The search party, each armed with a torch, whistle and baton, could not penetrate the underbrush or frighten the tiny, glistening eyes that occasionally got caught in the crosshairs of a flashlight.

A man named Abbas, a Moroccan immigrant, spotted the soles of Babita's sneakers sticking out of a nest of broken branches. It took everyone, a group of ten, to pick apart the nest and carefully retrieve her mangled body, rolling her onto a stretcher. Wrung out of shape.

Saisha rolled her yoga mat up and placed it in the corner. The electricity was back, and all the electronics (TVs, stereo, refrigerator) sang with newfound life. She made herself some tea and sat on the back stoep. The yard was still drenched; it gave the illusion of liquid sunlight dripping off everything. A breeze blew across her face, titillating her nostrils with a musk of damp earth. She recalled Babita in the hospital after the first surgery, stable, but not out of the woods, face so swollen that only the bottom part of it looked vaguely familiar. Ishaan basically lived in the hospital's waiting area for days, consistently trying to weasel packs of Simba chips and Cadbury chocolate out of the vending machines. When she eventually found him, he had bags of chips and slabs of chocolate on the seat beside him. None of them open.

'Mexican Chilli,' he'd said, breaking down for the first time since the civil case. She helped him open a packet, pulling his head to her shoulder. She thought long and hard about what Ishaan had done for them: taking the full blame for the composting. Of course she had known what was going on in the Wendy house; she was the one who ordered the equipment. They were equal visionaries in their exploits, but she was the pragmatic manager. It was Ishaan's job to experiment and report back. She understood her duties just as Ishaan understood, without them needing to discuss it, that he would take the fall.

Sitting beside Ishaan, with Babita fighting for her life on an operating table somewhere in the hospital, an unlikely idea settled into her. She *would* divorce Ishaan, but that didn't mean they couldn't be there for one another – walking into, and through, old age together. After all, before they were lovers and business partners, they were friends, compatriots, who believed that what counted was connection. The authentic kind, forged not with fire but breath.

'Askies, aunty, sorry to bother you, but can you help me?' A teenage boy of about sixteen stood at the fence.

The boy's voice drew her back to the tea and dripping sunlight. She listened to his request one more time – eyes downcast, fingers pulling at his hair – then she made him a deal. If he swept up the garbage that the rain had funnelled from the surrounding streets into their cul-de-sac, she would give him the money he was asking for. The boy dutifully agreed and, with a yard broom supplied by Saisha, swept the street, stuffing the trash into black plastic bags. Saisha watched from the stoep, listening to his distinct, melodic whistling. It was upbeat.

MUSTAFA DECIDED ON the long route home. They needed to talk before they arrived back at the institute. The Mortician scrolled through the radio stations, unsatisfied, before switching the radio off. He refused to make eye contact or say a word until she made the first move. He was done with being the one always begging her to come out of herself and share. For once, she would have to do the work, put their teachings into practice, forget her pride.

He drove through Braamfontein, wanting the sudden jolts of the city to remind him of the many lives so different from his, all with their own survival methods. Sometimes, people subsisted through escape and sometimes escape propelled them off balconies and roofs.

He had followed the trend of jumpers in Joburg central with a macabre interest ever since Swanepoel revealed to him that, as a baby, he'd been found near a dumpster, outside Ponte City Tower. In the year he turned eighteen, Swanepoel had shown him a newspaper clipping of the day. Mustafa had made page four. A dumpster baby, one of the many featured in newspapers that eventually landed up at the bottom of recycling bins, shredded, fading into blotches of black on white.

Ever since Swanepoel's revelation, he felt drawn to the building, not least for the number of people said to have leapt from its many storeys, the most recent being the case of a fifty-five-year-old man who'd leapt off the thirty-third storey. There were days, in his early twenties, when he thought his birth mother was one of those jumpers. It was Victor who had asked him why he assumed his mother to be a jumper. She could as easily have become one of Ponte's landlords. Destined to battle unruly tenants for the rest of her life.

Mustafa decided that Victor's story was better and left it at that.

A hollow, cylindrical tower of Babel, he thought, as they drove past. He'd visited Ponte years ago; stood on the ground floor, at its centre, looking up into a sky cordoned off by unforgiving concrete. It was like standing at the bottom of a giant well – although here was no water, just garbage thrown out of windows, disintegrating on the way down. At ground zero, in the five-storey-high rubbish heap, the hot odour of decomposing cats made it difficult to breathe.

He thought about how the combined efforts of the jumpers had succeeded in renaming the tower 'suicide central', about the countless articles written on the landmark: the fascination with its life mirroring the lives of the people that moved through it. Perhaps the building had been nicknamed 'heaven on earth' by its architect not because of its 360-degree luxury views of the city, previously reserved for whites, but because its design lifted its inhabitants up to dizzying heights. Any person standing at the top might very well hear a small voice inside their head, curious to see what it would be like on the way down. Curious to know if heaven lay a ledge away.

'Are you ready to talk?' said the Mortician, staring straight ahead at the intersection besieged with traffic.

'I've *been* ready.'

'If I'm going to explain, I'm going to need an explanation too.'

'What do you mean? Explanation for what?'

'You and Lucas.'

He looked from the robots to her and back again in a quick swerve. From the look on her face, it was clear that her surveillance had picked up his transgression. The car behind hooted for them to move as the lights turned green. He returned his attention to driving, speechless.

'Well?' Her tone bordered on triumphant.

'You're comparing me having a little fling with you violating people's rights to privacy? Is that your move?'

'All I am saying is that we've both taken liberties, some more disastrous, admittedly. At least mine has given us insight into what Vicky is capable of. What has yours done?'

Her voice had that familiar shade of certainty in it, drawing lines in the sand between them. As they drove past several student accommodations, Mustafa said a prayer for the students who had jumped from the buildings, and the crowds of people gathered on the pavement below who'd egged them on. Those students needed certainty too, needed lines in the sand drawn around them, for protection.

'At least I'm able to say sorry. That I let myself be taken by Lucas when I shouldn't have.'

'And what about Daniel? What happens to his progress once he learns this?'

Mustafa punched the accelerator, raced ahead of the traffic, and took a dramatic right turn into a deserted side street. He parked the car. 'What do you think our residents will do once they find out what you've been doing?' he shouted, banging his hands against the steering-wheel. 'When you convinced me to sell Frank's hospice, you promised we'd do things together. You knew what Frank meant to me! That man made me and now I see. I should have never left the hospice for your dreams.'

She was running out of sand to draw in. As she saw it, there were two options: either allow Mustafa's emotions to carry him away or forget her lines in the sand, jump in those murky waters, and go swimming after him. 'All right. I understand what you've given up. I do. It's just …We can't fail, Mustafa. I've seen what it does. With my parents. And it's not like I've always been this secretive. Remember when I first started my sessions with Prinsloo. Remember those recordings?'

'Everyone in the room consented to those. I reviewed them myself.'

'Yes, and when residents started coming, I thought some form of insurance would have to be taken to keep them quiet. What if they left and chose to expose us, for whatever reason? Or if we wanted to look back over the treatments to see where we could do better? To learn. That's all I want to be Mustafa. *Better*. I have no desire to compile or publish anything. To risk exposure. My father made that mistake. I won't.'

The pair sat, eyes finding corners of the roof and floor where they could be alone with their feelings. Mustafa pulled on the hairs of his forearm. A beggar came up to the driver's window and asked for some change. He waved the man away, without looking into his eyes, as was the habit. 'What does this mean for us, then?'

'We hold space for our secrets. What else can we do?'

His gaze was drawn into the street ahead, unwilling to focus on anything in particular.

'I need you. I can't do this without you. You *do* know that, right?'

She had finally admitted it. Then why didn't he feel any better?

'From now on, there's nothing between us. Everything's out in the open. No hiding.'

He heard the fissure in her voice, the swell of fear thickening her vocal cords. 'Okay.'

'Okay?'

'Let's go home.' He put the car into gear and turned the radio on.

THEY STOPPED AT an intersection a few blocks from the house, music swirling between them. The Mortician watched an all-girl troupe stand in front of the paused traffic and flip one another into the air, all singing a song she hadn't heard before. When the girls landed back on the ground, they spun on their feet and lunged forward into a synchronised handstand.

Some of the cars waiting at the intersection cheered and hooted; other drivers held out their hands, dropping coins and notes as the troupe came round. In the car beside theirs, a man held onto one of the performers, refusing to let go, sizing the girl up. She couldn't have been older than fourteen. The Mortician rolled down her window, reached over to the steering-wheel and hooted.

Seeing the Mortician, the man let the girl go, driving off as soon as the traffic light turned green. The girl caught a glimpse of the Mortician as Mustafa pulled off. Before she could acknowledge what had happened, her troupe pulled her onto the pavement; in their hands were fisted rainbows of banknotes, speckled with coins.

They pulled into the driveway a lot later than they expected. Mustafa wanted to check in on how the marijuana and mushrooms were doing; the Mortician felt like she needed a walking meditation through the hedge. Mustafa peered into the rear-view mirror. Four armed men stood behind the car.

Neither of them had been paying attention.

LUCAS

When I said goodnight to Dianne last night, she asked me to join her in the stained-glass room this morning.

I haven't prayed in years, but she insisted. Getting up before the sunrise was reminiscent of the early morning workouts I used to do before track practice. So here I am, unable to turn down a dying woman's request. The room is quiet. Dianne and I sit together, eyes closed, her lips moving too fast for me to catch the words. One thing is for sure, the lady has got faith.

After the accident, everyone said I'd been blessed. I hated that. Who gets blessed by a busload of death, as one of the survivors? What kind of Creator gives that story to one of their creations? Daniel says that 'a subsystem cannot understand the macrosystem that it's a part of'. He says it's like asking the keratin in your hair to understand the plasticity of your brain. I get where he's coming from. I mean, here's Dianne, believing that what she's saying goes somewhere special. And maybe it does. Maybe prayer doesn't go up, or out, but in. I don't know.

The room slowly gets brighter. The paintings on the wall are clearer. She has set up a vase in front of us, placing incense sticks in white sand. I help her light them.

'I've brought some of the fulgurite from the garden,' she says. 'Pretty, isn't it?' She hands me some and I follow her lead. We balance them, one on top of the other, in front of the incense.

'This is harder than it looks,' I say. The fulgurite feels like coral reef. The other day, Mustafa gave me a pure white specimen just like it. *Extreme energy changes the memory of a thing, at the smallest scale*, he said. I hid the fulgurite between my clothes, in my suitcase, where Daniel wouldn't find it.

'There, that's how you do it.' Dianne shows me the cairn she has made. She balances my pile in seconds, claps her hands together when she's done.

'Thank you for inviting me. You know I did pray before my races, but it was more of a habit, like checking if my shoes were tied. I stopped after the bus accident.'

'Why?'

We help each other up. 'I guess it felt weird to say things like "serving God, praising His one and holy name", all that stuff. It was like speaking to a lover who always acted like they knew better. You never know if today God's gonna throw some goodness your way or leave you out in the cold,' I say, as we walk to the door.

'Are you sure you're speaking about God?'

I don't answer. As we enter the passage that leads to the kitchen, the smell of baked bread makes us hungry.

'Smells like olive bread,' she says, sniffing.

'Only Mustafa would be up this early.' I say, chirpier than I mean to. When we enter the kitchen we find Daniel, bent over the oven, adjusting its temperature.

THERE IS A swing under the avocado tree, just outside the meditation room, that I like to sit at. The avos are ripe. Tear-shaped fruit hang ready for the picking. I gather as many as I can into a shopping bag and place them next to me on the swing before I make the call. 'Unjani, Ma?'

'Ngiyaphila mntwana wam'. uRight?'

'Yebo, Ma.'

'The monkeys must be having a wedding. Elzane! Come say hi. It's Lucas.'

263

Elzane isn't Ma's husband; they've been living together since I was a teen. I exchange pleasantries with him whenever I'm there, but we have not ever shared a meaningful conversation. He's all right, as far as men who live with single mothers go. We say our rigid hellos before he disappears into the background.

'I just wanted to check up on you, Ma,' I say. 'We're at a retreat centre like I told you.'

'Oh, okay. Why now again?'

I can tell she's getting ready to go somewhere because Boom Shaka's blasting in the background.

'Relationship things. And just general wellbeing. A little escape. We both needed it.'

'You must see to those relationship things now before they become marriage things and divorce things.'

'Hawu, you think we are ready for marriage?'

'Angazi. I also thought your father and I would work through our things, kodwa starting a family is complicated. Don't rush yourself, boy. And uDaniel une nhliziyo enhle. His heart is in the right place. And fighting can be good for love sometimes. Have you been teaching Daniel to speak isiZulu?'

'I'm trying. He says he wants to learn, just that life is hectic for him right now.'

'Oh, okay.'

There's silence on the line. I want to ask about her marriage to uBaba, but then Elzane shouts, 'We're going to be late, babes,' and I know our time is up.

'Ngiyaxolisa, boy, we're going to Midrand. Elzane's friends, they're opening a new restaurant. We're already late. Call me again tomorrow? All right?'

'Kulungile, Ma. Have a good time. Love you.' The phone cuts.

I begin to think I'll never get to ask her about what I found the last time I was there by Elzane's house. Daniel and I had been dating for a year. I was looking for old baby photos – some of my cuter days – to surprise him with when I found a water-damaged notebook with *Victoria* written across it. Ma's diary: the one she kept when she was pregnant with me.

Finding it was wild because somehow, in all my efforts at building myself up – coming out to family, running track, loving Daniel – I had somehow forgotten that the woman who had raised me for eighteen years had had a full life, before me.

I took photos of the passages that struck me most. I'm not proud of doing that, but at the time I thought that as much as it was Ma's history, it was also kinda mine.

… Doctor Mahlangu says the baby isn't the right way round …

I was a breech baby, my head not facing her mucous plug, like I was meant to. My parents tried all the tricks to force me the right way round. *Inversions* was the word she used. She wrote about performing handstands underwater in our swimming pool, and, at night when she went to sleep, she propped her pelvis up under two continental pillows. All of these midwife methods failed. Then Dr Mahlangu tried an external inversion.

… the doctor worked the baby so much today, trying to get the child to face down. It didn't work. Mahlangu says there is too much amniotic fluid in my womb …

I was stuck skew for nine months. The doctor advised that a Caesarean would be best, something Ma made clear she didn't want.

… to give birth naturally. At home. Pushing my son into his father's arms …

Her insistence on natural birth, despite the risk, was something uBaba admired, though she still sensed his hesitancy. When I was born, the labour left severe scarring in the lining of her uterus. A few days after my birthday, the 30th of April 1998, she wrote, *Lucas has closed me up for good.*

I wasn't sure how to feel.

That day by Elzane's I'd taken the diary with me, knowing Ma wouldn't realise. For the next week and a half, I read sections from it every night. It was like finding a wormhole into the past. Of all the reasons I was given over the years about why they got divorced, what was in that diary made the most sense.

… Solomon keeps his distance. He's not present. We talk about groceries, birthdays, the things Lucas needs, but never about us …

I never thought Ma could write such vulnerable stuff: describing the *degrees of ambiguity* between uBaba and her and how, when I turned two, the coldness in their marriage was *a grotesque feature of what love could become.* Whoever said having a baby brings a couple closer was missing something.

As hard as it was to read all that, I continued. The hardest part was reading about their sex life.

… His hands find me late at night. Half asleep, an instinct wakes us. Sex is simple. No need to talk. No need to cuddle afterwards. Different to making love.

I had hoped that whatever she saw in Elzane, that at least he loved her, in and out the bedroom. Near the end of the diary, I read the part where Ma met Elzane. They were colleagues in the bank, often crossing paths during lunch. I think Elzane reminded her that life was still worth the laugh. That it was okay to act foolish, adolescent even.

… When I'm with El I don't feel like a mother or a wife or even a woman. I'm a goddess. I don't know how he does it. I must come clean to Solomon.

She did. Ma wrote about it. As much as it seemed to inflict pain on him, she said telling my father finally broke through the distance between them.

… He is still passionately in hurt with me. I see that now …

It's funny. When I first read that, I thought it was a stupid phrase because things with Daniel were so effortless. I get it now.

I couldn't read any more of it. Not because I didn't want to. The back pages had water damage: all that was vaguely legible were the headings – session one, two, three, right up to five. I assumed it referred to their couples counselling sessions. At least Ma had mentioned that in conversation.

I check the time. Shit, I was supposed to open the greenhouse an hour ago. I text Daniel and ask if he can pick up the bag of avos on the bench before I make my slow way round the house.

I can't wait to be done with these crutches.

THE TIMER GOES off when I enter the greenhouse. I open the shutters to let the sun in, winding back the slats so the air from outside can filter through. The greenhouse is set in quadrants, the first two divided between male and female sativas, the second two for indicas. Mustafa showed me how to tell the difference: sativas grow tall and spindly, mini-Christmas trees, and indicas shape into short, fleshy bushes. They usually flower quicker than sativas, so I gotta keep a closer eye on those ones; already most have an amber hue to their leaves, as if they have been storing the long summer. Take a closer look and you'll see hints of violet running through the flowers while others will have a dirty-burgundy tinge.

The plants respond to the morning light; by eleven, their limp leaves stiffen in the direction of the sun. I check the moisture sensors in each quadrant, make sure the soil isn't too wet or dry, and then record the readings in Mustafa's notebook. Once that's done small fans, stationed on ladders that tower over each quadrant, are turned on to simulate airflow. It can get real stuffy, with the plants' pungent terpenes and the humidity from the evaporated water locked in here all night.

Mustafa says terpenes are their way of communicating their

readiness to us. When I started tending to them, the assault of their stench gave me a headache. It was overpowering, like the groins of furry animals on heat. I've grown to appreciate the scents though, learning that some of them give off damp, citrus aromas, and others pepper the air in spicy, woody notes. I never thought I would be the type to speak this way, but watching how Mustafa is with them, noticing how they react to the slightest change in the environment, how can I not?

The timer is set to go off after eight hours. I give the place a good cleaning, collecting fallen leaves, sweeping up any dust that's found its way in. I also keep an eye out for rats or pesty little beetles that try to eat the buds. Mustafa said that is how the plant was first discovered in Asia. People observed how pigeons who ate from the leaves and buds behaved strangely. So much so that humans had to try it for themselves.

Later, when the timer goes off, I'll have to close the blinds and turn the UVB grow lights on. This bathes the plants in alien-purple light. Apparently, it ramps up oil production, similar to how sun exposure increases melanin in us, I guess.

When the grow lights go on, Mustafa will come to check on the day's progress. *It's all about environment. Being a gardener teaches you that. A tweak here, a little discipline there, and a whole chain of reactions is kickstarted*, he had said when he first explained the need for this daily ritual to me. I told him then that the beeper reminded me of a fitness test my track coach made us do once a month, in off season.

'Ask any athlete about the beep test and they'll tell you about the pain it puts you through.'

We were alone, walking the rows of purple-lighted plants, pruning leaves, pouring shots of fertiliser solution into drip buckets. The beep test was a simple exercise, I explained. You run between two stations that are at least ten or so metres apart; the air of the exercise is to make it to the other station before the next beep sounds. As you progress through the levels, the intervals between beeps get shorter and shorter until you're full-out sprinting to make it to the other station before the next beep. It was one way of knowing just how much stamina you had as an athlete and, if you had little, how strong your will was compared to the hurt ricocheting between your legs and chest.

'I had a reputation for always being the last one standing,' I said.

'Does that mean you had stamina or will?'

'At the start of the season, it was definitely willpower that got me through. Once you have that history of winning, you'll do anything to keep it.'

'I've always admired that about the best athletes in the world.'

'What's that?'

'Their ability to go into uncharted territory within themselves. Even when the body is begging for reprieve, even when all the sirens are going off, they trust that one voice, which is not really a voice. No, it's a force. Something *vital*, that wants … expansion. Something that's prepared to leave the body utterly spent, so that it can be salved into vigour.' He tipped a plant towards his nose, inhaled, then glanced at me like he wanted to sniff me too.

Should I have resisted? Walked out of the greenhouse, then and there? I could have. Mustafa would have understood – would have understood and not treated me any different. I wanted him to treat me differently, though. To treat me like the indicas and sativas he cultivated so methodically, taking pleasure in their resin, the stickiness of their vegetal needs.

The plants watched as we took each other to the floor. In the purple glow, the shadowy corners of the greenhouse turned in upon us. The plants' serrated leaves waved nonchalantly above, fans blowing cool air around. Everything shaded purple, it seemed like Mustafa wasn't kissing *my* body. I closed my eyes and imagined him suckling on the tip of some secret teat, deep inside me, a place that hadn't been squeezed for so long. Not once did he make me conscious of my injuries or the fact that I couldn't move as much as I wanted. Not once was there pity in the way he handled me. He was unapologetically rough, in a way that made me feel myself from somewhere other than my own two hands.

WHEN THE MORNING ritual is done, I go and sit in the sauna. I've gotten better at sitting here for fifteen, sometimes thirty minutes. I wonder if it's me or if my body has gotten better at it. Is there a difference? When I'm in the sauna, I imagine my own drip lines running through me, my skin hanging just a little looser than before.

When I come back to the greenhouse later in the day, I turn down the water pressure for the indica quadrant. It's harvesting time. Mustafa hasn't returned with the Mortician yet, so I guess it's up to me.

The trick is to inspect the trichomes. Are they clear, cloudy or amber? I hear him in my head, more here than anywhere else. I take a jeweller's loupe and inspect the trichomes. The indicas' leaves and flowers are covered in curvy crystals; if you look closely, they are like hundreds of domed towers pushing through the plants' skin. Mustafa says he wants a mixture of trichomes: some cloudy, some amber. The more amber, the 'heavier' the high. I use a jeweller's loupe to get a good judge of the trichomes' colour, then snip the ripe buds, placing them in separate glass jars.

When I'm a quarter of the way through I hear yelling, glass breaking, and loud banging coming from the main house. I stop and close the shutters, then seal the jars I've filled with buds and hide them under a loose concrete slab in the floor, Mustafa's words echoing: *plants with these powers don't discriminate. They attract all kinds. That's how they survive. That's how they're demonised.*

With the room dark, I grab my crutches and move towards the door. Peeking through, I spot the Mortician and Mustafa; they're back, but they've left the car doors wide open. Something's not right. From the greenhouse, there's a clear view of the gym's wide windows and, through it, a passage leading to Dianne's and Angelique's bedroom.

I watch for movement. Nothing.

Again, a bang. And the Mortician yelling: 'Take what you want and get out!' Tobias and Dianne are shoved by two men with guns; they're shuffled down the corridor and into a reading room.

Where's Daniel? When I last saw him, he was in the kitchen with Angelique. On the back patio two men lead Mustafa and Daniel out. They tie them to the railing's wooden beams with their backs to the greenhouses. One of the men waves his gun in Daniel's face while the other looks towards the greenhouses.

I duck back inside, shining the torch of my phone around to see if there's anything I can use as a weapon. There's a set of small spades on a nearby table (I don't know what kind of damage those will do). I peek out again; the men have gone back inside. I can't call the cops, not with what's in here; I'll have to get close enough to untie them. We'd have a better shot then, but wait – where the hell is Angelique?

'Fuck you!'

A distraught voice screams from a second-floor bedroom. It sounds like it's coming from Daniel's and my bedroom. I gotta do something. Now!

I creep out of the greenhouse, sticking the crutches into the lawn like two vaulting poles, and lunge forward as fast as I can carry myself without hurting my wrists. The crutches make a strained, clicking sound quiet enough to go unnoticed, I hope.

I'm halfway to the back patio when I hear footsteps coming

back down the passage. Changing direction, I vault towards the gym's windowsill, my right leg doing most of the leaping and balancing. My left hip flexor aches (I can't give it the comfort it needs right now). The ache spreads across my pelvis as I pick up speed towards the windowsill. The burning in my right calf rips right up into my lower back.

When I hear the footsteps hit the wood of the patio, I let my crutches go, sliding arms first across a patch of grass, hitting my left side hard up against the brick of the house. Before I think about my bruises I scramble back for the crutches and pull them towards me.

'Hey! Is there another someone here?' says a man, his voice like a lawnmower.

'No, there's no one,' says Mustafa.

'If we find someone else, it's your gat, ja,' another man says.

I can't do this. I can't take them all on.

Another one of Angelique's high-pitched screams rings over head. Tobias is the one I need to get to; he has probably been situations like this more than any of us.

'What's over there in those buildings?' the Lawnmower Man asks.

'Just gardening equipment and compost,' says Mustafa.

'Colonel, go check that there.'

Soon as Colonel gets on the lawn all he'll have to do is turn around and he'll see me. I have no choice but to make a move. Putting my crutches on the windowsill, I try and find a good enough grip to pull myself up through the window. My legs can do some the work, but most of it has to come from these arms.

I paste my body flat against the brick, feeling for the best grip before pulling myself inches off the ground. My right leg finds some leverage in the grooves between bricks. There's no time for a delicate landing; I'll have to jerk up and over at full speed.

When I do, the brick drags across my belly, cutting me. I haul myself over and into the gym. My tracksuit pants are torn down the side. There's blood dripping off the hem. The scraped skin on my stomach burns. I'm in. Safe. For now.

No one seems to have heard my landing. I look over the windowsill and see Colonel walking towards the greenhouses. Shit. Once he opens the marijuana greenhouse all of their attention will go there. That could work to my advantage, actually.

'General! Come see here! Hulle het dwelms!' shouts Colonel.

'It's medicine,' says Mustafa.

He's really in no position to argue, I think.

'Drugs is medicine, domkop,' says the man they call General, the Lawnmower Man.

A loud thud smacks the air.

'Mustafa! Mustafa, are you okay?' Daniel shouts.

They've hurt Mustafa. I draw myself up on the crutches and head for the door. When I look through there's another man with a balaclava on; he's going through one of the cabinets in the passage. As I lean against the doorframe, it creaks, and balaclava man turns. He's coming down the passage towards me.

I stand back against the wall, hiding behind the door, when my foot touches a set of dumbbells. There's no time, the man is outside, about to walk in. Bending awkwardly, I reach for a dumbbell and swing it across my chest. It hits Balaclava Man in the head.

He falls. Blood leaks through the floorboards.

I don't know where the patio men are; my best guess is the greenhouse, sizing up the plants. I have to find Tobias.

I reach for Balaclava Man's weapon: I've only ever held a gun once in my life, and I was nine then, I don't remember much. This revolver has a silencer, something I've only seen in movies. *Point and fire, Lucas, like a video game.* I have to make it across the corridor to the reading room.

Carefully, I make my way there, gun in one hand, a single crutch supporting the left side of my body. My right leg has gotta come through for me here.

'Hey, solider! Soldier! We hit gold here, my boy. Soldier!' Lawnmower Man shouts from the greenhouse.

I think he's calling Balaclava Man, I'm not sure. They'll be coming back to the house. I gotta move.

At the reading room I open the door to find Dianne and Tobias tied up and gagged, back-to-back. They're stunned to see me. Tobias gestures to untie him first. Once untied, he helps me loosen Dianne's restraints.

'What do we do now?' she says.

'Angelique,' says Tobias, looking at the gun in my hand. 'Give that here. I'll get her.'

'There's two by the greenhouse. Are there more?' I ask.

'I counted four,' says Dianne.

'I knocked one out in the gym. The other two will be coming back soon.'

'The dagga will distract them. One's with Angelique and the Mortician.' Tobias checks how many rounds are in the gun, then he runs out of the room.

'Is he just going to leave us here?' asks Dianne, tugging at my sleeve.

'It's okay. Listen, I can't move as fast as you. You're gonna have to run to the kitchen and get the sharpest knives you can find.'

'Okay,' she says, unsure.

I hold her face between my hands. 'You can do this. Be quick.'

We stagger to the door, my right leg failing to hold my weight anymore. I get down on my knees and hold myself up, my arms rigid against the wall. 'Go. Now!'

Dianne exits, turning left towards the kitchen. There's a major cramp coming on in my right hamstring. I try to stretch out, but it's too late, the cramp builds, swelling to an excruciating ball in the centre of my thigh. The muscle throbs; I bite into my forearm. The cramp has me. I'm alone, just like on the day of the accident. Me and the pain again, fighting for a way out.

'Lucas, Lucas, are you all right?' Dianne kneels over and rubs my right leg. Her hands are cold.

'Not so hard,' I say breathily, feeling like I'm about to pass out.

'Stay awake!' She slaps me a few times, waving the knives from the kitchen in my face, one for each of us. 'I can't do this alone.'

I press her hands into my thigh; the cold helps the muscle a bit. 'Help me up,' I say.

She places a crutch underneath my left side and supports me from the right.

'Soldier! Where are you?' It's Colonel, coming down the corridor.

We both keep quiet.

'Oh fuck,' says Colonel, before several gunshots snip through the air. A body falls to the ground.

There are minutes of silence before Tobias cocks his head around the door, telling us to come out. When we do, the man called Colonel is lying outside the gym, bullet holes in his neck.

Angelique and the Mortician stand behind Tobias. Both bruised. Angelique has a busted lip. She rushes forward and takes Colonel's gun. Her shirt has been ripped and the bra strap is broken.

'What're you doing, girl?' says Tobias, going after her.

Angelique sprints across the patio, down onto the lawn, towards the greenhouses. We follow them out. The Mortician gets to Daniel first; she goes to work untying him while Dianne and I untie Mustafa.

We all watch Tobias catch up to Angelique on the lawn. She tries to resist, wrangling against him, but Tobias holds her tight.

'Tobias!' yells the Mortician, pointing.

Lawnmower Man comes around the corner of the mushroom greenhouse. But before he can get a clean shot off, Abbas goes for his heels from behind.

'Abbas, no!' Tobias aims and fires, hitting the walls of the greenhouse before the gun stops. He's out of bullets.

Lawnmower Man takes aim at the dog and fires, twice. Abbas lets go. Before the man can turn on us, Angelique points and shoots, missing several times, but hitting the man once in the arm. He doubles back behind the greenhouses and darts through the bushes, towards the driveway.

'He's getting away!' shouts Mustafa, turning to the Mortician. They lock eyes and then, out of nowhere, the Mortician hurdles over the patio and sprints after Lawnmower Man.

What is she going to do?

'Are you okay?' asks Mustafa. He begins separating the torn fabric of my tracksuit from the gashes on my stomach and legs.

I touch his forehead, bruised purple from the butt of a gun.

'Eina!' He holds my hand, keeping it there.

The Mortician comes back round the bend. 'The fucker is gone. Damnit!' she says.

Tobias is over by the greenhouses, kneeling over Abbas; Angelique is in the middle of the lawn, frozen. Dianne has her rosary in her hands, whispering 'thank yous' into her beads. Mustafa gets up and walks over to the Mortician to hold her. I turn to Daniel, who is sitting, silent, against the railing. I reach for him, avoiding eye contact. He shifts away. When our eyes eventually meet, it's as if we cannot remember where we began or how we got here.

He has no cigarettes to offer. I have no races left to win.

The sky was mottled blue and grey when rain fell over Northcliff. Like children tossing tinsel on a Christmas tree, delicate and haphazard, fine strings of water broke upon entry, raising the soil's mineral damp. Through canopies and across the bodies of garden gnomes, drizzle eked its way into mulch made from peels, hair, pits, teeth, dead flowers and bone.

Mustafa and the Mortician had worked tirelessly preparing the men for planting. The residents with stoic stomachs were encouraged to either take part in the process or observe. Everyone, except Dianne, gave in to curiosity.

Angelique got involved with the man who had left bite marks on her right breast. Mustafa had helped her put the body in a large wooden barrel, similar to the kind whiskey is fermented in. The Mortician made sure the man fitted inside the barrel by breaking his joints with a hammer; she showed Angelique how to mix the corpse in with wood chips and bucketsful of pampas and buffalo grass. The recipe for composting was tried and true, she'd explained. He would be nothing but black gold, soon.

It took roughly four weeks for the man to decompose into compost. Amongst layers of mulch, moth larva bred by Mustafa gorged themselves on the organic waste. The lava slowly ate themselves to bursting – rupturing their flesh several times over, until they moulted into fat, furry caterpillars too big for their bodies. Plump and ripe, they burrowed into the soil, burying themselves for pupation.

When it came to Balaclava Man, the one who succumbed to his head injuries, Lucas opted to observe. Though he helped Mustafa assemble the pods beforehand – egg-shaped lattices of biodegradable wire packed with moist earth – he couldn't bring himself to fold the man, like a wombed baby, inside it. Everyone, except Daniel and Dianne, was present for Balaclava Man's planting. It was agreed that Lucas be the one to pick where the pod was planted and what tree would grow on top of it. He decided to plant the man behind the sauna, and on the spot where the pod was buried, a young, pale grey camphor bush took root.

In the surrounding soil of the camphor bush, trails of cater-pillars did not make it to their underground cocoons. Crossing paths with maggots, wriggling in between the manure Mustafa and Tobias had sown, the caterpillars had mistaken the maggots for food and subsequently ingested them. But maggots are a tenacious horde; they guzzled their hosts' gooey viscera without hesitation. As they matured inside the dying caterpillars, they ate their way out, emerging as pupae eager to fly.

The man who Tobias had killed in the corridor was burned, piece by piece, in a large firepit that Mustafa and the Mortician had built just after Prinsloo had handed over the property. The firepit stood in a secluded grotto near the west wall. The area was overgrown with prickly leafed Mexican poppies, which deterred anyone from wandering there. After some work clearing the space, the Mortician and Mustafa made it mandatory for everyone to at-tend the cremation of the man referred to by his fellow burglars as Colonel. The burning lasted three nights. At each cremation, Mustafa brought out a piece of the man, shrouded in white linen, and called on a resident to help him place it in the fire. This was done while the Mortician played her most-prized flute, made from the wood of the mopani tree.

Dianne refused to get involved. Not only was her condition deteriorating faster than either Mustafa or the Mortician expected – leaving her with less vigour as the days wore on – but she also insisted that, if her soul was to be saved, she would have to fast and pray for her salvation. No one questioned her reticence; after the violence they had survived, a traumatic kinship seemed to solder them together. By any measure, it was becoming clear that Dianne would be the first to depart, whether she left through the front gate or was carried out. Her imminent passing seemed to grant Dianne a translucent, almost ghostly aura in the way she languored about the property – sitting, as she often did, in the solitary nooks in and around the house.

On the first night of the burning, Mustafa and Tobias each placed a thigh in the firepit, stepping back as the flames rose to eye level. The next night, Lucas and Angelique heaved the man's torso into the hearth. On the third night, Daniel was charged with dropping the head into the blaze. Each time the fire crackled, spat and billowed smoke, temporarily blackening the sky about their heads. By the third night, a luminous moon won out against the soot.

It was on this night that moth pupae surfaced from being wound, tightly, in the earth's embrace. To get to this point, the pupae had had to dissolve their innards with digestive enzymes, awakening specialised cells that reorganised their interstitial miasma into wings, eyes, abdomens.

Rebuilding, the pupae swished and gurgled in subterranean cocoons, spinning time into tissue. When their disparate parts (head, thorax, tail) locked into each other, they rose. First in dribs and drabs, then in a flurry, flapping their leathery wings against the starry sky, in search of mates. Mouthless, male moths had only the source of their former fattened selves to sustain them as their antennae tracked the pheromones emitted by females residing on the ridges of tree bark.

Gathered around the firepit on that third night, everyone was enthralled by the swarm about them – tiny wings crinkling air into fine static. The moths circled the firepit, and the tower of smoke above it, before dissipating.

Dianne was so taken by the spectacle that her rosary fell from her hands.

ON THE DAY after the bodies had been seen to, Dianne woke before dawn to a persistent fly buzzing at her shoulder. She reached for a can of Doom on the bedstand and doused the fly in insecticide.

The maroon-eyed insect rubbed its limbs together, grooming itself, when the air around it became diffused with a harsh mist which prevented the fly from relaxing its muscles. In seconds, the fly seizured, its lungs unable to expand.

Dianne watched the insect squirm with sleepy interest. Something about its fruitless efforts, how it hummed in random spurts, made her wonder if it was more merciful to just put the creature out of its misery, once and for all. Picking up her slipper, she bent over and was about to flatten the fly, when, suddenly, it stopped jittering. Lifeless, the insect stirred a strange sense of admiration for the metallic-green pest. It was the bane of domesticity, a harbinger of disease and yet, in the dim light, the fly's characteristic exterior was quite (dare she think it?) beautiful.

It had been a long month and a half for Dianne. Every day messages from Karabo, Tshidi and Lavinia were relayed to her through Mustafa, who she'd charged with keeping her cell phone (fewer reminders of what she was missing, she figured). Since the burglary, Dianne had taken to fasting on weekdays, drinking only water and tepid coffee throughout the day, breaking fast only after sunset, the way Muslims did during Ramadan. The burglary had renewed her faith in a way she hadn't expected – how had they survived if not for the grace of God? So, in addition to fasting, she renewed her practice of saying a decade of the rosary at the top of every hour – sometimes for the souls of the men buried on the property, other times for the sisters she'd left back in Nkandla.

If only she had had this kind of dedication in the convent, she thought, maybe she would have stayed on to become a nun and not leave to join Hopeful Horizon.

Perhaps she was simply too young for the convent then? The nunnery's insular lifestyle – always aching for a kingdom to come – had, over time, grated against her, like dusty clothes that made one itch.

Pray. Clean. Cook. Garden. Clean. Eat. Read. Pray. Sleep. Repeat.

The grooves of that world were stifling. No wonder some of the older nuns took a vow of silence; the goal, it seemed to her at the time, was to eradicate all personality from their lives, until they no longer had the need for speech. She had admired the older nuns' resolve. It was a steadfast focus she assumed one only got in old age.

No, if she had stayed in the convent – retreating not only from the world but herself as well – she wouldn't have discovered the velour love possible between women, for women, by women. Perhaps places like convents were only necessary when the end was near, and one had nothing but soft, drawn-out days.

Surviving the burglary in the frantic fashion in which they had, reaffirmed that God was sparing her so that she would have enough time to prepare her spirit for its reception into the heaven of the Holy Trinity. Every day following the burglary, she reassured herself of this.

Sometimes, during her daily prayers, people from her past sprang up in her mind's eye, underground springs shattering the earth she knelt on. Like Naledi – the girl who had created an aura of menace around them both when they were children. Dianne tried tracing back to the origin of how it all unfolded, but all that surfaced, initially, was an image. *Naledi holding a ripe plum to her face.*

It was breaktime. She had been sitting beneath the statue of Mary, not bothered by the boys playing soccer on the field, or the girls clapping over by the benches.

'Want one?' Naledi, so sure of herself, made the question sound like an instruction. Dianne took the plum and offered the girl in braids a choice of her animal biscuits. Naledi picked the elephant one, popping the entire animal into her mouth.

The two girls ate in silence, considering one another with brief, furtive glances: Dianne sitting sideways on the steps of the alcove with Naledi leaning on the wall made of slatted stone. When Dianne asked if she wanted to sit, Naledi obliged, turning her attention to the statue of Mary poised with arms open on the top step. Spotting her interest, she told Naledi all about Mary, the way a spokesperson might conduct a press briefing for a celebrity.

It was the way Naledi keenly listened that made Dianne happy to share the alcove. On rainy days during breaktime, the girls sheltered close, delighting in fingering their names on the moss that grew at Mary's feet. On sunny days they would press their cheeks to the statue's bosom to feel the clamminess of the stone. At the end of the month, when they both got tuckshop money, they would host tea-parties in the alcove, with juice boxes, rolls of multicoloured liquorice and doughnuts dusted with cinnamon sugar. At the start of their tea-parties, they made sure to address Mary as the VIP. But, over time, the girls became so involved in their shared bounty that the placid statue shrouded in white and blue, watching from the top step, was forgotten in favour of the giddy rush that refined sugar gave.

How had Naledi spun the rumour so effortlessly, thought Dianne. How had she convinced the kids in their grade that she had the untrammelled favour of the Mother of God? It was too ridiculous a story to tell anyone.

Dianne got dressed, her restlessness disturbing Angelique,

who was moodier than usual these days. Wasn't she happy that the man who'd assaulted her was now literal dirt?

She walked across the room and readjusted Angelique's blanket up over her shoulders. Angelique pulled it over her head. Then she left for the kitchen, ignoring the hunger in her stomach (she would give anything for a liquorice roll or cinnamon doughnut).

Walking down the passageway, she heard arguing coming from the central atrium. The Mortician and Mustafa had not been in accord since the burglary; the tension between them had spilled over into the institute, making it uncomfortable to be around them at the same time. Though the surrounding gardens remained docile as a wristwatch in a drawer, Dianne sensed a tug-of-war afoot. The institute no longer felt like the place where one's spirit might find repose. The air felt charged with desperation.

In the kitchen she poured herself a glass of water, squeezing the pulp of a lemon into it. *If you mess with Dianne, Mary's gonna get* you – Naledi's voice, always so direct, protecting Dianne from the kids who teased her about her friendship with a statue.

Naledi had such a biting nature at times; it often cut through any teasing that came their way. She could picture Naledi flicking her braids across her face – cackling – telling the other kids that Mary was coming for anyone who made fun of Dianne. She hadn't thought Naledi was serious about any of it. Not until Naledi asked her to pray for something 'bad' to happen on the playground. Something that would scare the name-callers.

She was reluctant at first. But as soon as she tried it, young Dianne felt a strange pleasure, born from the jolt of possibility. Soon, it was all that she asked for. It got to a stage where she didn't even have to ask out loud for it; all she had to do was look into Mary's unyielding eyes and she knew. Mary was listening. Mary was going to make something bad happen.

It took Mary listening to the same prayer for the better half of a year for something to happen. Kagiso – a boy who had named them 'the virgin disciples' – slipped off the jungle gym's pole, falling face first on the concrete. Tiny quartz in the concrete cut across his face, roughened his knees and streaked dirty bloodstreams down his shins. She never admitted it, but her delight grew in tandem with Kagiso's hysterics.

Like cotton candy whizzed around a stick, Naledi had gathered coincidence and intention into a haze of speculation that made them infamous. And she handed that cotton candy to all the kids willing to believe in the so-called 'virgin disciples'. The children ate of the sugary speculation. To their hearts' content.

Sitting at the counter, Dianne wondered what had become of her manipulative friend. Probably went into politics, she thought. A string of birdcalls lilted through the open window, brass polishers on metal. She closed her eyes and listened to their melodies. Was she going mad? Were the birds saying her name?

Diiiann. Anndii. Diaan.

She rubbed her forehead and drank more lemon water. The longer she focused her gaze, the fuzzier it got, no matter how much she blinked. She didn't need a doctor to tell her what was going on.

'Everything okay?' asked Mustafa, opening a breakfast bar from the pantry. He wasn't his usual self. He seemed distracted. Every day since the cremation, he'd been shovelling ash from the firepit into a wheelbarrow and emptying it along the hedges.

'Mustafa, I've given it some thought, and, I think I'm ready to leave.'

'Leave?'

'It's time.'

'But, our work, *your* work. Are you sure you feel … ready?'

The question seemed directed at someone who hadn't just

witnessed the transformation of three men. She wasn't completely ready. Did that matter? Things happened whether one was ready for them or not. She didn't know how to put what she was feeling into succinct statements – memories, bits of conversation, feelings, it was all so sticky. If she thought too long about it, she was certain molasses would drip from her ears.

Mustafa sat across from her, the thought of shovelling ash pushed aside. 'If this is what you want, and you're sure. I'll speak to the Mortician.'

'Thank you.'

'There's one thing I want to show you before you leave. Something I've curated for you.'

'Oh? Can you show me sometime today?'

'Later, say tomorrow night? We can arrange your trip back afterwards.'

Mustafa left the kitchen. On his way to the firepit he passed a mound of freshly dug earth – on top of it lay an endless knot, carved out of cherry wood, that had been pressed into the mound to flatten it. He hadn't expected Tobias to take Abbas's death to heart the way he had, insisting that the dog be buried, not cremated 'like a piece of rubbish'.

They had buried Abbas in the morning, after breakfast. Mustafa and Tobias took turns deepening the hole, dug near the flowerbed that Abbas loved to pee on. They dug a lot deeper than needed, but Mustafa didn't voice this. The act of shovelling appeared to put Tobias in a genial, trance-like state.

He handed Abbas's limp body over to Tobias, who cradled the dog, making soft clicking sounds with his tongue. A lullaby of gibberish. Then Tobias crouched into the hole and placed Abbas in the centre. For a dog with such fight, who never liked to be held for longer than a minute or two, there was no protest – just two wilted buds for eyes, four sets of cracked onyx for paws, and fur that ran black, on account of the dried blood.

When Tobias hauled himself out, the guinea fowl were circling the hole and, a few metres away on a low-hanging branch, the cat from next door groomed itself, watching. Mustafa knew how animals cautiously stalked dead things. Abbas himself had done something similar when he'd found a dead rat near the mushroom greenhouse a few months back. On that occasion, like this one, Mustafa believed he was witnessing the tacit comprehension that some irreversible line of flight had been taken, leaving putrescence in its wake.

Now Abbas was that putrescence. A crumbling absence.

Finally reaching the firepit, Mustafa began the morning's work of shovelling ash into the wheelbarrow, thinking it must have been the Mortician who had placed the endless knot on the dog's grave. Typical, he thought. All symbol. No action.

THE MORTICIAN REACHED under the bed for the X-rays. Her body limber, full of vitality, the morning's fight with Mustafa filling her with adrenalin.

She needed release, but her mind couldn't free itself of its incredulity. Mustafa *actually* believed the burglary was not a planned assault orchestrated by Vicky Prinsloo. How could it have been a random twist of fate? That, out of all of the lavish houses in Lancaster, the institute was the one targeted. It was so blatantly clear that Vicky had the capacity to order a hit and make it seem like a burglary. Vicky was a shameless woman who had made frequent, public claims that the Prinsloo wealth had not been derived from the nation's unequal and traumatic past.

Apartheid – the tenebrous bogeyman that most people agreed had had a fruitful life for a select few and, post '94, had gone about disguising its fruits in plain sight. This bogeyman had transformed itself with such equanimity over the last decade that today the majority were left wondering where all the fruit had gone, while leaders seemed stumped as to how to take it all back without snapping the stems from which the fruits grew.

She remembered when Jan Prinsloo had first come to them, right after Frank Ledwaba had passed and left the hospice to Mustafa. Prinsloo came seeking palliative care for his pancreatic cancer, explaining that Frank Ledwaba's mother had been their housekeeper and that he was so 'taken' with the way Frank had lifted his family out of poverty with the success of the hospice.

Both the Mortician and Mustafa believed the old man sitting across from them in Mustafa's office to be borderline delusional. Could he honestly think that running a hospice earned enough money to lift entire generations out of servitude? Mustafa was on the verge of turning Prinsloo away, but the Mortician calmed him down enough to see the opportunity in front of them, begging to be cared for.

Over the course of an hour, it became apparent that Prinsloo's cancer was belligerent. The man spoke so feebly that one had to lean in close to hear him. The disease was hollowing him from the inside out. This drew their pity.

Prinsloo paid the hospice for in-house care, and the Mortician went to live in his home for the remaining months of his life. Most of her days were spent feeding, bathing and reading to Jan Prinsloo. She didn't see much of any of the other family members; the Prinsloos treated her with a distant coolness, the kind reserved for cleaners, cooks and gardeners. However, the Prinsloos' attitude suited the Mortician just fine.

There were times, in the middle of the night, when Jan would wake to rapturous, fever-dream visions – which he went on to describe as decaying Rothkos that oozed a thick sludge. She found it ironic that for all the African art in the house (beaded ornaments, lino etchings, ornate calabashes) Jan's deteriorating mind clung to Rothko.

Nevertheless, the Mortician indulged Jan's visions, often sedating him just so she could have a full night's sleep. Usually, she put visions like his down to the psychic exhumation of an individual's past near the end of their lives. Such terrors would pass, she had reasoned, the closer he got to the end. But Jan Prinsloo was different, for even near the end his night terrors continued unabated. This was when the Mortician, against her better judgement, suggested an alternative therapy to alleviate his distress.

By then, Jan was in a desperate state – his skin like stale pastry, his ears leaking a consistent waxy fluid, no matter how thoroughly they were cleaned. For all his deterioration, Jan was sure of one thing: he wanted the visions to end. And so, on a night when they were alone, the Mortician administered a careful dose of shroom tea, sweetened with honey. The tea summoned the decaying Rothkos after an hour of Jan drinking it. The paintings towered over him until they were all he could see.

He wept, incessantly.

All the while the Mortician held his hand, sometimes holding it with such vigour that she was afraid his fingers might snap.

Prinsloo stayed in that state of horrific awe until the diseased Rothkos emptied of their sludge and faded away. He then attempted to describe to the Mortician what the sludge around the bed looked like. A kind of tar, he said.

That was when the Mortician, seated on the edge, heard Jan's confession, and recorded secrets she had no business hearing, let alone recording. Jan rambled on about his past and how, as a businessman with political connections, he had negotiated his way into being a silent partner in the ownership of all the drinking halls in coloured and black townships. Through the profit he made with his more public associates, Jan Prinsloo slowly became part of an empire of alcohol – an empire that spread into distribution chains, advertising and even the illegal markets supplying alcohol to the men who worked in mines and factories.

Investment in alcohol went way back in the Prinsloo family. In fact, one of Jan's ancestors were credited with inventing the 'dop system' on the Cape farmlands – a system that paid blacks in alcohol instead of money, he explained.

Back then, Jan knew – with the country-wide uprisings and mass shootings – that the regime would become a smouldering carcass no vulture could claim sole responsibility for. That was when he sold his shares in the empire of alcohol, moving millions offshore. He proceeded to offer similar services to his business associates, who soon realised, like him, that the political tide was turning.

They paid us for their oppression, Jan explained that night, unable to look up from his yellowed fingernails. He reached for a photo album on the bedstand and pulled out a sepia-coloured photograph of a young white girl, in horse-riding pants, feeding a child labourer with a wine-filled ladle from a large tin drum. In the background, the young Mortician saw the regimented vineyards – how they seemed to want to go on forever, were it not for the mountains lifting the horizon into the sky.

That's my mother, said Jan, rubbing the girl's face with his pinkie.

It was all too much for the Mortician to take in. She wasn't entirely sure why she had pulled her phone out and recorded Jan's ramblings. Something about the nature of the confession felt monumental.

Later, when Jan was asleep, the Mortician listened to the recording, wondering what she might be able to do with the information.

The following evening, alone with Jan, she played the recording and watched his wrinkles peel away to reveal the young, shrewd businessman he had once been. That young man, buried in a decrepit, curdling body, was not defiant or defensive.

He was relieved. 'I'm glad someone like you knows.'

The Mortician was annoyed. She told him it was not enough, that the debt of history was not so easily repaid. How dare he think she could stand in for entire generations ground down to bone broth. 'No, Jan. Do more than apologise. This is your pound of flesh.'

'It's so long ago,' Jan stammered. 'Money can't turn back time. And where, to whom or what, would I give it all to now? There are new elites out there. Just now they talk the talk of democracy, of liberation, while they cannibalise their own.'

'Give it to me,' said the Mortician, softly at first, before repeating it with certainty. 'Give it to me and I'll put it to good use.' She sat back against the bed's headboard and detailed her ideas for a place she could only describe then as an institute.

IN RETROSPECT, JAN was quite impressible near the end, thought the Mortician, as she climbed down from the treehouse. At the end of the day everyone was susceptible to some form of influence. What she did was simply seize an opportunity; give her elevator pitch. Plus, she didn't use the money for personal gain: every cent went into making the institute what it was. In fact, once Molefe managed to get the litigation of Jan's will thrown out of court, there would be enough for several institutes, just like this one, across the country.

There's no evidence linking Vicky to the robbery. We have nothing – Mustafa's words pecked at her. She shooed them away, tucking the X-rays taken from her parents' house under her arm and exiting the atrium. Voices reached her from the kitchen; she turned and walked in the opposite direction, towards the kokerboom staircase.

Her phone vibrated. 'Hi, Shona, what's the latest?'

'I'm sorry for the delay, but I just had to make sure of everything before I came to you with the news.'

'Oh my God, what's happened? Was I right? Is Bonginkosi dead?'

'He's sitting right in front of me actually. Here, speak to him.' There was a shuffling of hands before an older, scratchy voice came on the line.

'Ms Babita. Good to hear your voice.'

'Bongi, where have you been? We thought the worst.'

Bonginkosi chuckled. 'Can you believe it. I fell in love.'

'I don't understand.'

'Love, mam.'

'Yes, I know what you said. But *where* have you been?'

There was silence. The Mortician carried on to the second floor, stepping into a passage filled with hundreds of ceramic dung beetles inserted into walls.

'I was by family in Clarens. Met a beautiful lady who runs a guesthouse there. What can I say, when love hits, you must move. I'm here to sell my flat. Ms Shona found me there.'

At the end of corridor, on the south-east side of the house, she rounded the bend and climbed the ramp to the third floor. 'Did she tell you about what's been happening?'

'Don't worry. I will testify for you. It's not right what Vicky is doing. How's Mustafa?'

'Sorry, Bongi, can you give the phone to Ms Molefe quickly.' The Mortician stepped onto the third-floor deck and strolled along the aerial walkway, disappearing behind a tall jacaranda tree in full purple bloom. 'This is *it*, right? This is what we need to prove everything.'

'It will be near impossible to claim forgery with Mr Mahlangu's testimony.'

'Gosh, Shona, I don't know where we'd be without you.'

'Don't thank me.'

There was another shuffling of hands. 'Please tell Mustafa I say hello,' said Bonginkosi. 'Tell him that this old man's lonely years are behind him. And to expect a wedding invitation!'

'I'm sure you'd want to tell him yourself when you see him. We'll probably be seeing you and Shona soon so this whole ugly affair can end.'

'That will be nice, ja.'

'Bye, Bongi. Thank you again.'

Shona came back on the line. Before ending the call, she explained that a court date would be set up soon and that she didn't expect the litigation process to be too drawn out. There was nothing left to do but let justice take its course.

In the south-east corner of the property, the Mortician stepped into her private treehouse. The treehouse was lined with many trinkets that she had collected over the years; some ordered from dark tourist websites, others taken as tokens from her travels, and a few had personal significance. La Santa Muerta statues from Mexico. A sign from Aokigahara forest that read, *your life is a precious gift from your parents.* Samples of pale green and red trinitite, quasicrystals made from nuclear blast sites in New Mexico. A branch from a tree that had survived the atomic bombing of Hiroshima. A photograph of herself standing in a sea of bioluminescent algae. A bronzed appendix in a glass jar. A nineteenth century trepanation tool in a muslin-lined box. A taxidermy ostrich, hatching from its egg. A black granite scarab. An abalone shell with dried ochre paint from the Blombos Cave. A strip of tyre from the very first suicidal swing Gaby ever nailed.

She felt overwhelmed.

Vicky hadn't gotten rid of Bonginkosi like she thought, and, perhaps, she hadn't orchestrated the burglary either. Was the crime dumb chance? A chance anyone in Joburg had of being scouted for violence. Still, in the wake of the impending triumph, she felt that Vicky needed to know the side of Jan that she got to see.

She leaned her X-rays against the wall, beside the three computer monitors, and sat down on her roller-chair. Scrolling through the last month and a half's worth of video footage, she deleted all evidence of the robbery and the burglars' transformations. Then she opened a file labelled 'Jan Prinsloo' and played the video.

In it, Jan, Mustafa and the Mortician all sat around a table as Jan looked straight into the camera and stated, quite calmly, that he was giving a sizeable lump sum to the work that 'these two pioneers' would be undertaking. Important work, he said. *Work that has become dear to me.* Jan held their hands throughout his speech. Smiling.

The Mortician didn't expect to tear up at the sight of the pixelated Jan. To her surprise, she had grown fond of him at the end. How could she not?

She copied the file to a USB drive and sealed it in a brown envelope, savouring the taste of the gum seal. Perhaps Vicky would appreciate this. A last vision of her father, speaking from the grave.

DIANNE

'Aaah … the beginning of the world,' says Mustafa, rubbing the sleep out of his eyes.

We're seated at a picnic table on the back lawn, waiting for the others to join. It's midday but it doesn't feel like it because we've slept for most of the morning. 'Last night was one hell of a thing,' I say, groggy, though the freshly squeezed orange juice and blueberry muffin lifts my spirits.

'I hope it gave what you needed,' he says.

The Mortician comes out of the house, balancing a tray. When she reaches the table, she places bowls of steaming shakshuka in front of us. The smell of tart tomatoes seasoned with cumin and simmered in garlic and onions whets my appetite.

'Dig in.' She sits down beside me.

When the others arrive, the mood is light for the first time since the break-in, but maybe it's because Daniel hasn't joined us. Angelique says he's gone for a run and will only be back later, after I'm gone. I don't take it personally – he and Lucas have been avoiding each other despite the Mortician's best intentions to get them in the same room.

From what I heard last night, it's clear that the Mortician and Mustafa put on brave faces when they're around us. They don't sit close to one another anymore; they don't spar in their typical, playful way.

'So, tell us. Last night, how was it?' asks Tobias, slurping the maroon stew with a spoon.

The Mortician and Mustafa don't look up from their bowls as

I speak. 'It was scary at first. Mustafa curated such an experience. I couldn't help but feel safe, once I was used to the feeling.'

I try to be as vague as possible because Mustafa asked me to, leaving out that both he and the Mortician joined me in the ceremony. Though I was going through my own journey, the mushrooms did allow me to see into the dynamic between them.

'In another week or so we'll have another one. With us all. Mustafa and I first need to see to some legal matters. Nothing serious.' The Mortician raises her glass of orange juice. 'I want to make a toast.' She turns towards me, her eyes glossed in a feeling I think is pride. 'Dianne, I admire you for the choice you made coming here. For preparing yourself for the nothing, out of which everything springs. We are far from perfect in the running of the institute, but we do our best because it is Mustafa's and my belief that there has always been a better way to die. Dianne, we will never meet again in this form, and that's okay. Where else could you go but here, in this expanse of chiliocosms.'

'Cheers!' says Lucas, clinking his glass with mine.

Everyone chimes in and wishes me well, even Angelique. Mustafa is reserved, even when Tobias talks us into drinking mimosas. Everyone is trying so hard to be jovial, but when they settle down to eat, there's a forlorn undercurrent. Is my leaving a reminder that they'll have to do the same?

'How do you think you'll do it?' asks Angelique.

Mustafa answers before I can. 'There's a syringe filled with what she needs. It'll be painless.'

'Aren't you scared?' asks Lucas.

'After all of this, and last night, a lot less. I won't do it right away. I'll have as much time with my sisters as I can before … before it gets unbearable.'

We carry on eating. Angelique and Mustafa bring out picnic umbrellas to shelter us from the heat. Above, a plane glides through a thin patch of clouds, trailing engine sounds behind it. It's funny: I feel as if the world is pressing in on all sides – like soon it will press so hard that I'll be snuffed out and filtered through. Like this orange juice.

AFTER BRUNCH MUSTAFA helps me with my bags. I've given most of my clothes to the Mortician. She'll give them to a charity. I've left two of my rosaries for Tobias and Lucas, though I doubt they'll use them. Angelique's given me a tube of lipstick from one of the commercials she booked years ago that apparently gave her a life-time supply. Lavinia will have better use for it than me.

I'm not sure if I like Angelique any more than when I first met her. She's a prickly person to get to know and I suppose, in my own way, I am too. Is that why they put us together: to have us prick each other till we soften. And yield? Whether I like her or not doesn't matter. Like anyone, she wants a world that can hold her as she holds it.

I DON'T GET to see Daniel before Mustafa and I set off for the air-port, which is fine because we didn't really connect. 'What's going to happen between you and Lucas?' I ask Mustafa as he turns into the main road. After the break-in, everyone eventually caught on to what had been happening; it was impossible not to overhear the arguments between Lucas and Daniel.

'There's a lot I have to consider. I'm not sure I want to be in this anymore. Too much has happened. It feels … tainted.'

I know what he means. 'When I left Bethlehem Primary, things felt the same for me. No matter what I did from then on, the episode with Aluwe would always get brought up when people spoke about the school, or my career. There was no school I could go to that wouldn't have heard something about me. True or not.'

'Some of us aren't brave enough to stick around and see our dreams go up in flames.'

'And others are brave enough to leave.'

He makes a muffled, throaty hum with his voice and turns the radio up. There is a white pimple on the fleshy part of my arm; it's a big one, the kind Tshidi would love to pop. I press the thin gunk out till it leaks. We drive on towards the city centre. Once we cross over into Braamfontein a man in a plush pink nightgown offers to clean our windows at a traffic light. Mustafa lets him, giving him coins. The man bows as if healed from some horrible affliction.

We head on deeper into town. Everywhere, people criss-cross roads and pavements, carrying groceries, school bags, themselves. Even here, amid fast feet, broken glass, dubiously stained pavements, there is green growing. In the cracks, it can't help itself.

At an intersection we spot two drunk men, on either side of the street, shouting at each other. They encourage one another to dance, the tongues of their shoes lapping up the beer that falls from the bottles they've hidden in small plastic bags. The one man crosses the road to meet the other. Hugs him. They walk into a bar that looks so dark from the roadside it could easily be mistaken for a dungeon. Will it be day or night when they go home? Will they know the difference?

On the highway again, we pick up speed towards the airport.

'Who's meeting you on the other side?' asks Mustafa.

'I'll be alone at arrivals. I'll have to take a bus through to Nkandla. They'll meet me at a bus stop.'

'Dianne, what I told you yesterday –'

'It's all right. I don't have any intention of telling.'

'Thank you. That means a lot.'

Last night, in the thick of the ceremony, Mustafa told me everything about Jan and Vicky Prinsloo, the Mortician's recordings, the lot of it. I'm not sure why; if he hadn't, I'd have been none the wiser. People seem to always come to me with their secrets, as if I have some priestly quality that could absolve them. I don't believe I do, but the quality has stuck with me my whole life.

'Aren't you mad at her?' he asks.

'You still are, clearly.'

'What she's done defeats the whole purpose of the place. The sense of privacy is a lie.'

'It does, I'll admit. Then again, I'll be gone by the time any of it comes out. If it comes out. I hope. What is privacy when you're on track to be worm food?'

For the first time since the start of the drive Mustafa smiles. 'You sound a little like her now.'

'God, I hope not.'

We giggle, returning to our windows.

WHEN WE ENTER the airport, there are people hugging and kissing, waving and saying goodbye. Toddlers cry with their faces pressed to the departure glass, people carry signs decorated in glitter. Others trolley expectant faces into the arrivals terminal, offloading themselves the first moment they spot a family member, a lover, a friend.

'There's nothing like walking through those doors, having spent whole days with strangers, bagged and zipped up, and then having familiar hands reach out and take your luggage for you,' Mustafa says as we walk past arrivals.

At departures it's a different story. Strangers stand beside one another to watch the boards above their heads for signs of delays and cancellations. It's more frenetic – make sure you have everything you need; let go of what's too heavy to take on the plane. Be nice to the people at the counter; your job is to make them believe you're more than a name on a screen.

The check-in process goes smoothly. We walk back past arrivals towards the main departure gate. The crowd at the arrivals gate has tapered off. One by one, everyone's found someone. When we get to my departure gate, I can't help but feel short-changed. 'I thought she said she'd be here by now.'

'I thought so too. She never usually misses saying goodbye. Guess she got tied up at the Postnet.' Mustafa checks his watch. 'It's almost time.'

Just as I get ready to leave the Mortician comes down the escalator from the Gautrain entrance and walks briskly towards us.

'I'm here, I'm here! Sorry about that. Postnet was a bitch.' She takes a breath and adjusts her hair. 'All ready?'

I nod. 'If you hadn't knocked on my window all those weeks ago, I –'

She hugs me before I get the words out. Are they my friends, or am I just a successful client? I go ahead and stand in the queue between the frosted panes of glass. Soon, more and more people crowd around me, and I can barely see Mustafa or the Mortician.

There's a point in any journey where you have to look ahead and turn away from those who are waving goodbye.

When I walk through the security checkpoint, the past closes behind me. Turnstiles lock in place. The future opens before me. I take my seat on the plane.

I'M SITTING AT a small café near the station, waiting for my bus back to Nkandla. A few tables away there's a father with his baby girl. The dad's drinking water with slices of lemon in it; when he's not looking the baby reaches her fingers into the glass and pulls out a slice. When the father returns to his drink, he's more amused than anything. He watches the girl put the slice in her mouth.

The world is so new for her, I imagine him thinking. Let her be surprised by it, as much as she can. Lord knows, the older one gets, the less awed one is.

The baby squints at the sour taste; she bunches up her face the way an oyster might slam shut on an irritating grain of sand. Once the taste dissipates, her face relaxes. Curious, she tries again. The same result. This carries on until her father pulls out his phone and records the small event. I get so wrapped up in watching them I almost don't notice the bus waiting outside the station, across the road. I gather my things and leave enough money for three meals on the table.

The moment I step outside, noise batters me from all sides. Men chop grass by the roadside, the wind whips across my face, a burp travels up my throat and bursts in my mouth like a wad of gum, chewed soft, pliable. I've never been this aware of the undulations of things. I'm not sure what it means.

When I'm in the line for the bus the awareness strikes me again. Wheels of luggage bags against the asphalt; the zing of a zip being opened and closed. Knuckles cracking. I want to sit down and put my headphones on to cancel it all out. Once inside the bus it gets a little better. I sit near the back by a fogged-up window that I wipe clean with the sleeve of my shirt. A boy of around seventeen sits next to me. He acknowledges me and puts his headphones on. He has the right idea.

A few rows in front of us, across the aisle, the father and baby from the café sit down. The baby's face softens slowly into sleep. Most of that age is spent sleeping; it takes far too much energy to stay awake in the world, especially for something so fragile, something raring to grow. Most adult life is spent fighting sleep and craving it. Choosing who to spend it with. The world of sleep is just as large as the waking one; we're drawn to it because it's easy, so natural, to just … stop.

On the bus now. Should be about four or five hours. Will let you know, I text Karabo.

Okay see you soon, she says, with a heart emoticon. There's so much more I want to say but I'll wait till I see them. I want to tell them about the ceremony, about what the mushrooms unearthed; how they took me back to the time Lavinia found my test results in my suitcase. Back to when Tshidi walked in and saw us curled together on the tiled floor – me sobbing, Lavinia wiping my tears.

Tshidi, Karabo and Lavinia, they joined me on that floor. I was scared. Life had short-changed me. The day after, they made me breakfast in bed, cancelled my tutoring sessions with the kids and told me that they were going to 'take care of me'. I could see the burden I was becoming.

The bus starts up and we're off. The landscape morphs from brown to green, to brown again: at this speed the mountains in the distance are towering waves of rock. I don't know how I want to spend these last days, but I know that I want to spend them with my sisters. I want to eat Karabo's salmon pastries, dance to Whitney Houston while Lavinia and I sweep the house, watch *The Bachelor* with Tshidi as we bet on which guy is going to take home the girl. I want to do the laundry and smell it when it comes out clean, warmed, scented. Plant a new flower or two in the garden. Get to see another one of Hopeful Horizon's kids go off to university. I don't know if I'll get to all of it. I know they'll say I've changed, that I'm less rigid. I'll tell them there's nothing that can undo inhibition more than death's call sheet.

I'll tell them about my ceremony too. How Mustafa took me to the stained-glass room, blindfolded. How he removed the blindfold, revealing a completely redesigned space. At the entrance stood the Mortician, waiting for me beside a teapot filled with tea leaves, herbs and crushed mushrooms. She poured a pot of boiling water into the teapot, and I watched as the water turned from yellow, to orange, to deep red. She handed me a cup. It was bitter, with hints of nutty flavour. I gulped it down as instructed and, because I hadn't eaten anything that day, immediately started to feel different.

I'll try and describe to Karabo, Tshidi and Lavinia what it was like though all I have are the bits and pieces my words can stick to. I know for sure that there was a feeling of *rising* – like I was being filled with helium. And I wanted to laugh, but I held it in until Mustafa told me to *go with it*. When I finally let out my laughter, my body and mind seemed to separate into Tetris blocks. I wasn't frightened.

The Mortician and Mustafa each drank a cup too. We walked the room together and it was magnificent. The floor was covered in gemstones. Jade. Carnelian. Topaz. Yellow jasper. And others I don't know the names of. Each one with its own texture, each reflecting the candlelight. And the candles all around: black, purple, rich pinks, filled the room with scents that transported me to the seaside, then a field of roses, then to Lavinia's bedroom pillows. Everything my mind latched onto passed through me and changed my world from the inside out. But nothing was more breathtaking than the shelves and rows of ornaments they'd stacked in cascading fashion up the walls.

Tibetan singing bowls laid beside statues of angels, some kneeling, others wielding swords. Salt lamps of different shapes illuminating Egyptian figureheads, labelled Ra, Nut, Ammit: the sun. the sky, the devourer of the dead. Amulets made of copper and gold, symbols I'd never seen before, nailed to the walls; sculptures of fairies, laughing Buddhas, dragons, dancing elephants. Each ornament had a pulse, something in the way it had been made – like someone had whispered a prayer into each thing and that same prayer was on repeat for anyone who looked close enough. I felt … tied to the objects, as if the stakes for us were similar, as if I was a symbol, a thing just like them, pointing to every possibility. A myth too provocative to ignore.

I had forgotten all about Mustafa and the Mortician before I stumbled on a statue of Mary. *Look familiar?* the Mortician asked, her eyes different, glazed with an invisible honey. Yes, I thought, but it can't be.

It was the statue from Bethlehem Primary. The school I attended. The school I returned to as principal. Moss had grown up from around Mary's feet to just below her bosom. Her face had been weathered out to mere indentations in the stone. I rushed up to the statue and looked behind it. They were still there, Naledi's and my initials. Small. Inconsequential. In black permanent marker just above her coccyx.

I'd hugged them both, my skin lighting up at the points our bodies touched. Mustafa was teary-eyed. The Mortician took my hand and sat me down on a cushion. Then she invited me to chant with them. She said it didn't matter what I chanted, but that I should chant something that mattered. Mustafa sat down across from us near a handpan and began beating it. Gently at first, alternating between his fingers and palms. Both of them chanted in a language I didn't understand. The words rippled out of their mouths.

I searched myself for something I could repeat and that's when Funani walked across my heart and sat down on top of it.

Seashells remember the air for what it was. His words. A line from a game we used to play. He would offer a word and I would say one back and we'd continue like that until we felt like we were saying something smart, or funny. Most of it was nonsense; some of it was funny, but that line was our favourite. I chanted the words, getting louder and faster each time. By the time I keeled over and stopped, I'd lost their meaning.

EVERYONE SWAYS IN sync to the motion of the bus. The baby is awake now, begging for attention. The teenage boy beside me smells of too much Brut. He tries his best not to brush up against me, but it's impossible at this speed. We're at the mercy of the driver. This bus could be in better shape. Every nut and bolt protests each time the driver does something sudden. I am tired. My eyes play tricks on me: there's double the number of people that should be in here.

We take an offramp and turn down a road that leads past Funani's school. Almost home. The bus stops at an intersection that overlooks the playground. It's in better shape than it was five years ago. Across the playground are brick-and-mortar toilets; four blocks in a straight line: two windows in each, a concrete basin outside. Four gagged, decapitated heads with vacant eyes. If I had worked harder, they could have been built sooner. I should have made people listen, even when they didn't answer my calls. I should have told each child in the aftercare programme to go to the toilet in pairs, to watch over one another as they sat on the pit latrines. Why didn't I go down there myself? I had told Funani to hang on, to wait for help, to find something to hold onto. I couldn't imagine ever climbing down in there with him – the drop was too tight and narrow. I don't know if that's true anymore.

Now the pit latrines have been built over. Shiny blue ribbons of transformation have been cut. Congratulations awarded.

The bus pulls off and leaves the school behind. Pressure builds in my head and I reach inside my bag for a bottle of water (almost home) and take several gulps. I watch myself drink; this hand isn't mine; these lips belong to someone else. The boy beside me puts his hand on my thigh and I want to brush it away, but I don't. I can't. I watch myself turn to the window and it's foggy again – all the windows are fogging up.

A woman who looks like me stares at her feet. Her feet tap-toe vigorously to a melody only they can hear. What kind of melody has one kicking the underside of the seat in front of you? What kind of melody makes everyone in the bus turn and gawk? Everyone on the bus is looking at the woman who looks like me. I'm trying to tell them it isn't me; that if they stop looking maybe she'll calm down, come to her senses. Maybe her body will hang on long enough for her to get home.

The passengers take the woman with my face and lay her down on the floor of the bus. The teenage boy puts his bomber jacket underneath her head. The man with the baby girl offers tissues for the spit and foam bubbling from her mouth. The passengers are frantic, shouting orders, exclaiming, muttering to themselves, covering their eyes.

The woman who looks like me doesn't calm down like I thought she would. She forces me to lie down inside of her and look up at a rim of worried faces. Crashing, the sound of crashing, falling bookshelves, shakes the roof of the bus.

None of the passengers react.

The sound of falling bookshelves rips the roof right off the bus.

No one reacts.

It's a clear sky. Clearer than I've ever seen it – one can almost look through the blue. The baby girl cries for her father, who is lifting me up, above the seats, out of the roof of the bus, hovering over the road. The edges of things pull at one another – lengthening, distorting. The blue sky recedes into a long canal.

Plump. Moist. Sheer. I am absorbed into it. Broken down by it. Shepherded apart by its cilia.

DIANNE'S BODY LAY atop a table draped with linen in what h[...]
been her bedroom. Lavinia, Tshidi and Karabo had removed wl[...]
furniture they could, decorating the room with air freshen[...]
made to resemble gazanias, and pots of potpourri.

The sun pawed through the room – from the enamel-wh[...]
door to the windowsill decked with framed photographs. Dian[...]
as a child with watermelon smeared across her mouth stood bes[...]
Dianne on top of a rock with one arm round Karabo's shoulders[...]
the foreground of a forest – sisters pointing, making out a shorel[...]
in the mist.

Two buckets of milky water stood on either side of the bo[...]
blue and brown sponges floated on the surface. The sisters ca[...]
in, sleeves rolled up to their elbows. Dunking the sponges, tl[...]
washed their sister. Lavinia began with Dianne's feet, pressing[...]
sponge to the soles – squeezing – until the lily-scented water gusl[...]
through Dianne's toes. Karabo patted along the thighs, right up[...]
Dianne's belly button, the rigorous scrubbing removing a thin fi[...]
of scum that had accumulated. Tshidi focused on the midsecti[...]
up to where the neck became the jawline. They washed the body[...]
meticulously that an outsider would think they were attempting[...]
rid it of something ineffable.

Limp and gradually stiffening, it didn't matter how lovin[...]
the sisters addressed the pale flesh. It would not respond.

In between the gulping sound of their dunking, the squish[...]
their wringing, the dull splat of sponge-on-skin, a kind of rhytl[...]
entranced them. The corpse was washed as though it were a he[...]
less child. By the end, milky streamlets had soaked into the fo[...]
of the linen, making it heavy. When they deemed the body cle[...]

the sisters wrapped the linen in bundles and placed it in a washing machine. It would be hung out to dry the next morning.

Daniel's eyelids couldn't stave off the morning sun slipping through the blinds. Cells in his retina responded to the incoming light and, changing the shape of their protein membranes, opened a channel for the morning to climb along his optical nerves, back into the different regions of his brain, waking him up.

He collected himself underneath the sheets. The dream he had been having blotched his mind: ill-formed, photographic negatives. In the dream, he was walking around the institute in the middle of the night, the moon like an open drain in the sky. His walking brought him to the mushroom greenhouse, lit by candles with flames twice the size of their wicks.

Amongst the logs growing with different mushroom strains were Lucas and Mustafa. Naked. Embracing.

Though he had wanted to interrupt, his body refused. He looked on, unable to penetrate the scene. Mustafa put his hands on the small of Lucas's back; Lucas spread his fingers into Mustafa's hair. Their hands disappeared into each other and, out of every orifice, a strain of fungi fruited. Reishi. Changa. Cordyceps. Lion's Mane. The air filled with spores.

It was suffocating.

Daniel got up to brush his teeth. The solid thud of feet-on-road would make him feel better, he thought. He put on his cycle shorts and trainers and made his way out onto Frederick Drive.

Before the burglary, he had typically asked Mustafa to join him, but that was impossible now. How could Mustafa have agreed to go on all those runs, all the while knowing what he was doing behind his back? (Not just massaging his back but stabbing it.) How had Mustafa given him those deep tissue massages – cracking his joints, manipulating stubborn fascia, realigning his connective tissue, bringing him to the point of weeping – without once trying to come clean?

As he started his run, Daniel tried to focus on his breathing. Thoughts of his fights with Lucas kept slowing him down. *You're such a fucken cliché.* Lucas had had no comeback for his affronts; variations of 'sorry' weren't able to soak up the anger.

Picking up speed, he lost track of his route. He took lefts and rights at whim, doubling back at dead ends and rounding corners without keeping track of the way back. Fatigue set in; he'd been in this position before. From experience he knew that if he held on a little longer, the exhaustion that was holding him back would give way – his arteries expanding, glands exuding endorphins that blunted the pain. If he kept pushing, his heart could beat Lucas and Mustafa into a paved surface, one that he met with the sheer force of his musculoskeletal system.

He ran on through the neighbourhood, currents of blood zig-zagging through his body, just as he was doing between the numbered houses. Pushing beyond fatigue, his viscera sought sugars to feed his muscles; the perforating pain would signal where future capillaries should take root, where more mitochondria were needed.

Daniel came to a stop in the main road: hands balled to fists, the chug of his heart in his fingertips. Cars whizzed past. After the ceremony, he would leave the institute. But first he would have to find his way back.

UP IN THE institute, Angelique was happy Dianne had left, leaving her the bedroom. Dianne was far too motherly for her liking – always checking that she 'took care of herself', wanting to know if she was certain about wearing *that* skirt or *that* halter top.

The truth was that it had become hard for Angelique to fit into her usual clothes. High-waisted pencil skirts. Crop-tops with bum shorts. Bodysuits that accentuated her best assets. She had dropped so many dress sizes that her once voluptuous figure was now just imagined recollections superimposed on the bathroom's full-length mirror whenever she stood naked in front of it.

Since the burglary, she was more disciplined about drinking the Mortician's plant powders. Some tasted like watery mud, others like seawater, but all were promised to rejuvenate her skin, while helping with the removal of harmful toxins. Standing in front of the mirror, she wondered, if she could go back in time, would she stop herself from taking that first snort of coke Todd had placed before her? She drank the muddy tonic, envisioning Todd's nonchalant expression, scooping coke onto the tip of his car key.

And poof! he'd say, with a triumphant sniff. *All better. Brighter.*

Things were brighter, for a time. High-end fashion shoots on private jets, on yachts, on Table Mountain; commercials where she was lavished in diamonds, or painted gold, or made into an Afro-Modern Aphrodite (a cracked calabash for the seashell, her body adorned in San rock art, an afro on her head dotted with peacock feathers). Things were so bright they had started to blind.

There were days, cooped up in her Rosebank apartment, when her phone's incessant beeping and vibrating would send her into an anxious spiral. That was only sometimes. With the help of what Todd called 'white magic' she blasted through her anxiety, becoming more than herself. With white magic she could be *the* Angelique Mlungisi: exactly what the photographers and PR wanted. Politically 'woke'. Insanely beautiful. Seductive.

After she drank the muddy tonic, the seawater came next. She needed to pinch her nose and swallow quickly this time. It was impossible not to gag a little at the taste. As she drank, she couldn't remember any of the answers PR had made her learn for those snotty-nosed journalists that were always looking to trip her up on some pressing social ill.

What are your feelings on colourism in the industry?

How do you think beauty standards and social media lead to the overwhelming cases of mental illness we're seeing among young women?

In a country with epidemic proportions of alcohol abuse, can you honestly be involved in a vodka campaign without a second thought?

She once was asked her opinion on 'pretty privilege' and she had responded confidently, explaining that her role was to uplift people that didn't feel pretty through her own prettiness. She thought the answer sounded exactly how any other social media activist would approach it. It wasn't long before she was dragging herself through threads on Twitter, watching camps of people dissect her interview from her body language to her tone, to what she was wearing, to how she pronounced words like 'Roedean High'. Truth was, she didn't even go there.

How many times did she have to tell PR that she wasn't a spokesperson for Human Rights Watch? She didn't want to be the face of Amnesty International either. She just wanted to take stunning photographs. Nobody got that, except Xolisi. And look how that turned out.

Since his bail release, their love story was back in the spotlight, discussed on every pop culture podcast trading in the latest gossip. There were those who believed in her abuse claims and those who labelled her a vengeful ex. It was true, she had told the detectives, that money from Xolisi's barman job kept his designer dream alive while she worked on her career with Todd. It was also true that Xolisi was the one who'd introduced her to Todd one night after her live set. Maybe Todd would have found a way to introduce himself either way, but she always liked to stress Xolisi's importance in her being discovered.

When work with Todd started raking in the big bucks, Xolisi

JARRED THOMPSON

leaned on her. She supported his dream until it started making serious dents in their finances. She asked him to scale things down for his first show so that they could maintain their lifestyle. Xolisi did as he was told, begrudgingly. Their relationship took on shades of resentment after that.

It got worse when Todd advised her not to take part in Xolisi's first show. *Darling, if you want to play in the big leagues, you can't relegate yourself to the park merry-go-round.* Todd's analogy stung, and, if she was being honest, she agreed. Was Xolisi ever going to be in her league? Did she need to upgrade?

When the first trio of scathing fashion reviews dropped, Xolisi spiralled. He disappeared for entire weekends, partying with friends, only coming back to the apartment for a change of clothes. He skipped shifts at the bar too, enough for the manager to send through a final, written warning. She had been patient enough to convince him to go back to the bar, apologise to the manager, and work overtime.

Going back was an admission of failure for Xolisi; going back meant dealing with overly friendly drunk people who burped in your face, who never tipped enough and never knew when to go home. The bar's live music was its saving grace, no doubt, but how could music save catatonic dreams?

One night, Xolisi had snapped – blamed her for pulverising his career. He actually used that word: *pulverise.* Angelique walked away towards the staircase in the apartment; he threw the Louboutins, charging after her. Only later, when he was helping her up from her fall down the stairs, did she recognise that the excuse of 'slippery tiles' could not explain the situation away.

When details of their altercations leaked – probably from so-called friends – most men on social media sympathised with Xolisi, their arguments congregating around the idea that it was Angelique's job to make Xolisi 'feel like a man'. Men on Twitter demanded clarity on the definition of 'abuse', fearing that if they were to ever break up with their girlfriends they would be accused of either sexual, physical or emotional abuse.

Angelique tried to shield herself from the comments while simultaneously searching for threads from followers claiming to believe her.

Though she didn't express it, she knew there were no 'sides' to the story. There was only *the* story, and that contained everything: from their tumultuous coke habit to her calling the police on him, to the terminal diagnosis – all the way back to the first time a man assumed that women, in their entirety, were changeable props in their lives.

Every part of the story had weight to it, the exact measurements beyond what any Insta Live could capture.

THE TONICS MADE her nauseous. These days most foods did too. This, in addition to the increased time on dialysis, worried her. She asked Mustafa if the nausea was a symptom of the burglary trauma; after all, the bite on her right breast wasn't healing. Mustafa said it might not heal entirely, that, because of her kidneys, she might be left with it for 'some time'. Afraid to ask, she wasn't sure if that meant a lot or a little.

Angelique didn't like looking at the scar. Every morning she applied foundation to it, even though yesterday's foundation was still there. Each time she applied it, the man appeared, forcing her down, spit collecting in the corners of his mouth, a clutching shadow of pubic hair sticking out the top of his underpants.

Recollections insisted on being replayed.

While covering the bite, she filled her mind with the same thing that her eyes had held onto when the burglar was standing above her, pants at his ankles. *A bee hovering above a glass of cran-*

berry juice on the dresser. A bee mistaking fruit juice for nectar.

She believed that when the man removed his pants, it was over. Death could have taken her and she would celebrate it like the second coming. Never in her life was she so reconciled to corpse-hood (not even when she overdosed and woke up with tubes running into both nostrils).

A sudden shatter of air, and Tobias had killed him. She looked up from the bed to see Tobias fire another round into the man, who fell at the foot of the bed. Tobias didn't look at her exposed breast or her torn panties. He simply reported that there were two men left to 'see to', before running out of the room.

Was that the right thing to have done, she wondered? Treat her like a fallen soldier in a war: one expected to dust themself off and get on with the business of killing? She wasn't sure. Tobias's demeanour suggested that there was an expectation for her to be accustomed to the situation. Impervious to whatever men threw at her.

She wasn't impervious. Knowing that, she had gotten up from the bed, determined.

'ANGELIQUE? CAN I come in?' said the Mortician.

'It's open.'

The Mortician walked in and sat on her bed. 'How are you finding the powders?'

'They taste shit, but my skin likes them. I just can't get rid of these dark circles under my eyes.' She pulled a pillow to her chest and crossed her legs around it.

'Excess fluid in the body. I'm afraid the powders might not help with that. I just wanted to make sure you're prepared for the ceremony.'

'Why wouldn't I be?'

'Mustafa's expressed concern that you might not be able to handle it.'

'I mean, if Dianne could go through with it, then I want to.'

'I understand. I want you to be sure about the risks, that's all. There might not be a way back after this. Dialysis can only do so much.'

'What are you saying?'

The Mortician grabbed hold of her knees. 'When is Xolisi's trial date?'

'Few months from now.'

'Okay.' The Mortician looked disappointed. 'During the ceremony, rely on the breathing techniques I taught you.' Then she kissed her on each knee and made her way to the door.

'Before you go. I wanted to thank you for giving me that treehouse to sing in. I've been really enjoying belting out the Mariahs and Whitneys and Dions.'

The Mortician stopped. 'I've enjoyed listening to you. If it was up to me, I'd sponsor your EP.'

'It's too late for that.'

The Mortician came back to sit on the bed. Angelique knew that if she were to lie back and invite the Mortician to hold her, the Mortician would not refuse. 'I know the risks when it comes to the ceremony. Isn't that what this whole thing is about?'

Surprised, the Mortician leaned forward: 'I believe you.'

Angelique turned to rearrange the pillows behind her head. 'I'm going to take a shower before we start.'

The Mortician got up, curling hair behind her ears. 'We'll call you when we are ready.'

Once alone, Angelique called her gogo, Ma Edith. A woman she hadn't seen since moving in with Xolisi. The phone rang several times. It went unanswered.

THE RESIDENTS WERE called out to the back lawn. On a low circular table seven small teapots were stationed in perfect symmetry. The Mortician and Mustafa sat at opposite ends: she played her wooden flute, and he ushered each resident to their seat.

A draft swept through the property, hushed breathing tossing sunlight from one clump of waxy leaves to another. In the sky, hadedas in V formation pressed on through cloud, the leader creating zones of free lift for those trailing.

'Welcome,' said the Mortician. 'This has been a long time coming. I know it's been hard. And I want to thank each of you for staying. You could have easily left. I like to think that you stayed because you believed in the work we do.'

Daniel mumbled. Everyone cast their eyes in his direction, except Lucas.

'Right,' began Mustafa. 'We'll each pour boiling water in our teapot and let the mushrooms steep.' He lifted a kettle and poured the hot liquid. Then he passed the kettle around for others to do the same. In each crystal teapot, the crushed mushrooms and slivers of ginger root danced in a throng of illegible punctuation before settling to the bottom of their infusers. 'Smell the tea leaves you'd like to add,' said Mustafa, passing several woven baskets around.

Lucas picked dried hibiscus. Angelique was drawn to almond-coloured leaves that had a feral fruity aroma. Tobias reached for peppermint, its smell reminiscent of the ice-cream he shared with Aunty Charmaine on Friday nights. The cool rush of sage in Daniel's nostrils jolted his brain to attention and, for that reason, he sprinkled a handful into his infuser. The crocodile green of lemon balm leaves were the Mortician and Mustafa's choices: its delicate zest invoked the spirit of the lemon tree they had planted beside the sauna.

The Mortician resumed her flute playing as Mustafa sat his

Hang drum between his legs. Everyone closed their eyes. Air moved through the man-made cavities of the instruments, throbbing inside the unique geometry of each. Music unfurled on the residents' eardrums the way a stranger might unclench their fist, offering a child candy.

'Ask for what you want. Accept whatever comes,' said Mustafa.

Tobias never kept his eyes closed for more than a minute at a time. When he tried, the nocturnal dread that he had been feeling returned: the heaviness of knowing what he was responsible for. A week after the burglary, the Mortician had made him sit in the composting greenhouse and contemplate the corpses he had made. He could only stomach it for an hour at a time, which was weird because he'd seen a dead body before. Stephen's: a stray bullet from drug turf wars had struck him in the neck. The blood had lashed across Tobias's face – a bullwhip of crimson.

Tobias wondered what the men he killed were like as boys; what dreams they might have had for themselves. Do boys who dream of violence grow up to be violent men? Was it that simple? Every violent act Tobias ever witnessed, or committed, collapsed into the same dank turd. What did it matter, he thought, words are useless when hunger demands *taking*.

'Okay,' said the Mortician. 'Drink up.'

The residents poured their teas, bringing brims to their lips. Once everyone finished, Mustafa suggested a game. 'We sit in a circle and clap, passing it along until someone double-claps, changing the direction. The aim is to go as fast as you can, without hesitating. Whoever makes a mistake is out.'

It didn't take long for the group to get into the rhythm of the game, their attention focused on watching one another, on reacting as fast as possible to trip each other up. It got harder for them to focus as time wore on. Tobias felt the roughness of his palms more keenly and began to pick at the calluses along the base of his fingers.

Lucas noticed the criss-crossing lines of his handprint and how the creases deepened or faded depending on how he moved. He couldn't do anything to remove the creases completely and realised that, like crumpled paper, there was no way to smooth things out. He glanced over to Daniel, feeling an inexorable urge to pull him aside so that they could talk. What could he say that he hadn't said before?

'I got a game,' said Tobias. 'Something I haven't played in long. We're gonna need some pantyhose and a scissor.'

The Mortician went back into the house with Tobias to fetch what they needed while Lucas took Daniel aside.

'How are you feeling?'

'There's a rumbling in my stomach,' said Daniel.

'Same. My face feels weird.'

Daniel nodded, unsure of what to say.

'I know I've said this, but I just –'

'Do we have to do this now? I want to experience this without having to think about us.'

'There's still an "us"?'

Daniel saw the expectation in Lucas's face. How was he supposed to answer that? He looked at his feet. Was the grass pulsing? He got down on his haunches and decided that, yes, the grass *was* pulsing. Almost waving. He got down lower, his face above the blades. An entire forest underneath my feet, he thought.

'Daniel,' called the Mortician.

Tobias's game had started. Mustafa and the Mortician held the repurposed pantyhose around their ankles; Lucas and Angelique took turns jumping into and out of the ring made from pantyhose string. When had Lucas walked away from him? How much time had passed between that and him getting on all fours? Daniel felt anxious; he didn't like losing time this way.

Angelique knew the game as skippini. To her surprise, she was still good at it. Whether it was ankle or shoulder height, she was better than the others at jumping over the pantyhose and into the ring. It had been that way since primary school; no one could beat her at skippini because she'd worked out how to run up, leap, and bundle her lower body in order to twist it in one, sure thrust, before landing safely in the ring. Getting out was always trickier.

The band of fabric moved up Mustafa's and the Mortician's legs. Soon it was around their necks. Tobias and Daniel tried their luck, failing at different heights. Angelique was the last woman standing.

The higher the jump, the tighter the tuck, she thought, jumping. She didn't make it. Her body had not been that high on strength alone in years. When she fell to the ground, the impact dislodged a chuckle from her stomach. 'What next?' she cried out, between giggles, elbows and knees smeared in lawn goo. Euphoric murmurations billowed through her body's shutters.

She got up, took Daniel by the hands, and spun them around until dizziness set in. As they spun, Daniel shut himself off from the blurred surroundings. When they stopped, their eyes struggled to refocus; the world became a blank canvas, slowly saturating with paint. They both wanted to throw up. The Mortician offered to take them inside, out of the sun, until the nausea subsided, leaving the three men behind.

Mustafa was familiar with the whirlpool shrooms created. Even though he'd gone through ceremonies before, each one took on a different shape, because the people were always different. The Mortician was the only constant.

The shrooms had a knack for reminding Mustafa how little he knew: about himself, the world, the people he tripped with. Even that word, *tripping*, suggested a kind of holiday where one lost luggage in transit. 'I've got a game,' he said, finally.

'We're listening,' said Lucas.

'The maze. First one to find its centre, wins.'

'That's unfair. You grew it so you know where the centre is,' said Tobias.

'Fine. Just you and Lucas then.'

'What does the winner get?' said Lucas.

'Whatever they want.'

'Anything?' Tobias got up to stretch, a boyish giddiness animating his limbs.

Mustafa nodded. 'The maze isn't about speed.'

'Ja, ja, ready when you are,' said Tobias, patting Lucas on the chest.

The pair set off into the hedges, each choosing different entry points, the spirit of the mushrooms in full swing. Mustafa knelt in front of a nearby rock, picked up a pebble and drew a circle on the rock's flat face. Then he gathered several stones in the centre of the circle and played a game.

ACROSS THE LAWN, over the back patio, down the passage and opposite the central atrium sat Daniel, reclined in a reading nook. The after-effects of the spinning had worn off; his skeleton began to take on its usual compact weightiness, pinning him to the seat.

He tried to imagine what the mushrooms were doing to his nervous system, how molecules of psilocybin activated serotonin pathways in his brain, inducing mammoth electrical storms that thundered over the uncharted parts of his psyche. There, on the shores of his imagination, lay the jetsam of his language:

> *of which I am composed*
> > *I shall be dead*
> *still performing*
> > *the universe*

the change not important

in the presence of the sublime

the body is failure

understood by no mind

make your world

wherever you are

He had never felt this energised, searching the reading nook for a sticky note to write on. Not only was his mind aflush with ideas, but his heart felt emboldened to take its own detours, lub-dubbing to echoes in its chambers.

No echo was clearer than Sarah's. He wanted to text her. Tell her what he was doing. He expected her to laugh and call him a hippie, like her.

At the clinic, Sarah described depression as a 'flat feeling', a rolling pin that won't stop till you're spread too thin to function. She said, for people like them, it was easier to lie there and take the levelling: have the clinic erase all difference between you and the next person in the lunch queue – everyone gorging on food for a sense of fullness.

Sarah's biting wit was what had saved him. Her comments about clinic staff always made him laugh. Like the heavy-set cleaner who never wore a belt, who she nicknamed *crack of doom*. Or Dr Vermeulen who she labelled a *Woolies glue snorter*. Beneath the deflecting wit, Daniel knew Sarah didn't want to be around anymore. Could he blame her? He had steeped himself like an overused teabag in the minds of dead white men for most of his twenties, and what did he have to show for it? An intellect able to put together a logical argument and take empirical reasoning as far as the available science allowed. A brain that mapped the world in concepts and theories. A mind, bereft of wonder.

An ache in his chest launched him towards the kitchen. A notepad and pen was stuck to the fridge. He sat at the counter ready to write, knowing that, before this, he had always pictured language as a loaded gun. Trained, as he'd been, to aim words at ideas, rustling in the brambles of his brain. His studies were about bringing home the kill to dismember, and reorganise, into theses, evidence, and conclusion.

Is this what he should have said when Pa refused to fund his postgraduate degrees? That philosophy and butchery led to the same thing, a cut of meat, prized above the rest of the animal. He could see it so clearly. Both endeavours strove for the most logical cut – the one that slipped between the joints, letting meat fall from the bone.

It was decided. This time he was going to write towards failure, letting one word bleed into another. He scribbled furiously, refusing to listen to his inner cynic.

> *Beneath paradoxes, small wanderers gather, are moved*
> *by everything I can't see. While I, pendulum body, am housed*
> *in my father's wristwatch, unable to break his hands.*
> *Among anagrammed strangers, love never belonged*
> *to anyone. Umbilical cords have not been knotted,*
> *pretty bows in joint graves. Love's viscosity splits*
> *shadows from their frames. That is its gift.*
> *Punctuate hollows. Puncture solids. Be*
> *in this, as long as the weather permits.*
> *Foggy flesh, straddling the heart of cities*
> *and cited hearts.*

He folded the paper several times and put it in his pocket.

'There you are,' said the Mortician, leaning against an archway. Angelique sat on the staircase a few metres away, running her hands along the crook of her neck. 'Come, I have something to show you both.'

They walked up to the third floor, taking the aerial walkway to a large treehouse held up by palm trees. 'We've never been to this one, have we?' asked Angelique.

Daniel held her hand. 'No, we haven't.'

'Welcome. To the aftermath of eternity,' said the Mortician. She opened the door, leading them into a pitch-dark room.

As soon as the door shut, the space was lit with the honeycomb glow of lanterns dispersed throughout a room made of mirror. Lanterns hung from the ceiling at different lengths, the reflective illusion making the room appear larger than it could ever be. And the quiet – opaquer than a well-crafted lie.

The Mortician, Daniel and Angelique tiptoed forward, cautious in their delirium.

ANGELIQUE

'Are you okay in there?' The Mortician knocks on the bathroom door.

I'm gonna vom. I shouldn't have spun so fast, though it felt good at the time. Like if I went fast enough, I might just lift off the ground a little.

Standing in front of the bathroom mirror, I remember my breathing – deep and full. Watch as I expand, contract, expand. Weird to think that parts of me I don't control are still me, in agreement. A contract. Most of the time. I'm a sinewy thing, not laminated or airbrushed, not styled into an idea. I hate thinking this way.

I sit on the toilet seat and notice how clear the screen of my phone looks. My eyes are 3D glasses. The colours are so sleek, I lose track of time just scrolling Facebook, Insta, Twitter.

'Angelique?'

The Mortician's voice feels nearer, though she's behind the door. The room's textures distract me, Terry Lustre towels draped over a beige washing bin. Hand creams and fragrant soaps beside the black faucet and basin. A single orchid in a pot on a shelf. It needs water.

'Okay, I'm coming in.'

'No, sorry, I'm fine. My stomach's working, that's all,' I say.

'I'm going to find Daniel. Don't wander off when you're done.'

Her footsteps grow faint. I get up, pour some water in a glass and tip it into the orchid's pot. The water bubbles, soaks into the soil. A warm tickle travels from the top of my head down to the base of my spine. Everything I touch seems able to melt into me. The mahogany wooden panels, the stand-alone chrome bathtub, the stone patterns in the ceiling – they want my attention. Want to be the VIP.

The cramps start up again. Real bad. I'd rather shit than throw up. On the toilet I push, hands on stomach, begging for whatever's stuck to leave. The mushrooms reorganise my insides. Finally, I fart, and the cramps subside. It doesn't smell as bad as I thought it would. I haven't eaten for the day, but it still feels like something wants to come out. I take my phone off the cistern and scroll through Insta.

Todd's posted an image of him and Malik having a picnic on top of Northcliff ridge. The caption: *#powercouple #foundtheone*

If I had told them where I was, they could have visited. I call Todd. The phone rings for a while before it's answered. There's no voice on the other end, just white noise. My ears are at the bottom of someone's handbag, jiggling round with their keys and coins. I make out voices in between the beat of a house track.

'Hello, Todd? You there?'

Still no answer. It's a party. People chatting, bottles clinking, the random outburst of a laugh. I was probably butt-answered. The white noise is better than nothing so I put the phone on loudspeaker and rest it on the toilet mat.

'Hey, Todd, make a toast!'

People gather. It sounds like a crowd. Where am I? In Todd's back pocket? On a random shelf behind sculptures of naked torsos? Fallen down the side of Todd's beloved turquoise Dahlia single-seater?

'Okay, okay. Fine.' Todd's voice and, from the sound of it, he's wasted. 'I just want to say thank you to all you fuckers for putting up with me long enough to see this mad hatter find his mate.'

'Balance us, Todd!'

'When I first met Malik he was fresh out the womb, coming into a tough industry. Believe it or not, we didn't like each other at first. You all know how uncompromising I can be. But this man right here melted my rough edges. He's the sweetness I need. A beauty I can stand by. To my fiancé! I love you, babe.'

Applause. Laughter. The pop of champagne corks and the whoops that follow. Their engagement party, and they didn't invite me! I didn't even know Malik wanted to be a Ben Ten. Typical. I pick the phone up and hold it to my ear. Now I need to be balanced.

'Malik! Speech! Speech!' people yell.

I imagine Malik walking across the room, champagne flute in hand, taking his time for everyone to see what he's wearing before cosying up to Todd.

'Most of you know, Todd and I met because of my friend Angelique Mlungisi. One of the hardest working models you'll ever have the luxury of meeting. She always told me how much she admired this amazing photographer – who she said was a real dictator by the way.'

There's giggles and witty comebacks from Todd trying to come off innocent. If I was there, I know Todd would have given me a dirty look for calling him a 'dictator'. The crowd dies down and Malik continues. 'But, more than that, Angelique said this guy was a maverick. A trailblazer. A firecracker. And now, my lover.'

Malik's voice softens on the last word. The party gushes – I imagine young women leaning on their boyfriends' shoulders, smokers looking in from the balcony holding their joints in mid-air. A sloshed guy breaks the tender moment by asking where 'this Angelique is today?'

'She's been having a rough time of late. Messy media break-ups. Drugs. Urgh, let's not get into it –' Todd says abruptly. Malik quickly draws attention back to him and makes a toast to himself and Todd in the third person.

'Cheers!' a woman shrieks, and the party echoes.

I end the call. Mouth dry. I stick my mouth under the faucet, drinking till a burp stops me. Is that all Todd saw in me? Did he forget how old news he was before I came into his life? How much I needed his name, and he needed my look. Why is it that anyone who's ever gotten somewhere in the world is made to seem like they became their iconic self all on their own? I was never like that. Was I?

I run my fingers along the slight cracks of the screen protector and the dents in the phone's cover before removing the cover and peeling off the protector, bit by bit. There's the black window, the one I stand by, yelling *I'm still here. Like me. Love me. Look how far I've come. Still I rise. Right? If I can do it, then why can't you? Work Harder. Be Happier. Be Positive! Don't rest on what you are. Go. Go. Go. Be about that luxury. Be about your life. Fetch your muthafucking life, gurl!*

This is the longest I've ever had the same phone. This Samsung, with its hairline crack on the flashlight, a busted recorder mic, a battery that doesn't last longer than six hours. This phone that's forever asking me to clear space and delete memories. If I force it to do too many things at once, it'll reboot randomly; if I don't give it attention, it searches for notifications, anything to make it vibrate. Calling me back. Some version of me lives inside; the places I've been are written into its microchips. All that can be erased with a factory reset.

Truth is, this phone's circuits are in me – a billion little feeds, PowerPoint presentation lives and memes multiplying the meaning of any moment. It feeds on me. And I like it. I'm made potent from its charge. Fanged. I hate thinking like this.

I place a palm to my forehead. I'm burning up. I haven't been on dialysis yet. Mustafa usually reminds me. My chest is tight, and even when I try to deepen my breath my lungs resist. A shower. Yes, that'll help.

The water runs hot. Undressing in front of the mirror, my feet feel swollen on the cool tiles. I'm tired, not just from today, not just from the trip. It's the exhaustion of always being on the move. I open my phone's camera and try to find a natural angle that is the Angelique Mlungisi I remember. Fish-scale skin on my neck. Itchy redness across my jawline. Darker bags under my eyes, a pale yellow to the cheeks. Small bumps along the shoulders. I open Snapchat and go through its filters.

Me with perfect pink skin.

Me with sparkling doe-eyes.

With skin supple and tight.

Me in cute dimples, crowned in flower wreaths.

Goddess. The perfect combo of pixels.

The real me. The me I could be.

Breathing through the wound.

In the shower, I let the steam take me and my phone. Through the steamed-up lens of my Samsung I'm the kind of bad bitch who demands that you put respect on her name. The bad bitch burning up catwalks. The bad bitch with her Louis Vuitton logos all facing the same direction – up. Up to the penthouse suites, the presidential rooms, the boardrooms where I sit as executor of the lux life. The life of American, British and French *Vogue*. The city girl who runs circles around any man, whose gogo made her practise jaguar eyes. Whose gogo made her sing Top 30 Disco Hits while we cooked samp and beans in our plush nighties.

The water short-circuits my phone. I'm calm. It's kind of cool to watch the phone fight for control. The screen dissolves into bright lines of green. The phone won't win; there's too much water here, for us. A few seconds and it's shut down. Malfunctioned. I lay it at my feet and do what the Mortician said I should after a hot shower. Turn it cold.

I have to hold the ledge of the niche to stay upright. I'm awake. 'Here! Here!' I shout through water, holding back tears.

ON THE LANDING, I wait for the Mortician to fetch Daniel. She has something to show us. Something we'll enjoy. I trust her. She's like no one I've met. She wouldn't treat me any different if I showed her my ugliest sides. What do you call that?

'Are you feeling okay?' I lift my head from my hands and they're standing in front of me, Daniel and the Mortician. She touches my cheek. 'Can you make it?' she asks, her face inches from mine, lips wet with gloss.

I nod and Daniel helps me up. We walk to one of the tree-houses on the walkway. Daniel takes my hand and I think of Xolisi, wondering what he's doing right now. Why the fuck do I always have to do the most? I could slap myself for thinking about him; for wondering if, beneath all his flaws, there was really just a boy, afraid of never becoming a man. That doesn't mean I'll forgive him. I won't. I can't.

The Mortician opens the door to the treehouse. There's just enough light to make our way to the centre of the room before she shuts the door.

'Why's it so quiet?' asks Daniel.

'Soundproof walls.'

We wander around the room, walking on mirrors. The flickering lights in the dark make me dizzy. It's as if I'm falling and standing at the same time. I take a seat on the floor for control. My breathing is short; it's an effort to lift my arms. The spit in my mouth, my swallowing, the flinch of blood up my neck: I can hear all of it. I lie down. My insides purr.

The Mortician sits by me and strokes my hair. I crawl up on

her lap to rest. Too weak to speak, I listen. 'There are times when I can't stand being alive this way. In this world. And when that hits, there's an exercise I'll do. I'll smoke a little weed, lie here, in this room, and zoom out.'

'Zoom out?' says Daniel.

'Out of the spiral arm of the Milky Way. Out of the wave of interstellar dust our sun rides on. Away from the supermassive black hole at the centre of our galaxy. Far enough so I feel as insignificant as …'

Daniel taps a lantern and its soft light breaks into fractals. They look like honeycombs. I can't take my eyes off it.

'And that helps?' he asks.

'Being here reminds me of the immensity that is oddly quite comforting. Depending on what story you're telling. The supercluster of galaxies that we're part of – Laniakea – has given us these few billions of years, to play.'

'What does Laniakea mean?'

'*Immeasurable heaven.*'

Daniel walks the room, tapping lanterns, sending fractals my way.

'Why don't you sing something for us, Angelique? You've been practising, haven't you?'

The Mortician lays my head on the floor, gets up. I don't see where she's going. When she returns, she hands me a phone with its Spotify app open. 'Pick a song. Sing for us.'

'I know what you're doing,' says Daniel.

'She knew the risks in her condition.'

'I'm fine,' I manage to say. 'Tired, but fine. I wanna sing.'

Daniel looks to the Mortician, who has moved my head back onto her lap. 'I can't,' he says, shaking. He bends to kiss me on my cheek and walks out the treehouse. It's just me and her now. The Mortician sits me up, pops the cap of a small bottle and a harsh, chemical whiff wakes me.

'Sing. Sing for me,' she says. 'Here, pick a song, let me type for you.' She shines the phone's light in my face.

I squint and whisper a title into her ear. She types. 'Gogo and I sang this often. She loved disco.' I swallow hard, leaning on her. The snare drums come in fast, keeping time with the electric keyboard.

I won't take this lying on the floor.

I'll stand here and sing down the door.

(Buzzing in my throat. Voice croaky. The Mortician lifts me. The beat bops and I wanna dance.)

My boo stole my brand-new violin.

 Now there's little that'll cleanse me of this sin.

(Music rises from my groin. I'm shaking. The melody forces its way out.)

And it's hard to find

Any view to cure my mind.

Oh, I'm just swooning, turning these shoes to soles.

(Eyes open. We're dancing, the Mortician's hands in mine. She moves us back and forth. Twirling. I can't stop. It feels too good. I'm a girl again, dancing with Gogo in the kitchen, a pot of samp and beans on the stove. We don't care. We wanna dance. Jump on the bed. Break its springs.)

Tires are slashed, there's no way to get ahead.

and to pump their schemes the world starts selling dreams.

(Crescendo. Dizziness. I almost fall. But the melody, the Mortician, they keep me on my feet. We knock against the lanterns. The room fills with honeycombs. Each note climbing up my throat is a bee. There are hundreds of bees. My voice box is their hive.)

I'm so happy, turning these shoes to soles.

(Bees flying through the fractals.)

 I'm just swooning ...

(Air in lungs. Reverb on vocal cords. Fire in my feet. The hive is empty.)

It's in my hands,
I'm just swooning, it's in my feet,
I can't take it, it's all over me …

I don't feel a thing when I hit the floor. The Mortician glimmers, bends over me and strokes my face. Then covers us with a quilt. From this angle, I see Gogo.

I unlatch her wire gate, walk past the outside tap overgrown with coriander. On the stoep, under the red roof, Gogo is on her knees, smearing black polish. She doesn't say hello. 'Ku no kudla ekishini. Se oxtail, namadombolo. Just how you like it.'

'Ngiyabonga, Gogo.' Have I been playing skippini in the street with the girls from next door this whole time? The streetlights aren't on, but I walk into the house anyway, hungry, school shoes in my hands.

I've never left.

THE HORIZON SPLIT the sun open across its middle, spilling tangerine yolk across the blue pan of the sky. Evening approached. Lucas was nowhere near the centre, the grass beneath him shorter in the hedges than elsewhere on the property and resembling a cricket pitch. He propelled himself on his crutches, trying to deduce the turns he should take to beat Tobias.

The hedges were tricky. A left turn that seemed to lead in the right direction doubled back to the outer rim. A right turn that led to the upper north-east corner of the maze curled into a dead end. In a remote part of himself Lucas concluded, having spent a good hour wandering, that there was scant reason for choosing left or right turns; every decision felt imbued with a strange aura of irreducible 'common sense'. What was beyond that sense, he was not sure.

What Lucas hadn't anticipated – as he manoeuvred up the incline of a corridor running obliquely to the one he'd just exited – was the wreck he would stumble into. A wreck made to look like a bus accident. He recognised Mustafa and the Mortician's intentions: the scrap metal strewn across his path, shattered panes of emergency glass, taken from old buses, sticking out of the hedge walls. They were taking him to his limit. To make him panic. They couldn't have known for sure that he'd come this way, he thought. Yet here he was, forced to return to that day when, driving home with the athletics team, the driver had lost control, spinning off the road and overturning on the bank of a dam.

He tried to hold onto what the Mortician had said in their sauna sessions as he navigated the replica wreckage. She spoke of how one had to 'stay with' the discomfort, sit down, and befriend it.

What is unbearable is already being borne. As he walked the oblique corridor, her voice resounded in his head. Even when he envisioned the bodies of his fellow teammates as fleshy slush trapped in metal, he held onto her advice. *Ruined. Ransacked. Somehow, you begin again.*

They're projections, he told himself. Hallucinations.

When he reached the end of the corridor, he looked back, relieved he had made the trek through the wreck. Was the accident finally over? Or had the shrooms only temporarily given him their mycorrhizal power, as Mustafa had said they might, so that he, like them, digested the dead? It was getting dark. He didn't want to be in the maze any longer.

He lowered himself to the ground and leaned against a hedge, the same way he had done after the accident. Except it was a tree stump that time, a stump at the top of the embankment. Four other athletes had survived with him; others who had happened to choose the middle rows, closest to the emergency windows. They had all crawled up the embankment as the bus slid down and sank into the hyacinth-filled water. Officially a survivor amongst survivors, he watched the bus sink with the other four – their adrenalin levels receding into a hospital-ward's-worth of injury.

A wind swept through the maze. The hedges undulated. Lucas saw a weak spot, a section that hadn't taken to the soil very well. It was worth a try. He made his way to the thin skein of hedge and used his crutches to carve out a crawl space.

A FEW METRES away, Tobias sprinted through the green corridors. The psilocybin slowed him down, making him fixate on the woven branches running alongside him. He fought the impulse to stare at them because he wanted to win, even if it was just a game. Out of all the addictions he'd fallen into and out of over a lifetime, winning was the true exhilaration.

It was the thrill of winning that made The Fountain of the Active Grace of God Ministry a successful venture. After Stephen's murder, he became well known in the community for appearing several times on eNCA to give his eyewitness account. People in the community began to trust him out of a sense of familiarity, one that Tobias used to inculcate his first group of congregants. A week after purchasing a fake certificate in Bible studies, Tobias was at the pulpit, in Aunty Charmaine's garage, expounding doctrines on the 'evils of money' and how giving it away to God's church was a way to 'purify' this evil, this 'tainted water flowing through our cities', as he called it.

He became a pro at Bible-speak because TV at Aunty Charmaine's had stayed on TBN Africa, even when no one was watching. It was this extensive exposure that made speaking in divine riddles, prophesying imminent calamity and shaming people out of their money second nature. When the growth of his congregation slowed after six months, he knew he had to change the message. So, he got more radical, preaching that God was *abundance* and if people gave what little they had to his ministry it would come back tenfold in material blessings. If they didn't get their blessings, it was because they were still unworthy, their minds too attached on earning a living instead of living *in* the Lord Almighty.

Over time, he became a virtuoso at consuming all forms of suffering from his congregants, regurgitating their confessions, using scripture as an admonition of their lack of faith. Yes, no one believed as much as Tobias did, which was why God had blessed him with a profitable church, a house, car, a fridge packed with Woolies groceries. The suffering of the people, he liked to stress, was a holy burden God placed upon them for not focusing every part of their life on praising Him – The One, Eternal Father – and doing so exclusively at The Fountain of the Active Grace of God Ministry.

The Bible, Tobias discovered, was a handbook: a tool used to capture people's minds and scam them blind. The stories had mythical force; he could not argue with the eloquence of the book's verses, so poetic it answered the yearnings of millions in catch-phrases, perfect for the mass production of bookmarks, key chains, bumper stickers. Near the end of the ministry, just before he was arrested, he took on the view that hidden in the Bible's memorable verses was a book on how to run a profitable enterprise based on the stoking of collective shame, and the evocative plot twist of a God that went above and beyond to save even the worst of people.

Though I walk in the shadow of the valley of death, no evil shall I fear.

He often ended his Sunday miracle services with this verse. These were the services where crippled women walked, deaf men heard, and the occasional poisonous snakebite was rendered futile in the face of passionate prayer. Sometimes, the men he shared a prison cell with asked why he chose a church ministry, and Tobias would explain that, really, his church was a business like any other. It had expenses, it needed income, and it produced profits, which he never fully disclosed to SARS. Like any business model, The Fountain of the Active Grace of God Ministry tapped into a gap in the market, a gap it had to fulfil, but not satisfy completely. The whole point of the church was to hook people into coming back. No point in saving people's souls without slipping in the fine print. And for redemption to stick, people had to cough up more for heaven's coffers.

EVENING THICKENED TO night. Tobias had covered large swathes of the maze and still had not found its centre. Breathing heavily, a pounding pain in his abdomen, he stopped to consider how he'd know when he reached it. Was there a sign? Some sort of altar or sundial that would confirm his victory? He felt stupid: how he imagined his congregants had felt when news broke of his faked miracles. He wanted the mushrooms out of his body; they brought up too much. It was useless to vomit, he thought.

So he continued, too weary to sprint but walking at a pace. He came upon dead end after dead end. A sadness overcame him. He was a loser, even if he found the centre. Even if he'd been made the centre of the world – by his father, mother, Aunty Charmaine or the white woman in his recurring dream – he was a loser. He had nothing to show for his life. No university degree. No house in his name. No walk-in cupboard filled with suits, cufflinks, pocket squares, rows of cologne. Not even the instant affection of Abbas.

All the running had made his feet swell; his shoes chafed against them. Blisters, he thought, thinking back to the day Aunty Charmaine was buried. Though her extended family had always treated him like a bastard – the spawn of an alcoholic father and play-white mother – they didn't mind letting him cover Charmaine's casket with soil. The shovel he'd used had no rubber sheath to protect his hands; the blisters it left on his palms later turned to calluses. He didn't mind. The love Charmaine had given was equal to the wounds her death inflicted. For once in his life, pain made sense; it equalled something other than blind cruelty.

The family watched him, Tobias the bastard, fill Charmaine's hole from the shade of their gazebo. They enjoyed putting him to work like that, a labourer without pay. A couple of the uncles came up to him after the hole was closed to commend him on his tribute. He knew there was no place in the family for him. Who would want to be in a family that clutched funeral pamphlets to their chests, singing *Amazing Grace* off-key, while he shovelled dirt under the welts of the sun?

Tobias turned a corner and landed up in the centre of the maze. His speculations had paid off; there was a sundial. If only he had found it earlier, he could have tried to tell the time. With the day spent, the sundial was useless. He called for Mustafa several times, exclaiming that he'd won. No reply came. So he sat on the sundial, convinced that retracing his steps was the best way out. Bats darted above his head, hunting for their first meal of the night; light from a half-moon pinholed the hedge, casting lunar spiderwebs. If Mustafa wasn't coming to get him, then he was lost, with very little energy to make the trip back without help.

He was scared, the fear a different quality to the one that had focused his energies during the burglary. Killing those men had sourced the last dregs of brutality in him, the kind of blunt force he now needed to force himself out of the maze. The descending fear was too enigmatic to be curtailed by fists or gunfire – there was no antidote for the sinking feeling that, at the moment of his passing, there would be no one sitting by his side. Life was so fucken hard, made starker by the random malice, naturalised by greed, humanity's highest form of progress. Why did it have to be this way?

The answer baffled Tobias. It had always baffled him and always would. It was this that made him tough, the exact way the world wanted him to be. All he had ever done was reflect back what life wrote into him.

His body tingled. A shiver crackled up and pressed against his skull, demanding an exit where there was none. He touched his distended stomach, felt for his liver, picturing years of drinking condensed to scars, black and bulbous. Scar tissue was supposed to heal a wound, wasn't it? What kind of body made scars that blocked the removal of toxins with their stubbornness? He chuckled thinking that, in fact, he was a fraudster, through and through. Scamming years off his liver was just something an alcoholic did.

He stood up, legs shaky, and dragged his body back into the corridor he'd emerged from earlier. After walking several metres, he fell to his knees. The maze was ghostly quiet, crickets rang in his ears. He got up, blocking his ears with his fingers to soldier on. He had taken two lefts and doubled back to take a right before his vision began to tunnel. Only the grass right in front of him was visible. Then he felt it. The breath of papa waggies on his shoulder.

'Nee fok!' He got on all fours and scrambled to the end of the corridor. Another dead end, the hedge too dense to force his way through. Face it, he told himself, turning, certain papa waggies was there. It could be no one else but papa waggies.

Tiny air bubbles had formed in the canals of his ears. Sound reached him as if he were wading through an underwater cave. He screamed in an effort to unblock his ears. It seemed to work, but he needed to scream longer, louder, for his ears to pop completely. Papa waggies was almost upon him. There wasn't much time. He wasn't sure how he knew this. Perhaps it was the pressure in his chest that wouldn't let up, the same pressure he felt while asleep and paralysed, an unbearable weight upon him, like a grown man crouched on his chest. Or was it a grown woman?

The atmosphere rolled and rippled with his screams, silencing the crickets, sending bats into their roosts. Something was coming at him from the end of the corridor. He screamed louder, his chest screwing tighter, limbs stiffening against the consciousness that animated them. The wringing in his abdomen was excruciating. His lungs strained for air. Was this what it felt like to be submerged underwater, or stranded near a summit, the air too thin to force into him?

Whatever was coming from the other end of the corridor bellowed, hundreds of war drums in unison. As Tobias emptied his lungs, what emerged from the darkness was no figure, no unbearable weight. Water. It was water. A deluge that knocked breath out of his body: a donga in the landscape.

Mustafa watched Lucas and Tobias enter the maze. They'll be all right, he thought, believing that everything they'd experienced so far would see them through whatever they faced in the hedges.

A weaver bird settled on the grass nearby. He watched the bird snip a blade of grass, carry it off in its beak and perch on the largest thorn tree on the property. It had amazed Mustafa how, when they had first moved to the property, several thorns trees had sprouted without any hands planting them.

Well, that wasn't entirely true, he thought. Air currents are their own hands. Leave a patch of soil alone and something will grow. Always. The weaver threaded the blade of grass through a tightly wound knot of twigs and leaves already fixed to a branch. Mustafa watched its head bob as it wove, making decisions as instant as breathing. Then the bird stopped to survey its handiwork, pulled apart what wasn't working without ceremony, and flew off to scavenge for more material.

Over the course of a few hours, that nest would grow from a flabby tryst to an oval of green, drying out into a pale brown. There must come a point, he thought, where the bird said to itself 'enough'; when its meticulous prodding and double-checking had led it to a feeling of satisfaction – even if that satisfaction came in the form of a chemical signal firing in sections of its brain. The weaver must have some sort of plan, a dream, compelling it to think that a home could be made from garden scraps.

The nests were always temporary – torn apart by a male companion or worn down by the weather – and yet the weaver continued with the same dream, throughout the seasons, believing each build could coax a female, bringing the nest that much closer to perfection. Or maybe it wasn't about perfection. Maybe it was about the thrill of imperfection: seeing how long one's efforts held, how much of a home one made for oneself by the light one had to see by. It struck Mustafa, a tap on the shoulder, that life had a vein of insanity running through it – a desire to assail and subdue unknown wilds that always won in the end.

What if it isn't a game, he wondered. What if it's an orchestra, the largest any mind could hold in one thought? An orchestra without an audience. An orchestra in a concert hall where the walls crumbled to their elements and, in the next sheet of music, rose to Byzantine magnificence. Forever flirting with silence between the notes, the octaves of the cosmos vibrated in related frequency – whether in petri dishes under a microscope or from a bird's eye view of the salt plains of the earth.

'Mustafa! I need you!' shouted the Mortician from the deck of the third floor.

'What is it?'

'Angelique. It's her time.'

He staggered into the house, the shrooms made him feel like he was gliding without legs. When he entered the treehouse, he found the Mortician sitting with Angelique, muttering. A prayer? He hadn't heard her pray in a while.

'Let's get her to a bedroom.'

'She's still –'

'Barely. Not much longer now,' said the Mortician, holding Angelique close to her chest. Angelique's eyes were closed, her chest lifting the creases of her sweater slightly. 'Quick, her breathing is faint.'

Mustafa held her upper body and the Mortician took her legs. They moved her to an unused bedroom on the third floor and laid her on top of silk sheets. 'I'll stay with her,' said Mustafa. 'Where's Daniel. Wasn't he with you?'

'He ran off. I couldn't stop him.'

'What do you mean you couldn't stop him?'

'She was having a breakthrough. I had to stay with her.'

'Go and find him.'

Mustafa spoke with an authority, the tone reminiscent of her time working under him at the hospice. 'Fine, I'll go.' The Mortician walked along the aerial walkway, checking each treehouse. It was only when she came into view of the last treehouse, in the south-east corner of the property, that she knew where Daniel had gone.

The door had been flung open and a light was on inside. She crept up to the entrance and peered in. Daniel stood amongst her most cherished possessions, in front of the monitors. Walking across the threshold, her foot caught a crick of old wood, alerting him.

He didn't flinch. Instead, he turned his head to one side, recognising the outline of the Mortician in his peripherals. 'So, lab rats, is it?' He spoke slowly, restraining his voice to a neutral tone.

The Mortician sucked her lower belly in, pulling her navel towards her spine. 'If the institute is to continue and grow, it needs memory. Something to compare itself to. A lineage. Like any organism. I'm sorry, but you must understand … when people know they're being watched they aren't authentic. And I needed authenticity, or else our work here –'

'You remember when you spoke about electrons and their particle-wave nature?' Daniel turned, a fiery sheen in his eyes.

'Uh, yes, sure I do.'

'What you failed to mention is that an electron will appear however it wants to, depending on what you put it through. But no one, not even *you*, will ever know what an electron really is. All this' – he gestured to the monitors – 'experiments. It's not us. Hell, you could have been taping me from the time I left the womb but you'd still never get close to knowing what it is like to be inside my skin.' He made his way to the exit, walking past her.

'Before you leave, there's something I need to show you.'

Daniel stopped between the treehouse and the walkway. The

Mortician walked up to the desk and scrolled through several files before finding the ones she wanted. On two separate screens she replayed two scenes. The first was Daniel, huddled over a phone, masturbating. The second was Mustafa and Lucas, on the floor of the marijuana greenhouse.

'What the fuck is this?' he shouted, coming towards her. Though he wanted to, he didn't shove her. After what she'd done to Tobias's hand, he wouldn't risk it.

'Put aside your anger and tell me what you see,' she said, standing to the side.

Daniel watched a version of himself cum into his hands while a version of Lucas let Mustafa whisper-kiss him, from the neck down to the scars on his knees. Daniel's videos cycled through the many times he'd taken his phone with him into the bathroom. Lucas had only one video; in it, he and Mustafa lay beside each other, naked, abandoning themselves to the unbearable tension in their pelvises, two cobras entranced by the flute charmer between their legs – heads tilted back, necks flared into hoods.

It was a beauty arousing in its dilatory intensity. 'I'm leaving,' said Daniel.

'I know.'

The Mortician stepped forward and turned the monitors off. By the time she turned around, he was gone.

DANIEL PACKED HIS bags within the hour. Anything he and Lucas had bought together he left behind. He lugged his backpack down the kokerboom staircase, out through the front door, across the lawn and past the rock pools, stopping underneath a willow tree at the top of the pebbled driveway that led down to the black lattice gate. He called an Uber and rested on his luggage, feeling ashamed for being turned on by the sight of Lucas with another man.

He was not the type to cause a scene, though every part of him was screaming for one. Shove Mustafa down the stairs. Break a cupboard of wine glasses. Make it felt, somewhere other than his heart, that damage had been done. The trip was subsiding. His body felt limp. He was hungry, but he needed to make it to the Uber first.

'Where are you going?' Lucas stood just beyond the rock pool, a darkening sky behind him. There was mud streaked across his clothes and leaves in his hair.

He was about to reply when his phone vibrated. The Uber was outside. He caught the straps of his luggage in the crease of his arm and made his way to the gate.

'Wait!' said Lucas, standing at the top of the driveway, looking down.

The lovers contemplated one another, one highway of neurons intending to stay, another set on leaving. Both men scanned for bodily cues, their mirror neurons discharging futures that no longer included the other.

If either of them had ever truly been in love, it was here where love relinquished its gridlocked hold for a dirt road through the wilderness.

A WEEK AFTER the ceremony, Lucas, Mustafa and the Mortician were lying on separate couches, drinking hot cocoa under blankets, sharing their shroom experiences, when the intercom rang. The Mortician, sluggish from a heavy lunch, walked over to pick up the phone. In the intercom's monitor she saw a stocky lady standing in front of an Omega Plumbing van.

'Hello? Yes, good afternoon, ma'am. I'm Thenjiwe Khumalo, from *Bull's Eye*. I was wondering if I could come in and ask you some questions?'

The Mortician couldn't believe it. Thenjiwe Khumalo, award-winning investigative journalist, was standing by the gate. 'Uh, what is this in connection with?' she asked.

'I'd rather we talk face to face, if you don't mind.'

'I'm afraid I do mind.'

'Okay, well, this is in connection with a tip sent through to *Bull's Eye* that you and your associates are running an illegal palliative care centre.'

The Mortician asked Thenjiwe to repeat herself before it all sank in. Was this Daniel? Or had Vicky Prinsloo figured out her final sucker punch, using her contacts in media? 'I have no comment to make at this time. You can relay your questions to my lawyer, Shona Molefe,' said the Mortician.

'Ma'am, if you won't speak to us openly, we'll have to take this up with the relevant authorities.'

Thenjiwe Khumalo didn't disappoint, thought the Mortician. She knew how to turn the screw on a mark, even via intercom. 'You'll be hearing from my lawyer,' she said.

'And you'll be hearing from the Health Professions Council of

South Africa,' said Thenjiwe.

She watched Thenjiwe get into the plumbing van, take a photo of the gate and the high wall that hid the unnumbered house from the street, and drive away.

The Mortician came back into the lounge, shell-shocked. 'We have to leave,' she said, the words estranged from the mouth that had made them.

'What are you talking about?' said Mustafa.

'That was ... Thenjiwe ... outside ... Khumalo. We have to leave!'

The Mortician's amygdala, manufacturer of fear, hijacked her nervous system, raising the hairs on her body to attention, saluting soldiers. But she had no rousing speech to give, no call to die for a flag on a pole. She drew a firelighter from a side drawer and held it to a lace curtain, explaining how it was only a matter of time before a blue-light brigade forced themselves through the gate. The lace caught alight, flames spreading faster than the eye could follow, determined as she was to scorch the earth.

Mustafa lunged for the firelighter, reaching almost simultaneously for the pitcher of water on a coffee table. When that didn't douse the flames, he ripped the curtains from the rail, burning his hand, and stomped till the fire was out. 'Just take a moment,' he said, holding his injured hand. 'Call Molefe and explain the situation.'

'Yes, you're right.' The Mortician got on the phone, every few minutes checking the intercom's monitor. 'Mustafa, call my father!' she shouted back.

Sitting on the couch, Lucas was stunned by Mustafa's quick thinking, as if he had always known it would come to this. He watched in fascination, receding into God's first language. Silence.

LUCAS

… Thanks, Cathy, I'm here at the Galleria in Sunninghill where Angelique Mlungisi is being remembered by family and friends, among them the newly crowned Mr SA, Malik Groenebald, and world-renowned photographer, Todd Nubile. The Mlungisi family have confirmed that Xolisi Makweto will not be in attendance. As we know, the couple was embroiled in a messy break-up, that involved a case of assault being levelled at Xolisi Makweto. To this day, the case sits in courts unresolved. Experts say the case will likely be thrown out of court. Speculation has been rife surrounding the circumstances of Ms Mlungisi's passing. Police say she was found in a bathtub at her luxury apartment in Rosebank. Investigators have ruled out foul play, but sources have revealed that the autopsy report has found that Angelique Mlungisi had high levels of an as yet undisclosed drug cocktail in her system when her body was found …

I turn the volume down. The percolator is almost ready, ground coffee smelling of nuts and citrus. Coffee poured, I head onto the Airbnb's balcony, propping myself in a wrought-iron picnic chair, an uncomfortable piece of furniture, but the view is worth it. A cloud on Table Mountain rolls down over the city. Yesterday, a tour guide spoke of the legend of the Dutch pirate who had a smoking contest with the devil up there. Dutchman and devil smoked for several days until the devil lost. Out of spite, the devil took the Dutchman wherever devils with bruised egos go. Moral of the story? Don't pick a match with a devil. You might win.

Through the sliding door, I spot Todd Nubile on the TV. Below

347

him, in white capital letters, a quote from his eulogy: *An education trust for young girls pursuing modelling careers will be established in Angelique's honour.*

I go back inside to turn the volume up. I wonder if Daniel is watching. Angelique never confided in me; I had heard about the photographer from Daniel: how eccentric Todd was, how much he demanded. A perfectionist. He definitely looked the part on TV – draped in a long black cape with silver and gold sequins that began at the collar and disappeared at the waist.

I've had many muses in my life. Angelique was my most prized. It's devastating to lose an immense talent like her. But her work, my work, will live on. Which is why the requiem of her life, our shoots together, will be on show at the Zeitz this spring.

My suit for the wedding has been tailored and pressed. Looking at it in the wardrobe builds anticipation. After living under the radar for months with the Mortician and Mustafa, it'll feel good to get dressed up and a little turnt.

I hop in the shower, alternating between hot and cold water. Under the hot, I close my eyes, quiet my mind, focus on the feelings, just like the Mortician taught. Nervousness, a slight tension in my neck. I turn to cold; the shock of it is something I've gotten used to. If I contemplate the sensations, I can almost feel the switch from my sympathetic nervous system to the parasympathetic. Would Mustafa be impressed with how much attention I pay now? At first, the cold can be unforgiving. It strikes like bricks. Then one day it doesn't; in fact, one day you crave the shock, wondering how you ever lived without it. I guess the parts of you that were unable to handle the discomfort are the parts that slough off.

I check my phone once out of the shower (still on time for the wedding). Daniel's been viewing my stories on Insta since I arrived in the city. He started doing it sporadically after the institute, resurfacing on my viewer's list, not saying a word. Watching.

I couldn't help myself, so I watched back, grateful he wasn't the type to block me. Mustafa and I had to be in a good space for me to even think about checking up on Daniel though. When things got a bit dicey with Mustafa, I dreaded clicking on that circle with Daniel's face inside. What was I scared of? That he was doing fine without me or, more than fine, that he was thriving – going on vacations, pursuing his academic career, finding love.

It was only when I left the Mortician and Mustafa and got a job as an assistant coach for the TUKS track team that I got the balls to listen to the podcast he'd started. He called it *The Pendulum.* The description on Spotify said it was 'the pragmatist's guide to dealing with life's questions. Desire. Pain. Pleasure. Disorder. And more.'

It was weird listening to him. I only managed one episode: something about the Roman god Janus and how, in a 'post-postmodern world', people could invent their own rituals for personal transition and new beginnings. These rituals didn't have to last forever. They could change and adapt to the demands of the moment. We'd both been affected by what we had experienced at the institute; Daniel never mentioned the place on his podcast, but there were moments where I felt he wanted to – where he seemed to second-guess himself, perhaps wondering if the Mortician or Mustafa were listening.

I was stunned when the invite for Sarah's wedding came. With her and Daniel being best friends, I was sure I'd get the snub. Maybe Sarah still saw our friendship as something separate; maybe they argued about it, and Daniel lost. She's a strong-willed woman. She usually gets her way.

Clean-shaven, tailored black paisley suit on, rose gold accessories around my neck, fingers and wrists, Chanel spritzed in the creases of my arms and a cane to match. Ready.

A family playing in the B&B's pool stares as I get into my

rental car. They must be living in the other cottage on the property. I greet, but they don't wave back. European, I think, or from someplace where people spend entire winters in the dark. I type the address into the GPS; it shows a snapshot of the winding journey I need to take.

Here we go.

The houses in Woodstock look like luxury cakes decked out in pink and white marzipan. Above a sign for Cassiem's Shop a giant hand graffitied on a white wall points to a flag of Palestine. Bright oranges and yellows mark out cafés, houses and curio stores. Graffiti has its place here. It surprises you with a woman's head made of lilacs, a majestic eagle swooping down against a black-bricked building, elephants swimming underwater behind a barbed-wired fence. Even the abandoned buildings and makeshift homes with corrugated roofing strain towards something forgotten.

Driving up towards Table Mountain and down towards Clifton, I'm less surprised. Glass structures turned towards the Atlantic, raised above street level. *Cough Syrup* playing on the radio. I try to sing along, but the ocean distracts. Look how it shatters the sunlight. Merciless. I try not to think of Mustafa, but when people break away from you, they leave evidence. *One more spoon of cough syrup now ooohhh ...* Singing isn't helping. It only makes me anxious. I drive along the coast towards the Twelve Apostles Hotel and Spa. The waves mimic the clouds, each a ship that the wind bends out of shape.

Finally, I arrive, feeling like I shouldn't have come. I follow the signs for *The Union of Sarah Tarr and Jeremy Sithole* to the garden, where I'm offered a choice of a tequila shot or some orange juice. I choose tequila. The only people I know here are Sarah, Daniel and Sarah's other friend, Tau. I always felt Tau had a thing for me because whenever we hung out as a group, he'd find any excuse to touch me – handing me a drink (and caressing my hand), coming up from behind (and touching the small of my back), laughing (and reaching out to squeeze my arm). Daniel said it was all in my head.

I see Tau sitting near the front and wave as I take a seat near the back. The venue is all cushioned-white wedding chairs on a pristine lawn, surrounded by flowers, of which I can only name chrysanthemums. There's an abnormal number of butterflies; I think they've been ordered for the occasion. Tau keeps turning and glancing my way. We lock eyes an awkward number of times before I put my shades on.

When the bride's wedding party arrives, a string quartet begins the wedding march. Daniel walks out as Sarah's man of honour. His hair's a lot shorter, and he has got a bit of a tan. As he walks up the aisle and stands under the arch, he doesn't notice me. All through the ceremony, the things we used to say about our potential wedding comes to mind. Like wanting to write our own vows. Or walking up to the wedding arch together, our families handing us over to each other at the foot of the aisle. Or not having a wedding at all and just getting married in court. Saving for the most lavish honeymoon we could think of. He told me marriage was never a possibility until he met me. I never took him seriously when he said cheesy things like that.

When the ceremony is over, the certificates signed, the wedding party goes off to take photos. I don't think Daniel's recognised me yet. While the families and friends take photos, greet and mingle, I fill up on champagne and carpaccio crostinis.

'Wow, and here I was thinking I'd never see you again.' Tau taps me on the shoulder and waits for me to turn around before he puts his arm around his date: a good-looking hunky guy with a septum piercing.

'How are you doing, Tau?'

'Great, great.' He sneaks a peek at my walking stick, then

looks up at his date, nudging him forward. 'This is Amir.'

I shake Amir's hand, filling him in on how Tau and I know one another. He nods politely, clearly bored.

'No plus one?' Tau asks, enjoying himself.

'Nope, don't need one. Excuse me, where's the restroom?' I grab hold of a nearby waiter, who directs me. It isn't long before I'm locked inside a cubicle. Safe, for the moment.

What did I want to prove coming here?

Wounds deserve their dignity. Mustafa's voice, clear as it was on the day he left. Am I here for dignity? Is coming alone to a wedding where your ex is the man of honour that much of a carnal sin? Here's the deal: I'll stay till the speeches are over. Then I'll make some excuse, write a sweet note in the wedding book and leave. Sarah will understand.

When I return to the festivities, everyone's moving inside for the reception. The wedding venue is decorated in frosted crystal and shades of blue. An ice palace. We welcome the bride and groom with cheers and applause; they sit at a table with their backs to the ocean. I've been placed at a table with Tau. When Daniel gets up to speak, I sip on a full glass of white wine. Tau taps me on the thigh. 'I heard he didn't put up a fuss when Sarah told him you were invited.' He winks, satisfied that that nugget of information was delivered at the right time.

I drink and listen to Daniel's speech. It's a lot funnier than the others. He talks about the time Sarah locked the keys in his car on Long Street on New Year's Eve, and that period in 2015 when she forced him to go on a liquid diet for six weeks. And who could forget the time she caused a ruckus at Home Affairs when she stopped a bribe from taking place right in front of her.

Sarah glances over to me during the speech. I raise my glass to her, mouthing 'Congratulations'. I need to leave.

WHEN THE SPEECHES are done and the mains eaten, I'm at the bar waiting for service. Daniel comes up behind me.

'Hi.'

'Great speech.'

'I didn't want it to be too serious.'

The barman takes our orders at the same time. We insist that the bill be separate.

'What's up with the cash bar?' I ask.

'Sarah's not a drinker anymore. She wanted the money spent on other things.'

'That's your friend, pulling everyone along. Kicking and screaming.'

Daniel considers his hands for a moment before asking where Mustafa is: '… I thought you'd bring him with. She did give you a plus one, right?'

'Oh, yeah. But no, I wanted to come alone.' I walk away towards the patio. It is dark and overcast, the ocean like a sleeping belly. The air is sobering; from where I'm standing I can see the silhouette of the wedding arch off in the distance. On the ramp leading to the garden a group of teenagers are huddled together. Before I can speculate about what they're doing, some of them start coughing loudly.

A hand reaches over my shoulder and drops a handful of berries in my gin and tonic. 'You've always liked yours with fruit.'

I lean against the railing, facing Daniel. 'Why did you let Sarah invite me?'

'You know how she can be. When it's her event, you gotta roll with the punches.'

'Fuck, she'll never change.'

Tau comes onto the patio, alone, and offers us cigs.

'We don't smoke,' says Daniel.

'Not tobacco, at least.'

They both turn to me, surprised.

'It's not even a thing to smoke weed anymore,' I say.

'That's true,' says Tau. 'What do you bitches think of Amir?' He is giddy for our response.

'Charming. Very proper,' says Daniel. 'What did you say he does?'

Tau starts raving about Amir's accomplishments. Doctoral degree in marine biology, doing postdoctoral research on optimising phytoplankton farms for absorbing CO_2 from our atmosphere. 'The man is obsessed with the smallest creatures. What kind of gay talks about the millions of bedbugs living on a single mattress right before he fucks you?' Tau looks at us, exasperated.

We burst out laughing.

'Anyway, let me go, gurls.'

We watch Tau join Amir at the table. 'It's all bullshit,' says Daniel.

'What?'

'Sarah says Tau always brings these Adonis characters to snazzy shindigs.'

'You don't think –'

'Oh, yeah. Rent boy.'

I drink. The wind picks up, making the water choppy. 'There's something I've been meaning to ask. Was it you?'

'It was whoever the Mortician seriously fucked over. Which could be a lot of people, let's be honest.'

The teenagers walk back to the reception from the ramp, giggling. We let them pass. 'I'm so –'

'You don't have to do that,' says Daniel. 'Things are, so different.'

'Did you know that we went into hiding, the three of us? I legit felt that being with them was what I was meant to do, looking after marijuana and mushrooms, sharing in their mysteries, practising their techniques. It felt … meaningful.'

Daniel turns towards the wedding venue, his face lit in laughs and dancing light. With all that joy shining onto him, he still hasn't shaken that sad look. 'I've thought a lot about those months. About before … your accident. My spell in the clinic. If I were to offer a theory –'

'You do like your theories.'

'Indulge me –' a glint, briefer than flint on stone, shoots across his face '– my theory, is that we held on too tight.'

'We didn't want things to change.'

'They *had* changed. We refused it. It was right there, and we couldn't see it. How could we be together if we couldn't bear our *own* lives?'

A fine drizzle comes in from the ocean. Neither of us want to go inside. 'When I was lying low with the Mortician and Mustafa, things weren't always great. There was a lot of blaming going on. I was in the middle of it. The Mortician wasn't happy about Mustafa and me; she suspected that you had something to do with the leak. Mustafa took it all to heart. He felt guilty. Instead of healing and bringing us together he'd broken us. Realising that made him push me away, I think.'

'Why'd he do that?'

'I don't know. He's a good guy, though. Complicated, yes, but caring. Him leaving the Mortician and I hurt, a lot. I had gone through losing you and then losing him. Everywhere I turned there was just … loss. I had to find some morsel of myself that didn't depend on affection from someone else. I had to realise that my story was one of millions, in a place that would continue creating stories, like mine; as if, with every story, the earth found new ways to see itself.'

Daniel's laugh starts in his throat and travels to his stomach.

'Yup, you've been spending too much time with those two.' He reaches for my arm and kisses me on the cheek. 'I get it, though.' The kiss happens so fast that by the time I touch my face he is already walking back inside. The newlyweds are cutting the cake.

ONE BY ONE, headlights turn on and leave the parking lot. I'm in my car, waiting, watching raindrops race one another to the edge of the windscreen, some engulfing others in the process. There's a knock on the passenger window.

'I told Tau I found another ride home,' shouts Daniel. I unlock the door. 'He didn't ask questions?'

'He was too drunk. Amir's driving.'

'Okay then.' He gets in and I turn the radio on. While I drive back towards the gleam of Clifton Daniel tells me about the success of his podcast. I listen, not sure what I'm doing right now.

When we get to his rental apartment, he gets fidgety, faffing around in the kitchen, asking if I want coffee. 'I can make you Nespresso.' He points to the machine.

At our basic level, we're grown-up children. The Mortician's voice blooms into my mind. She's right, I think, watching Daniel fiddle with his machine. But she's wrong too. There are parts of us, neither young nor old; parts that have always followed what tugs, tempts. What abides.

I go over to Daniel, hold his face in my hands and kiss him before he manages to put the machine to work. We tumble our way to the bed, clawing off our clothes. Naked, we wrap ourselves around each other, wary of my left leg.

He's inside of me, then I am inside him, our mouths hungry for any body part that may fit inside them. Elbow. Tuft of hair. Love handles. We want to climb up into the same body, the friction making us try harder. We cum at the same time, slimy ponds in our belly buttons. For once, I don't feel like a star in a porno. It feels awkward and silly, as if we've found a dusty box full of trinkets in our bodies' basements.

I don't know what to do with these trinkets. I don't think Daniel knows either. He idly pulls on the small hairs of my beard; I play with his nipples, watching them turn hard, then go soft again. We fall asleep that way.

WHEN I WAKE up, it's five in the afternoon and the bedroom window is slightly ajar. Daniel is motionless beside me. It's so quiet there's not even the background whirr of the fridge to disturb us. I sneak a peek out the window, from behind Daniel's chest, and make out a section of sky. My eyes stay fixed to that blue as I drift off to sleep.

Daniel's cooking wakes me. It's nine. I've slept the day away. Gathering my clothes from the floor, I walk into the kitchen.

'Breakfast for dinner?' he asks.

'I'm gonna get going.'

He leaves the eggs to go hard in the pan. Hugs me. 'I understand.'

'Thank you,' I say, finding the car keys in my suit pocket.

ON THE DRIVE back, I think about Mustafa and what he said when he left the Mortician and me. *These techniques, they're all traps. The trick is to let yourself get trapped. Then have the traps go up in flames, leaving you with nothing, save the chance to find a love to live in.*

When I get back to the B&B I run myself a bubble bath. I put my phone on charge while the water runs and roll a spliff. Three missed calls from the Mortician. And a message: *How was the wedding? Let's meet for coffee soon.* I don't reply.

Bath ready, I sprinkle eucalyptus oil in the water and light aloe vera incense. Joint lit, water warm, I get in, clouding up the room with steam and smoke. I see us, the Mortician, Mustafa and me, in Victor's lounge, watching the news.

On the TV, Thenjiwe Khumalo was front and centre, as the logo for *Bull's Eye* faded to the background.

It's one of the most mysterious stories Bull's Eye has covered to date. Following up on an anonymous tip-off, investigations may have uncovered an illegal palliative care centre in Northcliff, Johannesburg.

Several attempts to contact the owners of the alleged care centre were met with evasive responses from their lawyer, Shona Molefe. However, Bull's Eye has uncovered that the property was previously owned by well-known business tycoon, Jan Prinsloo.

When asked about Jan Prinsloo's possible ties to an illegal health care facility, Molefe denied all allegations, evoking her clients' right to privacy. Bull's Eye's investigators have the names of the current owners of the property, but currently a legal gag order prevents us from disclosing this.

What Bull's Eye can reveal is that the current owners are former hospice caregivers who had administered end-of-life care to Jan Prinsloo. One of the caregivers in the matter has ties to Ishaan Moosa, the disgraced former funeral parlour owner who, in 1996, was found guilty in a civil case of mishandling human remains.

The question Bull's Eye is asking: if Ishaan Moosa was involved in the running of this facility, why hasn't he been brought in for questioning? And why wasn't a criminal case brought against him all those years —

The Mortician had turned down the volume of the TV. She asked Mustafa how long Victor would let us stay at his place.

'Don't worry about Victor. He's a divorcee. He needs the company.' Mustafa abruptly walked out the room, uninterested in the report on the TV. In that moment his disinterest signalled trouble.

The Mortician turned the volume up.

– all attempts to reach Jan Prinsloo's daughter, Vicky Prinsloo, have been unsuccessful. We were, however, put in contact with Ms Prinsloo's lawyers, who referred us to case documents in which she has disputed the legality of how the owners came to be in possession, not only of the property, but large sums of money, 'donated' by Jan Prinsloo to his former hospice caregivers.

The presiding judge in the matter has since ruled against Vicky Prinsloo. Her legal team have stated that they will be studying the judgment closely.

Several attempts to interview neighbours in the area have yielded mixed results. Some have reported a steady stream of people leaving in a hurry, during the night, over the last two weeks. Although this hasn't been corroborated, some of the neighbours have reported strange noises, like banging and screaming, at odd hours, coming from the house. Although no reports to the police were filed at the time.

Currently, the property is occupied by squatters, who claim they have permission from the owners to take up residence here. Some of the neighbours speaking off camera say they are not happy with the development and are seeking legal recourse.

Questions abound. If this was an illegal care centre for the terminally ill, why has it taken so long for the Health Professions Council of South Africa to hear about it? Where are the facilitators who ran such an establishment? Are police going to investigate? Most importantly, if people came to this facility seeking end-of-life care, then where …

The Mortician turned the TV off. She said there was no reason to worry, that all *Bull's Eye* had was speculations. I wondered about this Ishaan Moosa, and the whole Jan Prinsloo debacle. Would she ever let me in on that? Would she ever trust me the way she trusted Mustafa?

I don't want to think about Mustafa. I don't want to think about the last couple of months, hiding out with the Mortician. I don't even want to think about myself.

The weed and the warm bathwater help me imagine all the lives I'm not living. I try to fix my mind on them. Maybe, in one of the houses in this street, there's a mother making school lunch before she goes to bed. Or a teenage boy taking selfies in his bedroom. Maybe there's an uncle falling asleep on a sofa, dreaming about the first time he rode a Ferris wheel.

All I know for sure is that there is something in each of us that wants to be our friend.

I ash the joint and sink below the bubbles.

Tobias sat beside the white woman on the dishevelled bench, wondering if the train would ever come. It was no use, he thought. She wasn't going to say anything new. This was her dream. It was clear now. He was a figment of her imagination and probably always had been.

An easterly wind swept across the ruined station. Dandelions growing through the concrete swayed west, against the wind. Afraid to face her, Tobias looked straight ahead and asked in a soft, pleading tone, 'Are you my mother?'

The woman held his hand but did not look at him. 'This is my dream,' she said.

He tried to pull his hand away, disgusted for even thinking she could be Mommie Ellen. But when he looked down, his hand was not there. Her hand was his hand.

The sound of a train drew nearer. The woman jumped up, clicked her heels, and strutted over dandelions towards the tracks. Her brisk walking kicked up hundreds of dandelion heads, tiny white umbrellas circling above, pocketing the air in whorls that rotated in on themselves, scattering seeds.

Tobias got pulled along with her. Unable to define his hand from hers, he looked for something sharp to sever himself at the wrist. There was nothing.

At the tracks, the woman leaned forward and turned east, in the direction of the oncoming train sounds. Eager to board, her platform shoes well over the edge, Tobias fought against her, trying to pull the woman back to safety.

'Ssshhh,' she said. 'You're in my dream, now ssshhh.'

When the train arrived, it came from the west. She had been

looking in the wrong direction. 'You're in mine!' shouted Tobias, clasping her with his free arm and jumping into the path of the oncoming train.

The station turned fuzzy with dandelion dreams.

THE DRIP OF a morphine bag was the first thing Tobias woke up to. The usual aches and sluggishness of his body felt distant. He manoeuvred himself upright and saw that he was in a room he didn't recognise. The curtains were drawn, bordered by bands of light; from their intensity he assumed it to be the middle of the day. There weren't any birds singing or rustling trees; just the faint gnaws of car engines, so faint they seemed to stem from another world.

The room was plain. Eggshell walls, brown carpet, a ceiling fan whose pull-chain switch clinked against its bulb in time to every revolution it made. On a table at the foot of the bed there was an envelope, balanced against a vase of tulips, their pollen-powdered anthers having stained the paper.

The envelope had his name on it.

Thinking back, Tobias saw himself in the maze, screaming. Remembered the feeling of being wrung out to dry like clothes left in the sun, baked hard by the sapping heat. He pulled the covers off and considered his body. How deflated. How in need of something it could never get back. His legs responded feebly to his commands, as if the covenant they'd entered into at birth was now scrambled letters that didn't want to be put back into words.

He sized up the room. By the looks of the ceiling, it was a Dutch-style cottage. Where were Mustafa and the Mortician? Had they found him in the maze and brought him here? He gripped the sheets and pulled them into a mound he could use to lift himself to standing. Who would have guessed that he would live this long?

He thought of Stephen: *Ja, you old cow, happy you outlived me? At least I died with a bush on my balls.*

Hearing Stephen's voice, he wasn't happy or sad. Naming feelings was a tiring business; by the time he deciphered them, they would have changed, swept along in a stream, all of it flowing into …

Was this the morphine? Some good shit.

Holding the drip stand with both hands, he stood and wiggled his gangly toes. As he made his way to the envelope, he thought of Moses: staff in hand, parting the Red Sea. Of all the stories he'd preached about, that one lit up the faces of the children in the pews. It was magical. Absolute faith, overcoming the elements. He had come to know better. Wishful thinking, prayer, only went as far as parting the sea of one's mind, for a time, before cathedrals of water collapsed. They always did.

He reached the table, huffing. The note inside the envelope read:

Tobias,

I must first apologise for not being there when you wake up. It was not a decision I took lightly. When we found you passed out in the maze, I was certain you wouldn't make it through the night. But your resilience continues to exceed our expectations.

We have had to pause the work for a while. While you were recovering, reports of the institute were leaked to the media. We can't be sure at this time who is responsible, but, frankly, I don't care. The result is the same.

Not sure what this might mean for Mustafa or me. We worried that we would not be able to take care of you to the end, so we had to leave you in the hands of another while we evade the scrutiny of the media and probably the police. Don't worry, we've left you in the hands of someone Mustafa and I trust. Someone who has worked with us before.

Can you recall our last session together? I ask because if you look outside, you'll see I've kept my side of our bargain …

The paper trembled in Tobias's hand. Holding onto the drip stand with the other, he limped over to the window. He pulled back the curtains onto an overgrown back yard, tall grass obscuring the bottom half of a house metres away. The roof was rusted and a pigeon bathed itself in the overflow container of the solar geyser. He continued reading:

We couldn't secure Charmaine's old house with the money you chose not to destroy. But, lucky for us, the family in the main house are renting their back rooms. All it took was a cleaning crew, buckets of paint and new furniture to give the place the love it deserved.

We won't see one another again and for that reason I must say that, with you, it was hard for me to measure the success or failure of our journey. I wish we had had more time. Alas, things take time, and time takes things, and life is a mixture of both trying to become the other. I'm not sure I am making sense, but no doubt sense is the least of your concerns. I only hope that you don't feel short-changed, that staying for the ceremony, like we agreed, was worthwhile.

PS A bit of history (I can't resist). Did you know that Roman soldiers while on long and treacherous journeys kept small satchels filled with personal trinkets, amulets, bits and pieces of loved ones (living and dead) to comfort them as they warred and bled for the empire? They called these loculi, meaning 'small places'. This is my gift to you. Our bargain. A small place.

There was a knock at the door and a woman dressed in a nurse's uniform walked in. She introduced herself as Gretta. 'I'm in the next room. If you want anything, just call out my name or bang on the wall.'

'Wait,' said Tobias. 'I'm not sure –'

Gretta sat Tobias down at a table and handed him a glass of water. 'If you want, I can take you around the yard.'

'Ja, let's do that. Later, I think. Thank you.'

'Oh, before I forget,' said Gretta. 'I was told to let you know that the fridge is stocked with your favourites. Don't be shy to share some, ne?' She winked before leaving the room.

The back quarters had always been off bounds for Tobias growing up. As boys, Stephen and he would sneak a peek inside when the windows were open.

My room is bigger than this, Stephen had bragged.

Even as a teen, Tobias knew these rooms were rented out to down-on-their-luck strangers – men working in the shoe or furniture factories who'd gambled themselves into disrepair, women on their way out of Joburg looking to make a life elsewhere. These people couldn't pay much rent and, when money was scarce, offered to take care of Charmaine's yard. Some tenants didn't do much but cut the grass down to its roots. Others worked the soil, planting cabbages, pumpkin, lettuce and the odd dagga plant. Then there were those who lied about the rent they could pay or the gardening they would do.

Charmaine had too much patience for other people's poppetjies, thought Tobias. He thought about what Gretta's wink meant. A cool rush of air greeted him when he opened the fridge; it had been filled with all kinds of alcohol. Brandy. Cognac. Savanna. Wine. Beer. Rum. Tequila. Vodka. Shuffling back and forth to the table, he emptied the fridge bottle by bottle, then sat down before them with the sun on his face.

Shadows of water spread across the table, through each bottle. His finger itched. A translucent insect (a spider, or maybe a small beetle, he wasn't sure) scrambled down the length of his ring finger. It was a baby, he thought; made from a pin-drop of blood.

Was that blood his? Would he have noticed the spider if he wasn't sitting here, like this?

'Gretta!' he called, listening for footsteps from the adjacent room.

Mustafa sat upright, asleep, his notebook opened on his lap. The words, *through it, with it, in it* written in the margin. A female mosquito flying through the room was drawn, mid-flight, towards Mustafa's gaseous emissions. Tracking the gases towards their origin, she settled on a patch of skin soiled in lactic acid, ammonia and sebum: Mustafa's forearm. Spitting on the skin to numb it, she inserted her proboscis, probing Mustafa's tissue for blood flow, releasing her saliva into him. Finding a blood vessel, she consumed twice her bodyweight in blood, pulled out of Mustafa and flew away.

Mustafa woke, itching. He held up his notebook and read some of what he had written. Without the institute, ideas felt useless. That place focused him, had framed his life towards eternity, which somehow felt graspable behind those walls. Hiding out at Victor Dlamini's house, the force of the weekday plagued him. Was he missing out on something? The tides of productivity, he thought, scratching the mosquito bite.

He rested against the headboard. They would be all right, he reassured himself. Time had been bought, thanks to Molefe. All evidence of any kind of 'health-care facility' had been discreetly deposited in storage containers, thanks to Ishaan and his 'no-questions-asked' approach. Mustafa walked out of the room to find Victor.

He was in his study, meticulously adding up the assets to be divided in his divorce. 'It's quite a thing, to see the world you've built with someone cut up by cold math,' said Victor, lying back in his Eames chair, sipping Inverroche gin. 'And you? Something wrong? You've been taking your meds?'

Mustafa fingered the books on the shelves. 'I've set an alarm every night. And a reminder for my refills.'

'It's not advisable to go as long as you did without them. I know I had a part to play in that. I'm sorry.'

'It's not your fault. I was getting tired of the whole thing anyway.'

'That thing called life,' said Victor, sitting up. 'You know you can't live without them, right?'

'That's where you're wrong.' He stood behind Victor, looking out the window at the glossy red Mercedes in the driveway. 'I *can* live without them. Just not for very long, and not very well. Can I ask you something?'

'Since when do you need permission?' Victor poured himself another gin.

'At this stage, what hurts more? Losing your wife or losing half of everything?'

Victor swirled the gin in his mouth before swallowing. 'At the beginning, I'd say her. Now, it's losing the things that remind me of us. That's a trick question, I suppose. Losing the one is an anagram for the other.' He clicked his tongue and refilled the half-empty glass.

Mustafa sensed his friend was uncomfortable with the line of questioning. 'We won't be staying long. After I leave, I don't suspect my friends will want to inconvenience you.'

'Wait – you're leaving?'

Victor's face was puffy from the day's drinking. He needed a shower and a litre of water before bed, thought Mustafa. 'I need to be on my own for a little, away from Lucas and her. You understand?'

'What about this venture you were all involved in?'

'I don't think I can go back to it. Not after what's happened. It's better you don't know the details.'

Victor handed his gin to Mustafa. 'You can always crash here when you need. Even if I only have half of what I used to have. Guys like us need to look out for each other.'

Mustafa sipped the bitter tonic and put it down on the desk. He left the study and went back to the guest room he had been sharing with Lucas. The Mortician was waiting on the bed, beside swimming trunks that she had laid out for him. In her hand she held an old ceramic ladle. 'Molefe called.'

'Oh. What does she have to say?' he asked.

'The remaining funds from Jan's lump sum should be coming in any day now.'

'That's good.'

'At least we can put all that Vicky stuff behind us.'

'That's if her lawyers don't manage to find more loopholes to use in their favour.'

'Vicky sent this, via Molefe.'

Mustafa sat down and took the ladle from her.

'It's the kind her ancestors used. Wine dished from a barrel.' She took the ladle from Mustafa and threw it to the floor. 'She sent that to me after I sent her the video of Jan explaining how much he believed in our work. I thought seeing her own father give credibility to our work might persuade her to let things go. I was wrong. Again. You saw *Bull's Eye*'s report. If it wasn't for Shona's manoeuvres we'd be in real shit by now.'

'Do me a favour. Don't respond to Vicky. She's just taunting you. You have what you need to start again.'

'That's me. What about those who don't have what they need to start again? Will their time ever come?'

'When everyone has their own ladle. Their own barrel to dish from. Maybe.'

The Mortician turned to him, dangling her feet above the floor. 'Come swimming with me. Please.'

'Let me get changed.'

VICTOR'S POOL WAS icy. Their bodies redirected blood away from their skin and in towards the core organs, keeping their temperatures steady. The Mortician swam down to the bottom of the pool and stayed there, watching Mustafa float on the surface.

She emptied her lungs and sat there for as long as she could before rising. 'I have to say –' she began between gasps '– if it wasn't for you, I'd have made a bonfire out of the property.'

Mustafa lifted himself out of the waters's delicate hold and swam to the edge.

'You want to leave. I know. When were you going to tell me? Or did you not think our friendship deserved that?'

'Friendship?' Mustafa climbed out of the pool and sat on the hot paving. 'Whatever this is, it's not real friendship.'

'Real? What is *real*, Mustafa? Owning up to the things we have kept from one another, even when it hurts. That's real.'

'With it. In it. Through it,' Mustafa whispered.

'What?'

'We knew, didn't we, how fine the line was between liberating people on their own terms and dishing out another catch-all cure.'

'We can learn from this. Make better choices. *Together.*'

'Babita, you can't stand having to depend on others. Knowing that you don't have all the best solutions.' He picked up his towel.

'Don't leave. I am the only one who accepts you. All of you,' said the Mortician, eyes red, water dripping off her chin.

'If death was the thing that brought us together, why not let it be the wedge too?' Mustafa strolled into the house, drying himself off.

As she watched him leave, the Mortician felt their friendship obtain a kind of sacredness. A wall had breached between them, and all she could do now was write little prayers, roll them up on tiny pieces of paper and fit them, snugly, in its crevices. How many prayers would it take to scrape the cement out from between the bricks? Would the wall even collapse, if it was, indeed, prayers that made it crumble?

She floated on the water, wondering how she'd counselled the residents with such equanimity and yet couldn't save herself from the loss invading her. None of her techniques could salve the wretched feeling. And even though she'd trained herself to accept loss as the immovable state of the world, she nevertheless wanted to lie down. Grieve for its limits.

A feeling, as imperceptible as an electric short-circuit across water, jittered through her. For as long as she was alive, the self she thought she had a handle on would surprise her with its fixations and orderings. There had never been a handle to grasp at in the first place. Only best guesses, eager snatches, until death showed life just how vibrant it really was.

She placed her towel down and stretched out on the hot paving, listening to the raised voices coming from a nearby bedroom. Mustafa was no doubt telling Lucas he was leaving. She didn't mind Lucas. If he were up for it, they could rebuild the institute together. She could do with an apprentice. In Cape Town, perhaps?

Sitting up, she scratched at the pimply-red rash that had developed on her hands over the last week and a half. Parts of it had evolved into tiny, fluid-filled blisters that she took small pleasure in popping. Stress. Time off was needed. A detox from the lives she'd been submerged in. Each of the residents had to be forgotten – reduced to journalled observations and video recordings so that she could embrace a new cohort.

Time was needed for the past's stranglehold to go limp, for the sharpness of individual lives to blur into pattern. For the wounds of the residents' leaving to harden into healing, sealing a body made for holes. This was the difference between cured and healed, she thought. One you leave behind, another you live with.

Sunlight lay in shards across the unnumbered house: a patina of gold-plated jewellery left to rust by an open window. Gardeners, car guards, waste pickers, car washers, beggars and street sweepers were asked, by an unusually friendly couple, if they wanted to stay in an abandoned house. Most took the opportunity with caution.

The car washers and gardeners brought their families to the property. Some waste pickers and beggars came alone. Each group had their choice of en suite bedrooms. The kitchen became communal, though there wasn't much of a cleaning schedule, so it was often piled high with dirty dishes, potato peels and sticky skid marks on the floor from boiled-over milk or gravy.

A family of four moved into the reading room, and the mother (a trader on the streets of Blackheath) took it upon herself to be the steward, lending books out to those who asked, forbidding the children on the property from using them as bricks for their make-believe castles.

The children who came to stay took to the trees, renaming the treehouses in a game of Avatar. The central atrium was for the Air Nomads. The treehouse that held the sense tank was home to the Water Kingdom. The room fitted with mirrors was named the Fire Kingdom. There were days when a child, left on their own, would get lost in the hedges, having ventured too far from adult supervision. This happened so often that, collectively, the new inhabitants decided to cut the hedges down. For safety. In their place they planted maize, sorghum, tomatoes and green peas, and built chicken coops and an enclosure to nurture young goats.

After *Bull's Eye*'s exposé aired on television, the unnumbered house drew attention, which the new inhabitants of the property added to. Neighbours complained about the 'doof-doof' music that went on from Thursday to Sunday. Complaints were lodged at the municipal offices against the unsanitary agricultural conditions of chickens, goats and people living in such proximity. Wasn't this how disease spread? Wouldn't these animals bring rats or rabies?

Rats were drawn to the unnumbered house, but so were Northcliff's cats, who mapped their way to their prey, scaling Northcliff's walls to hunt on the grounds. After several complaints and health inspections, the number of chickens and goats had to be reduced to half. The spilled chicken blood soaked into the vegetable patch for a good month, smelling of hard-boiled eggs.

As a result of the increased attention paid to the property, residents of Lancaster Drive began to observe the unnumbered house with interest. Episodes of children falling off the aerial walkways and breaking their legs, reports of drunken fighting that ended in name-calling that went on for hours, along with the odd firecracker, occasionally mistaken for gunshots. All of these were added to the formal complaints, made not only to the municipality but to the metro police too.

Despite the neighbours' best efforts, there was no legal remedy for removal. The owners of the property were apparently overseas and had written a letter to the municipality stating definitively that *the occupants are welcome to stay for as long as they wish and are permitted to inhabit the premises of number eight, including the attached property at the back.* It was made clear to those living on Lancaster Drive that the owners were still paying the rates and levies for the property. No one on the neighbourhood WhatsApp group understood why the owners would go to such lengths to safeguard a group of vagrants.

On the WhatsApp group, neighbours discussed the *Bull's Eye* episode, where it was revealed that the unnumbered house was, in fact, registered under number eight Lancaster and that this house was owned by the same couple, who signed their letters to the courts as Mr. and Ms. M&M.

I told you something fishy was going on there.
My husband said the owners looked like druggies.
It was a lolly lounge. That's how they operate.
Or a half-way house for human trafficking.
I'm telling you, it's one of those State Security safe houses.

Nightmares were generated as fast as fingers could type. The WhatsApp group went as far as suggesting that similar activities were *still* taking place. No one at the Randburg police station took these allegations seriously.

This is not to say mind-altering substances weren't being consumed at the unnumbered house. Sorghum beer was brewed weekly on the back lawn, its sour aroma bringing the occupants of the property together to share in the brew's spirit of conviviality. A few surviving marijuana plants stuck their stems out of the cracked floor of a ransacked greenhouse, yielding buds that grew achingly slowly and were of poor quality. The mushrooms left behind in the other greenhouse were eaten by pigeons adventurous enough to try them. The fungi coaxed the pigeons to dance on the brim of the rock pools, as if at a disco. The children on the property thoroughly enjoyed the spectacle, especially when the adults ate those same mushrooms and stared up into the trees – believing the faces of their dead parents lived there. Eventually, the mushrooms outgrew their greenhouse and spread across the lawn and into the surrounding gardens, weaving the soil together into a damp mulch, consuming whatever fell to its death.

Once the residents of Lancaster realised the occupiers were not going anywhere, they decided to have a meeting to discuss the way forward. Sitting down with the new residents in a meditation room that had been turned into a depot for sorting recyclables, the two groups discussed, and agreed upon, the appropriate times to play music, and the days of the week where garbage should be taken out for removal.

Some of the new residents expressed the desire to go back home to their families that lived in other provinces and countries. It was decided that the municipality would be asked to foot the bill for their transportation. Others asked to be added to the neighbourhood's WhatsApp group. It was agreed that wanton intimidation of the residents would stop and that the new residents would keep the number of people living on the property to an agreed-upon maximum.

An uneasy treaty was reached that day. It held for as long as either side understood, and respected, what the other needed.

SEVERAL MONTHS INTO the new treaty, while packing the house's gym equipment into the back of a bakkie, traders living on the property noticed a man in tie-dye yoga pants walking up the driveway with a handful of groceries. The man respectfully greeted the traders who gathered and offered them the groceries. Some of them recognised the man from before and, softened by the groceries he'd offered, let him wander, room by room.

Mustafa noted that the residents had kept the artwork on the walls; some of the framed prints did have smudges on them, but he didn't mind. He walked on into the stained-glass room and found the panes had been gouged out. Tennis balls. Soccer balls. Stones. Kids, he laughed, walking out towards the sauna beside the lemon tree. There he found a group of women chopping wood and piling it in neat bundles, tying the bundles with rope. He greeted the women and asked what the wood was for.

'For the braai meat,' they replied.

Then Mustafa strolled over to the room where he had typically offered his deep tissue massages. He found the room locked and, after asking for the key, saw that termites had eaten their way through the wood. The panels were ravaged by the little burrowers, a job that must have lasted weeks. He imagined the blind horde navigating the wood together, detecting signals of threat, or competition, communing with the frequency of their hunger.

When Mustafa finally exited the main house, he thanked the residents for their hospitality. Word spread fast that 'the owner was here' and by the time he was walking down the driveway to his car, he was being thanked by throngs of people he didn't even remember inviting.

As he drove down the alleyway into Lancaster, butterflies meandered through the trees. That is what callers on the radio had been phoning in about all day, he thought. Apparently, swarms of them were travelling up from the Cape, and flying on towards Mozambique, aided by the warm air currents of the Indian Ocean. Butterflies had gained a popular association for bringing luck, or were read as a sign that one's aura was 'pure'. Was this why the schoolchildren at the bus stop were trying so hard to stand still, just so that the fragile creatures could settle on them?

The truth, as he knew it, was that butterflies are drawn to the salt in our sweat. Some see that as a less romantic idea but, for Mustafa, it was just as romantic, if not more so.

He drove on into the main road – winged kaleidoscopes settling on a billboard emblazoned with the words *It Could Be You Escaping the Lift Club*. He took the offramp, merging with the highway traffic. Cars and trucks drove at similar speeds – petrol pumping through pistons – geared towards human homes, for now.

If it wasn't for the dancing landscape, it would have seemed that traffic stood still, pleats in the planetary fold, bodies sewn to hold, imperceptibly fraying, and coming undone in a world that always delivered itself. Caul to caul.

ACKNOWLEDGEMENTS

Michael, Justin and Jocelyn Thompson, thank you for stocking my life with treatises on love.

Alan Watts, for the spiritual entertainment that led to this.

Bronwyn Law-Viljoen, Phillippa Yaa de Villiers, Ivan Vladislavić, for your fine-tuning critiques, conviviality, and guidance.

David Mann, Ahmed Patel, Moira Vimbainashe, Chloë Reid, and Babette Gallard, for your community and insights.

Allwell and Confidence Uwazuruike, for seeing the potential.

Andrea Nattrass, for keeping a watchful eye on me.

Alison Lowry, for asking questions in the right places.

Thango Ntwasa, for holding space for my dreams, jokes and complaints.

Catharina Roux, who stoked the spark from the beginning.

Thank you.

This novel would not have been possible without financial support from the Chris van Wyk Creative Writing Scholarship and the National Arts Council of South Africa.

Yellow means stay
An anthology of love stories from Africa

Yellow Means Stay is a collection of enthralling love stories from across Africa and the black diaspora. The stories are a dynamic blend of the poetic and narrative, the spousal and familial, the suggestive and explicit, the dramatic and measured, the straight and queer, the sad and humorous, the past and future, life and after life.

"... these stories of connection, intimacy and lust are a delicious read."
—Megan Ross, Author of Milk Fever

RECOMMENDED READING

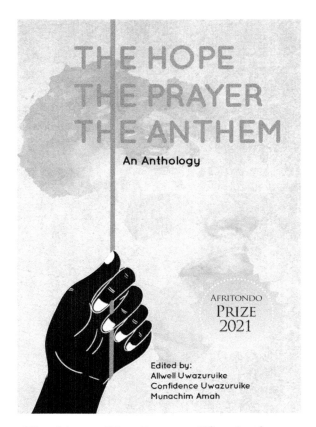

The Hope, The Prayer, The Anthem
An Anthology

The Hope, The Prayer, The Anthem is a collection of short stories on identity, love, hope, and self-discovery. Told by rising and award-winning writers from across the African continent and beyond, the stories are a rich blend of suspense, humour, drama, and romance.

"... It is complex, exciting, full of surprises, and brimming with brilliance."

—Maneo Mohale, Author, Everything is s Deadly Flower

RECOMMENDED READING

Rain Dance
An Anthology

Rain Dance is a collection of short stories on identity, love, hope, and self-discovery. Told by rising and award-winning writers, from across the African continent and beyond, the stories are a rich blend of suspense, humour, drama, and romance.

"... *These are exciting voices I hope to continue hearing from.*"

—'Pemi Aguda, Winner, Deborah Rogers Foundation
Writers Award 2020

Printed in Great Britain
by Amazon

18567340R00226